Brinemark-Bienemann Publishing 2011

Library of Congress Catalog-In-Publication Data
Brine, Mark
THE CAROL and the True Folk Legend of Jack Frost
Grateful acknowledgement is made to Linda Schuder for the use of her frontrcover charcoal drawing of 'Jack'..and to Linda Joseph for her drawing of 'Leah'..and to Keeve Brine, for his likewise 'stick man' sketch..and his further and initial graphic design for the front cover. And finally to Lillian Abernathy (LACreative).. for her assembly and layout of the final printed edition.

ISBN 978-0-615-54548-6

Artwork Credits:
Front Cover Charcoal of Jack Frost by Linda Schuder
Back Cover Photo of Mark Brine by Robert Willasch (Re-worked by Mark Brine)
All other drawings are by Mark Brine (except, in second book..
'Leah' by Linda Joseph Pitcher and the 'Confounding Sign'-Man by Keeve Brine-age 4)

CONTENTS

THE FIRST BOOK (THE CAROL)

THE SECOND BOOK (THE FINAL PAGES OF THE CAROL)

"THE CAROL"

- and –

"The True Folk Legend of Jack Frost"

- by –

Mark Brine c1979, 1992, 2011

- THE FIRST BOOK –

For my Father and Mother

AUTHOR'S IMPORTANT & "CRUCIAL" INTRODUCTION!

In all honesty, I must admit.. I do have my doubts that you are truly going to believe (or fully comprehend) this following account of the most overlooked and mis-understood hero in all-of Christmas History.

Why should you?

With as many facts and truths as there will be presented... Really... Why should you?

You, of sound mind.. and me, of.. me, of what?

Who am 'I' to believe?

And just 'Who am I' to begin with? You don't even know me!

Well, one thing's for sure.. when you've concluded this story, you're gonna know a whole lot more about me and 'Who I am'!

Then again, maybe you still won't!

Either way, what I'll do.. is start by telling you 'Who I was'. It'll be safer that way. I'll tell you some normal things about myself and how this story began.. then gradually I'll work into the abnormalities and complexities as we go. Yes, by then, maybe I'll have gained your trust enough to convince you of the extreme importance and factuality of what I'm about to confide in you.

THE FIRST CHAPTER

~ VOICES IN THE WIND ~

It all began in New England. My life and story both. Cambridge, Massachusetts to be more specific. Oh, there is just so much that can be said of New England! Its ever- plentiful and beautiful rural settings. Its cities and towns. The scenes and images that one might conjure up in their mind! And then.. the people.. their styles and ways! A Union-of-States apart and 'cubby-cornered'- away.. from the 'Great' Union-of-States! Hear of it.. in the works of Longfellow, Thoreau, Alcott, to name but a few! See of it.. in the works of Rockwell, for one! I will leave that for your own research or already- acquired knowledge of the region though.

Christmas always being such a very special time of the year for me, it is quite the expected that during this family- time, festive season, I instinctively migrate home. Returning to re-live and re-make the memories that I will carry away with me into each of the coming New Years to follow.

Cambridge is the immediate town north of Boston. And they.. divided only by the waters of the Charles River.

Being of a musical, poetic and artistic-loving nature, I always find it especially rewarding to take long strolls about Cambridge and Boston. For they both.. each in their own distinct way.. reek with inspirational qualities. Many of the Famous Poets made their homes here.. and still do.. for that very reason! There is a certain magic that settles in the air here.. an unexplainable thing! But, whatever?.. it most certainly exists! And likewise seems to remain, in spite of all time and modernizing changes!

So a foot-trip about these two towns is a 'must' for me, no matter how bitterly-cold the weather. Not only that, but with my musical business having me living afar through-out the remaining pages of the year's calendar, I find myself continually 'nagged on' by my fear of missing the 'whatever-limited-chance-I-might-have-to-do-my-exploring' before I'm once again on my distant way.

It was at the end of one of these casual hikes.. on the Eve of Christmas in the

year of 1978, that a most unusual event took place in my life. One that would considerably change my entire outlook (..and as well, all of the beliefs and opinions
I had up to that time acquired) concerning the world and its more-than-not regular
course of happenings. Yes, 'the world' that (up to this particular stage in my devel-
opment) I had felt quite sure that I had known and reasonably understood.

I had (for a number of years prior to this date) been residing in Nashville,
Tennessee, pursuing a songwriter/artist position.. and the immediately-preceding
year, more so than any, had seemed completely unfruitful career-wise for me. All
of my efforts had proven to be in vain.. and compounded by a most-recent marital
failure, I had slumped into quite a depressive state of mind. One that (from right
upon my arrival home) had been continually and very naggingly pre-occupying
my thoughts. All happening, ironically enough, during what should have (and
normally would have..) been one of the most happiest, joy-filled times of the year
for me.

This particular 24th-of-December-Day had been spent roaming about the streets
of Boston and Cambridge dodging hurried, last-minute shoppers and snowdrifts
with a reasonably 'above-average' amount of success. Doing a bit of purchasing
myself, in between my exploring and reminiscing. In and out of cram-packed

stores, racingly I went, trying to avoid
collisions of any nature. And very suc-
ceedingly at that!

Yet with all of my fortunate evad-
ing, my black cloud of depression
faithfully ensued, no matter how hard
I tried to lose it. Almost as if it was determined to destroy my holidays! And
then, more ultimately.. me!

As I departed from Harvard Square
to begin my northern sweep up Massachusetts Avenue (in the direction of
Rindge Avenue and my parent's house

there) it seemed that.. with the darkening and fall of the late day.. so too did my black cloud of depression seem to intensify and darkeningly-descend further upon me.

Winding through the noisy commotion and bottle-neck of 'inching along' traffic at the corner intersection of Mass. Ave. and Church Street, I scatted up and onto the sidewalk affront of the large First Unitarian Church. There I was greeted and momentarily eased by the harmonic entry of "Hark, the Herald Angels Sing", that was being rendered by a handful of carolers (who were situated to my left and standing at the foot of the structure's stairs). Edging my way through the congestion of passers-by and listeners, I dropped my last-of-change in their tin.

Continuing along the walkway and black-iron fence that borders the 'Old Burying Grounds', I trudged.. having now (as a result of the street choir) 'music' on my mind. And in so, my thoughts started to drift back to Music City (Nashville) and the previous year's events. The only happiness in my recall of it (at that particular uncomfortable moment) seeming to be, the few handful of friends that I'd made there throughout the years. Re-enactingly I cracked a frozen smile at one of the more-humorous of moments that we had shared, by-gone. A smile.. that was rudely met by a gust of bitter wind, hitting me head-on, as I made my hurried way onto the grounds of the Cambridge Common. Emotionally buckling myself, I forced on through the graying void.

As I made my way across Waterhouse Street to continue up and along Mass. Ave., a pleasant recall from my childhood came. One that brought forth many others before my much-further-ahead ascent over the railroad bridge at and lead-ing into Porter Square. But each (like its previous), being soon forgotten and dis-regarded for instead 'more dismal' thoughts. It seemed useless! Even my brief stop-off for coffee there in the shopping center did 'little-to-nothing' in soothing my depressive-inner chill and discomfort. No, the dark cloud kept sinking further and further down on me!

So, snuggling my 'Beale-Street-Big-Brimmer' hat (as I'd nicknamed it) tightly down onto my lower forehead.. and tucking my chin into the scarf-wrapped collar of my winter coat, I resumed my Mass. Ave. journey deeper into the heart of North Cambridge.

As I made my slippery left-turn onto Rindge Avenue, a fresh snow began to fall, chilling me all the more. Down the left-hand side of the through-fare, I soon overtook Fairfield and Haskell Streets.

Making my way off of the curb to cross the junction of Yerxa Road (just beyond the M.E. Fitzgerald School), it came to me that one of my shoes had sprung a leak, allowing the entrance of some tingling-icy slush. With all that had been pressing on my mind, I wondered if it had been leaking all the while.. and that I just hadn't noticed it until then! Before I encountered St. John's Evangelist School (on my im-mediate left, not even a half a block away), this thought too had been disregarded for deeper-gloom.

Trudging by the Bakery Shop (with its masking-taped-in-the-window 'Closed

Tomorrow.. Christmas Day' sign), I proceeded onto the Drugstore there in the tiny center (James F. Walsh Square) at the intersections of Cedar Street, Rice Street and Middlesex Avenue. Coming to a stop at the fore-corner of the latter, I contemplated my next move. Turning and looking about and down the five axial streets

(From my position.. Rindge Ave. itself being two of the spokes), I noticed a strange hush come over and upon the earth. Re-scanning the very limited square, I came to likewise notice the total absence of people and traffic. The thick silence puzzled and frightened me. To divert the perplexity, I instead concentrated on where-else I might go rather than to my parent's house (just several more buildings up Rindge, on the right). I needed time to think! To be alone.. and sort myself out! It came to me that I could continue across Middlesex Ave. and go three blocks up Rindge to the North Cambridge Catholic Cemetery. My first-born, three-month-old baby girl, Michelle was buried there.. and I could pay a visit. No.. I needed relief.. not more sorrow! Besides, to do that I would have to pass by my parent's house. And being as confused and depressed as I was.. well.. I just wasn't in the proper frame of mind for any confrontations or explanations. Yeah, my luck.. they'd definitely spot me!

In frozen desperation (internally, as well as externally!), I frantically searched my thoughts for where I might go.

Then.. it came to me! There.. right in front of my nose.. extending enormously-out towards the main-ways' five-street junction.. stood my so-needed haven.. the Our Lady of Pity Church! When depression and mass-confusion of this serious-a-nature sets in.. where better might one seek and find help, than from the Almighty! Yes, that would serve my purpose just perfectly!

But then (to crush my momentarily-relief), in squint I came to see that the huge, black-iron gates guarding the outer-lobby's arched entranceways were closed. De-

termined and assured I'd find no better and more appropriate a place to thaw.. in a leftward motion, my eyes followed its massive structure away from Rindge, down the edge of Middlesex. There, in the near distant offset.. behind ill-defined, naked trees and bushes, stood the Our Lady of Pity Chapel! This tiny assembly hall being connected and wedged into the side of its parental-like counterpart. Without the slightest ado, I crossed Middlesex and along the chain-linked fence began my way towards the chapel front. Tucking my face further down into my scarf and collar, I neared at an increasing rate.

Now I will mention here .. that, upon my entry to the chapel (as I made my rapid ascent up the last of the few stone stairs), a very strange feeling instantaneously came to possess and stun me into a momentary state of paralysis. As I very light-headedly halted my footsteps at the doorway to recollect it, it came to me.. very oddly enough.. that I had run through something! Yes.. run through something.. or somebody! Something invisible.. but, yet.. something very much there! Yes, there… at the top of the last stair! I turned back around to find.. not a thing! For the life of me, at the time.. I couldn't even vaguely comprehend what it might have been. All I knew was, that I had felt it! It being.. and feeling like.. a very cold vapor of some sort.. that, with its brisk out-of-nowhere arrival, had passed through my-person with a sudden flash too quick to properly gauge, due to my un-aware-of-it-being-there speed and encounter of it.

Turning again forward and trying to re-gather my thoughts, I snapped the bronze latch on the chapel door. Then.. taking a deep breath (for the lack of better relief), I slowly edged inside, attempting to ignore its confounding-me dilemma.

With night rapidly falling and the chapel being only barely-lit by the flickering devotion candles on the front altar, the atmosphere was very uncanny. I quite honestly had even considered turning around and forgetting the visit at first sight of it. Apprehensively and very shakingly, I did continue on down the main aisle though, for my burdens outweighed my fears considerably!

Step by step, I found my way to the center of the chapel, taking a seat in the middle of a long wooden pew on the left-hand side. There I sat very reserved and all alone in the deathly silence, nervously studying the surroundings.

At last (with the lapse of time), my mind became distracted from all of my inner and outer discomforts. And my mood came to be quite the opposite.. drifting slowly, but surely into a very serene mental state. It was just so peaceful there! The quiet (Which I so badly needed!) helped me to meditate above my anguish, putting me in a much clearer, more self-sympathetic frame of mind.

So, with a lump in my throat and an extremely-melancholy heart, I knelt to begin my soul-searching conference with the Lord.

Becoming, at times, a little bit irrational (I'll admit), I found myself begging.. and then, more ultimately 'demanding' God's response to my inner doubts and fears-of-failure...

"Lord.. Father.. Tell me.. Please!... Why.. Why did you put me here?

What was my purpose?... I've always felt there was one! ..Ever since I was just a little boy.. it's been there! ..Yes, I know it's been there! But.. but...

Well.. I mean.. If I've got something to do here.. something that you put me here to accomplish with my work, then how come it hasn't happened yet?.. How come you've made it so hard for me?   ..Father.. Please.. please tell me.. why? .. Why haven't you helped me?.."

I knew how unreasonable I was being, but I just couldn't contain myself. Emotionally out-of-control, I persisted on...

"You know.. Yes, You know how hard I've tried!.. You, above any, would know that!...

If there's a message in my work.. one that would help and enlighten mankind.. and give this world better hope.. and faith.. then, why.. why has it gone unheard?...

I've always tried to use my art with good intent! ..You know that I've been sincere in my endeavors and have never purposely tried to steer anyone wrong! ..I know that my own personal and human failings are numerous.. and in light of that, I'm probably the 'ultimate of hypocrites' .. but I can't remember now ever trying to capitalize on them or mislead people! ..Maybe when I was younger and unaware of all that, I might have done so.. But once I realized the harm that could result from it.. and the 'Power of the Arts'.. well, you know, I tried to correct it and make it right! .. Yes, I've always sought to make you proud of me.. At least in that department! .. and to the best of my limited abilities!..

And my Earthly Parents.. I've always hoped to make them proud too! ..I know, like with you, I've at times let them down.. but I didn't want to! ..I had always hoped to 'do good' for them! ..You know how important it is for me to 'succeed'.. for my Dad! ..all of his dreams were… well.. I've just got to!.. Yes.. you know what I'm talking about!…

And my Mom.. she's been so kind and understanding to me.. for just.. just so long! ..encouraging and supporting me and my efforts! …always going out of her way! ..You know as well as I do, I want to be able to someday repay her for all of it!..

And, well.. just both of them!.. it's important God.. Can't you see?…

Then there's my own little family.. my daughter and all of that!.. It's such a mess!.. And I'm truly sorry for that!.. But it kills me to think, if I'd have only been successful.. and been able to afford them the things that they needed.. then it might not have been like.. like this!..

Can't you see?.. Can't you help me?.. You know how hard I've tried!.. So, why haven't you.. Why?"

On and on I attacked with the like.. my mind racing through and blurting-out all of the built-up frustrations that had been without mercy tearing at my very heart and soul, for so long!

It felt good, I'll say, to release it. But after a time, I at last surrendered to the un-answering silence and slid my way back onto the pew. For.. other than my own self-pitying gratification, it seemed completely useless. No voice came with the so-badly needed reply I awaited. But then really, what would I've done had it come? I think I would've been so afraid and appalled ..well.. I.. I.. really don't know what I would've done!

Then.. very rightfully.. it came to me of just how selfish I was being. Guilt-fully considering all of the many.. yes, so many.. poor souls that there were in this world, being even 'more' less fortunate than myself.. 'Much more' less fortunate! Those with afflictions and the like. Those who couldn't see.. or hear.. or walk and talk, etc., etc.! Or even greater.. those having all or several of these or other handicaps! And the hungry! The Needy! The Sick! And here I was.. perfectly healthy.. fed and clothed.. and asking for 'success' and a reward for something that was already a 'reward in itself'! I felt kind of foolish, to say the least! So that ended that. And to make sure it did, I began instead studying the surrounding, still-vacant chapel as a diversion to any further thoughts on the subject.

Searching about the inner walls, I found just so many things to escape in.. Statues.. Stations-of-the-Cross.. Holy Pictures.. and Relics just everywhere! And the mood and lighting of the chapel made them seem, at times, to be actually moving. A flickering light will most certainly give that affect.. and I found myself double-checking quite a few times.

For such a small place of worship, there was just so much to see! And the more I searched and studied everything, the more lost I became in the suspended silence there-in. My conference with God became completely forgotten, as my eyes curiously moved about, totally absorbed in the dim and awesome-ness of it all!

Then.. gradually.. as if out-of-nowhere.. I became aware of a very faint whistling sound. It was coming from somewhere behind me, in the rear of the chapel. And I began to listen to it, very pensively. As I did, it seemed to become all the more louder and distinct. In no time, it completely captivated my interest.. and I turned back around to try to locate its where-abouts.

After a reasonable search, my eyes at last came in contact with a large, stained-glass window that was just barely opened a crack.. just enough to allow the outside winter winds to come squealing in.. and in the process, stampeding millions of tiny goose-bumps across even the most-clothed-parts of my trembling body.

Being that the window was up too high for shutting, I unwillingly surrendered. Instead I spun around forward in my seat and arrogantly tried to ignore it. But its persistent shrill made the latter virtually impossible to do. For as its volume increased, so too did my chilling awareness of it!

Trying desperately to shut it out of my mind, I began looking everywhere and anywhere about me for anything of interest. But it was just no use.. all I could think of was that insistent whistling! So eventually I just gave in to it and sat there listening, disgusted and shivering.

In the beginning it was all that I could do to control my trembling from the eerie, high pitch-ness of its sound. But the more I listened, the more I noticed that there was a definite melodic flow to it! And being a musician, I found myself quite naturally humming along and following its note progression. I became totally awed by it! For even though its melody line was quite basic, it still had a very pleasant-to-the-ear appeal to it! I'll add that it was a very 'catchy little tune' too! For after all, it had surely caught my interest!

Convinced I wasn't hearing things (Although I must admit, 'insanity' did cross my mind at first!) I sat there staring at the large window, listening attentively. It was just so beautiful and touching a melody! I wondered why I'd never noticed the wind to sound like that before! It reminded me of a penny whistle. You know, like the kind that children play with.. Only, the musical structure I was hearing was definitely more complexed-a-tune than any penny whistle could manage! There was no doubt about it.. It most certainly was the wind!.. For I searched for all and any other possibilities imaginable to no avail!

As I continued to be its audience, it came to me (and sort of to humor myself), I thought…

'Boy.. Ole Jack Frost sure is going to town tonight.. Whistling up just one heck of a Christmas Eve storm!..'

I smirked to myself, drooping my head and swaying it back and forth at the ridiculousness of the thought.

Then.. suddenly.. I froze in motion.. as the most overwhelming-est of brain-storms I'd ever (.. and I must repeat.. 'ever'!) had.. came crashing down on me! A million ideas, like pennies from Heaven, crashing down on my mind, all at once! Ideas.. images.. and what-seemed-like a fantastic concept that I could use to mold with my art into something that the world had never heard before! Something profound! Something that needed to be said and never had been before! Eureka! Why hadn't anyone ever thought of it before? Then creeping in.. 'Maybe some-body had?' I immediately rejected it.. 'no ways!' Re-assuring myself with .. 'Who could ever dream-up something this heavy?.. No.. just no ways!' Ideas.. Ideas.. crashing down!.. All happening so fast that I became confused with trying to remember each of the previous!

I frantically began searching my pockets for a pad and pen, that I might jot down some brief outlining notes.. that I (at a more convenient time) could return to, to begin my artistic-godsend. Then it dawned on me that I hadn't carried one with me that day. I had to get to one and fast, before it was all lost!

Grasping my forehead (holding it firmly, as if the thoughts might escape if I didn't!), I quickly scrambled my way to the end of the pew. Down the main aisle-way I hurried, like an over-excited kid on Christmas morn.. tripping and carelessly-fumbling every inch of the way! With my hands up and covering my eyes, I could barely see.. not to mention the pitiful darkness all about me, making it all-the-worse a feat!

Just as I reached the first exit (to the outer lobby of the chapel), I realized that my prayers had been answered.. and that God (despite my selfishness) had after all came through and sent me the help I'd asked for. So coming to a dead-stop at the arched-entranceway, I turned back towards the altar and let out a loud.. "THANKS GOD!"…that reverberated so many times, I didn't see fit that it needed repeating.

Then without any further ado, off I rushed through the vestibule and out into the now-pitch-black night.. all the while holding my fore-crown each leap-and-bouncing step of the way. My brainstorm pulsating away (and I praying it wouldn't clear!), down the snow-covered pathway I dashed.. slipping and sliding every-which-a-way and nearly breaking my neck too many times to want to recall!

Screeching to a stand-still stop just before the front-end of the larger church, it very-discouragingly came to me that.. in all of my hurried-search through my pockets for the writing tools.. I had unthinkingly taken out and left on the pew-seat a miniature wristwatch that I had purchased that very afternoon for my daughter, Jenipher. It was to be a Christmas gift that she had wanted desperately.. and I'd finally fell upon it that early-day, after a long season's search. It was the kind of child's watch that really works! She'd wanted one so badly (Asking me on a number of occasions prior!) ..and I knew fully well that no matter 'whatever oth-er'-presents she'd receive (that following morning), if that was not amongst them, she would be very much saddened. And God knows, how much 'my disappointing her', in turn, depressed me! So you see.. it was a very crucial moment here! For this being.. T.H.E. Main Gift! The U.L.T.I.M.A.T.E. in her eyes! And Thank God (again!) I had 'just lucked on it' that very, just-in-the-nick-of-time day! And when I had (Instead of having it gift-wrapped like I probably should have!), I'd simply set it to the proper time and slipped it in my coat pocket. I was sure I'd forgotten it, because I still could see it there in my mind.. laying on the wooden seat.. face up.. ticking away.. reading 'Seven O' Clock'! Even in all of my confusion, it had made an imprint that vivid in my mind! I fought with myself to return to the chapel to retrieve it, for I'd definitely need it that night if I intended to give it to my little angel the following morn! But then again, I hated to think of my losing any of the 'never-to-return-again' ideas either. I had to get to a pen and paper first! Then I'd return for the watch. Nobody would go in the chapel before I'd get back. And even if they did, they'd probably never even notice it. I was sure it'd be all right! So I resumed my direction and hastened flight towards my parent's house. 'Besides.. All I have to do is go right across the avenue.. then I'll return within minutes to get it!..'

Within seconds I was in the same state of high-acceleration and disorder as I'd been shortly before.. running through the night like some madman on the loose.. completely thought-blinded and unaware of all and anything in front of or about me.

Several elderly ladies (Who had been conversing there in the churchyard) became very upset, grasping their hearts as I dashed by, hands still up and covering my face. Assuming that they had thought I had hurt my head (and not to be responsible for giving anyone a heart attack.. especially on Christmas Eve!), just as I reached the avenue, without halting any of my speed, I turned back and yelled…

"It's just an idea!.. You know.. a brainstorm!.. That's all.. just a brainstorm!.."

This unquestionably was the worse mistake I'd ever made in my entire short life. For the next thing I heard was the ear-piercing screech of automobile brakes. Simultaneously I felt my body fly limb-lessly through the cold night air.. Only to conclude with the vibrating sound of my head crashing down on the icy pavement of the opposing sidewalk (directly in front of the shop-site that has been known for years as 'Phil's Barbershop').

The banging echoed. Then turned into what-was-like a tremendously-loud and reverberant ringing in my ears. Finally it became a long, low sounding drone that lasted far into my unconsciousness.

A long, dark silence followed. One that was interrupted occasionally by the wavering sounds of people's voices distantly calling my name. It was as if I were drowning into something.. and the voices were calling and reaching to rescue me, as I sank further and further below the surface of life. I'd inaudibly hear them.. like blares of mumble. Then they'd fade away.. off and on.. more and more faint, each time.. as I kept falling deeper and deeper into what was a vacuum-like blissful sleep and dream. A type of sleep that I'd never-before-then experienced. It was just so peaceful, I remember wishing I'd never have to awake from it. Nothing seemed to matter anymore. I just kept on drifting further and further away.. into thin air.. for what-seemed-to-be…an endless forever!

Then.. there was nothing! Absolutely.. Nothing!

THE SECOND CHAPTER

~ LIFE'S JUST A DREAM ~

My first recovering memory was that of the sound of distant whistling, echoing from the far-corners of my mind.. and interrupting the tranquility of my depthly unconsciousness. It being.. once again (you guessed it!).. that same high-pitched melodic shrill that I'd heard back 'in the chapel'.. making its entrance as unex-pected (and intruding to my peacefulness!) as it had done prior!

The more its volume increased, the more awake I became.. almost as if it were beckoning me to regain consciousness. Calling me onward, it persisted.. like an un-welcomed bugle in the not-yet-visible morning. I fought with it at first, as if it were in fact the metallic annoying sound of an at-dawn trumpet! But soon again, it had me captivated (just as it had before!) with its beautiful and touching musical flow. I was, in short, totally enlisted by its pied-piper-ing magnetism!

"Wake Up".. "Wake Up"… it seemed to be saying.. as gradually, more and more, my eyes blurred through the un-describable and mysterious gap that seper-ates the two adjoining worlds of consciousness and sleep. Hypnotically engrossed I followed.. and when finally my eyes did begin to focus properly, its sound ironi-cally-enough began to rapidly disappear. The more I cleared my mind, the fainter and more distant it grew! Until simultaneously it ended and I awoke.

Quickly I looked up and about me, in search of where it might have vanished to. Upon doing so, I found myself totally marveled at the notice that my head was not in the least bit of pain or discomfort (considering the traumatic blow it had just received in my most-recent mishap)! Quite to the contrary, it felt lighter and better than ever! Making me wonder if I'd even been in an accident at all! 'Maybe it was just.. a dream?'

As my eyes searched about from my laying position, into view came the dark covering of the night-time sky above me. There was a very dominant scatter of white, drifting haze that was obstructing great sections of it.. that, likewise (and in the same), was totally engulfing my entire ground level. Still (as limited as my view was), when I lifted my head to survey the area, I immediately deducted (beyond a doubt!) that this.. 'where-ever-it-was?'.. was definitely not North Cambridge anymore! No.. it seemed as though (as ridiculous as it might sound!), I was on.. on top of the clouds!

Rubbing my astonished eyes, I pivotingly jolted my head in every possible direction! But the fog all-about-me was simply too thick to see a thing beyond my immediate enclosure. The haze also was causing an awful glare that made it all appear very-dreamy and eerie-a-scene. And the swaying-ness and drowsy-state of my just-awakening-frame-of-mind didn't make it (in the slightest!) any more the clearer or more-comprehendible-a-situation either! I hurriedly jumped to my feet to attempt a better look.

When standing I could hear (coming from the nearby distance) what definitely was the sound of human voices. Lots of human voices! As inaudible as they were, it was apparent to me that there was a beach close by. And the happy, continuous laughter.. splashing and shouting.. all jumbled together.. made it seem very pleasant and inviting.

Being the most appropriate and logical thing to do when one is lost, I began walking in its direction. The thick but soft mist.. rising and floating in front and all about me.. made it hard (if not near-impossible!) to see where I was going. But I trudged on faithfully despite.

Then for a quick instant, the night breeze blew open a clearing.. allowing me a momentary glimpse of what-I-was-sure-were the vague images of people!

Very anxious to discover my where-abouts, I began trotting in their direction.. fighting the blinding, glaring haze and picking up speed as I went. I could actually feel the mist lightening as I neared, making the images all the more distinct and audible with each step forward.

And when at last it disappeared enough to no longer hinder my near-approaching view of them, I came to an immediate, jolting halt. For these were not people! These were not people at all! No, not at all! Why, these were.. these were.. Angels! Real honest-to-goodness, no-other-way-to-put-it Angels! Little ones.. big ones.. old ones.. and in-between ones.. all walking around and bathing in this huge crystal-clear lake that was settled into the massive-supporting, cloudy surface. Some were wearing long-white robes, while others were shamelessly parading about in their birthday suits.. All, just having a simply grand-time! As beautiful a scene as it was, my total state of shock completely over-powered any enjoyment of it!

In the near-distant background of them (and the opposing edge of the lake) I could see an enormous, glowing emerald wall of unbelievable height and width.. that continued and disappeared into the far-off, cloudy horizon. An unbearably-shining gateway (made entirely out of pearl!) stood wide-opened in their general vicinity.

I started putting two and two together.. "Pearly Gates".. "Real Angels".. coming up with.. "I've Died, It's Heaven!.."

I felt to run. I just couldn't accept it! "I've got to get back to North Cam-bridge!.."

I turned around and started. But the mist had thickened even more miserably now. My mind fearfully grasped at any possible solutions!...

"How will I ever find the spot I started from?...

And even if I do.. how can I reverse the process of Death!...."

'Death' struck so deeply, I had to pause to catch my breath at the sound of it! Death.. Yes.. I'd.. I'd really died! There was just no other way about it.. I'd died! I felt to cry. I simply wasn't prepared for this! But then again.. Who-ever is? Still.. there were just so many things that I'd planned to do on Earth! Important things! Things that I hadn't finished yet! What about my career.. and that brain-storming idea that I had had in the chapel? How could I ever complete them or anything now? They'd just have to remain undone, like so many other plans and dreams that I had had! It wasn't fair!

Self-pityingly I argued with myself.. Until finally I realized that there was just 'no other way about it'.. I was here.. and all the reasons otherwise that I could find that I shouldn't be, were in no way going to change the cold, hard facts! So justifyingly I consoled myself with.. "At least I've made it to Heaven".. and sur-renderingly began walking back in their direction.

Following the long cloudy shoreline, in no time I was in their midst. Finding myself (as I continued through them) going completely un-noticed! For they were all so busy about getting spotlessly clean for some reason that I hadn't the foggy-est idea of. I sensed it to be of great importance though.. which was more-than evident (I must admit) by their over-concern and un-controllable excitement in so doing.. washing and re-organizing anything and everything within close range, whether it needed it or not! And all.. with such detail and care!

Becoming more and more mountingly curious over 'What was going on?' with each step, I at last stopped to single-out a conversation that was going on between two elderly lady-angels who were resting on a silk blanket by the shoreline. Both of whom were polishing stacks of halos and verbally carrying-on a mile a minute. With all the noise and simultaneous conversations going on about us, it took my deepest concentration to hear…

"He's going to be Emmanuel!.. means 'God with Us'!…

Anyway.. it'll be sometime in the morning.. no one's sure yet just when the exact time will be.. but we're all going to be going along!.. Oh, I'm so excited!…

I wonder what He's going to look like?.. I bet He'll be the most beautiful baby ever!…

Mary and Joseph are on their way to Bethlehem now.. They're somewhere about five miles out of…"

I didn't need to hear another word!

So this was the cause of all the excitement. This was the Eve of the First Christ-mas! No wonder there was so much commotion and cleaning-up going on! That answered one of my two questions.. the other being.. 'How in Heaven did I get here?'.. I mean.. I was from the twentieth century! What was I doing 1,978 years into the past? It just didn't make any sense! But then again, death had always been a great mystery to me! Maybe this was just what happened to everybody when they died? I mean.. How was I to know what others had experienced during and at the time of their own deaths? Maybe this was just routine?

What was even more baffling to me was.. when I asked several of them.. 'If it was all right to just go inside the gates?' (figuring you'd no doubt need some kind of permission first or something), they just simply ignored me!.. Acting like they couldn't see or hear me in the slightest! I always knew that people couldn't see Angels.. but couldn't they see each other? I mean.. I was an Angel, wasn't I? They sure could see each other plenty fine.. carrying on just perfectly!

Assuming that maybe they just didn't warm-up to newcomers easily, I decided to take it upon myself and just casually proceed on in through the un-attended gates anyway. For even if I was to get scolded, at least I'd get some kind of a response from them!

Although the misty fog had cleared considerably, when I'd reached the shore-line of the beach and its bathers.. now inside of the gates, it completely had dispersed. The glazey-like glare remained though, due to the shining buildings and streets that held me spellbound. I breathtakingly paused to take it all in. It was easy to see that God's vast and wondrous city was in an awful, hectic uproar! Angels were chaotically running every-which-a-way, up and down the winding, hilly streets-of-gold in happy expectation! All preparing for the birth of the Baby Jesus, only a morning away! And of course for all of the joyous celebrations that would, in turn, follow on the 'First of Christmas Days'!

'I bet Heaven hasn't seen this much commotion since Satan and his band tried to overthrow the throne of God, many years ago!', I considered. It was just such an unbelievable sight! What a night to arrive in Paradise!

Being in no great hurry to stand my judgment with God, I decided to take my time and discover the city, instead of trying to search Him out. Not only that, but I was fully aware of the nervous frame of mind that is commonly-associated with 'Father's-to-be' in the final hours before the birth of their offspring.. and thought it in my best interests to be patient and wait! Besides.. a stroll about the city might not be such a bad idea.. Just in case, ultimately.. I was refused citizenship! So I ventured forth sneakingly.. fearfully expecting to, at any given moment, be discovered and brought to my final trial with the Lord.

Oh, what a beautiful, beautiful city it was!.. As dreamy and enchanted a place as all of the stories I'd heard told of it! Buildings made of pure gold bricks.. and others, constructed entirely out of tremendously-oversized slabs of sparkling diamond! Each and every one of them radiant beyond description! I became lost in the magnificence of it all. While all of those about me (on the streets) seemed to be 'quite use to them'. They being much more involved in their own immediate chores and pressing affairs. Even if they hadn't have been, it wouldn't have made the slightest bit of difference 'what I thought of it all'! As I'd finally (after many attempts at trying to communicate with them) come to the realization that.. they weren't ignoring me.. No, that wasn't it.. They just simply couldn't, in fact, see or hear me in the least! I (for some strange reason) was completely invisible to them! It was mind-boggling! But with no one there to consult with about it, I just (instead of worrying myself) went about my business. For, quite honestly.. I was much too wrapped-up with all of the 'miracles' unfolding right-before-my-eyes to even care!

Up one of the many winding emerald-cobblestone alleyways, I sped.. coming at last to the entrance of what-was-like a huge department store. I wandered in undetected to take a quick look. As would be expected, the shelves were stacked with everything imaginable. And it being, of course, all for free! For there was not a cash register to be found. There were many apron-clad employees about though. But only there to assist the shoppers in locating things more readily. This definitely was 'the most ultimate bargain store' I'd ever seen! For sure! And no questions about it! Prices unbeatable! It was no wonder that the place was cram-packed to the ceilings. Yes.. all the way up to the ceilings! There were angels everywhere, flying around with bundles full of presents and food in their arms. And the floor-level was none-the-less crowded either! Just a complete madhouse, right in the middle of Eden!

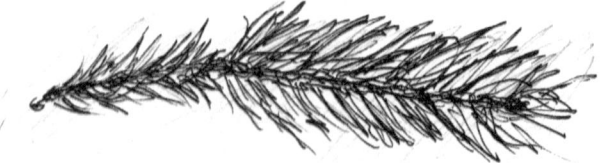

Ever present in the outside air was the tantalizing smell of evergreen pine. Upon my exit, I caught its sudden whiff.. and in so, closed my eyes to envision the darkest and most richest forest-green color imaginable. Had it not been for the slight nip of the night, this smearing-further introspect might have carried me away endlessly. But with its 'cooling aid', I at last forced myself to 'snap to'. The enticing fragrance was drifting from just a ways up yonder in the near distance, where great bunches of tied-together Christmas trees (freshly cut ones!) were being dragged and carted-up an inclined street by groups of merrily toiling angels. All headed ascendingly up towards (what was) a magnificently, glowing castle, that was crowning the further-set hilltop. This absolutely-beautiful structure, sending off a thick glow that was reflecting off and onto the above clouds like an oversized searchlight. It (I easily deducted as..) being.. the Palace of God!

The evergreen scent (along with the aromas of cooking foods, coming from the nearby opened windows.. blending together with the brisk night-time air..) had me enthralled in an ecstatic Yuletide trance. Roasting peanuts.. cloves.. angel-food sponge-cakes.. cherry pies.. boiling hot fudge.. to name a few, had my imagination going like a motion-picture camera, at a ridiculously rapid speed! Melancholy memories of all the Christmas's I'd ever experienced in my life flooded my thoughts! Only it felt like I was re-living them all at once, in a matter of minutes! Feeling all of the wonderful sensations that they had brought me; plus many more that I hadn't even yet to live! I'd never felt so 'full of Christmas Spirit' in all of my existence! This, in both senses of the word, was.. Heaven!

To top it all off, in the nearby distance I could hear a beautiful sounding choir.. singing in the closest knit harmony I'd ever attuned my ears to. Like the soundtrack of a movie, it backed my Christmas-sentimentality perfectly.. sounding just so 'Angelic'!

But then again.. what-else?.. they 'were' angels!

There was no question about it.. I had to get closer!

- UNDOUBTEBLY ANGELS -

So I hurried, following the sound up a long, curving dark side-street.. until finally I came to a gigantic cathedral front. It being supported by greatly-sized,

peach marble pillars. The large columns enclosing the main entrance-way (at the top of its long stairways) were centered by two wooden, nail-studded doors. One of which was conveniently propped-open halfway, allowing the captivating melodic sounds to escape freely. Also coming from the half-cracked opening was the thick ray of an inside, yellowish light.. that was bursting-out and onto one side of the upper level platform of the stairways. Intriguingly it lured me up step by step.. and in I went without the slightest concern for being caught. For by now I had become quite comfortable with my invisible-ness. As a matter of fact, I'd sincerely come to enjoy it, you might say!

Once inside the doors, I could easily see why it had appeared to be such an overly-sized building from outside. For it housed (what I'd have guessed to be..) no less than five thousand choir angels! Or at least it sure seemed to be that many! All.. singing away.. at the top of their lungs full force. And practicing for the most joyous of all occasions ever to be. And right smack-dab in the dead-center of them all, leading the rehearsal, was none-other-than the Angel Gabriel himself, in all his ultimate glory. He being, quite the exact image you'd expect.. a very obese black man.. a cool cat in every extreme of the word! Dressed (or maybe I should say 'tented'!) in a long-white, floor-level robe. Dangling in his left hand was a bigger-than-trumpet-size golden horn. A handkerchief (in the other) flaggingly waved as he jolted his arm abruptly, directing the all-eyes-on-him choir. Absolutely in-trigued, I watched as he jumped about.. completely lost in a dance that only one being (in the entire universe!) could've possibly managed! Yes, the one that God had bestowed 'all-of-the-rhythm-in-the-world' upon! The High Priest of Music himself.. Gabriel.. doing all of the movements that musicians and entertainers (for years and years to come) would imitate! Across the floor and back.. in and out.. and just all about! Yes, Gabriel.. the Angel of Soul!

Considering my inconspicuous state of being, I saw no reason why I shouldn't move in closer for a better view. So I did just that, making my way towards the center-floor of the enormous auditorium.. heading right into their midst, as carefree as (I felt sure) my at-present condition could afford.

Just as I came to (what-normally-would-have-been..) 'too close for comfort'.. I was rudely startled by…

"WAIT!... WAIT!... HOLD IT!... " as Gabriel halted the as-equally-astonished choir.

I froze in mid-step, afraid that maybe I'd been caught. Then...

"WAIT.. HOLD ON HERE!.. WAIT!.. WAIT!.." echoed the large inner chambers again. I started to back-up, as the angel choir came slowly and very-unevenly to a stop.

I stood there shivering in the long cold silence that followed, as Gabriel raced back and forth, lost in his deep and anguished thought. The choir was as bewildered as I was.. giving each other confounded, puzzled-like looks with their pale-fearing faces.

Eventually a faint scattering of under-their-breath conversation broke out, that was immediately deterred by...

"THIS JUST AIN'T GONNA MAKE IT!.. NO WAYS!.. NO, JUST AIN'T GONNA GET IT!.."

Then Gabriel (in all of his exploding frustration) began stomping his way out of the cathedral, leaving the choir still-as-confused and as-baffled (by his moment's-before unexpected outburst) than they had already been.

As Gabriel stormed out (still mumbling to himself), I decided that it might not be a bad idea that I follow him. For after all, maybe he had seen me and was going to do something about it? Something I should know about! Even if that wasn't the case, I still just had to know.. 'What was going on here?'! So (with the angel choir still questioning each other), I began pursuing Gabriel's trail out to the street.

Just as he met the street's edge, I too simultaneously reached the main entrance doors of the cathedral.. only to come to a screeching stop! For just as I caught the sight of his backside, so too did I see (standing right there in front of him, as if He'd been waiting all along and expecting Gabriel!) God, the Father, in all of His Almighty Glory! I was completely overtaken emotionally by His mere presence! My eyes became glued to the sight of Him, no matter how hard my inner guilt fought to turn away. The magnetism in His mystical appearance being totally un-describe-able and beyond the word definitions of even the most authoritative of dictionaries available to mankind! I only wish that I could touch on and relay one zillionth of the feeling I received from the sight of Him to you, that you might be better prepared for when your own time has come!

Still numb, I watched as God and Gabriel slowly took a seat together on one of the cathedral's bottom stairs. I (nervous and shaking like a leaf!) sneakingly made my way down pass them along the banister, making a U-turn as quickly as my legs could manage into the dark stairwell to hide. Which (when I later thought about it) seemed a completely ridiculous thing to do.. For God knows everything.. and even though He hadn't once made eye contact with me, I'm sure He was fully aware of my presence there! But at the time (considering my fearful frame of mind), it seemed the only thing to do!

So, hidden away in the dark (behind the solid stone baluster), I timidly waited.. to at last hear a very solemn and understanding voice break the silence with...

"All right, Gabriel.. What's the problem?.. What's bothering you?.. Tell me.. and I'll try to help... C'mon, now.. We can work it out.. "

"Well, Lord.. Sir.. it's...

it's just that...

Well, it's just that.. I can't get the sound I want from the choir...

I mean, it's them Hymns.. They're old ones!

I like 'em 'n all.. Don't get me wrong.. but.. but they just don't have nuthin' t' do with this special occasion!...

This is gonna be somethin' new.. and big!.. and them old hymns just don't get it!

Father, Sir.. I.. I wanted so bad to make you proud 'f me 'n all.. Y' know.. It meant a whole lot t' me.. but, there's just nuthin' I can do!...

Really, Lord.. Sir.. just nuthin' I can do!.."

"Well, Gabriel.. I sincerely appreciate your concern.. but you don't have to get so upset.. You know I can help.. All you ever have to do is ask.. You know that!...

Now wait.. Let me think for a minute here..."

About this time I had regained my composure and courage enough to peek out over the stone banister, catching the view of the back of God's head and Gabriel's staring-at-Him face. God was quietly concentrating.. and I could see that Gabriel was very pensive, nervously twiddling the hem of his robe. As the silence thickened.. dragging on and on.. he began biting his fingernails.. and I could tell (just by the expressions on his face) that he was thinking something like…

'What if He makes another me!…

Maybe He thinks I'm incompetent?…

Or.. what if He makes a whole other choir.. with another leader!…

Maybe I asked the wrong thing!..'

It was obvious that Gabriel was gripped in sheer suspense. And I couldn't rightfully blame him either. After all, he must have been very happy and content with his high-ranking and authoritative position in Heaven.. and I'm sure he didn't want to lose that, after all this time! And with God always being known for 'doing things big'.. Well.. Anything was possible!

Gabriel (lost in thought) was still staring eye-wide.. when all of a sudden (You could tell).. it struck him that 'God could read his mind' if He wanted to. An immediate dumbfounded look covered his face with the realization of it! Then.. out of nowhere.. God jumped up, only to startle the livin'-Heaven-out-of-him with…

"GABRIEL.. YOU GAVE ME THE GREATEST IDEA!.. THAT'S IT!.."

Gabriel's face dropped immediately with the saddest 'Boy, that's what I get for'- look I'd ever seen!

"No.." God reading his mind again.. "Not you, Gabriel.. I won't make another you!…

No, I'll just make you some more Angels!…

That's it!.. I'll make ones that can make-up hymns!.. Experts in the field of Hymnody!.. A very special sort of angel.. with an almost 'Human-ness in them'!.. That they might better relate to and fully understand.. and be attuned to the ear of mankind!.. As well as, to that of 'The Divine'!

Yes.. and they'll be able to create beautiful hymns.. ones all about my Son that's coming to save the world!…

And the whole choir can join in with them, as they teach and lead the singing!.. Under your authority, of course!…

They'll create hymns for this and each and every Christmas here-after!..

They'll herald the coming and birth of my Son!.. Yes, and.. that's it!.. We'll call them.. Sure, what-else!.. 'The Herald Angels'!..

Yes, and each one of them will be named after all of the different qualities necessary to make songs and to sing them!.."

Then God (in all of His excitement and without any further ado) rose to His feet to begin the creating.

Turning and looking up the cathedral stairways, He pointed His finger to the platform (inside the pillars of the main entranceway). An immediate flash of light impactually followed that lit up (as well and in the process) the entire inner auditorium. Gabriel (now also to his feet and staring up) appeared as curious and as nervously pale as, I'm sure, I must have looked!

When the explosion and its smoke finally cleared, there in the doorway stood a very tall angel. His lanky build.. together with his silver-trimmed dark hair and sleepily-appearing facial characteristics.. brought to mind someone of the Abraham Lincoln-type. Only, to the contrary, he was beardless and clothed in a long white vesture that was completely scattered with deep-scarlet-colored musical insignias.. notes, staffs and of-the-like.. which instead made him appear to have a unique look of wisdom and seriousness all his own. I watched as he very-drowsingly surveyed his new surroundings, only to be distracted when God announced...

"THE ANGEL OF NOTES!.." (Being a very fitting title, I thought!.. Except for maybe 'The Sleepin' Angel of Notes' which seemed even all the more suitable and

descriptive! For as I again glanced upward to catch sight of him, he was covering a yawn with his extremely-boney, 'perfect for finger snapping', cupped hand!)

"He.. Gabriel.. my first of Herald Angels.. will be blessed with 'perfect pitch.. an uncanny memory.. and be a perfectionist in all things pertaining to notes and their reproduction'!"

Before my eyes could return to the street, there was another exploding flash in the entranceway! Only this time (when the smoke cleared) there stood instead, a very jolly and fat angel of medium height.. sardined into a bulging (and splitting at the seams!) long white, only-loose-at-the-bottom robe. He.. looking quite the extreme opposite of his flanking partner, the Angel of Notes. His facial appearance was that of a wide opened-mouth smile, which immediately caught my eye! One that made all of his other features seem to only center-around it! The others be-ing.. his long silver-ish-like silky hair and beard.. his pink and protruding cheeks.. and his very kind and warm-filled eyes. His tremendous pot-belly took to an awful shaking, as he burst into one of the heartiest and most-pleasant laughters I'd ever set ears to! One that was so contagious that (upon hearing it) both Gabriel and I

uncontrollably joined in on to ac-company, losing all track of 'where we were' and the seriousness of 'what was going on' all about us! Only coming to our senses, when at last God's solemn, commanding voice proclaimed...

"THE ANGEL OF MUSICAL MIRTH!.." (Again, very fitting!) "..to bring happiness and joy to all angels, old and new alike! The Kindly Spirit.. with a Job of Many!"

By now, a very numbered and excited crowd of angels (from the street and all of its adjoining ones) had gathered around and in back of God to watch 'His creating' of these 'Herald Angels'.. with all of its fire-working, Fourth-of-July-like, breathtaking mood! Slowly but surely, the above cathedral-deck became filled, due to the (also-looking-on and crowding-outward) inner choir angels.. who, like everyone else, were tanglingly converging for a better view. With each flash of light, the in-process growing crowd would gasp and cheer.. only to subdue, just long enough, to hear the special title and blessing that God would bestow on them upon completion.

Then.. KAAABBBOOOOMMM!.. in the doorway.. another angel!.. In white, but he shorter of height.. yet still firm and with stock.. with a beard of dark.. and glasses.. stunned himself at his arrival there!

"THE ANGEL OF A CHORD!.." A brief pause…

"Harmony is his Absolute Existence!.. To flow in unison always!.. together with.. never alone!.. His ears hearing only the Fellowship of Sound!.. Yes, the forever supporter!.."

Without hardly a moment's pause.. KKAAABBBAANNNGG! And there.. Another! This one.. a nervous-looking and fidgety character! With a very flexible lankiness.. and smirky smile.. and pompadour-ed with light-colored, ever-wavy short-length hair! Having also (and very oddly enough) a sort-of business-man's-ness about him! "THE ANGEL OF THE MUSICAL SPIRIT!.."

Then, on God went.. giving him His 'special blessing'.. after which He continued to create even more of these 'Herald Angels'!

KKKKKRRRAAASSSSHHHH….. KKAA.. RRRUMMMBBLLE!
KKAA…PPUUSSSHHH…… KKAA…BBUMMMBBBLLEE!

After (what now in my recall seemed like..) a half-hour-or-so of this 'continuous creating', God at last took silence. Yet He did not say that He was done. So, all just waited. The stern-thinking nature of His look, made all very un-certain of what was on His mind! Would there be even more?

At last…

"The most important part of singing, Gabriel.. is Breathing!.."

That, of course, was the choking clincher! He wasn't done!

"I know it seems like a small and petty thing.. But.. it's the most vital and intricate part of it all!.." He added.

Then again He returned to His concentration, while all about Him began gaping at each other in wonder.

When God, at last, raised His finger and pointed it up.. even the most hidden of choir angels (not to mention Herald alike, who'd been squeezingly-forced back into the cathedral's outer-vestibule) held their breath in agonizing silence!

Like-as-if a tremendous bullwhip had been snapped onto the 'suspended-in-mid-air' mood of the on-lookers..So, too, was the impactual effect of the zap-flashing explosion that soon followed. None could comfortably await the smoke to clear! What would it be? It had been such a great flash, it seemed to take forever to disperse!

When it finally did.. all, excluding none (except God, of course) were completely and overwhelmingly amazed!

Disappointingly amazed, I should say though! For there in the cathedral doorway stood this tiny angel, no more than two and a bit feet tall! A glazey-eyed, pathetic-looking thing.. with a pointed-ish sort of chin, that protruded outward.. as in the same fashion did his arrowed-upright, ski-slope nose! Dressed completely out of angel-style to boot! Garbed (to the contrary) in an over-sized black Top-Hat-like Brimmer (At least, it was much 'too-over-sized', in consideration to 'his' limited stature!). And coming from it.. his long, jagged-and-shaggy, un-even dark hair darted down and out, just every-which-a-way! The hat and hair seemed to surround and outline his too-young-to-be-taken-serious, pale-looking face. Except for, of course, where his hair was parted on the sides of his head.. allowing for his ever-present and un-cover-ably, definite ears! A miniature, too-tight, black coat came to just below his waist.. half concealing an off-white (long john-type) collar-less shirt.. that was, in turn, made harder to see by the presence of a long, black choker scarf (that was hanging down and in-front-of-it from around his neck). His shirt sloppily tucked-into his pair of (almost black-ish too..) forest-green trousers.. which sort of stove-piped (too short) just below his fragile-looking shins! These being met by a pair of horizontally-striped, dark red-and-green knee socks (continuing from underneath his trouser-cuffs).. that were, at last, implanted into a pair of brand-spankin'-new, black-and-white tennis shoes. Yes.. That's right.. Sneakers!

What a sight! No robe! No wings! Not an angel-trace about him! And.. in a way.. looking about as out-of-place as if 'the Devil himself' had appeared instead, right in the exact spot!

All the angels (the street crowd and choir alike) began whispering. It was more-than obvious that they (each in their own way) felt that God had made some kind of awful mistake! Of course, none were prepared to tell Him so though! I mean, this was ridiculous! It had to be a joke! Yes, just had to! It sure seemed to be a laugh to them! For, in no time, the scattered sound of giggling became evident and began infesting the crowd's number increasingly. And in so, alienating the tiny little newcomer, who readily-enough picked up on their un-welcome-ness and ridicule (despite his just-being-born naïve-ness). He immediately became intimidated and very awkwardly un-comfortable. Yes, he too realized that he was 'different'.. there was no question about it! But the 'why he'd been created?'.. and even better, 'why like that?' was as much a mystery to him as it obviously was to the disorderly on-lookers!

I found myself (despite all the turmoil surrounding me) becoming deeply sympathetic to him, as I watched his fear-filled eyes dart all about the getting-very-unruly crowd below. More and more I could see that his ill-at-ease expressions were turning into what was an out-and-out embarrassment! It all just seemed to be so tragically unjust! For after all, the poor little fellow hadn't asked to be made and to be put into this awkward position! No, it just didn't seem fair!

Oddly enough, the more I studied his (seeming familiar, yet not grasp-able?) face.. the more, in turn, it came to me (in a very eerie and strange way!) that I could actually and in-fact read his mind. Yes, his thoughts! The deeper I concentrated, the more clearer and clairvoyantly I could reach in through the turmoiled jumble, finding and hearing..

'Why.. Why did God do this?.. Why?..

Why'd He make me.. like this? What'd I ever do to deserve this?..

I mean.. What am I supposed to be.. some kind 'a clown or somethin'?

Shoot!.. I just don't get it at all!.. It's gotta be some kinda mistake!.. Yeah, that's it.. some kind 'a mistake!… It's just gotta be!..'

As I listened in, the becoming almost-boisterous-now crowd began to distract me. Until, at last, I lost all perception. So.. surrendering my concentration, I instead turned back out to the street and its masses. Just as I did, I heard the commanding (and a-little-bit angered!) voice of God put an end to the commotion…

"THIS, GABRIEL, IS… THE ANGEL OF THE WIND!…

Yes, he will control the very wind that we breath from the skies!..

That same wind that we so desperately need to sing…"

Pausing to emphasize the seriousness of His next-to-follow lines, He resumed in a very dictating tone with…

"And.. because he has been received so un-accordingly by all of you.. I will also impart on him.. the extra blessing of the 'Will' and 'Power' that only the Great Wind itself has!.. They will be as one!…

Their determination.. and Their Gust-like Creativity will be as one within him!.. And more ultimately.. he will be 'The Catalyst'!.."

A dead-hush remained, even long after the ringing of God's speech. No one.. not Gabriel.. or even the newly-created little angel himself..(nor anyone, for that matter!..) fully understood what God had meant by His words. Yet no one.. and I mean, no one.. would question Him! For all knew that He had been upset and somewhat disturbed by their behavior.. and out of guilt and fear, held their silence. All mutually knowing though, that 'whatever it was?' that He had said.. it, for sure, meant business! And they best not doubt that!

Still hidden in the shadow, I glanced about their mouth-dried faces.. from one end of the tense-filled crowd to the other.. back and forth.. until (all of a sudden!), my eyes stopped-on and made an impactual contact with God's! No words were spoken! It was like 'time stood still'! And with a mental telepathy of unexplainable intensity, I was told..

"This is the reason I have brought you here…

You are to be.. and to serve as.. a guardian and constant companion to this new, little Herald Angel, 'the Angel of the Wind'..

It is for both of you that I have done this!…

You will follow him.. never letting him stray from your sight.. until, when the time comes.. I will call upon you, again, for a more ultimate purpose!

You have already become aware of your ability to see into his mind.. But never must you consider that you can change or alter his course.. for his Will is as strong as it is free!..

Your part in the journey ahead.. is only to observe and witness.. Remember that!..

Go now and follow.. And don't forget.. never let him stray from your sight long enough to lose his path!…

Time and Destiny are mine.. I control them and for-see them now as clearly as our next conversation!…

Never.. Never.. Never lose his path!..”

Then like the chill of an evening's dusk immediately falling upon me without warning, our telepathic conversation abruptly ended.. leaving me shivering and insecurely dazed! And emotionally drained, I might add! It was as though I'd awakened out of a beautiful, long dream.. with the water still blurring my eyes.. and wondering if it all had been real or not. But it had to be! For there, right in front of me.. was God.. now instead, looking very proudly up the stairs at the Herald Angels and once again acting as unaware of my presence as before. Not one eye in the vast crowd even merely glanced in my direction. It was as though God had stopped 'Time itself' to address me! Then, without another soul present knowing, He resumed it when He was through. I was sure He had! Because I could tell that none of the others there were (in the slightest) aware of what had transpired!

As I came more to my senses, I could hear God explaining to the Herald Angels what their purpose and task would be for this and all other Christmas's to follow.. Concluding with that they should first become acquainted with their supervisor, Gabriel.. and then go about their work. Adding that 'time was short' and that soon 'the Silver Star of Bethlehem would be in the Sky' and they must have their assign-ments completed and ready!

With His final words.. “That will do for now.. I must rest!..”, God began on His way up the long and winding street in the direction of His palace.. leaving the crowd (and its surrounding area) in the same mad-state-of-confusion that all-of Heaven had been in only moments before His unexpected appearance, and the captivating events that had taken place! Yes, all running crazy again! And only all-the-more excited and hurried, as a result!

Yet with as much as each one of them had on their minds.. and with all of the things that they had to do.. they still (in spite of God's being upset over the 'Angel of the Wind- incident') stopped for one more quick, 'gawking' look at the different-and-odd, little angel. Then (with a sort-of snicker) away they'd go.

Occasionally glancing back over their shoulders (and wings!) at the poor fellow..
Who had, by now, timidly worked his way in-and-behind one of the large columns
in the cathedral's entranceway. Sporadically he'd chance a quick peek out at the
crowd, only to again dart back!

Then (by accident), one of the descending-to-the-ground Herald Angels bumped
into his back, causing him to awkwardly fall out into the upper-level's open light.
This.. blushing the 'little misfit' beyond words!

Oh, the sadness in his hurt and fear-filled eyes! It couldn't help but linger in my
mind, even long after he'd again retreated back into the dark shelter. Why? Why
did it have to be like this? He'd never done anything to them. So.. Why? It sincerely puzzled and upset me to the max! And to think.. 'God was allowing all this
to happen'! Why? I could see Him, in the near distance, unconcernedly walking
away. And I just knew He was aware of it all. He had to be! Yet still, He wasn't
doing a thing about it! Why? I felt to call Him.. In hopes that He'd return and
help. Still though.. deep down inside I knew.. that there was some reason for all
of this. However unjust it seemed! But whatever it was.. I just, sure-as-Heaven..
couldn't see it, at the time!

THE THIRD CHAPTER

~ REBEL ~

"OKAY.. LINE UP HERE, YOU HERALD ANGELS!.." shouted Gabriel (now all-the-more 'in his glory' over his even-higher-ranking authoritative position!).

"LET ME GET A BETTER LOOK AT YOU.. and well.." moving in closer as they grouped.. "Let me see.. I think I'm gonna…

Yeah, that's it!.. I'm gonna give you all names… yeah, names that'll be shorter.. like nicknames!.. You know, so's it'll be easier on everyone 'n all!…

You.. Angel of Musical Mirth.. " who, by sheer coincidence, just happened to be standing closest-in-line-for-fire (and with 'nicknames' still on the 'tip of his mind')…

"We'll just call you.. ah.. Nick!.. Yeah, you know.. short for.. ah.." then, to himself..

"Ah.. What's it?.. Oh.. Oh, yeah!.." back out.. "Nicholas!…

And well.. Wait a minute!.. I tell you what.. Why don't you all get in order.. You know.. in a line.. like you's were created!.. Then I can think better!.."

They, re-shuffling. And when so…

"Okay.. now that's more like it!…

You.. Angel of Notes.." startling the lanky, dozin'-off fellow so much that he jumped at the sound of his name, as if he'd been rudely awakened and 'sleepwalking' through all of his prior movements. And in so, totally unaware of what had been going on all about him! Causing Gabriel to resume smartingly with…

"We ain't keepin' you up, are we?.." No reply.

"Well.. we're gonna call you.. ah?.. ah?.. let me see now?.."

As Gabriel thought on, it became evident to him that if he didn't hurry 'Mr. Notes' was going to definitely (and once again!) drift-off into an 'appearing awake', yet sound sleep! So just to say anything (without really even considering if it was an appropriate name or not), he forced out…

"Will!.."

And just in time too! For sure enough (not even a split-second after its execution) the newly-dubbed 'Will' did, in fact (and very unconcernedly at that too!) drift-off back into an 'eyes-wide-opened' slumber! His only (prior to that..) acknowledgement (of the name) being a 'sure.. that's fine with me'-nod!

Gabriel stared at him as if, either.. disgusted to the hilt.. or as if, maybe.. expecting a more-depthly reply. That of which, never came! So.. dropping his head and shaking it in disbelief, he continued on his way down the line. Sporadically shooting quick glances back.

Still innerly-perplexed, he reiterated.. "Nick".. as he passed the second angel in turn. It being receipt-ed with some hearty chuckles. But those of which, Gabriel never noting.

The Angel of a Chord stood firm and unflinching, staring keenly at his oncoming superior. This, in turn, snapping Gabriel out of his introspect and forcing him 'back on the ball'!

"Ah?.. ah?.. How's Len sound?.." This.. receiving stupefied recognition from the entire troop! And why not! What.. and I mean.. What could've possibly inspired that? Might it have been 'a show of arrogance' on Gabriel's part.. in rebuttal for the (what seemed defiant..) look on the face of (the now-baffled-appearing..) Len? Who knows? Anyway…

The Angel of the Musical Spirit, ever-flexible in his stance (twitchin'-and- gyratin' like as if some lilt was full-blastin' in his 'egg'-noggin'!), was world's away! Being that Gabriel was unable to hear (or likewise 'appreciate') 'the same', he offered very slowly and word-for-word-ly…

"Ah.. Excuse.. me.. but.. ah.. ain't you the Angel of the.."

Before he could finish, he was machine-gunned with…

"Yeah..Yeah..Sure!..That's-me!..Sure-thing!..In-the-Spirit!..Get-it?..Can-I-help-ya?.. Whatcha-needin'..Hmmm?..Hmmm?…C'mon, now!.." All said so fast, that Gabriel's initial response was to pull back stun-founded! When he caught his breath…

"Well.. you know.. We're havin' a meetin' here.. 'bout names and.."

"Yeah.. Yeah, I-know.. I-was-just.." cutting Gabe short.. and he in turn doing the same with…

"Yeah.. Yeah, I know.. just hold on a minute here!..   I can dig it!… But just cool-out for a bit.. 'k?.."

"Yeah.. sure.. I-wasn't-try'na-be-rude-or-nn.."

"COOL IT, CAT!.. HEAR ME?.. PUT A LID ON IT!.." brought a dead silence "Okay.. That's much better now!.. Don't you agree?.." Gabe smoothed.

It.. going un-answered. Uncaring whether it had or not, he resumed with…

"Now.. hmm?.. Johnny!.. Yeah… Johnny!.."   In another breath.. "That'll-do, who's-next.." (The latter.. all said jointly and like-one-word! And.. as a statement.. not a question!). Audaciously he moved onward down the remaining line of 'nickname-ees'.

Coming to a girl angel, Gabriel's brash disposition made a complete about-face. The ever-patient.. kind.. cheerful.. debonair.. soft-spoken.. (and you name it!).. 'Big Daddy' in him 'swaggered-in' taking its place. The whole transition coming off as 'fake' as his now wide-mouthed, googly-eyed smile! No one was buying.. (least of all, the girl herself!).. yet he tried on! In a way you couldn't hardly blame him. She was the cutest little thing! Shorter in length by far than her peers. Yet despite 'height', it was more than obvious to Gabriel (as well as by 'all') that her 'inner and musical stature' would be none in the least. The very way she carried herself re-confirmed it! Yes.. a giant in short! With an intense, vibrant glow!.. Un-beat-able charisma.. and a scarlet-red rose tucked into her jet-black, coarse-and-wavey, shoulder-length hair! She.. all the while.. bobbing her head about with the aire of 'cool' radiating out. Her definite nose and huge smile, the key-points of her face. Gabriel bent forward-and-down…

"Now ain't you just somethin' else.. you.. you.. just-sweet-little-'Angel of All Basics and Beginnings'!.." This being received by her (hip to him..) wide, show-them-teeth smile (Not to mention, by likewise.. some 'trying-to-be-choked' gags and snickers from the other on-looking Herald Angels; who quite honestly didn't appreciate, nor approve of, Gabe's style and approach. They.. thinking him to be instead 'Pure Corn' and 'Silly, to the Max'!).

"Let me see.." totally ignorant to this public-opinion (or simply choosing to ignore it?) .. "I know!.. What would 'you' like to be called?.." He smiled even wider.. cocked his head sideways.. and patiently waited (folding his hands, all the while, like the 'perfect' gentleman!).

"How's Mrs. Gabe sound?…" shot down the line from an unknown source. All gagged their laughs. Gabriel (on impulse) jolted his head to the left and the beginning of the line! Then sharply back.. to the right! He (steaming) scanned piercingly! The Angel of the Wind (on the end) seemed awful uneasy!

"HEY, YOU.. YOU DOWN THERE!.. YEAH, YOU!.." Gabriel belted at him.

He timidly stepped forward.. and paled even lighter in so doing.

"C'MERE.. YEAH, C'MERE!… FRONT AND CENTER!… PRONTO!.."

Reddening now with each painstaking step.. licking his dry lips.. and awkwardly wobbling his way, he at last reached fair distance of Gabriel.

"Did you say that?.."

"No, sir.." he mumbling-ly whispered, dropping his head to try and hide his face from the stares.

"Speak up, young man!.. The Good Lord gave you a tongue, didn't He?…"

"Yes, sir.." a tad louder. Becoming increasingly nervous, he tucked his trembling hands into his coat pockets and (to decoy his mounting, inner discomfort) began to sort of pace-in-one-spot.. as Gabriel snapped…

"Do you realize the importance of all 'f this?.."

"I guess.." still soft.

"YOU GUESS!.. YOU GUESS!.. WHAT'A YOU MEAN.. YOU GUESS?.."

"Well, I dunno.. I just.. well.. I just.. ah.. ah.."

"OUT WITH IT, BOY!.. YOU JUST.. WHAT?.."

Then…

"I said it!.. Yes, it was me!.. I said it!.." interrupted the girl angel.

Gabriel couldn't believe his ears! No one could, for that matter! How could she have possibly done it? I mean, first-off, it had been a male's voice! Or at least.. it sure had sounded like that! Secondly, it had seemed to come from 'somewhere's down the line'! No.. just no ways!

"I'm a ventriloquist!.. Didn't you know that?.." She added as convincingly as she could muster, under the circumstances… "Can throw it too!.. Make it sound like it's miles away, if necessary!"

There was a brief and meditative pause that followed.

Then Gabriel (still in astonishment and disbelief.. but, not to show it) offered…

"Oh, yeah.. Sure.. I knew that!.. Sure.. I knew it, all along!" When really and in fact, all he knew was.. that the first chance he got, he was going to 'check it out' with God.. and make sure that He had 'blessed her with that ability'! Either way, it had caught him totally off-guard.. and had, in the process, absolutely thwarted any further attacks on the (what he felt sure was..) little prankster at hand!

"In that case.. well.. you can just.. yeah, you can just go ahead on now.. Go on.. shoo, now!.."

With Gabriel's eyes ardently steaming-the-back-of-his-neck (despite his hat), the Angel of the Wind began his gradual retreat.. turning back only once (and very briefly at that!) to smirk a shy-'Thanking-like' smile at…

"Leah!.. That's what I wanna be called.. Yeah, Leah!.."

"Leah, huh?.. Well, why not!.. That's sure a pretty name!.. Yeah, I kind 'a like that!.. it's.. it's.. well, it's.. original!… Yeah, that'll be just great!.." Gabriel angled another smile. She (returning a quick one.. then snapping her fingers) sang…

"Leeee…aahhh!.." in a sort of falsetto. Tagging it with.. "Yeah.. That.. makes me feel all right!…"

Gabriel, once again, began down the line.. occasionally smiling back at her through-out all of his further proceedings.

When at last coming to the Angel of the Wind, he belted…

"ATTENTION!.." The little fellow.. practically jumping out of his skin!

"You ready, young man?…"

Catching his breath.. "yes, sir.."

Fact of the business, being.. Gabriel himself wasn't even near ready! His hastiness giving the impression that he already had a 'particular name' in store.. When truth-and-in-fact he hadn't the foggiest of ideas for one!

Glancing back down the assembly, he could readily see that all eyes were on him and waiting. He fought to shut them out and tried to concentrate. Desperately he searched for a 'proper and fitting' name. But not a one came that was even barely worth considering!

As the little angel grew more and more uneasy and self-conscious, Gabriel tried to think faster.. not wanting to purposely make it any harder on him (least of all himself!). Quite honestly, Gabe found even greater justification in the thought alone of (more than anything else) just 'getting it over with'!

Then it crossed his mind that 'Lack' might seem a very proper and fitting name.. considering all of the 'angelic qualities' that this little character was so lacking in! But, no.. What if someone (especially God!) were ever to put 'two and two' together. What a demoting thought! No ways! Besides.. Gabriel (with as much as he had it out for the little imp!) could never do anything that malicious or uncalled for!.. Regardless of whatever the reasons! He'd just have to think harder!

So, with 'Lack' still on his mind, he simply began reversing the alphabet in search of a rhyme word. From Lack to K.. 'Kack.. Kack?.. Nah, never do!..' To J.. 'Jack..

Yeah, sure.. Jack!.. Why not!..'

By now the Angel of the Wind was in the most pitiful of self-conscious states, over the 'all-eyes-on-him', suspended-in-mid-air situation he was being subjected to. So, when Gabriel at last (and finally!) exploded with…

"Jack!.." he, the Angel of the Wind (or.. excuse me.. Jack!) couldn't have cared less 'what he'd come up with'!

"Oh, thanks, sir.. that's.. yeah, that's just fine!.." served with a sigh.. "Yeah, that's sure fine with me!.." His response being so truly-grateful and sincere, that it made Gabriel feel somewhat guilty in knowing its real inspiration and origin!

Everyone else (down the line) didn't look so 'taken' or 'won' though!.. 'They're all songwriters.. maybe they figured it out?' Gabe worried. Then turning free from their gaze, he considered further.. 'I dunno.. maybe it's just my conscience?'. He spun another look.. 'No.. they know!.. Yeah, they know!..' . He looked at Jack (hands still in his pockets and scuffling).. 'I bet he does too!.. Why did I do that?'

To end any-further-thoughts-on-it, he yelled…

"OKAY.. LET'S ALL GO OFF SOMEWHERE'S IN HEAVEN NOW.. AND THINK UP SOME HYMNS!.. IT'S GETTING LATE.. SO LET'S GET MOVIN' ON IT!.. C'MON, NOW.. LET'S GET HOPPIN'!...."

As they all began dispersing in different directions, it was easy to tell (by the whispers and under-the-breath conversations, that were being carried-on-and-away with them) that (in spite of Gabriel's attempt at 'covering up') 'Jack's naming' was still the main, lingering thought on their minds! As likewise was Jack fully-aware of them 'talking about him' too! Though his 'natural stance' (head down.. scuffling.. hands-pocketed, etc., etc.) would have made anyone think otherwise.. Truth was, he was very, very perceptive! The study-er!

And being that they left in small groups (No one asking him, if he might want to join them..), it seemed like (to Jack) that even they, 'his peers', were against him! Even Leah (the friendly girl-angel who had 'bailed him out' earlier..) had been steered away! And the 'black-listed' thoughts seemed all-the-more-justified by the way they'd peeringly look back at him, as they continued on their ways. Yes, it seemed as though none wanted to risk being his friend.. in that, they too might become frowned-on by the others. Maybe in a way, you couldn't blame them. Still.. had only one of them made a greater effort... then the whole course of this 'Christmas History' might have been different. But none did. For whatever reasons! And so it stands!

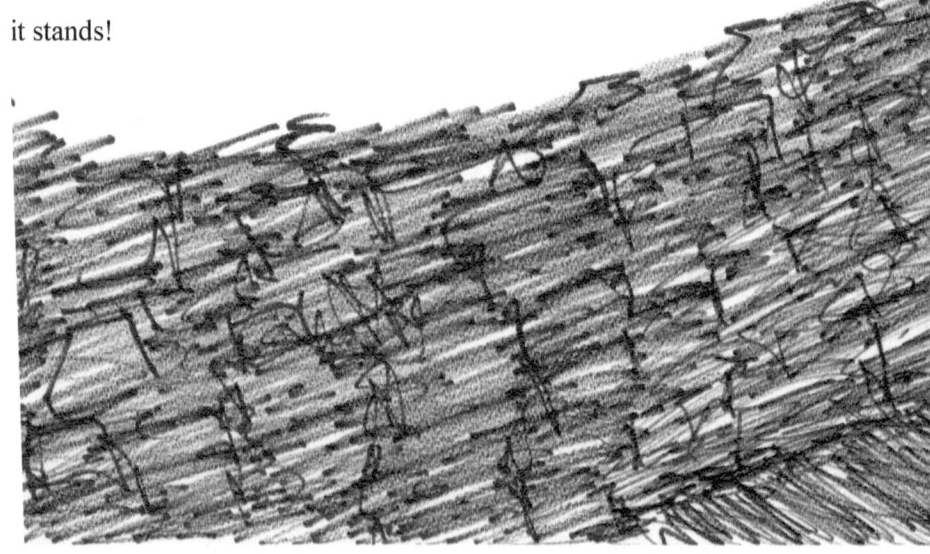

Jack plopped to the curb and watched them leave, sitting there feeling about as miserable-and-lowdown as no angel should ever have to feel in Heaven!

As Gabriel reached the top of the cathedral stairs, he addingly yelled to them all (now in the near-dimming distance)…

"BE BACK IN TWO HOURS!… THEN WE'LL PICK THE BEST HYMNS.. AND REHEARSE THEM FOR THE REST OF THE NIGHT, UNTIL IT'S TIME TO GO TO BETHLEHEM!.. GOT IT?.. TWO HOURS!.."

Then in he went, seeming very contented by the way things had turned out.

Jack (on the extreme other hand) was still perched on the curb.. head in hand.. absolutely miserable to say the least! You could've said 'he felt about two feet tall'.. but then again.. he was! Yes, he really was just about two feet tall! No.. seriously.. all kidding aside (For surely, Jack had had plenty-more-than-enough of his share of joking, through-out this night!)..

this was truly one of the most heart-rendering scenes I'd ever witnessed in my time.

For not only could I see his outward pain, but also I could 'hear inside' to the turmoil going on in his mind. This.. in turn.. bringing forth the most agonized-of-tears to his totally-depressed-covered face!

    -- I will interrupt and make note here, that… it wasn't until this time that I came to see (having been, in all other previous scenes until now, either 'behind' or 'too-far-away-from' him to detect), what was a gold-embroidered insignia on one of the ends of his scarf. It being a cursive J and F, back to back of one another.. with an up-swing continuing line on the left-side.. and a down-swing tail on the right. It appearing exactly as so…

    ..This, of course, being his initials! Yet, at first, it came to me as being and looking like.. a crushed (in sort of vertical fashion..) flower. That of which he kind-of was!

    Especially in these very moments, at-hand… --

Yes, the poor little fellow was in the utmost of distress…

"Why.. Why did God do this?…

Why did He have t' make me like this?…

Why couldn't I've been like all the other angels?.. just normal!.. But, no.. I gotta be like this!..

And.. these clothes!…

Maybe if I was t' find me a robe.. I might, at least.. Yeah, that's it!.. A Robe!.. Gotta find me a robe!.."

So.. down the winding street into the night, he went.. in search of his salvation.. A Robe! Or, you might better say.. 'in search of himself'! For really, was a robe going to solve all of his problems? Yes, it definitely would! At least, he was sure that it would!

I followed, tagging along behind him.. as he tried, as un-obviously as possible (and with the least of success), to walk the streets of Heaven unnoticed.. An impossible task for him, of all angels! For everyone he passed stopped to stare as he'd hurriedly try to escape on his way. His head steadfast-down all the way. He was simply too ashamed to look at anyone in the eyes! Eyes.. Ridiculing, laughing-at-him eyes. How he dreaded them! And even the deserted streets were none-the-less uncomfortable. At least, for me they weren't! For Jack's depressive state seemed to put a complete damper on all of the radiant beauty that Heaven had to offer. He.. with his hands tucked deep down into his pockets, mumbling and moaning to himself every inch of the way! And, me.. following faithfully and wishing that there was some way I could help him. But there was just nothing I could do to relieve his pain. Nothing.. except follow and sympathize! And a lot of good that'd do him! I had 'all the compassion in the (after..) world' for him. But what did it matter? He didn't even know I was there!

On and on, we went through the night-covered Heavenly City.. Jack's mind without-let-up dwelling on the abasing incidents he'd suffered. Up and down the streets and alleyways.. he, not giving even the slightest bit of thought effort to the hymn-creating that he was supposed to be doing. It was just the last thing on his turmoiled mind! And the black cloud surrounding him was so enthralling, that I found myself purposely falling behind to try to escape its ever-captivating effects. The more I lagged though.. and lost sight of him, in so doing.. the more I could hear the voice of God ringing in my ears… 'Go now and follow.. And don't forget.. never let him stray from your sight long enough to lose his path!..'

With those very words still echoing in my mind.. into view came the beginning of a massive crowd, just up and ahead of us. All gathered-about-and-facing what was like a speaker's platform, that was set-up just inside of the Pearly Gates. To say 'massive crowd' almost seems a totally inappropriate word-description though, considering its actual size. For the complete body of them absolutely filled the city's main courtyard there (in the nearing distance).. and continued (with barely any thinning!) out and into the surrounding axial streets! All-present were listening very-attentively to an addressing-them angel, who was 'handing down' instructions as-to the flight patterns (etc.) that they'd be following that morning, when their descent to Earth would take place. I panicked! For (just as I'd pre-meditatively feared) I'd lost sight of Jack, who had (for some strange reason stronger than his fear of crowds) made a bee-line directly into their midst! I (without a second's further delay..) dove in, as well, to try to retrieve his path.

Racing awkwardly through and about the gathering from one end to another, I frantically searched everywhere. Where had he disappeared to? What was he going to do? God was going to have my neck!.. Just started the job and already I'd blown it!

Just as I was ready to give up and sit down for a good cry, my eyes came in contact with the Pearly Gates again. Only this time I couldn't help but notice that (unlike only-moments-before) now they were not shut-tight. No, one of them was cracked-open just a hair. 'Yes, just enough to allow a small angel to…'

I rushed to them to look out and catch the fading, distant image of Jack.. running away over the misty, foggy clouds. "Thank God!". I took off in pursuit!

Running at the highest speed my legs could manage.. breathless and praying all the while that I wouldn't lose sight of him, I couldn't help thinking (with as much as was on my mind)…

'This… This is the Beginning!.. Yes, just the beginning of a lifestyle that's gonna remain with Jack.. for a long time!.. I can just feel it!…

Yeah, I can see it all now.. Running!… always running away!…

And the worst part of it is.. that he ain't only running away from Heaven.. No.. What he's really doing is.. Running away from himself!… Not facing up to it!.. Letting them and his own fears win over him, instead of standing his ground!..'

Yes, I realized right then and there that Jack's 'flee-dom' was going to be keeping-me-on-my-toes from that moment forth!

After a long strenuous chase, I at last came within close-enough-range to tune-in his thoughts.. finding (much to my amazement) that he was more-serene-and-happier than he'd ever been. Or never been, I should say! When only moments before I'd found myself condemning his 'to be' way of life, now to the complete contrary, I was justifying it…

'Well.. maybe he'll at least be a happy loner!…

For as alone as he is (or, in fact, thinks he is!), at least he's more at-peace with himself now!.. And there's a lot to be said for that!..'

I watched him up ahead as he slowed down.. with his arms-stretched like-as-if he were grasping the 'freedom of the air' and emotionally-lost in the 'inner relief of his heart' for the first-of-times ever in his short existence. A happiness and joy that he should've felt back in Heaven.. but, was un-able to! So.. really.. Was this escaping all so wrong? No, I agreed with myself, as I neared with a lump in my throat and tears mounting. What an over-powering happiness I felt for him! He was at last born! I was so pleased.. regardless of the whatever-circumstances that had made it possible! It was just so beautiful to see! He'd made it! He'd gotten away from it all! Far beyond the Crystal Lake.. the Angels.. and the Cathedral.. all way, way back now in the un-needed, un-wanted and forgotten distance!

After braking to a walk, he finally came to a stop when he reached the descending shoreline of what-was a tiny lagoon, engulfed-completely in a hazey fog. A fog, so surrounding, that the above-dark sky being the only visible different-setting the eye could find.

Alone at last (except for me, of course..), he sat on the water's edge staring-out forward across the pond, lost in thought. It was a lovely setting.. and the silence decorated and enhanced its mood perfectly!

Jack was in his own world now. A world that, step by step, he'd run into. A world that didn't have to deal with any society or its pettiness, problems and prejudices (etc., etc.). A withdrawn world of the mind! A peaceful world that.. all of a sudden (as if to rudely remind him).. was interrupted by the alarming sound of cathedral bells, coming from the near distance…

"The Hymn!.." He'd forgotten all about it!

An hour had passed and he hadn't made even one effort towards coming up with one! Thank God, the bells were close enough to hear! Actually, now that he'd thought of it.. they seemed too close, to tell the truth. I mean, especially considering the distance he'd thought he'd come! It didn't seem right? No, not at all right? It couldn't be! Just couldn't!

Jack quickly swung his head back around towards Heaven to confirm his distance.. only to be twitchingly startled by the small figure of a little-girl angel! She.. standing on the utmost ledge of the cloudy embankment, staring wide-eyedly back down at him! It seemed she had followed him? He couldn't believe his eyes! How could she have possibly caught up? It was totally unfathomable!

All that he could do was stare, dumbfoundedly, back at the adorably-cute angel and her very-sympathetic-looking, deep-hazel eyes. They.. being like magnets!

Eyes.. that seemed to reach right into him! Eyes.. so wide and compassionate, that even the most wildest, frenzied-est beasts alive would have had to yield to, at mere sight! She, too (like him), was small of frame. Even shorter than Jack.. with a much more petite of a build (Of course, she being a female, it was to almost be expected). And (only further accentuating her beauty..) she, having the longest of jet-black hair.. with scatters of reflecting rays (from the evening's limited-light) bouncing off of it, like a dawning sun. Hair.. so silky and fine, that it graced, softly-about.. even without the slightest movement of her head! And her face.. a very sensitive and youthful one.. with the fragile-est, punctuated nose and chin imaginable! Her dark-delicate features (so touchingly supported by her immaculate-white, ankle-length robe) made her a positive eye-catcher. Yes, it was no wonder that Jack was completely hypnotized! I knew instantaneously it was love-at-first-sight for them. It was inevitable! Their auras came together as one and shined in the dark reality, all about them.. Despite the fact, that they were actually a more-than-seeming-to-be distance apart! I waited impatiently for their first words. But not-a-one was spoken!

At last, she slowly neared. In so, Jack (finally coming to his senses) quickly turned away.. staring-out once more across the pond, in retreat. For the threatening possibility had struck him that.. maybe.. she, too (like everyone else), would find humor in him! What would he do, if she laughed.. or whatever? Why, it'd kill him! So.. rather than gamble the chance.. in a harsh (yet still noticeably hurting..) voice, he shot…

"What'da you want?…

Can't y' see I'm busy?…

I gotta get some work done!.. It's real important too!…

Gotta think up some hymns 'n stuff!…"

Jack's abruptness went as-if totally unheard.. seeming not to concern her, in the least. To the contrary, she appeared to be completely understanding of his anguished outburst. Continuing ever-closer, she at last took a half-sitting/ half-kneeling position on his front-right side…

"I just thought I'd come and join you…

My name's Angel Jane...

I'll be quiet.. really.. I promise!.. I won't disturb your thinking.. okay?..

Please.. I'll just sit here and won't make a sound.. all right?.. Please let me stay?.. Okay?.. I won't make it any harder on you.. Trust me!.. Okay?.."

Her pleadings were just so-sincere and emotionally-put, that Jack (in all of his 'fake' anger) couldn't help but surrender to them, without the slightest of retaliations!

"I'm one 'a the Herald Angels.. The Angel of the Wind..

But they just call me 'Jack'...

Well, anyways.. I'm suppose t'.."

"Yes, I know.." she whispered. Jack, near tears (.. and in spite of the brief interruption, that he never heard anyway) continued.. explaining his frustrating story, as she attentively listened...

".. create some hymns!...

'n well, y' see.. them others.. they left with partners 'n all, t' help them..

But, me.. well, I gotta do it all m'self!.. No help, what s' ever!...

Hey, they don't care 'bout me!.. They don't even hardly like me.. Much less, wanna help me!.."

Jack rambled on and on, pouring out his heart and soul.. as Angel Jane very patiently lent her ear. She knew fully well how badly he needed to express it to someone and get it off his chest. It was obvious too.. that she was someone that he felt he could trust with his utmost, deepest feelings. In short time, a very binding close-ness came between them. It was easy to see that they had something very natural and beautiful.. A friendship, as well as a Love! A true caring and sincere affection towards each other. Something rare and far above average. A God-given thing! I even considered (to myself.. being there to witness her all-of-a-sudden and out-of-nowhere arrival), that she had been created 'right there on the spot'! Yes, made for this sole purpose! That of, knowing.. loving.. and emotionally-supporting this complexed, little rascal! Who (more than obviously enough) was very much 'in need' of the like! God was showing an extra bit of mercy on Jack.. I was sure He was! But doing it, in an un-suspecting (to Jack) and disguised way.

I was positive it had to be that! I mean.. there was no puff of smoke or anything like that, when she made her entrance.. But, still.. I could just tell! For.. I (in all of my utmost effort to keep up with Jack's high-speed retreat) was, with first-hand experience, totally convinced that it would have been virtually impossible for her to have, likewise, just made the same trip. Not to mention, her at-present calm and cool (Not a hair out-of-place..) appearance! No ways!.. just no ways, in Heaven! Yes, there was simply no question about it in my mind.. She couldn't have! And besides, it was more-than-evident that they were 'made for each other'. Just the mere sight of the two of them huddled together, like so, would've brought a lump to even Satan's throat! They were the 'Perfect Couple'! It was just so touching, tender and pure! The innocence of true, young love.. so romantic and ideal! So beautiful, that one could say 'it was too good to be true'.. that it couldn't last.. Just like all other beautiful and ideal situations.. Doomed!

Jack (still sorting through his tragic tale) all of a sudden dead-stopped in mid-sentence, when he got to the part about hearing the 'too close' cathedral bells.

"Oh, man.. I forgot again!.." he gulped, becoming very notice-ably nervous.. and, in turn, thinking and talking-to-himself aloud...

"What am I gonna do?...

I gotta get t' work!... " turning to Angel Jane...

"Hey, you're gonna have t' leave... Really.. I ain't kiddin'!... I just can't think like this!.. I gotta be alone!..." back to himself...

"Boy, I gotta get down t' some business here!... "

Actually, it had been Jack who'd been doing all the talking! Angel Jane.. well, she'd just been listening and trying to help! But Jack was too twisted now to real-ize what he was saying. Upset and confused, t' caps! He needed privacy, for sure.. But his hysterics were completely unnecessary.. And only making Angel Jane feel like a 'completely un-wanted intruder'! By the look on her face, you could readily see that she felt hurt and unsure of 'exactly what she'd done wrong?'. She rose to leave, as he un-needingly persisted...

"What am I gonna do?...

You think they hate me now.. Man, it's gonna be ten times worse!...

Listen, Angel Jane.. I'll probably see you later.. back in Heaven.. in the cathedral.. All right?.. I gotta be there in a little while.. All right?.."

"I'm sorry, Jack.. Really!.. I was just trying to help.. I'd really.. I'd really still like to help, if.."

"No.. No.. Listen!.. I'll see you back there.. Okay!.." Jack swinging back around towards the pond, as if to not be listening anymore. His mind was made up!

So Angel Jane began her exit.. stopping occasionally.. hoping he would change his mind and call her back. But he didn't. She unwillingly continued.. off and, at last, into the horizon of haze.

As I watched her image disappearing into the distant fog, my first impulse was to strangle Jack. What a fool! She had tried so earnestly to help him. Listening endlessly and giving it her all.. And here he was, pushing her away! What an idiot he was being! And to stubbornly be ignoring her, on top of it all.. Why, he deserved to be alone! Oh, I could've very sincerely killed him!

I waited, praying he would realize his erring way. He'd call her.. I was sure he would! My head pivoting back and forth.. from him to disappearing-her, in the far. He'd call her, any second now. I (on the edge of my seat) waited. But, nothing. Then.. she was gone!

Jack remained steadfast.. elbows on his knees and resting his nose on his crossed fore-arms.. still staring-out across the shining lagoon. Not budging an inch! I continued to look back and forth between him and the now-vanished image of Angel Jane. How could he do this? Was he crazy? Back and forth, until my neck was beginning to sore!

Then.. at last.. when I looked at Jack and started to again turn away, my eyes returned ever-quickly for a double-take. For I had noticed (in my former glance) that his sunken eyes were now completely filled-to-the-brim with tears. These, as glistening and 'sparkly shining' as the pond that they were staring into! I immediately tuned into his thoughts.. and they were (as I would have hoped them to be) of Angel Jane and the awful mistake that he had made in sending her away. I was so glad that he had finally come to his senses!

Being torn between the job of remaining there alone and making-up a hymn.. or instead chasing after Angel Jane, he tangled through himself trying to make a decision. The more he thought on it, the more confused he became. And all the while and as well.. in so doing, the more he emotionally-'broke-down'.. bringing about and with it an audible whimper. Until so overtaken by it all, he at last slid down into a laying-position (curled-up like a newborn) and began crying uncontrollably. The hymn meant so much to him! It was more than just a hymn! It was 'proof-of-his-worth' to everyone back in Heaven (not to mention, to Jack himself)! They'd respect him and 'like him' for sure, if he could only accomplish that 'one great masterpiece' that he was so desperately hoping to! Yes, 'a one' so great, that no one could deny its value. He'd be important then! Someone that they'd all 'look up to'! It could (and would..) solve all of his problems! Even better than any danged, ole robe ever could. You betcha, it would!

But, then again.. there was Angel Jane.. and Love and all 'a that! What if he never saw her again? And even if they did meet later, back in Heaven.. maybe she wouldn't care for him anymore? Maybe she'd feel so hurt and rejected that she'd never accept any of his reconciliations, no matter what he did to make-up! Maybe even the 'Greatest of All Hymns Ever' wouldn't turn her head in the slightest then? Could he afford that? To lose her? The only one who'd ever showed him any true and sincere compassion? So.. which would it be.. The Hymn.. or.. Her? Which was more important to him?

The minutes seemed like hours.. 'til at last Jack jumped to his feet...

"ANGEL JANE!.. ANGEL JANE!.. WAIT!.. PLEASE.. WAIT!.. ANGEL JANE!.." he began screaming at the top of his lungs, as he ran off, back in the direction of Heaven.

There was no reply waiting though, in the dark-of-night distance.

He trudged on, regardless.. continually calling her. He had to find her!

'She must be back in Heaven, by now.. or at least, pretty far up ahead..', he puffing-ly calculated.. as his legs picked-up speed, rapid-taneously! I myself found it ridiculously hard 'keeping up'. He was just too fast for me! And with each run, he seemed to be improving his speed-a-bility a whole lot quicker than I, for sure!

After what-seemed-like ten minutes of this 'full force' running, he came to a stop to try to catch his breath. Something (I'm sure) he'd have never done (or would've had to, I can very safely say now!) had it not been for 'his crying' (that was heavily-draining his normally over-abundant energy). But, whatever the reason might have been, I was just very grateful! For it allowed me to catch-up (among other things more physically gratifying). And catch-up, I did! And.. just in time too! For right as I did, I witnessed what-was one of the most truly remarkable and phenomenal events that I'd ever laid-eyes-on up to that moment in time! And a total revelation for Jack himself, as well, I might add!

Yes, just as I got close enough to see.. Jack (pitifully out-of-breath) inhaled what-must-have-been the greatest amount of air that I'd ever seen anyone ever breath-in, in one take. Then immediately following, I heard the shrill of the loud-est whistle that had ever made contact with my absolutely-unready-for-it ears. My eardrums rattled and distorted at the first sound of it. I was 'ear-shatteringly' shocked, you could say! As, too.. was Jack, I'll re-state! For little had he himself been aware of this 'ability of his' to be able to create such an impactual sound. He was beyond-stunned! I could just picture (even though I was in back of him) what his facial expressions must have looked like. It showed in the frozen-cringed posi-tion of his backside!

'If Angel Jane was anywhere's up ahead.. well, she'd had to have heard that!..'

He inhaled again.. only this time taking-in even more.. causing him to counter-arch his back and entire body-frame into what-was-almost the total reverse of a 'toes-touching position'. I thought surely his spine would snap! My face tight-ened as I painstakingly watched!

Then, an even-louder, more-piercing whistle cut through the foggy pitch-black night. Jack paused to listen to its echoing return, totally lost in the awe of his new discovery.

Slowly, but clearly.. Angel Jane came into sight. She'd heard! Thank God!

As she approached, Jack (despite her return) remained completely enthralled and 'lost in' the deep thought of it all. This, making her a little uncertain and worried over 'whether or not, something was wrong with him'? And also.. as to 'whether or not, (like she'd hoped) he had been trying to call her'? In other words, just what had been his intentions?

When she at last reached speaking distance, she halted and waited-out some kind of a reply. But none came. No, all he did was peer and gawk at her with a dropped-jaw-look that seemed almost-spooky! Yes, it kind of scared her! In so, making her a bit nervous and uncomfortable. What was the matter with him? What was he thinking?

Arching back again, he took in even more air than ever-previous. Holding it in, he stopped and looked at Angel Jane (who was, by the second, growing increasingly-paler and more-anxious-appearing over this 'crazed-like' state of his).

Then.. after a long, limbo-like silence.. it whistlingly came. Only this time, it was melodious. Yes, it had a tune to it! A very wind-ful array of pleasant notes.. with an ever- romantically-crooning and enchanting melody.. had swirled and echoed-back beautifully through the so-still evening!

When it ended, Jack was still staring into the frightened eyes of Angel Jane. Breaking the unbearable hush, he jubilantly exclaimed…

"THAT'S IT!.. ANGEL JANE.. THAT'S IT!…

It's cause 'a you too!.. You helped me find it!…

You.. Yeah, you really helped me to find it!…

That's it!.. That'll be my hymn for the Baby Jesus!.. He'll love it!

Just imagine!.. Yeah.. Can't y' just hear it now?.. The whole choir doing that together, at the same time!.. It'll just sound.. so.. so beautiful!..

It's.. It's.. Yeah.. It's completely new and original too!.. It's a new way of sing-ing!.. I'm sure that it'll be the one they'll choose t' do as the first hymn, right after Jesus is born!…

Then, you watch, Angel Jane.. Then they'll all like me.. and see that I'm not so small and unimportant after all!.. Yeah, then they'll all think different of me, 'cause 'a that!.. Yeah.. you betcha they will!…

And, you.. Angel Jane.. you.. you're the one that helped me t' discover it!.. Yup.. y' sure as Heavens did!…"

Jack rushed to Angel Jane and threw his arms around her.

"It's beautiful, Jack!.. Yes, it's a masterpiece of a Hymn!.. Really!.. I like it!.. It's such a different and unique idea.. I'm sure that they'll all have to agree!.. Yes, I'm sure that it'll be 'the first pick'!.. It's got such a true and sincere feeling to it!.. How could they not hear it!.. Yeah, I just.. I just.. really love it!.."

They began jumping and dancing and holding onto each other, acting just like two little children. Yes, giddy and lost-in-the-joy of Jack's soon-to-be recognition.

~ IF WE COULD ONLY RUNAWAY ~

Holding hands, they started on their hurried-way back to Heaven.. running faster and faster, as they went.. becoming more and more excited and anxious-to-unveil-Jack's-masterpiece with each dashing step. Over the clouds, together, they sped.. through the fog and night.. pass the now-abandoned Crystal Lake.. through the glistening-ever-bright Pearly Gates.. and up the streets towards the

cathedral. Jack, now, no longer ashamed to be seen by anyone on the streets. No, now his 'proud-as-a-peacock'-certitude was carrying his head way up high. He was 'esteem-filled-to-the-brim' over what he'd invented! And along with Angel Jane's belief-in-him, he was beyond-any-doubts convinced that he had something new and profound to offer! No, he was no longer, in the least, concerned or worried over 'what anybody thought' of his different clothes or appearance. Now instead, he felt that they made him stand-out-from-the-crowd! And after all.. Why shouldn't he stick out?.. He really was 'someone different'! And what was all-the-more ironic was.. the very same angels on the streets (who'd laughed at him, only a short time before..) were now instead.. following behind 'him'! Yes, all.. hurrying to see why he and Angel Jane were so excited. Very curious and concerned, they advocatingly ranked behind them in a group that snow-balled by the second. All.. heading up and in-the-direction-of the un-expecting cathedral!

Ascending the long stairway, in they went.. Jack and Angel Jane pied-piperingly leading the tremendous and boisterous following.

The other Herald Angels had previously returned and were in the 'start' of auditioning their hymns for Gabriel. What was only moments before, an 'orderly scene' (I'm sure!).. now transformed into a total state of mass confusion and hysteria! The rowdy, chaotic crowd of intruders (following Jack) entered without end.. squeezing their way in, completely surrounding Gabriel and his center-floor troop. In a matter of 'upsetting' minutes, the entire cathedral inners were filled to the utmost maximum! Jack (with Angel Jane right at his side) immediately took the floor.. addressing and looking at Gabriel (who was directly in front of him).. but, doing so loud-enough that all might hear…

"I HAVE IT!… YEAH, I'VE GOT IT!…

IT'S GONNA BE 'THE GREATEST OF CHRISTMAS HYMNS EVER'!…"

Over anxious and gasping for his breath, he persisted…

"I REALLY HAVE IT!.. IT'S THE ONE!.. REALLY!.. I AIN'T KIDDIN'!..

GOD AND THE BABY JESUS.. THEY'RE GONNA LOVE IT!…"

Gabriel (being put into an authoritatively-bad mood by the intrusion and the continual disruptions still going on, all about him..) demanded…

"WAIT!.. WAIT YOUR TURN!.. YOU'RE GONNA HAVE'TA WAIT YOUR TURN, JUST LIKE EVERYONE ELSE'S GOTTA!..."

Actually (the truth of it, was..) Gabriel himself was as-curious as everyone else to know 'just what this little misfit had contrived' that was so worthy of all this enthusiastic response.. and the legion of followers that he had already seemingly convinced. So, when one of the as-equally-inquisitive Herald Angels, 'Will' (the Angel of Notes.. who was first-in-line, of course, to be heard) offered with a yawn...

"Let him go.. I'll wait.. I don't care.. Let him.." Gabriel grabbed-at-it, without the slightest restraint.

Jack resumed his selling.. only, at a more subdued volume. For now, all eyes and ears were on him. The dead-hush heard...

"I've got it!.. Yeah, it's the one!.. it's a new kinda singin'!.."

The 'new kinda singin'..'–part of his statement caused an immediate outburst of gasps and a surge of whispered, echoing-it repetitions.. "new kinda singin'?.. new kinda singin'?". These, being instantaneously repressed when Jack still-over-enthusiastically reminded...

"God and the Baby Jesus are gonna love it!.. I'm sure they will, 'cause it's never been done before!.. It's somethin' new and different!.. And, well.. it's gonna be.."

Gabriel (having heard enough) interrupted...

"Okay!.. Okay!.. Hold it!.. We believe you!.. For danged out-loud, cut out the sales pitch and get on with it!.."

Jack pulled back. But then (recapturing his zeal and self-confidence), he glanced a sort-of 'cocky-'n-cool' smile at Angel Jane.. and, in so, bent forward to begin his slow-motioned (for theatrics!) inhaling. This, at last concluding with his entire backbone again bent into an almost-reversed position! Not one wide-eyed on-looker stirred (or even blinked), in the slightest.. in that they might possibly miss even one second of the 'whatever-it-was?' that was going to happen!

Then, the (you-could-hear-a-pin-drop..) solemn hush, that had held the cathedral gathering spellbound, finally (after what seemed like 'forever') climaxed!

All and every single soul present.. almost jumped-out-'a-their-robes, as the loud-est.. echoing-est.. melodic-filled whistle (I, not to forget everyone there, had ever heard!) soared upward towards the high chamber ceiling!

Ricocheting everywhere (from marble pillar to marble pillar on its way back down), it fell upon the astonished crowd more loudly and reverberantly than its impactual launching! 'Bewilderment' could hardly describe the looks on the faces of all! All.. excluding Jack and Angel Jane, that is.. who were just standing there, smiling away.. and awaiting the expected praise that they were so sure would fol-low.

But it didn't. There was only (and instead) a long, speechless silence that re-mained.. and dragged on.. and on.. leaving them dangling in suspense. It.. slowly, but surely.. changing the composure of their faces and trying-desperately-to-stay smiles.

At last...

"Where are the words?...

Y' know.. the words!.. Where's the words?.." asked Gabriel, in facial puzzle-ment.

"There ain't any words!.. That's it!.. Don't y' see.. It's a new kinda singin'.. remember?..

It's a new way.. that's never been done before!...

It'll just sound s' beautiful, when all 'a us..."

Before Jack could finish, it came.. like a tremendous avalanche.. The crashing-like thunder of repressed, dying-to-escape laughter from the crowd! Rumbling the entire cathedral's foundation.. like the 'Greatest of Cloud-quakes, in all-of Heaven's history' had just erupted! A laughter that persisted on and on, in spite of Gabriel's attempts to regain order.

Poor Jack was now (more than in any of his previously-traumatic situations) experiencing the most embarrassing moment in his entire short existence! How could it have happened like this? A total backfire! For he'd been so sure of what he had! The hymn.. he had been convinced beyond a doubt that it would be ac-cepted.. But instead.. this!

His face deepened a redder-and-redder blush, as he confusingly eye-darted the still-laughing-at-him crowd. He found it absolutely impossible to look at Angel Jane in the face. He just couldn't let her see him like this! And to think, she had believed in him and his outrageous idea. That made him feel all-the-more guilty and ridiculous! She just didn't deserve this! Why should she even have to be subjected to something this degrading! She was too good for anything this cruel-some!

Jack became sicker and sicker, by the second.. feeling so ill-and-tense, that he started becoming dizzy and nauseous. The laughter just wouldn't stop! It only seemed to get louder! He wanted to run and hide, but where could he escape to. His mind was exploding with total complexing anguish! Until, all he could see.. was red! Fire red! His heart and emotions pounded un-mercifully.. beyond all control!.. Red!.. Exploding red!.. red!… red!.. red!.. red!

Then, he went blank.. falling to the floor, limblessly.. and becoming completely unconscious.

When (out of a beautiful and peaceful dream..) he awoke, the laughter had finally ceased. Angel Jane was comforting him, kneeling right above and beside him on the floor.. while Gabriel (all the while) was repetitively commanding…

"GET SOME WATER!.. SOMEONE.. GET A GLASS OF WATER FOR HIM!.. Y' HEAR ME?.. SOME WATER!.." continuing and injecting (but nobody listening)…

"MOVE BACK.. EVERYBODY.. MOVE BACK!…

GIVE HIM SOME AIR!.. DON'T CROWD IN S' CLOSE!.. MOVE IT NOW.. YOU HEARD ME!.. WHAT'S THE MATTER WITH Y' ALL?.. CAN'T Y' HEAR ME?.."

At last, he blew his roof…

"JUMP BACK, JACKS!.." and that did it!

When (after a time) the crowd was more settled and organized, Gabriel began (the more awake-appearing Jack became) apologizing for the incident…

"It's a great idea!… But.. but.. but, I.. I just can't see it bein'.. Well.. I know what I'm lookin' for.. 'n well, when I hear it, I'll.. I'll.. Well, there's others that'a gotta be reviewed.. 'n.. well.. well.. ah.. ah.. well.. let me see.. Ah.. Yeah, let me think on it some.. 'n…"

Jack knew fully well what he was trying to say. It wasn't going to be used! Why didn't he just come out with it?

There was a very obvious and mutual feeling of guilt through-out the crowd. It was very notice-able that all felt bad about the way they'd acted. But it was too late.. the damage had been done. There would be no amends! At least, not in Jack's mind, there wouldn't! No, he was right.. and that was all there was to it! His hymn was a masterpiece.. and they were just emotionally deaf! They had to be, not to be able to hear the sincerity and pure love that had gone into it! He was also convinced that.. the real reason that they hadn't liked it and had laughed.. was not because it wasn't good.. But , in fact, because it had been he (himself) that had created it. They just simply didn't like him.. and no matter what he ever did to try to change it, he was just never going to be accepted by them! There was no need for him to try to fool himself any longer. They just didn't.. and weren't ever gonna like him! No.. never! So why should he be nice to them? Really? Why should he forgive them and act like nothing happened?

His anger and reverse-prejudice intensified with each recovering moment. And by the time he'd reached total awareness, a completely new character was to emerge. No longer (outwardly..) timid.. and shy.. and humble, etc., etc… But, now instead.. one seeming to be very openly-arrogant.. with a very bitterly-cold-nature! One.. refusing to listen.. or even let Angel Jane herself (nor any, for that matter!) tend to him. In a very overly-dramatic, pulling-his-arms-free fashion, he jumped to his feet and began scuffling his way towards a dark-and-hidden alcove in one of the far-corners of the huge auditorium. Head down.. hands in his pockets, he stormed.. occasionally 'sly-eyeing' a quick look back. Only to fire-ingly mumble something, then continue on his sulkin'-and-steamin' way!

Gabriel soon (and without a lot of effort) accepted that all communication was lost.. and instead began vacating the intruders that he might resume the 'hymn-auditioning'.

As I (soon to be followed by Angel Jane) tailed Jack into the alcove, the Angel of Notes yawningly stepped forward to begin the rendition of his hymn. This, causing me to stop (after a few feet into the dark) and momentarily lend it my ear.

"Ah.. It's titled.. 'Christmas-time is here again'.." I heard him say.

"Again?.." shot Gabriel.. "What 'a y' mean.. Again?.."

In a sleepy-like sigh of defense (with earnest)…

"I dunno.. Somethin' just told me that's what I was 'sposed t' write!.."

"It ain't even come once yet.. 'n here y' are singin'.. Again!…

Are you for real?.." Then Gabe, quickly to the crowd.. " Is this guy for real?.." Back to Will.. "Y' know.. I can't help wonderin' about you!.. Somethin'.. Yeah, somethin' kinda tells me that you're as weird a one as.. as.. him!.." pointing to the alcove.. "Yeah.. you'd better watch y' step, buddy.. or.. y' know what?.."

"What?.." This again-earnest reply of Will's, confounding Gabriel.. setting him off-guard and making him totally forget his train-of-threat…

"Listen you!.. Do your danged hymn and just.. just.." becoming so flabbergasted, he lost his conclusion.

Will sang it.

It was real nice! At least, in my book! I liked it!

But Gabriel, of course, nixed it in mid-notes with…

"Nah!.. Nah!.. Nah!.. Don't make no sense!.. Ain't gonna work!.. I don't know what could 'a ever inspired that 'Again' baloney!.. Can't even vaguely dig where you was comin' from, on that bit!.."

Will's head dropped, making Gabriel feel sorry for his harshness with him. But I knew (all the while) that he'd in-fact-'n-sure-enough just drifted off again. Yeah, to sleep! Despite, Gabriel resumed in a much more sensitive way, totally un-aware of this…

"Look 'it.. I tell y' what.. We'll catalog that one.. for later!.. Okay?.."

No response.

"Okay?.."

Still.. nothing.

It hit Gabe!

"I'M GONNA KILL THIS GUY, SOMEWHERE'S ALONG THE LINE!.. I

SWEAR IT!…

SOMEBODY!.. SOMEBODY, PLEASE.. GET THIS SLUMBER-HEADED.. SLEEPWALKIN'.. SNOOZIN'-EXCUSE-OF-AN-ANGEL OUT'A MY FACE, BEFORE I.. I.. I…"

To the sounds of etc., etc., I resumed my entry into the dark-solemn-like confines of the alcove. There, Jack sat.. in all of his anger.. floored, in the pitch-blackest far-corner.. face down.. and still mumbling away. As I took a seat on the opposing side and corner.. Angel Jane (now kneeling behind him) reached out.. touching his back.. to be greeted with…

"Why don't you.. leave me alone?.. Can't you see.. I'm trouble!…

Yeah, I'm different than.. all 'a them, out there!.. There's somethin' wrong with me!.. Super wrong!.. I.. I.. just ain't normal!…

So.. why don't you just make it easier on y' self.. 'n go find someone else!.. Someone who fits in with this ridiculous place!.. 'cause, I sure don't.. and.. "

"But I love you, Jack.. I really do!…"

"Words!.. "

"No, Jack.. I really do!…

And I still believe in your…"

"Why should ya?.."

"I just really do!…

It may take some time, but.. they'll all see.. someday!.. It's just gonna take some.."

"Someday?.. It's got t' be tonight!.. Not.. Someday!.. I wanted the Baby Jesus to hear it 'n well.. It's gonna be the one He loves the most.. I just know it is!.."

Jack paused to control his quickly-rising tears.. that were, in turn, beginning to make his voice crack. Then (in the amount of time it would take to swallow a throat lump), he insistently continued with…

"Listen out there.. Hear that?.. All that is.. is.. Old Hymn Music.. with some new words put t' it, 'bout Christmas!.. That's all it is!.. It ain't nothin' different or creative!.. or new!.. No ways!.. just the same old stuff!…"

"Jack.. now you know you don't really mean that!.. " Angel Jane realizing (better than he) the insincerity of his remark.. "You're just.. upset 'n all.. Well, you know you'd never say that if.."

"What 'a they know!.. They don't even like me!.." His tears showing now.. " I betcha they all prob'ly know I'm right.. 'n just don't wanna admit it!...

Boy, 'm I gonna get out 'a here!.. 'n soon!.. Yeah, I ain't stickin' 'round here, f' nothin'!.. Yeah.. 'n I ain't never comin' back!.. I ain't nobody's fool!.."

"Leave?.. Where will you go?.." Angel Jane heart-brokenly interrupted.. "I thought.. Well, I thought you loved me too?.. I thought we'd be together?.. What.. is your hymn more important than me?.."

Pausing to catch her emotional outburst, she softly returned with...

"I'm sorry, Jack.. I didn't mean that!.. I understand how important it is to you!.. I really do!.. It's just that.. Well, I'd just really like to.. to be with you!.. I don't want to see you go away.."

She began to cry. This, immediately 'cooling' Jack's anger. Moving in closer to comfort her, he began running his fingers through her dark, fine hair. Then, supportingly he lifted her chin to wipe away the tears.

"Angel Jane.. I love you too.. I really do!.. And always will!... I'll never love anyone.. the way I love you!...

Why, you could search forever-'n-ever in this vast universe.. 'n you'd never find another that feels for you, the way I do.. It's beyond all words!...

But y' have to understand.. I have t' do what's in m' soul!.. How can I ever love you totally, when I'm so at-odds with m' self like this?...

There's a road I have to follow.. No matter where or how far it takes me!.. And whatever-the-cost, I have t' be willin' t' pay it.. It's somethin' I've just gotta do!...

There's somethin' missin' here!.. Seriously missin'!.. 'n I gotta find it!.. But it has no bearin', what s' ever, on our love!.. Not in the least!.. No.. that's forever!.. Yeah, Forever 'n ever 'n ever!..."

As I continued to eaves-drop on them (being such a touching scene), I likewise found myself crying-along and breaking-down from the intensity of the mood. It was just so heart-breaking! I (at one point) even considered leaving for a while.. at least, long enough to catch my breath. Between all of their tender kissing and the romantic, Romeo-'n-Juliet tragedy they were being faced with, I couldn't hardly watch without being totally pulled-in to the melodramatic spell that was radiating from them. And as it persisted.. non-stop.. through-out the long night (accompanied by the most angelically-touching soundtrack that you could imagine), it came to me that my only-possible escape-from-it was going to have to be.. sleep! And being as worn-out as I was (from the earlier-evening's escapades), it took not the slightest bit of effort to comply!

When Gabriel's horn blasted reveille into the still-dark morning.. rattling the entire cathedral inners.. hailing all that it was time to leave for Bethlehem.. my nervous system became completely un-glued. It was, as though, all of the electricity in my body had short-circuited in my brain, awakening me instantaneously!

With the lids of my eyes opened to their absolute maximum, I jolted my pulsating head in the direction of Jack and Angel Jane, in fear that I might have lost them. They were still there.. Thank God! Yes, still there.. and still 'carrying-on' just exactly as they'd been, when my eyes had surrenderingly closed.

Immediately (at the sound of the horn) though, Jack was reminded of the previous night's episode.. and jumped to his feet, regaining all (and more!) of the fury that he had displayed at the time. Nervously pacing all about the alcove, he started in again with...

"Now, it's too late!.. They're leavin'!.. Now what 'm I gonna do?.. Oh, man.. What a mess this is!.."

Rantin' and ravin', he went on and on.. even long after the auditorium had been completely evacuated.

Eventually his non-stop 'verbal outburst' gave-'way to a deathly silence. One, that was only interrupted by the sounds of his sneakers squeaking as he continuously paced back and forth, from one end of the nook to the other. Now.. he was thinking.. deeply lost in his 'whatever?' strategy. Angel Jane and I impatiently waited to the echoing sounds of his shrilling rubber soles.. Squish, Squash.. Squish, Squash.. back 'n forth.. to 'n fro.. Squish, Squash.. What was goin' on, in that little mind of his?.. What was he planning?.. It seemed to be going on forever! Finally...

"They ain't getting the best 'a me.. No ways!.. You just wait 'n see!.. Yes, siree.. I'll show 'em!.."

Then once again.. deathly silence.. Squish, Squash.. Squeak, Squeal.. Only, this time, it didn't last as long.

"Angel Jane, I gotta move.. it's getting late!.. Yeah, I gotta get out 'a here, before they..."

"Where are you going?.." she interruptingly pleaded.

"Don't worry 'bout me.. There's somethin' I gotta do.."

The early morning mist and dew were beginning to settle on the still-very-grey streets of Heaven, as I followed them sadly to the Pearly Gates. Up and down the now-abandoned ways, we went.. until slowly (but not 'slowly enough for me') the beautiful shining entranceway came into view. Why did it have to be this way? Why couldn't he take her with him? I just couldn't justify it at all! Did he realize just-exactly what he was throwing away?

I could hear Jack comforting Angel Jane, just a few feet ahead of me…

"I'll be back again someday.. Really!.. Don't worry.. We'll be together then!.. After all 'a this is over!.. Then we'll be happy.. Promise!…

I really love you.. just remember that.. 'n never doubt it, n' matter what I ever do!.. 'cause that's one thing that'll never change.. No, our love is forever!.. It ain't just.. Words!.. Right?.." turning to her, questioningly. Then back to his original exclamation.. "I mean it, Angel Jane.. from the deepest part 'a m' heart!.. Yeah, it's.. it's forever 'n ever!.."

Jack's conversation ended as if it were ideally timed to, just as they reached the closed entrance. Pulling open one of the huge gates, he turned to Angel Jane.. planted a kiss.. and began on his way, trotting out and across the clouds.. through their still-present, rising mist.

Just as he started to pick up speed, in the near distance.. he interrupted it with a screeching halt, as Angel Jane yelled to him from the gateway…

"AND IF ONE OF US GETS LONELY?…

WHAT IF ONE OF US FINDS SOMEONE ELSE TO LOVE.. AND TO BE WITH?.. THEN WHAT, JACK?.. THEN WHAT?.."

Jack spun slowly.. to look at her.

She nervously awaited his answer.

He stared, emotionally lost in her.

Then.. taking a deep gulp, that his voice might not crack, he forced…

"MAY IT BE YOU!…"

It echoed through the silent night, sending shivers up my spine.

Then again…

"MAY IT BE YOU, ANGEL JANE… MAY IT BE YOU!.."

Then turning, he took off into the dark-morning's horizon.

Still standing beside Angel Jane in the gateway, I watched as she raised her arm to sadly wave to him.. now already far away in the distance.

Then it hit me.. 'I've got to catch up to him'! With tears streaming and the dense fog blinding me miserably, I began my pursuit across the clouds.

Not to lose him anymore than I already had, I forced myself on.. praying I wouldn't run into anything. Around the large Crystal Lake I sped, following just a faint and very distant echoing of his whistle, that I could hear up ahead in the un-see-able horizon. That whistle, being a blessing in disguise! For although I knew it to be directed at Angel Jane, it regardless helped me to locate and remain on his trail. And without it, that would have been a virtually impossible thing to do!

On and on, the chase went.. for what-seemed-to-be an eternity. Over cloud after cloud, we dashed through the aggravating haze. I.. tracking the dimmed sound of his up-ahead squeal, only!

Finally (and lucky-enough-for-me) the vague and blurred image of him came into barely-visible sight. It was this.. and only this.. that I fought to keep up with, for the remainder of the trip!

'Where, in Heaven, is he going?..' I kept thinking, through-out. 'Maybe he's never gonna stop?.. How long can this go on for?'.

I kept praying that he'd stop. Or even just slow down! My legs were killing me! It got to the point, where.. it was a good thing (for him) that he didn't stop! For.. if he had.. I sincerely believe I would've strangled him!

Whatever 'leading-me-on-curiosity' that I might have had, at the beginning of our journey (as to.. 'Where he was going?' and 'What his plans were?') was in no time completely lost! Being replaced (along the way, as the night's race-to-nowhere un-mercifully continued) with an 'I-couldn't-have-cared-less' attitude on my part. I was disgusted to the hilt!

And if it weren't for God's 'ordering me to follow', I'm sure that I would have just let his sustaining whistle (ahead) disappear into the distant darkness. Even regardless of the fact, that I was lost in the middle of nowhere!

But, no.. instead I forced on.. and on.. and on.. and on.. and on.. and on…

THE FOURTH CHAPTER

~ EMMANUEL (GOD WITH US) ~

Earth? I realized (when I'd finally caught up with Jack) that, for some strange reason, we'd wound up on Earth! I'd been so involved in the chase, that I hadn't even been watching where we were going. But however we had done it (as unanswerable as it was and remains to be), the fact was.. we were most definitely on Earth!

As Jack came to a slowing-down up-ahead, I (in all of my amazement) began turning my head in all directions to survey the abruptly-changed scenery. I couldn't believe my eyes. There were sand dunes everywhere! I thought I was hallucinating! I did an immediate about-face to find nothing but oceans and oceans of sand, with occasional palm trees scattered about and upon its vast and un-ending horizon. We were somehow.. all of a sudden.. in the middle of a desert! The heavenly fog had, somewhere along the way, disappeared.. and now instead been replaced

by a tremendous sand-storm. And a very chilly one at that!

Re-pivoting forward, I could see Jack still ahead, standing with his back towards me. His head was arched upwards.. and as I neared, I slowly came to realize that the cold sand storm (that was becoming more and more unbearable with each step forward) was, in fact, centering around him! I knew I'd have to keep a fair distance, for it was 'he' that was (for some reason beyond me, at the time) most certainly the eye of it! Yes, it was coming from him. I was sure it was! For each nearing step proved it so! I had to find out just 'what on Earth' was going on here. What had happened to him? And what was he looking at?

So I forced myself onward, squinting my eyes from the flying sand. When I was close enough (fifteen to twenty feet to the rear of him), I could readily see that Jack was studying a very beautiful-and-radiant, cross-shaped star, that was hovering above and in-front-of-him in the still-grey sky. There was a very quiet, anticipating eerie-ness about the entire early morning, that was very, very breathtaking! I could likewise see.. as I studied further.. that surrounding the same sky (and the earthly valley below) were thousands-upon-thousands of flapping-and-fluttering angels. Then it hit me.. this is Bethlehem! And all of the angels of Heaven were there, waiting to witness the greatest creation ever to take place on Earth.. the birth of Jesus, the Son of God! And there too.. was the Expecting Father, Himself.. God.. also very impatiently awaiting the soon-to-be arrival. What a thrilling sight it was for me to see first-hand!

I attempted a closer move towards Jack, for I could sense that there was something dreadfully wrong with him. I couldn't put my finger on it, but could just 'tell' that something wasn't right, and had to get a closer look. But the more I tried to approach him, the more I realized that any-further-advances-to-his-front would have to be made by encircling him. There was just no way around it! The fury and bitter cold he was giving-off was absolutely unbearable!

When I'd finally encompassed him enough to afford myself a 'good side-view' of his face, I sincerely wished I hadn't. For what I came to discover was.. just terrible! I don't know if it had been a result of his leaving Heaven like he had (Being a sort-of 'fallen angel', if you might classify it as such?).. or if it was because of the high speed he'd traveled at?.. Maybe it was due to the way he'd had to leave Angel Jane and all, making his heart grow tremendously bitter and cold, along the way?.. I just can't say!.. But whatever the reason.. the end result was devastating! Whatever had been 'the fault', I guess.. really didn't matter. All I knew was, he had under-gone some of the most drastic changes in appearance, character and general-nature that I'd ever witnessed in any one being (and in that short a span of time) in all of my days. My heart had gone-out for him, back in Heaven, during all of his 'trying times'.. But now, there was no other way to put it, except that I felt the worst of pity for him ever! For the poor little fellow had completely froze to the bone and heart! His chapped, pale-white, smile-less face appeared.. to the ultimate and extreme meaning of the words.. dramatically sad! There was an awful death-ly-ness to it, you might say! I couldn't help but shiver at the sight of it. What was once a so-youthful-looking face, now appeared weary-worn and older. Its shape and generally-elfin features remained.. except now, there was an entirely different

overtone to them. One that reminded me of a look that comes from the loss of in-nocence. His eyes seemed fear-filled, like those of a wounded animal. Glaring and distrustful! And hurt.. very hurt! Whiskers (that had ice on them) were poking off his pointed chin in every direction. And his now-thicker, even-more un-manage-able hair likewise had patches of frozen icicles that were dangling and hanging from it, like shining Christmas tree ornaments glistening to the still-dim-morning's background. All of his clothes were very-seriously weather-beaten.. either from his 'fast running'.. or from.. Well, I really don't know what? But.. there were rips, tears, scuffs and holes all over them!.. and a totally 'frozen-in' wrinkled-ness that went from head-t'-toe consecutively! His hands were chapped and extremely dry-appearing.. and the skin-cracks were in-numerable. As his head began to turn in my direction, I raised my own to meet his now deeper-sunk, terribly-piercing eyes. They.. sending an awful shiver through me! For.. although I knew he couldn't see me.. the anger and bitterness of his look, at first sight, gave me second thoughts. As he scanned back away, my eyes began again down his pitiful frame. I couldn't help thinking…

'He was such an awful misfit in Heaven.. If they could only see him now!.. Yes.. and if they could only see what their ridicule and non-acceptance had caused too!.. Maybe they wouldn't think it so funny now!..'

As I continued my study of him, my eye (in the process) caught the trembling of his hand. It was shaking awful! I quicked a look to his face and eyes to find that he was beginning to cry. The tears immediately froze upon facial contact.. and I could tell that he was desperately fighting-with-himself to hold them back. That being, of course, the worst thing he could do! But really.. what choice had he? What a terrible position to be in! For I was sure, with time, this dilemma (and retaining of his bad feelings..) would only make his already-miserable life all the more frus-trating and uncomfortable. This tragic sight before me was to be the way that Jack would remain (progressively getting worse!) in all of the years that I was to know him. And even after that, to this very day, I'm sure. The refuge from Heaven.. ex-iled by his own choosing (or maybe I should say, 'circumstances')!

Awe-stricken by the two phenomenons unfolding right before my very eyes.. the mystical sky and Bethlehem village in the below valley.. And, the other.. Jack and his unbelievable transformation.. I found myself looking back-and-forth like some 'observer of a ping-pong match'.. not wanting to miss a thing! While he, instead and all the while, just stood there glaring onward.. and not straying his sight, nor concentration, once.

Then.. in the sky.. the star and surrounding angels began slowly descending closer and closer down upon the Earth. It was time! The early morning event.. so waited for.. was about to happen! My heart began pounding unmercifully.. and a certain very-uneasiness came to my stomach. This was it!

Jack (at the sight of the descending angels) started creeping down the sand embankment towards the little town in the near distance. As he lowered off of the dune and converged closer, I could more focusingly see a small wooden shed (cave-set) just on the outskirts of the further-beyond-it, sleeping village. Jack crouched down lower.. almost to a walking-on-hands-and-knees position .. and scatted forward.. dodging in-and-out from behind rocks, bushes and almost-anything-else that he could get to fast enough to not be seen. I followed in the same fashion, so nervous that I could hardly think straight!

It was as-if the little structure (ahead of us) had some sort of 'magnetic field' about it, pulling everything in towards it. And the closer everything got.. God, the angels, the star, Jack and I.. the more rapid-a-speed everything acquired! And, all the while, I.. becoming more and more unraveled, the better-visible it came to view!

When Jack finally made his last move and stand, behind a huge boulder in the very near area surrounding the tiny dwelling.. I too stopped in a hidden position behind him, holding my heart from the running and overwhelming-intensity of it all. God and the angels continued in, even closer than Jack, to almost directly above the designated birthplace.. so that none (in their great number) would miss any of the proceedings. It was so quiet, I could hear the cows inside the shed, snorting and scuffing gently about the hay. The coldness (radiating off of and all around Jack) was starting to take effect on everything in the general ground-level-area surrounding him.. and I could see Joseph bringing a blanket to Mary and placing it over her, as she rested there in a bed of hay. I was trembling uncontrollably now. I just couldn't believe my eyes! For, all my life I'd read and heard about this event.. Only now, here I was, actually witnessing it take place! Only thing different was.. I'd never heard about Jack's part in the whole thing. There'd just never been any mention of it!

I had to stop and turn away for a minute to catch my breath. This was just too much for me! I just had to relax somehow, or I was sure that I'd explode from the tension! So peering back at the sand mountain that Jack and I had only-moment's-before been on, I fought to clear my mind.

Then.. from the manger.. cracking the dead-silence of the so-peaceful morning, it came. The loudest and healthiest of baby's cries that I'd ever heard!.. So startling, that I felt my nerves lightning-bolt to the limbs-ends of my body! My head snapped-back in the direction of the manger. I was stunned and speechless! For.. there.. right before my paralyzed-opened eyes.. was the Baby Jesus! And He.. as radiantly beautiful as humanly imaginable! His aura glowed like the presence of the Sun! And adorable?.. Yes.. absolutely adorable!

And, me.. I wasn't the only one stunned. For.. stuck right in mid-air.. suspended above us.. were all of Heaven's angels.. the entire choir included.. looking like mannequins.. jaws wide-open.. staring spellbound, down at the Blessed Infant! And, God.. well, He was just as happy and proud as any father would have been, at the first sight of his newborn!

It was all.. just so beautiful! Yes, all.. except for something.. yes, something.. was missing? Something wasn't right? No, something definitely wasn't right! The cold morning was echoing the Baby Jesus' crying and He wasn't stopping. God started looking worried and a bit confused. Something was missing? He started looking all about. But.. But.. What was it?

"That's it!.." He declared, as it came to Him. "The Choir!.. There's no choir!.. They were supposed to lullaby my Son!…"

He turned back to signal them. They'd practiced all night long for this sole purpose of comforting the Baby Jesus (who was still crying away, full force!).. But instead of so doing.. had now become awe-struck and completely motionless! Yes, they were in a trance! And even totally unaware of God's cue-ing them to begin their singing! I guess that they'd all been even more nervous than I was.. For, by now, I had regained my perception and was likewise aware of their absence.

God motioned to them again. But, nothing!

He began looking impatient and uneasy, as the crying from the manger kept growing louder and louder!

Then.. all of a sudden and out-of-nowhere.. with the chilling-ness of a brisk wind.. the loud, swirling, melodious sound of Jack's 'whistling hymn' pierced through the hush of the stagnant, eventful morn. It.. completely drowning-out the crying sounds of the Baby Jesus. In and about the manger scene.. and up with its cold, frosty air it went.. waking all of the choir and other-angels out of their immobile trance. Its plain and beautifully-unique melody dancing all about the Bethlehem stillness.. and lasting longer than it ever had previous!

When at last it did end though.. so too had the crying of the Baby Jesus. Now instead.. He was smiling away like every newborn should!.. and looking all about for where it had come from! Being (just like any other infant would have been) completely fascinated by it!

Within a matter of minutes after Jack's 'offering' had faded into the remaining silence of the now-awfully-chilly-morning, God was back to being His happy-proud-Father Self. The now-wide-awake choir silently awaited His command, all sensing that an approaching speech was at-hand…

"Which one of you created that beautiful hymn?.."

There was no answer.

"That beautiful hymn.. whose-ever it was.. will be.. and forever be considered.. The First Christmas Carol!…

For.. in all actuality, it was.. 'The First'.. to ever be sung to My Son!…

And.. none others would probably have ever followed, if it hadn't have been!.." glancing an implicit look at the choir.. who were all quite ashamed now, over what had happened there.. as well, as back in Heaven, earlier that night. For they were fully aware of 'whose hymn' that had been. Yes, all knew too well that it had been the one that they had laughed-at and refused! But now, the whole situation had turned things around. And God's proclamation made it all the more understood and regrettable to them. And.. all heard.. loud and clear! All, that is.. except Jack.. who had instead fearfully ran away, off towards the desert, the split-second after he'd whistled it! Afraid that all would laugh at him again, he just couldn't bear the thought of even more rejection. And so, instead, fled.. completely unaware of the acclaim his carol had received!

Catching just a fleeting glimpse of him, as he disappeared over the edge of the sand dune, in the distance.. I knew that I would have to hurry, if I didn't want to lose him. I ached to stay! Why did he always have t' do this?

Stealing one more quick look at the Baby Jesus, I unwillingly began pursuit.. hearing the angel choir singing (at last) behind me in the fading distance.

Again.. the 'catching up' was as difficult (and as physically exhausting) as the 'keeping up'. But the closer I came to his vague-up-ahead image, the more beneficial I found it to be. For the sand he left in his trail had crusted solid from his bitter-cold, making my footwork that much more steadfast and alleviating.

Up and over ridges and heaps of scattering sand at an amazing speed, we went.. While, all the while, I kept thinking..

'If I could only tell him just how unnecessary this is.. For God and all the angels have accepted his hymn!.. There's absolutely no reason or need to be running away!.. His dream of pleasing God and the Baby Jesus had come true!.. Not to mention.. that of having it be 'The First One' to be sung to Him!...

'This is ridiculous.. Maybe God will intercept this futile, high-speed craziness?.. Yes, I'm sure He will!...'

But nothing happened. The chase continued undisturbed far into the mid-day. I prayed for a moment's relief. But one never came!

As the dark of the first Christmas Day's night began to settle upon the Earth, we at last reached an ocean. The Mediterranean I calculated, considering our westward movement. I felt sure (as I saw him encountering it in the blurred distance) that.. now.. yes, now.. he'd have no other choice, but to come to a stop. My long-awaited rest was finally at-hand.. Thank God!

'Yes.. finally.. we're going to…

No.. No.. No.. Hey, wait a minute.. Wait a minute!…'

It froze! I couldn't believe my weary eyes!.. The water actually solidified!..
Yeah, Iced!

Without a second's delay, Jack un-encumberingly reeled out and across the
ocean.. as the water's of, at least, five hundred feet encompassing him froze solid
upon contact.. Paving a firm, but slippery way for his tenny-soles.. and likewise
my own, soon to discouragingly follow. I was totally disgusted, to say the least!
But I forced onward my velocity. For now.. I'd 'have to keep up'.. or drown!
Stopping to rest (regardless of losing Jack) was completely out of the question!
There was no longer any choice in the matter. It was then that I realized that..
short of God.. nothing (and I mean nothing!) could stop him! And how.. yes, how
I wished that something.. anything.. would. For the whole situation had gotten so
out-of-hand! And was just so un-needy!

Countless days literally flew without the slightest decrease in speed. And as we
continued, I became aware of a gradual change in our direction. Yes, it seemed to
me that our journey took on more of a north-western swing.

When at last we did 'hit' land, I presumed it to be 'somewhere South-Western
Europe'. I would easily have guessed Southern France (judging from the excruciating distance we'd come), but even Italy could be used and still sound dramatical-
ly-exhausting enough, I'm sure!

On the beach I dropped! But growing more and more fearful with each 'ticking'
minute (that I'd lose the still-continuing-on little imp), I made it a very brief stay.

When again I could feel the freezing cold, brisking upon my drowsy eyes and
face.. and breath the bitter air (in my pitifully-out-of-breath lungs) of his unthaw-
ing path, I felt ironically-enough comfortably re-assured that I was not far behind.

Again.. days passed.. Until another ocean came into view. At its cliff-overlook-
ing shoreline, Jack at last.. yes, at last.. stopped! His stay though, only being a

very short one. One that seemed (to a weary traveler as I) hardly worth being called 'a stop'! For within what-seemed-like five minutes, he fidgetingly began his climbing-descent down to the beach and out onto the now-becoming, stuck-in-turbulent-motion ocean! I (in teeth-gritting anger and whimpering repugnancy) followed over the treacherously-slippery frozen-waves in awkward pursuit.

And again.. days passed! I began to forget what land looked like. I felt like a sailor who'd been away at sea much too long.. Only difference was, I wasn't on a ship! It became where I could no longer think straight from the strenuous and unmerciful repetition of our flight. My mind (and behind) throbbingly ached from the constant falls and sliding spills. I was an absolute mess!

Then.. land. Yes, Land!.. Maybe a rest?..
God please.. A rest!
No such luck!
Up the beach into a vast forest with jungle-thick shrubbery, he plowed.. into this 'no-man's' land!   North America (long before it even became known as one of the Americas), I immediately deciphered!

The calendar continued to arrogantly flip before my seeing-things eyes. Mirages came.. of me 'standing still'. Not necessarily doing anything pleasant or exciting, just standing still!   In the dizzy-fever of my running-together, head-aching thoughts, I could hear my soul screaming…

'WHEN'S HE GONNA STOP?…

HOW MUCH LONGER CAN HE LAST?…

HOW MUCH LONGER CAN I LAST?…

WHERE ARE WE GOING?…

NORTHWEST!…

TREES.. TREES.. LAKES.. FOREST AFTER FOREST.. AFTER FOREST OF TREES!…

NOTHING BUT TREES.. TREES.. TREES.. TREES.. NORTHWEST.. TREES.. TREES!.. TREES!… TREES!… LAKES!… TREES!.. TREES!… TREES!.. TREES!.. TREES.. AND MORE TREES!…

AND THEN.. TREES.. TREES.. TREES.. TREES.. TREES.. TREES.. TREES.. TREES.. TREES.. MORE TREES!

Finally (and I'll joyfully repeat.. Finally) he slowed down! I could've cried at the beautiful sight of it. Yes, he was slowing down! It was a trick? It had to be! What would he stop here for? There was not a tree, nor plant insight! Just a totally desolate region of ice, snow and water. So.. Why? Well, then again.. Where-else would someone as cold and bitter as he was, want to be? In light of that, I suppose it was ideal! At least, for him anyway! For I sure had no use for the place. Quite honestly, at this point, it really didn't matter 'where' we were! All that mattered was, he was at last slowing down to a stop. Beyond that, I couldn't have cared less!

The more I could afford to take my eyes off of him and observe the surroundings, the more evident it became to me that we were.. in the Arctic. There was no question about it, it had to be the North Pole!

Jack concluded his 'Trans-Atlantic, Continental Marathon' by parking himself on the cliff's edge of an enormous iceberg, that over-looked a giant, lake-sized body of water. Upon his presence, the liquid instantaneously froze.. transforming its contents into what-became-now a large and vast valley of ice, directly below and in-front of us. He sat there staring out and upon it unflinchingly.

By this time, I'd become a bit more aware of how to deal with Jack's frost-nipping sphere.. and moved in to the more-bearable eye-of-it, ten or so feet to his rear. This being always the calmest area of the forever-raging-about-him tornado. Drained of all energy, I flopped down to a sitting position on the cold, icy surface.. surrendering within seconds, to a laying-position and a sound sleep.

When (after I don't know how long?) I came to, Jack (Thank God!) was still sitting right there in front of me, in the exact position and spot that he had been in, when I'd unknowingly dozed off. As I 'very-pacingly' tried to wake myself more, Jack's sudden leap to his feet 'worked wonders'.. and I came to reality in-stantaneously! He began grumbling and mumbling something.. and I could see (from our location on the ledge, above the newly-formed lower valley) that, in the near distance, there was what-appeared-to-be a small aircraft approaching to land. As far away as the oddly-enough 'open-top' air-vessel was from us (hovering over and around the dead-center of the lowland) the sounds of laughter, shouting and general happy-carrying-on's coming from it (and filling the sky) were more than distinguish-able-enough to hear from our position. I smiled on impulse. They were such beautiful, joyous and happy sounds! People that were in the giddiest of a mood. Beautiful.. delightful happiness! I loved it! Jack, on the extreme other hand, was cringing and totally upset by their un-expected arrival. Furtively (and fussin' every inch of the way), he began his climbing-descent closer.. as I tagged after, curiously absorbed in trying to see and figure-out just who they might be?

After very-clumsily reaching the valley-level.. and working our way closer (dodging and darting impishly from behind one snow-mound to the frozen-solid-as-a-rock next), it became more focussed that what had appeared to be an open-topped aircraft before.. was, in all actuality-'n-fact, a sleigh! Yes.. and a sleigh being led by reindeer.. carrying a small army of little people too, at that! One very large white-bearded gentleman (who kept on laughing and yelling "HO.. HO.. HO!") was at the head of the craft, holding the reins and steering it in, as it made its smooth landing on the icy earth. And there.. right beside him.. sat a likewise roundish-type little woman.. with auburn, trimmed-close-to-the-face hair. She.. wearing (in her soft, very-lady-like silence) a steadfast smile. A smile, that almost appeared to be more of a 'joy-filled, sincere smirk'! Yes, she.. a totally peaceful-composured-type being!

As we sneakingly-converged still-closer, Jack's grumbling became increasingly worse from the more distinct sounds of the ecstatic chitter-chatter. I thought surely he'd give himself away!

The jolly round man (in charge of the crew) looked very familiar. Yes, I knew I'd seen him somewhere before. And very recently at that! Where had it been though?

The nearer we got, the more I zero-ed in on him.. and the more certain I was that I knew him. Only, the red suit that he was now wearing kept throwing me off!

Then it hit me! It was Nick.. 'The Angel of Musical Mirth'.. one of the Herald Angels! Yes, it definitely was him! But.. what was he doing here? Maybe God had sent him to retrieve Jack.. and to tell him that his hymn had been acknowl-edged.. Yes, I just knew God would eventually step-in and fix this mess. I just knew he would!

When the sleigh came to a stand-still, Nick did an immediate about-face to ad-dress the crew (who I realized then were, in all actuality, Angels)…

"Okay, my little friends.. calm down now.." injecting brief 'Ho-Ho-Ho's' through-out.. "Here we are in our new, to-be Home-Sweet-Home-Land…

Now the Lord has, of course, sent us here with a purpose.. A purpose that we will all fulfill to the best of our abilities!…

And.. I'm sure.. you're all wondering just what that purpose is.. And, as well, why we are here of all places.. So, I'll give you a brief rundown of our mission.."

Pausing to control his compulsive giggling, he glanced at the (still seated) little woman flanking him. She.. still smirking away and looking like, at any given moment, she would explode into un-restrainable hysterics! To the absolute-contrary of her appearance, she remindingly offered (in the most calmest of ways)…

"Go on, Nick.. Don't leave 'em hangin'.."

Nick.. clearing his throat and quickly pulling himself together.. resumed ever-obligingly with…

"Okay…

Now.. What it is.. is.. We have only thirty-four years to prepare here at the North Pole for our task of supplying all the children of the world with gifts, each year, on Jesus' Birthday.. A job that will be forever-expanding.. growing more and more difficult to accomplish with each year that follows...

When Jesus' life in Heaven begins, God wants it to be, that.. instead of people giving Him presents on His birthday.. We are going to.. 'in His name'.. distribute them to the world!.. For God wants His people.. especially the little ones, 'The Angels of the Earth'.. to see that it is much more rewarding to give than to receive!.. And He knows that Jesus would want it that way too!...

Now I know you're all tired from the celebrations that were held in Heaven.. as well as from the long journey that we just under-took.. But we must start building our homes first.. Then later, we can rest-up to begin our work for the Lord.."

As Nick concluded his speech, I (still dreamingly-absorbed in the mystique of it all.. And forgetting that he wouldn't have heard me anyways!..) turned to Jack to say...

"Isn't that beautiful.." But, in so doing, noticed that he was gone!

I quickly looked about.. Then saw a snow-storm flurrying up on the distant ledge that we had just come from. Immediately I responded after it.

Other than the fact that this chase was aimed in a southward direction, there was only one other noteworthy 'difference' that I can offer. It being.. that I couldn't help, but notice.. that this time I was 'keeping-up' with him easier. Yes, finally.. I was adjusting to him and his too-fast-for-comfort lifestyle! I'd noticed (back on the ledge) that I could withstand nearing-him closer than I'd ever been able to, prior.. And, now this.. I was 'holding-ground' with him effortlessly. Well.. almost effortlessly!

Directly south we went. This time though, I could better understand and justify his reasons for leaving the Arctic. For after all, being around Nick and the whole merry-'n-yule-tide Christmas Spirit (that would prevail there. And constantly t' boot!) would be painstaking! Yes, it was obvious that he would only be forever reminded of his not-so-pleasant memories of that first night in Heaven. No, he needed to be alone and away from all 'a that. At least, for the time being!

As he dashed onward.. through trees after trees after trees, he contemplated (in all of his fever) what Christmas would mean to him. It would likewise be a time of the year for hard work! Only, in his case, a time when he would roam the Earth, whistling his tune to the population.. hoping that eventually they would 'catch on' and likewise begin whistling and singing it as a Christmas Carol. That.. would be his 'ultimate quest' from this moment forth! Yeah, then.. and only then, when that had been accomplished.. would he return to Heaven. For if such was the case.. then God and everyone there would 'have to' accept his Carol! They'd have no other choice! No matter what they thought of it! He'd prove that he was right! No matter how long it took! His persistence would only multiply! For although he'd been laughed at and pushed aside, his will-power was now as strongly-determined and self-righteous as ever! His stubborn-ness and inner-belief would only double!.. then triple!.. and on and on, until he'd win! And that was all there was to it!

As much as I respected him for his self-belief and determination, I couldn't help thinking how much of a 'pitiful shame' this all was though. If he only knew how wrong he was! Not to mention, his attitude! Double wrong! And if only he knew what unnecessary grief his rebelling would bring him. But, there was just no way for me to stop him. He'd have to learn for himself! Yeah.. just like every single one of us! No, there wasn't a thing I could do. Except follow, of course!

THE FIFTH CHAPTER

~ BLOOD ON THE CROSS ~

So.. south, it was..

Across the thickly-wooded, virgin forests of the North American Continent.. Never ever resting once!

The Gulf of Mexico.

South America.

Then..reaching a great ocean strait, in our non-stop hurry to..who-knows-where?

Ultimately, we came upon a very dark and abandoned, beautiful tropical island. At least, that's the way it appeared in the near-approaching distance. Of course, the closer Jack came to its very mountainous shores, the more it transformed into another Arctic Region. A region later to become known as 'Antarctica'. Or.. more off-handedly as.. 'The South Pole'! A frozen and barren land that would (and will..) remain this way for as long as Jack resides there. A very remote and secluded place from all of the other continents, where (ideally-enough for him) his bitter-cold can conveniently thrive, unchallenged by Mother Nature or any other natural forces. A frost-biting exile's 'dream-come-true'!

It was there.. deep into this deserted island.. that Jack was to build his home. A hide-out, where he would remain.. Only leaving bi-seasonally, during what we now know as 'the Winter Months'. And that, in fact, being exactly why we have Winter Months! For it is (at this particular time of the year), that Jack is in our midst, trying desperately to win our attention with his 'whistling carol'!

That first and very-lengthy dark night that we arrived there (somewhere south-side and at the foot-arch of, what-is-now-called, the Trans-Antarctic Mountains), Jack, without delay, went to work on raising his house. Or shack, I should more precisely say!

Using the surrounding trees and the newly-formed, first layers of ice for plaster-like insulation-and-seal, he labored endlessly, in-spite-of and through-out the (due to him) bitter-cold and lashing-windy night.

Trees?.. you might ask.. considering the present-day terrain of the Antarctic. Yes, I will re-affirm.. there were thickly-cluttered forests of them, upon our arrival! But, in the 'ice-capping' aftermath that was to follow, they, of course, were 'froze below'.. and in so, vanished from the face of the continent. Yet, still.. it was with these 'now-very-buried' trees, that Jack's miserable-looking home was construct- ed. Its window-less frame.. frozen from roof to ground.. giving off, in appearance, the most 'un-home-sweet-homey-ness' feeling that I can ever remember sensing from any other dwelling I'd ever set eyes to!

I vividly recall those shivering moments, sitting there on the ledge of the hill- side (that over-looked the site of his in-process home).. snuggling myself, while studying him pensively. It was then that I came to notice, how.. more and more.. he took to talking-to-himself, as he toiled along. It seemed as though he was totally absorbed in a constant self-argument.. an inner turmoil that became more heated by the minute! So faint and in-audible were his 'jibber-'n-jabberings' though.. that (to fully understand them) I found that I had no other choice, but to tune-in to his thoughts. And, that.. being something I really didn't enjoy doing. For after all, we're all entitled to our privacy. But sincerely, there was just no other way at times! He was a habitual mumbler! And lip-reading was also completely out-of- the-question, for his head was forever drooped down so low. Always sad and mel- ancholy! Withdrawn.. being hardly the proper word to describe him. Tangled in an intense self-love/ self-hate complex, that I could never quite fully comprehend. It baffled me to the ultimate! Most of the confusion.. as I saw it.. was centered around subjects, such as…

'Whether or not, he was doing the right thing.. in leaving Angel Jane, the way he had.. All for his selfish desire to find acclaim!…

Should he go back?.. Could he go back?.. Was it too late?.. Maybe she'd found another?…

And what if he did quit and return?.. Everyone that had laughed at him.. they'd only think all-the-less of him.. "Quitter!".. he could hear them now!…

Besides, he couldn't live like that.. being looked-down-on and mocked constantly.. He couldn't take it!.. Especially when, all the while, he knew what he had.. the Hymn was a masterpiece.. and that's all there was to it!.. He'd prove it!..'

On and on, he'd go.. his thoughts shooting back-'n-forth.. in and out of the most dis-according states of mind.. Traveling from general uneasiness to out-'n-out convulsive-like fits of inner anger. Then.. like the snap of the fingers, he'd be back to self-belief and stubborn defiance. From one extreme to the exact-opposite other. What a mess he was! Yes, it's easy to see.. why I didn't really like tuning-in.. making as little a habit of it as possible there-after. And doing so.. for only short periods of time, when I'd have to! Sometimes when I'd get involved in his turmoils.. and forget to tune-out.. I'd end up feeling nauseous and sick-to-my-stomach for quite some time after. Even considering to myself, on occasions.. that 'too-lengthy' a dose, of such.. might result in insanity! It was just that heavy a confusion! Yet he seemed to exist in it somehow. Still.. not to tax myself any more than I had to.. and out of respect for his privacy, the 'mind-reading' was kept to a very minimal practice. In the later years of our acquaintance, he became slightly more at-peace with some of his self-doubts and 'inner wars'.. and instead directed more of his thought-effort towards an 'I'm-gonna-do-it-this-year.. you-just-watch-me' attitude, that was much easier for me to tune-in to and digest. But in these early years, the 'thought-scans' were just unbearable for me!

During the thirty-four-year waiting period, Jack's days (or 'awake hours', I should say..) consisted of constant whistle practicing. And the tune he so-well-loved echoed repeatedly out across the surrounding valley of his Antarctic-engulfed (and rising, by the day!) homeland. And this.. hours and hours upon end! At first, aggravating me silly. I could've rung his neck! Over and over.. Over and over! But as time passed.. the more I heard it, the more I grew accustomed to its unending repetition. I actually even began missing it, when he'd occasionally catch a quick, restless nap. And before you know it (I must admit), I began 'living for it'! Yes.. the days wouldn't have seemed right without it! Ultimately.. by the end of the waiting period.. I myself was anticipating his winter-crusade north as much as he was. His will-power and drive were so intense, they were catching! I couldn't wait! I was all-with-him on it! When finally it had rolled around to that thirty-third Christmas Eve, I watched in gun-ho ecstasy as he prepared in his shack for the long-season's journey ahead.

Yes, you read it right.. the 'thirty-third year'! I knew that it wasn't right.. even then!.. But Jack had, somehow or other, mis-calculated. I think that in his mathematical addition, he had included that first Christmas as being one of the thirty-four? But however he had done it, I knew he was off! But in all honesty, I couldn't see where it would hurt whether-or-not he was jumping the gun. I was so sick of being where we'd been.. and for the length of time we had.. that I was more-than-glad to accept a change of scenery!

So, as I was saying.. on that thirty-third Christmas Eve, I impatiently waited and watched as he made-ready for the first of his 'Christmas Carol' Crusades. All about the ram-shacked room, he raced.. talking a hundred-miles-a-minute to himself.

Then, when finally he realized (after a good hour or so), that he had nothing to bring or do there.. and that it was only his nerves that were detaining him, he shot straight through and out the tiny front-door and on his way.

At first, it took me a little-bit-of-getting-used-to 'keeping up' with him.. for I was a 'reasonable' out-of-practice. Thirty-three layin'-around years worth, to be exact! But soon, I was tailing him easier and more-gracefully than ever. Off into the northern night-fall, we sped. I.. now.. his ever-believing advocate!

That first winter season (like all others in this era of history) was to be a concentration on the Middle East (as it is now called). This.. for 'familiarity' among other reasons, I assumed.

The greetings that Jack received on his visit and return to the Holy Lands were discouraging, to put it mildly. For the world (least of all, this section of it!) was not, in the slightest, prepared for him and his violently-cold nature. They completely shunned the bitter winds and freezing snow that accompanied.. and boarded themselves in.. making all of his hymn-whistling-efforts seem 'just a big waste of time'. No matter how hard he persisted, it was just hopeless! His caroling wasn't even heard, let alone ignored!

Regardless and in spite of the reception he'd received, Jack remained.. arrogantly whistling-away the thirty-three years of built-up frustration he'd festered-up inside. All through-out the holiday season.. and even long after, into the next new year to follow.. he held ground. He was refusing to take 'no' for an answer, you could say! He had felt so sure that he would succeed the first time 'round.. But instead, he'd flat-on-his-face failed and he just couldn't accept it!

Months passed in fruitless endeavor.. until Jack, by sheer coincidence, was to come upon the scene of a most-disheartening event. A happening so tragic and emotionally-penetrating, that I myself, to this very day, find it hard accepting and speaking-of, in retrospect.

It was a very dark day. At least, all-of-a-sudden and out-of-nowhere, it had very-strangely-enough fallen upon us. This.. confounding Jack (as well as my-self)! For oddly, in so.. and very rapidly at that.. it was becoming as black as night!

A very tense and uncomfortable chill came over me at the first sight of the up-and-coming-into-view Israeli village, that we were (on this particular mid-day) en-countering. I could just 'sense' and 'detect' in the air, that 'something terrible' lay in-store for us ahead. Yes, there reaked a 'scary-ness' in it! One, that I could tell, even sent a shiver through Jack himself.. as he cautiously stopped at the scent of, to survey the walled-in city in the distance. Even the about-him wind (that forever howled and hissed, regardless of whether-or-not he was whistling his Carol) came to an alarming subdued-ness! Almost as if to better blend with the awful-eerie stillness that was settled upon and into the surrounding darkness.

In the distance (with the walls of the city even-further back-set) came to view, the silhouette-ed-like images of people. They.. descending an elevating-to-our-right hill-side.. and making (in slow movement) their further-retreat towards the city's gates.

Jack neared warily.. and in so, I could see that some of these people were sol-diers. Roman soldiers, I determined by their décor. Civilians.. women and men of all age groups.. made up the greater number of them though. Most appeared to be very sad and forlorn. And even with Jack's further advances.. other than a few quick tightenings of the hoods of their robes.. his nipping coldness seemed to go completely un-noticed by their number. They.. very-obviously being much more concerned with and over some grave incident that they weighingly were carrying with them in their hearts, as they continued on their further descent.

An overcast was massively moving in, above all.. and just as we entered their midst, as if to shockingly force our eyes and attention up towards the peak of the hill.. came the violent-pounding crash of thunder and lightning. This.. bolting fiercely across the above-it, dark sky! It (with its sudden flash of light) making visible the images of three crucifix's atop of the huge-earthly-mound. All eyes (in fear-filled awe) compellingly stared upward. Jack (in naïve curiosity) began up the pathway.. While I (with some distant better recollection and insight as to what had just taken place there) unwillingly followed.

When (all-too-soon, it seemed..) he'd surmounted the hill.. I, at a chosen close-enough-for-comfort retreat, watched as he (in a state of over-powered emotional-paralysis and awe-struck disbelief) continued in closer.

In spite of my behind-him location, I could tell (by the position of his arched-upward hat) that he was staring steadfastly into the face of the man hanging on the center crucifix.

With all of the about-us rage of the stormy afternoon, there seemed to be a cold, deathly silence in our immediate area. A silence that was only interrupted occa-sionally by the in-agony, surrendering-to-death groans of the poor soul above and in-front of us. Jack (still uncertain of whom his eyes were beholding) whispered, in attempt to confirm his dreaded notion...

"Jesus?..."

No response came from the looking-up-towards-the-sky, pain-disfigured face on the crucifix. My heart pounded.. and my breath shortened. Adrenalin tingled the total-ness of my being. I wanted so badly to cry and scream-out. Desperation burnt my throat and nostrils. The darkness coldly thickened. I heard Jack's still-advancing footsteps squish and crunch in the ear-ringing hush.. and saw (through the misty haze) his scarf blowing snappingly to his side. A climaxing stir in the wind then, out-of-nowhere, fell. I twitched at the discovery of it. The tension mounted, tightening by the second.

"Jesus?.. Jesus?..."

Again, no reply. Instead the face stared upward-still.. now inaudibly speaking to the sky…

"My God, My God.. Why hast thou forsaken me…"

I could barely make it out. For I was much too tense to concentrate. And when (all of a sudden) Jack's whistling-carol made a brief entrance (ending abruptly after a few bars), I startlingly lost complete track.. directing my (whatever-was-left-of-it..) attention to its seeming-very-out-of-place melody instead.

What was he doing?.. This was no time for that!…

Surprisingly enough.. and much to my amazement.. the severely-bruised face of Jesus slowly lowered to half-consciously survey the below-Him surroundings. It was obvious that (in all His pain-drowsed condition) He couldn't see very well, for His eyes scanned and completely saw-through the image of Jack, only several feet in front of Him.

Another short version of the tune was rendered to help the Lord better-locate his exact whereabouts.. The guiding sound of it, leading His face forward and into the proper looking-down-on-him position. The moment's-before vacant-ness of Jesus' eyes became filled with the inner glow of a far-away, distant recollection. There was a sad smiling in them of a pleasant memory.. from another time.. another place.. another season of life. Something so deep in His conscious, that it was just barely recall-able. A vague, but precious scene from the past replayed. Something very 'dear to His heart'. Something 'chillingly warm'.. that awoke and embraced.. and brought back into view and perspective 'the reason and purpose of His creation'. The Beginning.. The End.. from Triumphant Moment to Triumphant moment!.. The pain and glory of Birth.. to the pain and glory of Rebirth!

Jack returned again with still another even-longer version of the hymn, realizing that it was more soothingly-effective than any possible (or grasp-able) words. And more enlightening, as well.. in spite of the voice-cracks and sadness in its normally-brisk melody. It quiveringly rang through the morbid day.

Then, surrendering the more-pleasant recollections to the excruciating reality of His predicament, Jesus raised His head and expressed the awful-est-sounding-of-them-all sighs of agony. It was mixed with words that I was 'too cringed' to hear. His head fell forward limply. Jack rushed to Him arms-stretched, clutching the base of the crucifix, pressing his grief-tightened face up towards the slashed and battered feet of Jesus.

"No.. No.. No... no.. no..."

Sliding down to a kneeling position on the gravel, he whimperingly continued...

"no.. no.. no.. no..."

Then.. a long drawn-out silence.

At last, shattered with...

"THESE.. THESE ARE THE PEOPLE I'M TRYING TO REACH?...
THESE PEOPLE.. WHO'D.. DO THIS!...

MURDERS!.. FOOLS!.. HATERS!…

THESE PEOPLE.. WHO WOULD DO THIS TO.. TO.. THE SON OF GOD!.. WHAT AM I DOING HERE?…

INSANITY!.. TOTAL INSANITY!…

GOD.. FATHER.. WHAT AM I DOING HERE?.."

Then.. another uncomfortably-long, wind-chilling silence.. after which Jack arose to his feet. Emotionally exhausted and lost in a thick haze of deep thought, he began on his way down the mountain's path.. head bowed.. not turning back once. There was no more for him to see.. No more to believe in.. There was just no more of anything in the world for him.. He was going home. Heaven had waited much too long. Maybe it had been uncomfortable for him there.. but, at least, he didn't have to deal with people.. People who killed!.. Sick.. Sick People.. Who killed! Sick.. Sick.. Sick.. Sick!

Through the tragically-shattered late day, he walked.. never once gaining speed on his foot-dragging retreat. On and on, it went.. into the late-night hours. I'd never seen him so desperate! So defeated! Even back in Heaven.. in spite of his depressions and heart-breaking, wearisome situations.. he'd always had some amount of remaining vigor. It was as though his will was completely gone! Traumatically crushed to smithereens! Nothing made sense to him anymore! He was lost! Totally and thoroughly confused! Drained.. Absolutely drained!

Following him over sand-mound after sand-mound, I found myself growing increasingly concerned over his condition. He couldn't quit! He just couldn't! I had to do something to help him. But, what? Besides.. God had warned me not to try to interfere! But I must! I mustn't! I prayed. Yes, that's what I did.. I prayed! God-beggingly prayed, too!…

'Lord, please.. please help!…

Please do something.. Anything.. but, please…

Please help us.. Please.. Oh, please help!…'

It was on the morning of the third day of our retreat.. when I had long-surrendered all praying attempts.. that, in the above-and-in-front-of-us sky, appeared a

Star. Yes.. a Star! Settling on the far horizon. A yellowish-orange, ever-glowing Star.. with a rich, florescent-like rainbow awning. It was absolutely beautiful! Breath-taking!

Jack (at last) raised his trauma-worn face to greet it. Its distracting brightness glared across the ahead-of-us desert, leaving him 'no other choice' but to acknowledge it. There was a strange-ness about it.. For although our slow-moving journey continued without let-up, it magnetically attracted our eyes and our direction. Yes, it moved.. compellingly dragging us along with it.. remaining as our guide through-out the long days and nights that revolvingly followed. It.. bringing direction. For, up to that point, we (or 'Jack', I should say) had been wandering aimlessly.

The speed of our travel remained a dead-lock slow.. But after a time, I came to notice a gradual south-western bearing in our movement. And when (after what-seemed months and months of walking) we reached Antarctica, I realized my prayers had been answered.

Jack relinquished his further retreat in the discovery of his cherished 'new-found' homeland.. and stood (steamy-'n-blurry-eyed) on the ledge of an enormous iceberg, staring out at it and across its vast and barren horizon. Still numb and unconcerned.. but now, at least, he was home! Yes, he'd gone far enough. He would stop and rest here in the familiar surroundings. Here.. away from the mania of it all. Here.. where he could better decide what he should do. He couldn't even think straight now anyways! His shack waited. He could board himself up in it and reconsider his future plans. Maybe he was being too hasty and irrational about it all? Either way, he would wait…

Throughout the following and very depressing year, Angel Jane and 'going back to Heaven' seemed to dominate Jack's thoughts. The disheartening scenes of the Crucifixion replayed over and over in his mind.. haunting his awake hours, as well as his very-few sleeping ones. Yet still, he hung on.. remaining in his South Pole home-base.

Recovery was very minimal, if at all! He had to force himself to rehearse..

often missing days (and even weeks) of it, at a time.. mumbling away the hours in his un-kept shack instead. In spite of his lack of enthusiasm 'whistle-wise' though, his inner battle raged on with its equal amount of drive. For now, not only did he distrust and feel alienated from those in Heaven.. but likewise his image of the people-folk of the world had been severely contorted. Along with his increasing self-consciousness and discontented self-image, his distraught suspicion had him trapped-and-cornered into one of the most-anguishing-of-all-types of mental states. Fear.. I must say.. was, as well, one of the main-contributing factors for Jack's 'staying-put' in the Antarctic and not retreating to Heaven. For.. as much love-and-devotion as he felt for God, the Father and Jesus.. his paralyzing doubts and uncertainty of being severely chastised for his mis-behavior held him in constant apprehension over his final confrontation with them. Yes, it seemed as though 'everything' was against him! At least, in his 'warped'-opinion it was. There was no place to go for relief! No where for comfort! No where to run! Just nowhere! And tell me.. How does one escape one's self?

- YOUR DOORWAY (CHRISTMAS EVE) –

At the dawning of the on-coming and following Christmas Season, I was still 'totally in question' as to what Jack's plans were. And mind-reading was a waste of time and effort, in regards to the matter.. For it seemed that Jack himself didn't have the faintest notion of what he was going to do! Of the three choices he had.. return to Heaven.. resume the Quest.. or stay put in the Antarctic, I discarded the latter on the December-chilling night that he made his speedy departure into the 'destinations-unknown' of it.

Onward I followed.. in the misty-wet spray of my ice-cutting-path-maker's far-ahead-of-me advances.. hoping that the blinding chase would ultimately find us in the Middle East.

When at last my coming-into-focus sight beheld the backside of Jack standing and over-looking the Crystal Lake, just outside of Heaven (In oddly-enough the exact location of my first-time visit, only a reasonably short number of years before!), you can imagine my discouragement! Why did he have to come back? It was much too early to quit! It was Angel Jane.. it had to be! The sad-eyed, boyish-'I'm-sorry'-look on his staring-at-the-Pearly-Gates face was a dead give-away. Yes, he just couldn't resist her. This was it.. the Quest was over! I just knew it'd wind up like this!

As I scuffingly followed him around the water's edge towards the Heavenly City, I came to more-and-more sympathize with him and his choice though.. Doing a gradual, but complete, emotional about-face. After all, love is something very precious and needed! Especially for someone like Jack. Not to mention his all-the-worse (at this particular time) need for someone to console him!

Tagging behind him, I recalled that first Christmas Eve night, when Angel Jane and he had (after discovering his whistle) ran hand-in-hand along this same exact pathway, en-route to the Cathedral. I remembered their joy and happiness in having each other. And then how everything had turned out so bad. And how their romance had been unmercifully cut short. Yes, it definitely was the better-choice that he had come back! It was meant to be this way! They deserved each other. This was.. all for the best! I was proud of his decision! Boy, would Angel Jane be surprised to see him. I could hardly wait to see the look on her face!

As we at last encountered the Pearly Gates, we came to hear the sounds of what-was-like a party going-on inside of them. Slowly pulling open one of the gates just-a-hair, we peeked-in our curious-filled faces.. to meet the sound of joyous Christmas Caroling! This.. coming from a massive crowd gathered just beyond us in the huge inner courtyard. I couldn't believe it, but amazingly-enough we'd returned on Christmas Eve! For the mood of all proved so. How ironic!

Jack seemed 'so controlled and pensive', I couldn't believe the sight of him. Not one display of distaste for the Christmas joy that non-stop unfolded before our eyes. No, he just seemed to be totally in-surrender of it all!

Silently in awe, he just stared.. until the thought of Angel Jane edged him sneakingly onward and into the un-noticing-him group. Face down and moving as fast and as inconspicuously as possible, he dodged his way through the masses. Miraculously enough, he was never once detected! Fully knowing his direction, he darted up a particular side-street.. leaving behind the merriment.. trudging faithfully on, towards the site of the Cathedral.

When ultimately he had made his way through the abandoned-alleyways and night-covered streets to the building's front, he found its doors wide-opened and its auditorium vacant-to-the-hilt.

Squeaking his way about the vast hall, he (in a moment's desperation) chanced

a.. "Angel Jane?.." that echoed so loud, he cringed in its return. He shot a glance at the doorway, trying to confirm that he had not given himself away to any, by-chance passersby. No one appeared. He resumed his search. Over to the alcove. She wasn't there. Of course, she wasn't still there! It's truly amazing some of the straws that we'll grasp at, under the gun!

After a more-than-fair inspection (if not, a far-more-than-fair inspection!) of the entire auditorium inners, he began towards the front doorway again.. Only to (upon reaching it) collide head-on with the Angel of Notes, who had like-out-of-nowhere suddenly entered. The impact of their crash made an awful noise.. and (although I'm not sure of how to properly describe its sound to you, that you might likewise vicariously feel it, I will say..) the sight of the two of them sitting opposite each other.. with stars circling their heads.. might give you some sort of a better-insight than any 'THUMP'- 'CRUNCH' or whatever-'sound-effecting' words that I might use to convey its extremity!

When after what-seemed-like a very lengthy recovery they were able to still-a-bit-drowsingly focus on each other, Jack offered with a lighthearted chuckle...

"Hey, where'd you come from?...I didn't even see ya!... I was just..."

"I belong here!.." interrupted Will angrily, turning quickly away and jumping to his feet.

"Hey, man.. I didn't mean f' that t' happen!.. It was an accident!.. I got hurt too!.. I mean, what's with you anyways?.." pleaded Jack, as he likewise rose to a standing position.

With no reply and an uncomfortable silence lingering, Jack felt obliged to fill it in...

"Well.. What's with you?.. What's the problem?.."

Still no answer came. Instead.. just a cold-shouldered hush settled on the very-confused Jack, as the Angel of Notes (without another word) walked away into the further inners of the dark auditorium.

"What-in-Heaven did I do?.. Was it somethin' I said?.." contemplated Jack, still totally dumbfounded over the incident...

"Ah, the heck with it!.. They just don't like me!.. None 'a them!.. Never did.. 'n

Never will!.. Who cares!.."

Down the stone stairways and out into the still-abandoned streets, he resumed in his search for Angel Jane.

Hours passed. At least, I would estimate hours. Up and down the narrow-ways, he snuck.. fortunately enough for him, not a soul coming into sight. The courtyard party must 'a been still in full swing!

Then.. out of the corner of his eye, he caught sight of her! At least, he felt 'pretty certain' it was her? It was hard to tell.. in the darkness, as it was! But he was almost positive it had, in fact, been 'his Angel Jane', who had only-split-seconds-before entered the doorway of a row-house-type, gold-brick building at the opposite end of the street-like walkway we were, at that point, reaching.

Rushing to the front of the dwelling, he made it there just in time to see the parlor light snap-on and glow through the above-panes. There was stenciled angels on the window glass.. and Jack very impatiently waited for the sight of her to come into view behind them. His heart pounded in the aching silence.

He couldn't wait another second, so he began on his way over to the apartment's stairways to go up and in.

Halfway up the snow-lined steps, he stopped and stared up into a Christmas Wreath that was hanging on the door. There was a cherry-red ribbon fastened on it. Below it (on the left-side of the door frame) was a silver plate with a name engraved on it. Moving up even-closer, he squintingly read it. The name belonged to no one that he knew! Maybe he'd been wrong? Maybe it hadn't been Angel Jane, after all.. just someone that looked like her? He'd better check!

Down to the sidewalk, he dashed. He was so excited, in spite of his confusion. He felt the Christmas Spirit, at last (at first!), touching him! He'd been a totally different angel from the moment he'd arrived.. But now.. yes, now.. he was all-the-more Jekyl-'n-Hyde-ly changed! Happy.. and as anxious as he'd been (as I recalled) only one other time in his whole existence. A distant 'Christmas Carol-like' ballad (out of nowhere) fell upon us.. entering as inconspicuously as that-of a soundtrack melody in some movie. It.. warming him.. and making him as-peacefully-melancholy internally as he could be. The cool night-air seemed to be flowing brisk-fully about us in heavenly balm. No longer turbulent. He was home! At last, home! Home for Christmas! Home Sweet Home! And in Love! Yes, so in Love!

In the window. She was in the window! Unaware of us outside.. But.. there she was! Staring out.. as if she were expecting someone. Someone.. who had been lost.. and gone. It showed in her eyes! Yes, there she was.. It had, in fact, been.. Angel Jane!

Jack froze. He couldn't move! He just stared at her. Tears started. His throat lumped. I waited for him to do something.. for she couldn't see him and he'd have to let her know he was there! Instead he just whispered, as if to himself, but aloud...

"I love you, Angel Jane.. God knows, how I love you!...

It seems like forever since I've seen you!.. Yes, the Lord only knows how much I've missed you!...

Oh, Angel Jane.. I don't know how to.. to…"

Before he could say another word.. likewise into view (inside of the window) came the image of a man-angel.. who (upon entering) caressed her and turned her away, leaving her back facing us.

Jack's face dropped. Being extremely confused, he turned towards the doorway. The name plate! The name! Lost in trying to comprehend the situation, he quickly returned his eyes to the window.. Only to immediately drop them to the sidewalk. They began to fill with pain-streaked tears.. and his nose began to run uncontrollably. He gulped hard, as a scene from the past flashed before his mind…

' "AND IF ONE OF US GETS LONELY?…

WHAT IF ONE OF US FINDS SOMEONE ELSE TO LOVE.. AND TO BE WITH?.. THEN,WHAT, JACK?… THEN, WHAT?…" '

"May it.. be you.." Jack whispered aloud.. slowly raising his head to the pane… "May it be you, Angel Jane.."

Turning, he began away.. oblivious to all about him.

Halfway down the block, he encountered Will, The Angel of Notes. Into the loud hiss of wind-mounting-and-lashing that was rapidly-increasing in his ears, came…

"Jack… Listen.. I'm sorry.. I didn't mean what I…"

Jack began to run, to try to relieve the intense 'pounding pressure' inside. It was overtaking him! It whirled.. and swirled.. and began to howl through his mind!

At last, grasping the words that he'd unnoticingly heard, but failed to address (for all of his turmoil), he yelled back to Will (now in the shrinking distance)…

"FORGET IT, MAN.. REALLY!… JUST FORGET IT!… ' AIN'T NO BIG DEAL!.."

Needless to say, we returned to the Middle East.

And if it hadn't have been for a small shepherd boy (on this particular, late-arriving, very-desperate Christmas Crusade), I feel quite certain in saying that

Jack (in spite of the 'whatever' romantic-failings that he had had with Angel Jane) would have returned to Heaven in surrender. For everything had just gotten to be too heavy for him! There was absolutely nothing else he could've done to have dodged it!

But it was on the third night after we'd arrived there (on our second of Crusades) that.. in a small field just southwest of the town of Capernaum.. Jack en-routed a young herds-boy who was tending to his sheep.

It just so happened that the boy was whistling (at the time) to a few of his 'strays', lost somewhere in the dark of night.. when Jack (who was passing in the nearby area) caught the sound of it. And in so, Jack 'mistakened' his intentions.. believing (or maybe wanting-to-believe, out of sheer desperation!..) that the lad had caught on to his Carol.

So, without the slightest delay or second thought, Jack searched-out and located the boy.. and, in turn, began whistling-up one-heck-of-a-terrific-storm to help him out. He was in his glory. He'd made a connection. At least, he'd thought he had! For when Jack had worked-up his frost-biting-blizzard, the boy (as to be expected) fled in frozen desperation into the night.. Completely abandoning his search for the sheep! And this, of course, for the warm-security of his in-the-village home!

Regardless of the more-than-obvious mis-interpretation, Jack remained totally convinced that he had made a definite breakthrough. And as a result, that particular winter-crusade lasted almost as long as the first and previous one. It gave him in-centive.. that, of which, was very badly needed, at the time. Incentive that carried his quest into the months that followed, even after that Christmas Season had long passed. It always seemed to be like that for Jack.. Everything would become so bleak and hopeless.. not the slightest sign of recognition or advancement. Then (at the darkest hour) something would happen! A light (like the Star we'd fol-lowed) would appear and shine in the dim horizon. A light of hope! A light to lead him just a little bit further down his path. Until despair again would overtake him. Then, once again.. that light! The light that always led him to nothing. Yes, nothing! It's only worth-while purpose being.. that it carried him that much further down the road to 'nothing'. Yet still.. in spite of its never-leading-to-anything consequences.. I thank God for that light! For I truly believed that that was exactly 'who' was responsible for its appearance. Yes, I was convinced that it was He that made it shine.. to lead Jack onward to whatever his pre-determined destination would be! And likewise I'd also come to believe, by this stage in our journey (and still do, for that matter!) that this 'was' Jack's purpose in God's Master Plan! All the events that had taken place (and were to come with the future) were most definitely inter-woven.. strategically-planned.. and happening for some more ultimate purpose! At this point, I can not divulge to you what that 'finalizing outcome' will be. But I will say, the more involved I was to become with Jack's Quest (and all of the unbelievable fiascos surrounding it!), the more I was to over-all come to a better understanding of 'why there was no-other-choice' but that it all 'had to' happen that way! Well for one.. What if it hadn't? Stop and consider it, for a minute.. What would the world have been like.. without Winter? And.. How would there have been any Winters at all.. without Jack Frost? Yeah, just think about it!

So you see, there are lots of underlying reasons for all of this. Some that are not nearly as obvious as the above-stated. But still, their existence and validity are beyond debate! Thus I will again repeat.. this 'was' Jack's purpose in God's Master Plan. As outrageous as it all might seem, it was (I sincerely believe) all pre-determined for some much greater result beyond our at-present reasoning!

As the years faded away into forgotten-day's-past.. so too did the just-as-lost Centuries. Quickly lived and discarded.. Quickly gone and departed! Yes, 'Quickly' being a very appropriate word for it too! For it seemed that we were constantly 'on the run' with Jack's Crusades. From village to village.. town to town.. then city to city, as the world turned forward the hands of time.

As a result of the countless escapades that we mutually experienced in these fleeting years, I (needless to say) became very emotionally attached to Jack. He.. becoming like an un-knowing and un-aware-of-me 'Brother'! I sincerely and very deeply came to love him and his for-never-ending project. In spite of the whatever- 'bitter grounds of justification' that it had been foundation-ed on! And as well, to 'whomever outside of his cause' it was momentarily being applied to. No, I just couldn't help but be 'all for it'! As the old saying goes.. 'All is fair in love and war'.. and this most-certainly was 'war' in my book! Besides, to say the least, his scheming, strategically-impish ways forever intrigued me. He was never at-a-loss for yet another of his outrageous pranks. Yes, despite his imprisoning shyness, he would gamble anything to further his goal! His sneaky (and more often than not.. clumsy!..) approach was amusing-and-entertaining in itself.. Not to mention, some of the 'hilarious calamities' that were to follow as a result. Hardly boring! The mischief and messes he'd get into.. Why, you just wouldn't believe! I had to be 'on the ball' constantly, for I never knew what he'd do next!

Yes, it was a life of total mystery and adventure. There was rarely a dull moment to speak of on any of the Crusades we made, regardless of the never-to-amount-to-anything outcomes they'd afford. It became compellingly important to me that I make the rounds with him each season. A treat.. never a task! I lost all sight and recall of my entire past.. becoming more and more obsessively absorbed in Jack's continuous battle, as the years moved forward. Yes, in the process, I completely forgot my previous on-Earth life.. including all of my own 'once-so-pressing' dreams and goals. There was no need for them anymore! They disappeared and faded.. and instead were replaced by a total focus and allegiance (on my part) to Jack and his never-winning cold war.

As the people of the world accumulated and spread out across the once-unsettled regions and continents of the Earth, it (in turn) enlarged Jack's areas to concentrate on. With that evolving factor, he had to devise a more appropriate schedule to include (and as well, be able to cover..) the entire world annually. This.. being easy-enough for a master-mind such as he! After his November through March shift in the Northern Hemisphere, he would return to the Antarctic for several months of rest. Then in June, he would attack the Southern-half of the Globe.. quitting in early September for another brief homeland-rest before his again-November journey. Yes, it all seemed to 'fit together' enough for him. Need I remind you (as I'm sure that Jack never would!) of Mother Nature's 'orbital contribution' to this ingenious (-of-his?) mapping and strategy! This, of course, making his Crusades all-the-more interesting and challenging. And, as well.. a 'whole lot more' promising too. The latter, at least, in Jack's mind!

Through the Medieval Times of Europe.. right on up to the Plymouth Rock Days of America, our expeditions continued without let-up. Every year, the same endeavor.. Racing from one place to another, in a desperate and fruitless search for recognition and acclaim.. surviving rejections that would have surely made a lot of others just give-up and abandon the thought of success all together! For, in these early times, there were hardly any breakthroughs at all. Actually now that I'm trying to recollect it, I can't honestly remember a one! At least, not a single solitary one worth mentioning or going-into here. Yet in spite of the desperate situation that Jack always seemed to find himself tangled-in, by the conclusion of every Crusade; each South Pole lay-over would find him again at the drawing-board 'making plans'.. all the more earnestly-determined and eager at the onset of his next quest. With each passing and vain winter though, he grew more and more bitter. And being there to witness and share his trials, I was inclined to sympathize and have a true understanding of his averse disposition.

As I had previously stated, these earlier years in history were quite unfruitful.. so I will not dwell on them here. I will, in so doing, apologize to any readers that would have rather that I had gone into a much-more depthly account.. and instead (for the sake of the general 'Christmas-Book-Reading-Public', who prefer it more 'short and concise') will concentrate on/ and deal with the more modern-day events that we experienced together. If not only for the breakthroughs and more-interesting facts that they afford; but also for the more-readily and vivid my memories are of them.

So I will resume our story with the 1900's. For it was, in these times, that Christmas was becoming a more popular and celebrated holiday by the people and nations of the world. Social consciousness was likewise expanding in these faster-moving, more-discovery-filled days.. and the probability of Jack's whistle ever being understood for what it 'really' was, seemed more likely and conceivable a thought. Yes, during this period in history, people were more 'open-minded' and inclined to accept anything, no matter 'how off-the-wall' it seemed. And if Jack was ever really going to make any breakthroughs, then now was the most-likely-of-all times that he would!

With all that seemed to be so-much-more in his favor in that respect, Jack (to the contrary) was growing awfully restless and discouraged by the time the Twentieth Century got into full swing. And I rightfully couldn't blame him either. It seemed like everything was against him. At least, that's the way he was starting to see it! Yes, it was beginning to seem as though too many other obstacles were standing in his way. Things that he'd started 'taking note of' that he hadn't previously. The 'appearing-to-be' out-numbering odds! 'Real' or 'Imagined'.. Whatever?.. But they sure did appear to be 'real enough' for Jack. For when you're feeling down-'n-out about things, it's quite natural to get nit-picky about even the most common of aggravations that (even in your best of moods) wear on your day. Well, for one example.. the Sun! Yes, it seemed to him that it was making him work further and further into the night. For it wasn't until night-time anyway that Jack had the chance (and the freedom) to turn-on his utmost freezing forces.. and that's when ninety-five percent of his prospective audience was inside, retiring to their dreams. Yes, it seemed like and out-'n-out conspiracy! For who could 'hear' his Carol, if they were all inside of their boarded-up, unlit houses 'sleeping'? Sure.. he could whistle in through the window cracks and doors.. But, still.. it just didn't seem fair at all! Then to top it all off.. after the long night's wait (when finally the barricaded inhabitants 'did' re-appear) they'd forever 'hurry out' and 'run-away' at the sound of Jack's high-pitched tune! Not to mention, the scarves and ear-muffs wrapped around and covering their lower heads.. and 'ears'! Just consider for a moment 'how that would appear to Jack'. How would you feel, if you were trying to sing to somebody that was doing that to you? Had I never brought it to your attention, you probably never would have thought of it that way. But just stop and consider how deeply that would offend you!.. Not to forget, someone as already-rejected-feeling and hurt as Jack! Now you and I both know that it's not an intentional thing.. But still, that's the way Jack takes it. And that (among a number of other seeming-petty-type things) was making him come to feel that there was some sort of 'big plot' against his succeeding in the works! Need I further elaborate by saying what the dawning of the term "Defrost" meant to Jack! So you see.. all things considered.. Jack was (at this stage) beginning to wonder if he had ever really had a snowball's-chance-under-the-Sun to begin with!

Yes, the Twentieth Century found Jack at an all-time low in spirits. He could hardly get people to listen, let alone get them to understand. And even more far-fetched, get the 'whole world' to whistle-and-sing along. It was becoming an outrageously, ridiculous idea.. Even to him! With all the odds against him, how on Earth was he ever going to do it? It seemed.. The Ultimate, Impossible Dream!

In spite of all the handicaps facing him (and above all, his own self-inflicted depressions!), I could see that Jack was now though acquiring quite a slickness to his style. A smoothness and approach that was a-whole-lot-more-together than it had ever been! Refined from years and years of experience and dedication to his work! I knew that (as crazy as the whole Crusade might have been becoming to the both of us!), if he was ever going to make a 'real' breakthrough, it was going to have to be now! It just had to be! Jack was failing! Losing touch with everything that he had once so believed in! One light.. just 'one light of hope' would have to appear. We hadn't seen even a ray of one in so long! One just had to shine.. to shed light on the so-dark future. And.. at last.. it did! And not a moment too soon either!

THE SIXTH CHAPTER

~ ORCHID LADY ELEGY ~

It was some time into the mid-twenties (of the Twentieth Century) that, by sheer coincidence, Jack lucked upon his first real, substantial breakthrough. The first in a line of others that would start the ball rolling for him and his quest.

It was at the forthcoming of this particular 'eventful' Holiday Season that Jack had decided he would get a head-start and begin his rounds earlier than usual. This.. due to the advance Christmas advertising; and consequently the Yuletide Spirit that it brought with it, which was becoming more-the-style of the times. And, not only for the more opportunities that the seasonal displays and general pre-Christmas mood might afford him.. But also, because he was becoming ex-tremely impatient, these days. His hyper-activeness had gotten the absolute-best of him! Having realized throughout the years that he would need to crack-out of his timid-shell-of-bashfulness, if he was ever going to make any headway (and having done so considerably!), he was now all-the-more raring to go! Yes, by now he'd become the scheming-est, little prankster in all of the history of the Universe (excluding 'Mr. You-know-Who'!). A master of his own bitter-ing deviltries!.. An art he could no longer patiently contain throughout his off-season voids. It was for these reasons.. plus the fact that he could sense that something was 'due' to hap-pen, that he left the Antarctic earlier than normal, this Crusade. Yes, he could just 'feel it' in his bones! You could say he had a 'premonition' that something.. yes, something 'big' lay in-store, down the line! A breakthrough! He just 'knew' it! Feeling right on the verge of it. He couldn't quite put his numb-cold finger on it; but still.. it was there. It just had to be! Yes, there.. and just waiting to happen! He couldn't stand the suspense another day!

So it was with this 'pre'-usual move that winter came to the Northern Hemi-sphere sooner than it ever had before on Earth.

Throughout the years, Jack had been analyzing his un-appreciative audiences quite thoroughly.. and had concluded that the most-promising (and most likely to relate to him) candidates were obviously going to have to be 'musical people'. For these were a breed of people with an extra hearing sense. Yes, if anyone on the face of the Earth was even 'near capable' of comprehending his whistle as being a Christmas Carol, then it would surely have to be one of these! Their eccentric and highly-sensitive nature.. not to mention, their more open-minded, inspirable imaginations.. made them seem (to Jack) to be the 'most promising' victims. Although in all actuality, this was (and still is!) not always the case.. it was, regardless enough, Jack's desperate reasoning at the time.

So with that, it was quite to-be-expected that on this particular untimely season, I followed Jack to a city in the southern parts of the United States of America. A small metropolis where many musicians and people of that trade lived and congregated. One of the major 'musical mecca's' of the world.

Jack's disposition (as cold and bitter as it normally was!) was now (as previously stated) at its extreme worst! His thoughts of Angel Jane, being stronger and more-melancholy than ever.. missing her terribly, these days.. making him all-the-more unbearable and uncomfortable-a-character to be around! His lonely frustrations had mounted to an inner fury, that I was sure would explode at any given moment! He was working harder and harder now, in hopes of completing his Crusades, that he might return to Heaven. But only to return if he was victorious! For it was too late now to change his mind. He'd come much too far and wasn't about to give up for anything! Besides.. maybe 'Victory' would help restore his losses with Angel Jane?.. There ain't nothin' like a 'hero' to turn a lady's head. Yes, it could change everything!

   In spite of all his undying self-faith.. his persistence.. and even his 'victory visions'.. the truth was, he was becoming more and more confused and unsure. This, as I had stated earlier. Yes, he knew all-too-well that this (his quest) was taking far longer than he'd ever dreamed it would. Yes, much too long! Something had to happen.. and soon! This was just getting to be too never-ending!

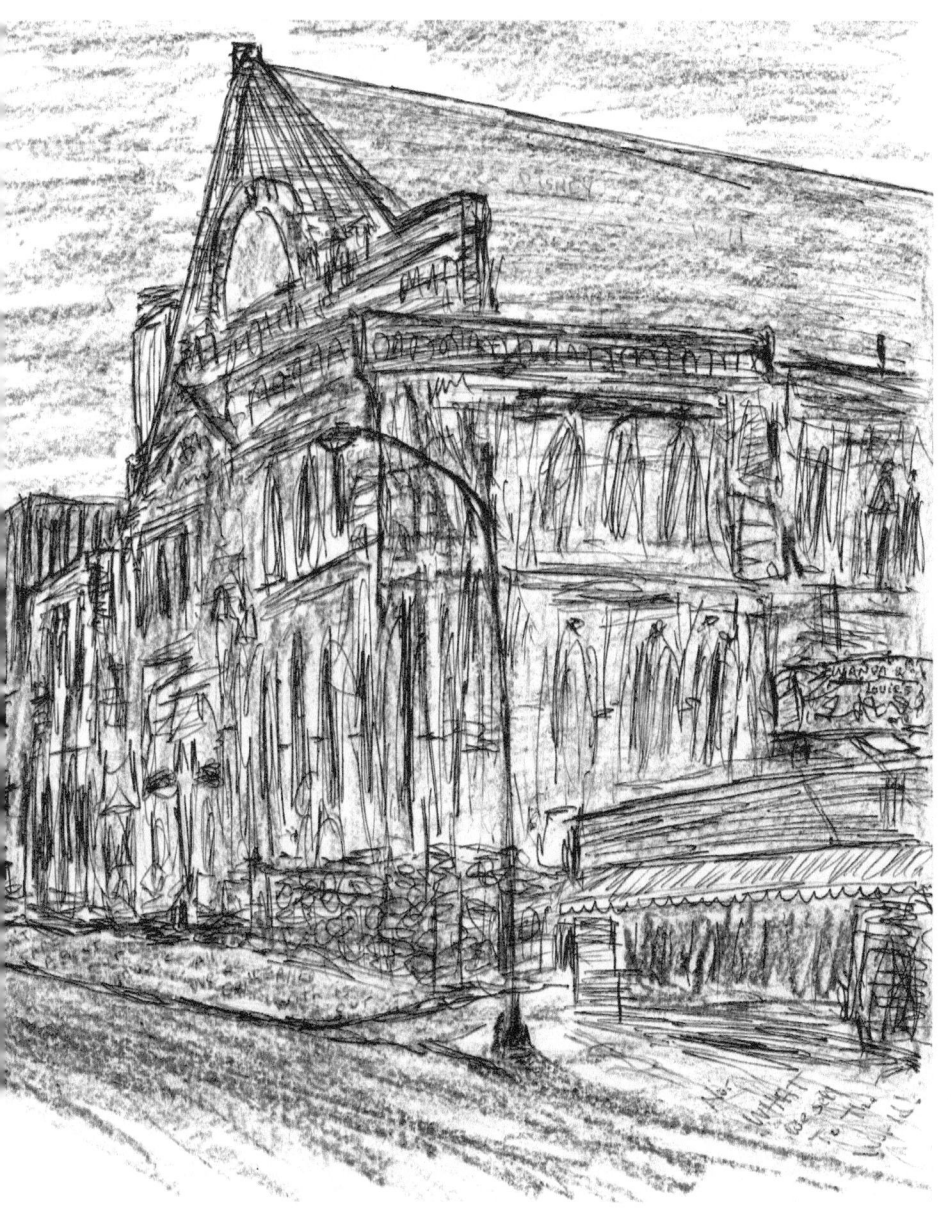

It was mid-November and raining that first night that we arrived in the 'Musical City'. A rain that immediately transformed into sleet and flurries upon our entry to the main downtown area.

There, on the front stairs of a huge cathedral-like structure, we rested from our long excruciating journey. This, being built oddly-enough front-angularly, facing an uphill side-street that ran north off of the town's main-through-fare.. The latter, located just to the left of our seated position.

Panting and retrieving our breaths, we studied through the silence that was settled about and upon our immediate area of the dark street-way. It was easy to 'street-wise-ingly' detect that this particular section of town was (for a lack of better words..) the down-trodden 'red light' district of the small metropolis. From the ever-presence of the surrounding's beggars, drunkards, streetwalkers and so forth (that we had encountered in making our tracks to our at-present stop), it took no great insight to arrive at this conclusion. Still, despite this deduction, Jack and I felt right-at-home here.. being not in the slightest uncomfortable. No, quite to the contrary, we were extremely content in the environment. Yes, it was much-the-norm for us to be found in-the-like! Feeling very much like 'family' to any other 'misfits' that we'd ever encountered! For with Jack's (not to mention, my own..) deep-disdain for high-browing bureaucracy, snobbery, prejudice and so on, it was quite 'the expected'! (Our feelings on that subject, being worthy of 'a Book' in itself!)

Then, to interrupt the quiet stillness engulfing us.. below (from the intersection of the lower-broadway), we saw four large buses entering our side-street.. making their awkward incline towards us.. pulling themselves up to our curb-area and stopping to exit their over-excited passengers. Tourists was our first (and correct) impression. Bunches of them!

As they boisterously made their way-free and off-of the metal contraptions into our direction, Jack jumped to his feet, over-enthusiastic over the prospects of the more-than-fairly-sized approaching audience at hand. The whistling came, filling the street and echoing into the adjoining alley-ways of the brick cathedral.

Then (to deter their nearing advances) came the sound of two street-minstrels, just below and behind their masses.. who were tamborine-bangingly, guitar-strummingly and heartful-singingly intercepting the crowd. The latter of whom were now (as a result) turning back towards the lower-main-street and gathering to listen to them. Jack (in a flash of frustrated anger) darted down the sidewalk into their shivering (yet, still pre-occupied..) midst.

Edging our undetected ways through the crowd (to the near-center gladed-few-of-them outlining the troubadours), we dead-stopped to likewise become enthralled by the entertaining two-some. Our faces (like all of those surrounding us) dropped in jaw-plopped awe! For here.. before our very eyes (propped just outside of the inter-section's cubby-cornered pawnshop).. were two of the most outrageous and unique singers we'd ever encountered in all of our travels! Both toothless-to-the-gums and viciously attacking and pounding their instruments, they (with the utmost sincerity and feeling) were singingly entrapping their audience in the most joy-filled-and-jolly-est-of-ways we'd ever witnessed.

Their side-splitting and humorous, antic-filled approach was irresistibly contagious. Everyone in the crowd (excluding Jack.. who has never really taken to Christmas Caroling, short of his own!) was happily laughing and singing along. Jack (I will mention though..) seemed quite subdued and pensive throughout, totally absorbed in their impromptu performance. For if he hadn't have been.. Well, need I tell you what he'd have done!

Boy, they were good! And different, for sure! Jack and I were spellbound. We just couldn't take our eyes off of them! Their earnest dedication shined like a radiant aura, all about them. In spite of their very-unorthodox and raw delivery, it was more-than obvious that their hard-worked craftsmanship completely over-ruled all, if any, shortcomings (in regards to 'musical prettiness') that they might have had. We were absolutely 'trapped' in the focus of them! So totally entrapped that.. when they at last concluded their performance.. upon our turning-back-and-around to the surrounding crowd.. we startlingly realized that they had somewhere-into-the-night dispersed!

As one of the two musicians knelt to re-pack his guitar into its case, Jack and I dumbfoundedly proceeded down onto the main avenue with all of its glaring lights and night-club-prevalent excitement.

Throughout the following hours, we roamed this cold-wet street and its surrounding ones.. endlessly searching-out a single ear that might hear and understand. But not a one did, in the slightest, it seemed! The music in the air (that blared repetitively all night long, out and onto the sidewalks from the nightspots-of-plenty) only made Jack's effort seem all-the-more fruitless and wasted. His whistle simply got lost in the 'drowning-out' din!

Jack (along with everything-else that was weighing-down his mind) was becoming increasingly disgusted and angered, as the in-vain night continued. And I was becoming very worried over what he might do with each passing minute. He was furious.. for he'd felt so sure that this would be 'the place' that he'd make his big breakthrough. But nothing was happening! No results at all! It was as though, his whistling was going 'right over their heads'!

"Was this all just.. a waste of time?...

Maybe I was all wrong about this place!...

Musical City?… They can't be serious!…" he mumbled in his arrogant way, as he trudged back down the city's main-strip.. passing the pawnshops, restaurants and hotels.. each being fronted with large store-sized, pane glass windows. These.. immediately frosting with a heavy mist from his mere-nearing presence.

The further down the dark-busy street we went, the more violently-upset Jack became. He was (to put it mildly..) 'steaming' from the reception he was receiving! He'd been so convinced that this was going to be it! His gut-feeling and intuition had proven wrong and it was killing him!

At last, when we reached a small combination Goodwill Store-and-Shrine (that was ironically-enough located near the end of the block, on the same side of the main avenue, heading back in the direction of the earlier-that-night's 'street minstrel-ing scene'), Jack's frustrated-fury exploded with all the violence of a cyclonic, Siberian buran! The unexpected and uncontrollable upheaval of this 'temper-tantrum', causing the wooden door (in the entranceway of the Shrine-Store) to pull wide-open from its unmerciful- vacuuming pressure. Jack (in all his anger) quickly looked inside of the Shrine (that was oddly-enough decorated-to-the-max with wall-to-wall, old-and-aging photographs.. not to forget, Christmas decorations of every sort!).. only to catch the compelling sight of a kindly-old-lady. She.. peering back out in his direction through the still-opened doorway, from behind the shop's counter. She.. having the most sensitive, little-old-lady-ish face I'd ever seen on any Nun! Both Jack and I could tell (in that mere split-second) that she would be understanding-enough to listen and help.. Despite the fact, that we were beyond her visible grasp! For she was the kind to help blindly! You could just tell! Yes, a very caring soul she unquestionably was. It read all over her! She, as well, having a sort-of 'motherly in-stinct' about her. A charisma that radiated a sympathetic-yearning-to-aid-and-nuture any (if not 'all', had it been within her means!) of the poor and less-fortunate, over-looked souls of the world. Truly a glad-to-assist type! The cloth-covering religious habit that she wore was (for some strange reason?) of a complete orchid color! And from the un-viewable background (further inside the Shrine) we could hear clearly-enough the sounds of other nuns, merrily Christmas Caroling away.

The furious wind from Jack's 'letting-off-steam' was causing all of the hang-ing pictures (etc.) on the walls (and throughout) to flap and fly like tree-leaves in a tornado. This.. causing the old lady to become extremely upset. She, in so, calling back to the others…

"HELP!.. HELP!.. SISTERS.. HELP!.. SOMEBODY HELP ME SHUT THIS FUNKY DOOR!.."

The seeming very-out-of-character 'Funky Door'-part of her statement caused Jack to crack a smile…

"MOTHER SUPERIOR ELIZABETH!.. SISTER ROBERTA!.. SISTER WANDA!.. HELP ME!.. PLEASE… HURRY!.."

Running to the rescue, they came.. all tugging away.. and at last slamming the door to the cold, unsettled night. And in the process, on our still-gawking-in faces.

Then it struck me.. Jack had smiled. He'd actually smiled! It was the first one I'd seen on his face since when he'd discovered his whistle with Angel Jane, back in Heaven on that first Christmas Eve. That little-old-lady had somehow-or-anoth-er found a warm-spot in his frost-bitten heart. And to prove me right, immediately after the door had been shut, he began 'caroling-away' at her inside.. Whistlin' up a tremendous storm, more melodious and beautiful than it had been in a long spell!

When he'd sporadically stop to catch his breath, he'd scramble up towards the window glass, trying to look in and see the 'Orchid Lady's' response. But the windows were much too steamed-'n-smudged to see a thing. So back and forth he'd go.. on and on.. on and on.. caroling like crazy in desperate hopes she'd hear. He had to reach her! She just had to hear, for he was sure she'd understand and help! He was positive she would! If only he could get through!

Finally (after much repeated caroling) the blurred image of a hand neared the window glass. There.. on the right-hand (-to us) pane! It.. trembling and shakingly.. cleared the thick vapor just barely-enough to allow a scant view. Jack and I scurried to the small opening to peer up.. and find the curiosity-filled face of the Orchid Lady squintingly looking back out and through us. It worked! She'd heard! She'd really heard!

As she searched-out through the clearing, we could hear her muted voice calling back to the others (who were, by now, returning back to their Christmas-Caroling-session)...

"Did you hear that?.."

They.. stopping.

"Did you?.. Did you hear that whistling sound?.."

"Yes.. and it sounds very depressing to me!.." cranked back Mother Superior Elizabeth, as she resumed her retreat around the far-end of the shop's length-wise counter.

"No.. really!.." returned the Orchid Lady.. "It sounded like music!.. Really!.. Y' know, like it had a little tune to it!.. Yes.. it definitely did!.. Listen.. Listen close!.."

Jack kept his face towards the clearing, not to lose sight of her.. and began again his whistling. He was making a breakthrough! This was it!

It was more-than obvious (judging from the expressions on the Orchid Lady's face) that she couldn't see us through the pane.. But she stared out into our faces so firm and attentively, that it made us feel like.. maybe.. just maybe.. she could, in fact, make out our images!

She continued motioning and calling to the others without turning her head back towards them, as they very slowly neared, now in-wonder...

"Can't you hear it?.. Sisters.. it's beautiful!.. Listen.. Come close and listen to this funky little tune!.. It's just so pretty!.. Hear it?.."

Jack was ecstatic! This was it! This was why he'd come here.. It was in his heart and destiny. He'd been right, all along! This was the place where he was finally going to get his recognition. She was the one he'd been searching for, all of these years. She was the one that would help him bring his Carol to the world!

Sure.. it all added up! It all made sense now! Sure.. now it all seemed so clear! Yes.. after all this time, his quest had finally led him to the 'key person'! He was at last face-to-face with her! He could see it all now.. She would convince the other nuns of its worth.. They would, of course, add it to their Christmas-Caroling Repertoire.. And then.. Yes, then…

Then.. like a nightmare.. it all began to fall apart, right before his very eyes. Something was wrong! It was the Orchid Lady.. she began acting dizzy! Maybe she'd just gotten too excited? She was raising her hands to her head and swaying awful. The other nuns came rushing.. comforting and supporting her.. and at last leading her to a nearby seat.

Slowly the window began to fog again. How could this happen? What was wrong? What was going on?

Jack (still aimed to the glass) began calling and whistling with all his might…

"ORCHID LADY!.. MISS ORCHID LADY!.. PLEASE!…"

His voice (emotionally cracking) persisted.. over and over.. until it slowly surrendered to a continual mumbling. Tears came. The clearing had long disappeared.. and he still whimperingly pleaded on…

"Orchid Lady.. please.. please help me…

Miss Orchid Lady, please.. please help me.. please…"

An awful-cold hush followed, when his pleadings had at last faded into the solemn-silence of the night. Jack's face (composure-lessly) still remained focussed on the window. He began to cry uncontrollably.. and whine to himself.. as slowly he sank to a kneeling position on the ice-covered sidewalk. Then, effortlessly he pivoted and dropped to a sitting position.. raising his knees and arms and burying his face in them, in child-like fashion.. totally lost in a bewailing outburst that he made no effort to restrain.

It was terribly heartbreaking.. for he'd just been so close! There was just no way I could justify the situation! It seemed like he'd always just about get there.. Then something just had to mess it up! You talk about 'being behind the eight ball'.. Man, this poor cat.. he was 'stuck under it'! It just.. just.. just seemed 'so unjust'!

Needless to say, I started (right then and there) agreeing with him and his fear that someone.. yes, someone.. was purposely making it hard for him! It was like there was a curse on him! What had he ever done, that was deserving of this? It was no wonder that his nature was so coldly-bitter and suspicious. In my opinion, it was quite to be expected!

The remainder of that concluding year was a sad and trying one. Jack's recovery was painfully slow and drawn-out from the Orchid Lady incident. Still.. in spite of the 'failing results'.. he, in justification, ultimately re-adjusted the outcome to say.. 'at least someone had heard.. and partially understood!' He hadn't had enough time to convince her that his tune was a Christmas Carol.. But felt sure that if he had, she could have.. and surely would have.. seen and helped! Yes, he was sure of that! Anyways.. the fact that he had been able to capture her interest.. and that 'strongly'!.. Why, that meant something! At least, it did to him! Not to

under-estimate his accomplishment though (as justifyingly- important as it was to him).. but, all and all, the search was still on. For no one yet was whistling his Carol, except he.. and that was a 'far-cry' from having the entire world on his side!

On several occasions during that same winter, Jack (in desperate hope) returned to the site of the little shrine. But only to never-again see the little old lady. All of the other nuns were still there.. But (for some strange reason?) the Orchid Lady had disappeared! Maybe she was sick and hospitalized? Or possibly she'd been transferred? If she was somewhere-else, Jack figured that by 'hanging around', maybe he might 'rake up' some clues. And if so, it would be more-than worth the trips. So he did just that, returning as often as he could, through-out the season. It was heartbreaking to watch him though, on these occasions.. pacing back and forth, up and down the freezing, snow-covered Broadway. Sometimes waiting far into the night.. and all in vain.

It was on one of these such nights though, that Jack did make a 'connection'

with his Caroling. And ironically-enough, it all sort-of happened by coincidence.

After diligently casing the outside of the Shrine-Store's front entranceway for an entire late-afternoon and half-evening, he crossed the avenue to momentarily es-cape the continually-mounting frustration. Now I will mention up-front here.. that it has always been (and remains-to-be to this very day, I'm sure!) a habit of Jack's to.. in times of void.. spend hours-upon-end, leaning up against lamp-posts (and of-the-like), staring forward into open space. And in so.. he becoming totally lost into 'what-so-ever thought' might be on his mind, at the time. This.. being very much the case on this particular, fruitless-dark evening.

In a directly-opposing position from across the street, he stood.. gawking stead-fastly at the Shrine.. never even noticing the side-walkers only inches behind him, that were hurrying by. They likewise-and-also being visually-unaware of his presence.

Re-living the night that he had captivated the Orchid Lady's interest, he began (unknowingly) whistling his tune, as he stared forward into the memories-of-it in his mind. It immediately caught my attention.. and as I turned to look at him from my position at the (to-his-right) adjacent lamp-post, I came to (as well) see a young man advancing on the now-deserted sidewalk to the left-rear of him.

With the continuing of Jack's whistle, I could see that the young man was re-ducing his speed as he neared.. at last coming to a dead-stop right in back of the still-un-noticing serenader. He (this young fellow) being a lad of medium build and good height, I would say.. and wearing a rough-grained, animal-hide, black hat.. with quite-curly hair pressed-'n-tucked under it (This hat, as well, be-ing shaped in a sort-of three-cornered style.. and momentarily reminding me of the old 'colonial-type' cap). Likewise.. he being dressed 'appropriate-enough-for-the-season' in a bundled-up, matching hip-length hide coat. Here (before my eyes, I could tell..) stood a very street-bred character, for sure! It showed.. in his stance!.. his movements!.. his every bit of nature! Yes, there wasn't a single question in my mind that he had every credential!

When he (curious-lookingly..) came to his last steps.. he, in search of some-thing, reached into his large coat-pockets.. while I (in uncertainty) waited and watched.

At last something shiny-'n-metallic came into view with the re-appearance of his hand.. and I saw him lift it to his mouth.

Before I could grasp for a quick-guess at what-on-Earth it was.. the beauti-ful, lonesome sound of a harmonica came to my ears, answering immediately my wonder.

Jack (at the first note of it) practically jumped out of his skin (or 'spirit', how-ever you'd have it)! But within minutes.. realizing the lad was playing along to his Carol.. he began whistling like crazy, to better acquaint him with the melody.

Oh, they sounded so beautiful together! Such a tremendous harmony of sound! A real 'shoe mover', you could say, as well! In short time, the lad had Jack's Carol mastered.. and was even improvising (in a blues style and fashion) the answer-lines in- between the main melody. What a duo! Pretty off-the-wall.. but uniquely good, f' sure!

On and on, they went. I couldn't hear enough of it! They were so wrapped-up in the music, I'm sure that I was the only one to notice, that.. behind them, approaching down the sidewalk.. was a small (but rowdy) group of people. By their curiously-spectating-looks, I knew that inevitably they'd be interrupting the musical two-some in but a matter of moments.

"THOMAS.. WHATCHA DOIN'?...

JUST WHAT ARE Y' DOIN', MAN?.." shouted one of the young men with an 'are-you-crazy' sound to his voice.

When they were within close-enough-for-speaking range, the same young fellow shot...

"What-on-Earth y' doin', cat?.."

"I'm playin' to the Wind, Earl.. Y' know, The Wind!.. Listen.. hear it?"

Jack (in spite of the interruption) was still whistlin' away.. Only now, a more arrogant forcefulness was being applied to what (only moments before) had been so casual and flowing.

".. Are you crazy, man?.. The Wind?.. Y' can't be 'for real'!.."

"Yeah, Listen.. Can't y' hear it?.. It goes like this.." putting his harp to his lips and playing several quick bars.. "Listen.."

There was a dead silence, while everyone in the group held their breath to hear.

Jack (having his audience now) forced on his melody, not to lose them. What better chance could he ever get than this to display his work. And work, he did.. feverishly.. whistlin' so powerfully and ridiculously that I thought surely he'd strain himself!

The street (and all upon it) seemed to shake from the violent-fury of his Carol. The pensive little group of listeners, one by one, tightened the necks of their coats and grasped their hats.

Then (in a near-frost-bitten tone of voice) Earl.. the same fellow who'd been their un-official spokesman, up to this point.. finalized the suspense-filled hush with...

"Brrrrrrrrr... rrrrrrr!.... Man, you're nuts, Thomas!.. Really.. I'm getting to think you're losin' it, all over the place!.. You got t' be out 'a your mind, standin' out here 'n 'playing to the wind'!.... Yeah, I think your reeds are getting warped!...

What you need.. is a good strong cup 'a coffee.. to clear y' head, Bro!.. C'mon.. let's get down to Linebaum's 'n get us one.. 'k?.. Before we all freeze t' death!.."

There was a small amount of good-natured chuckles from the group, then another young lad from their troop swung his arm around Thomas's shoulder and they all began down the sidewalk to a restaurant at the opposite end of the block. Jack just stood silent, watching them.. looking like he'd just lost his best friend.

When at last they reached the dining place, Thomas glanced back over his shoulder to take a one-more, 'I'm-sure-I-heard-it' look.. then disappeared with the others inside.

As if it were planned that way (to spare Jack of his grief), at the exact moment that Thomas went out-of-view.. into view, across the avenue, came the sight of two nuns leaving the Shrine-Store. Jack didn't waste a minute! Before you could say 'Jack Frost', he was right in their midst. It being Mother Superior Elizabeth and Sister Roberta. We recognized them from that first night immediately. On their way to somewhere, fortunately-enough-for-us they lingered outside of the entrance to bundled-up and have a few words, before they went on their ways.

"Y' know, Sister Roberta.. it seems like only yesterday that the Orchid Lady was here with us.. carrying on like her usual, happy self. I miss her so much! I really wish that she could've been with us for the Lord's Birthday.. She always made it seem so much more joyous and fun-filled!.. Christmas is always so beautiful a time of the year.. But she forever made it seem that-much-more-special an event, each time! Yes, I really noticed her absence, for sure!"

MOTHER SUPERIOR ELIZABETH

"Yes, Mother Superior.. I know just what you mean…

I especially missed her joking-around and witty comments.. 'Funky Tree'.. 'Funky Ornaments'.. 'Funky This 'n Funky That'.. Everything was always 'Funky'!.. Remember how that used to forever have us laughing!.. Yes, I truly missed her a lot too…

Well, I'm sure that she must've had a splendid time this Christmas though!.. Yes, I'm sure she was very happy.."

Sister Roberta

Jack was becoming as frustrated as I.. Where was she?.. Where did she go?.. Come on.. out with it!

Mother Superior tightened her black shawl.. for Jack was bittering, by the second, from the anticipating-tension of knowing.

Sister Roberta (after a moment's silence) resumed…

"Yes.. I'm sure.. she was very, very happy though…

Oh, what a beautiful and joyous Christmas she must have had, this year.. with the Lord Himself in Heaven!.. Huh, Mother Superior.. What a glorious Christmas she must have had!.."

Jack's face dropped cold. Or, I should say, a whole lot colder than usual! He let out a "Rrrr… rrr…rrrrrrr!.." of anguish. Then off he shot down the main street, wild and blinded in a violent rage! I chased after him, gulping at 'what he might do'!

When (after a time) we reached the southern suburbs (just outside of the city limits), he at last slowed down. Upon doing so, he entered (through the gateway) an at-random graveyard, that was just-off the road that we had been on. In a mumbling-whimpering-blinded fit of outrage, he began attacking the individual grave-sites.. scraping and brushing-off the frozen snow that covered them with his dirty, numbed hands.

Desperately searching and reading the tombstones, along he went. All throughout the flurry-filled, pitch-black evening, he continued.. non-stop.. looking for 'the one' that would prove to him that she was truly gone. He would refuse to believe it otherwise! How could it have happened? It just couldn't be so! He wouldn't believe, until he saw it with his very own, two eyes!

The wind howled and swirled.. making our location and our hour-of-being-there, all-the-more frightful and uncomfortable! I yearned (even greater than he!) its 'un-covery', in that alone we might depart from the 'eerie' premises, as soon as at-all possible!

At last.. it was in the graveyard's section designated as 'the Garden of Prayer' that Jack located the grim truth that he'd so-feverishly sought! Yes, the entire night's search ended with the discovery of a flat-to-the-ground, grey headstone that bore the inscription.. 'So Dearly Loved.. The Orchid Lady'.

I tremblingly watched as he stood there, above the grave.. staring down.. lost in deep thought.. trying to recollect himself emotionally. He said not a word. For after all, what was there to say? Nothing he could voice would ever bring her back! Nor would it ever change anything in any way! I will say though.. had he, in fact, had some few, last words.. I'm sure they would have been something very heartfelt and sincere (Despite himself). For although he'd only known her a very short time, she had been the only person on Earth that had (up to that point) actually touched into Jack's cold-being and found a warm-spot. A warm-spot that would burn 'eternally' in his heart and memory throughout all of his existence! Yes.. and I can say that with as much certainty and authority (on his part), as if I myself were, in fact… Jack Frost!

THE SEVENTH CHAPTER

~ THE CAROL RAG ~

There was no doubt about it.. Jack was at last beginning to get the attention he had, for so long, worked for! As limited as it was, progress was being made. At least, it seemed so! And in that, he was becoming more and more confident that his 'impossible dream' was not so 'impossible' after all! The Orchid Lady incident.. along with his on-the-street jam session with the harmonicat-playin' Thomas.. had proven that to him. Even though they had both ultimately fallen through, still.. things were coming together! Yes, on a 'musical level', of sorts! He could see now himself, how his style and approach had acquired a greater 'effective-ness' to them. He was definitely making headway! After all this time, he was starting to get through to people! At last, the barriers (that had so-imprisoned him and his unique creation for centuries..) were breaking down. Yes, it wouldn't be long now. He was sure of that!

There were, of course, many other less-significant occasions when Jack attracted 'humanely-attention' during these years (in the Twenties), but I myself would prefer to concentrate only on the more major events here-in. For it is they, that.. if any great public acclaim was going to result.. would be the responsible. The minor accomplishments being more like 'helpful encouragements' that Jack so badly needed.. But as for their actual worth in his still-remaining quest, they were not of lasting merit. Nor were they, in any way, size-able steps forward.

So it is with the above-stated reasoning that I will eliminate the trivia and bring you instead to the next impactual achievement (and the events surrounding it) in the lives of Jack Frost and his forever-constant-companion, yours truly...

North-eastern France. In the high-slope lands that carry-over from near-bordering Switzerland. The year.. 1928. You might wonder why I am so precise with that date! So I'll note.. likewise do I ponder the same! Maybe it's because the incidents that occurred there were so completely unbelievable and astounding, that even the most-minute statistics (relating to what-took-place on that Crusade) still remain vividly-intact in the imagery and recall of my mind. Indelibly-secured forever in un-explainable fragments that dart about the vastitude of my memory-bank. Whatever the reason?.. It stands.. 1928!

Yes, as if it were but yesterday, I still can re-live that dark-November night.. with us racing along the steep hillsides and through the snow-bulging forests upon them. Heading North. To Lorraine. To say the least, it was very slippery! And in so, quite a dangerous trip!

Although the about-us scenery of Swiss-trimmed cottages and farmhouses were very enticing to my eye, I found regrettably-enough little chance to enjoy them.. thanks to Mr. J. Frost! No, instead.. through the silent night, we hurriedly forced onward at aggravatingly awkward speeds and angles.

For very long whiles, there would be only wilderness. Then, into the far-off distance, would appear a light from an up-'n-coming hillside dwelling. It was at one of these such dwellings.. a cottage.. that Jack at last stopped to listeningly-heed an old man, who was playing a violin (and very soulfully at that!) out on the snow-lined deck of his protruding-out-and-above-us front porch.

The old-timer's Hansel-and-Gretel-type, blizzard-bound home overlooked a beautiful, mountain-ranged-in valley, that (at first sight) stole your breath away!

As bitterly-cold as the evening was, I believed that the old fiddler was doing so for the reverberant echo that the lower valley afforded (and replayed to him) his very folk-oriented, traditional music. Oh, how beautiful it sounded.. rebounding back and forth.. out across the vast opening.. And with no less the volume, return-ing more clarified-and-hauntingly to our just-under-him position on the hillside. And he (all the while) 'in his musical glory'.. smiling away.. completely absorbed in the ecstatic-joy of its magic. This making it all-the-more pleasing a sight to behold! His frail frame.. bowing back-'n-forth, up-'n-down.. as he swayed to the rhythm of his enchanting melody lines.. Bringing to mind, a mechanical, wooden-music-box-type mannequin with a painted-on, steadfast smile. An always-cheer-ful and ever-minstrelling character!

With the background light from the windows (of his cottage) shining-on and outlining him, it was all-the-more obvious to see.. that, here.. yes, here.. was a very eccentric man! A music lover, if there ever was one! Jack went to work!

Within minutes, his assumption proved right.. and the old man's violin was sawing-away his so-loved Carol. Out across the huge gap it flowed, resounding in the most touchingly-eerie way! Jack awed at the unexpected immediate response. I myself marveled at how quickly the old-timer had caught-on and re-captured it note-for-note-ly like he did!

Smilingly-away, he fiddlingly continued.. on and on.. as Jack (all the while) melodiously inter-weaved about his rendition. I held my heartbeat to listen even closer.. feeling, through-out, a compelling and overpowering urge (building up inside of me) to laugh freely with a childish joy. It was just that 'inner-tickling' and 'movingly-pleasure-some'! The rawness of the old man's style blended so perfectly with Jack's so-forceful and unorthodox whistle, that I couldn't help thinking.. 'what a natural marriage of sound'. Unrefined as it was, it rang true-er and ever-so-more sincere than any to-the-utmost-scored symphonic-piece I'd ever heard! Yes, it was becoming more and more evident to me, that Jack's Carol was quite-duplicate-able! I mean, it obviously wasn't beyond human capability. Far from it! Yet, despite, it was so pitifully obscure! I just couldn't understand it! Nor justify it! It was such a pretty tune.. it just seemed like such a shame! And hearing it now, echo so-beautifully-back at me (from across the valley) made it all seem that much more unfair!

Just as though it could have been for-seen, when the old-timer came to the concluding notes of Jack's melody, he began on his way back into the cottage. For (you could tell) the coldness of Jack's presence was at last getting to him. His slight build just simply couldn't withstand any more of the gripping bitterness of the night.

With the echo of his final efforts returning from across the valley, he retreated further into the entranceway of his snow-bound cabin. The violent tremor of his hacking-cough (that disappeared with him through the enclosure) verified the toll of his self-inflicted, musical gesture. But it was more-than-plain that a man-of-his-nature would have life no other way. Determined to find happiness and enjoy-it-to-its-fullest at any cost!

With the slam of his wooden door (causing a tremendous white avalanche that snow-mounded-in the entire lower-frame).. and to the clitter-clacking sound of him forcefully bolting the inside-sliding lock, Jack and I (without further ado) resumed on our slanted journey through the night.

As for 'any depressions' that Jack might've carried away with him (in regards to the once-again 'failing results'); all I can say is, it was hardly notice-able. For, by now, it had gotten to the point, where he almost 'expected' things to fall through! Becoming almost immune to it, you could say! After all of the rejections and dis-appointments he'd experienced, it was getting to be that it took a whole lot more than something like 'this' to get the best of him. I mean, he obviously didn't like it.. and always hoped for the best, deep down.. But with all he'd been through, you could hardly blame him for not letting himself get prematurely worked-up over every situation. No matter how promising it initially appeared. It was just too much to have to recover from every time! Besides.. being that his mind was al-ready made-up.. and his lifestyle, as well, 'chosen' and 'molded'.. Why should he waste valuable time falling down, each time he failed? Why not just keep moving?

He was right.. So why let anyone else's opinion or denial effect his still-going-to-continue-anyway quest? He'd simply refuse to let it bring him down! His attitude had finally evolved into an 'I'll-shrug-it-off' one. It was the only way for him to survive anymore! Though it had taken many, long fruitless years and innumerous hard-knocks to acquire that outlook.. he was ,at last, learning how to successfully apply it!

Of course, don't get me wrong now.. at times there still were dramatic outbursts and deep fits of depression. And as if to make me sound like a liar (ironically enough, after all of my boasting on his self-assurance), he was, at this particular point in our account, on the road (or maybe I should say.. 'on the slopes'..) to just-precisely one of those! Yes, one of those terribly disappointing situations that he forever seemed to be running into. And running.. being just so accurate a word to describe it too!

- TEARS FOR LYDIA –

It was not until very early into the yawning, next morning that we (exhausted and pantingly..) reached a little country-side village on the northern-most border of France. The inhabitants (as limited as they were) were already awake and quite-active on the roadways, upon our entry to the town's square. Horse-and-cattle-drawn carts fought exertingly to make their way through the cold-slushy, miserable streets.. While pedestrians (bundled-up and freezingly..) darted in and about them on their hurried ways. Jack and I (being there for no immediate reason) browsed-about, taking it all in for the lack of anything-better-to-do.

It was while we were idly standing at one of the main street's intersections (in the village's business/shopping area), watching the bustling passersby.. that, (when all of a sudden) into view came a middle-aged gentleman carrying a tremendous overload of bundles in his arms. Trying desperately to see in front of himself, he made his awkward way towards us, down the glazed sidewalk. It appeared, as though, he'd just 'bought-out' half of the shops in the entire village, judging from the over-abundance of the bundles that he was (with every effort!) fighting and juggling not to spill. The sight of him and his antics made us immediately stop to watch.. and wonder 'What, in tarnation, could he possibly have in all of them?'.

When at last he was close enough, we could see that, inside of them, were all types of musical accessories and gadgets. Pitifully stuffed-down-in and crammed-together were.. phonograph discs, sheet music, microphones and cords, a violin and a flute, a horn for a Victrola, guitar strings.. you name it.. he had it!

At first we just assumed it all to be Christmas Gifts, that he had purchased for the near-approaching holidays. But on second thought, it came to us that he might very-well be.. sure!.. Yes, there was a good chance he was a 'man of music'! He had to be! Needless to say, Jack went for it, full speed ahead!

With no more than four bars of Jack's Carol, the middle-aged gentleman's at-tention was captured. Despite the terrific excess in his arms, he stopped dead-in-his-tracks to listen further. The look on his French-moustached face was one of total bewilderment! Was he hearing things?

Shaking his head (as if to re-shuffle his wits), he resumed his foot journey to the next intersection; stopping again as Jack persistently continued. Then (when Jack's melody died down) he again be-gan for the next street corner to see if the sound-of-it would follow. Jack, of course, did! On and on this went, from one intersection to the mud-slushy next.. looking back for a minute, each time, with that same look of doubt on his face.

At last, a few miles out of the town's square, the Monsieur entered the front-yard of a little, home-sweet-home-looking cottage.. that was located just-along-side of the main road we'd been block-by-block-ly traveling. Jack and I likewise followed him, as he excitedly began his way up and unto the front porch.. and into the screened-in doorway of the dark-brown, cozy-'n-simple dwelling.

Reaching the porch, we stopped and focussed on a hanging-above-and-from-the-front-of-its-main-arch, chain-suspended sign, that read...

" 'M. Jean La 'Belle... Pioneer in the Music Recording Industry'.."

We were right.. He was a 'man of music'! And not only that, but a 'pioneer in the recording industry'! 'Wow, what a break this could turn out to be!'.. What greater opportunity than that could Jack ever get, than to have his Carol be recorded on a disc and be sent 'world-internationally' for all of the population to hear consecutively! Think of all the 'running' that would eliminate! Man-o-man, what a dream come true that would be! He'd never thought of having his Carol be recorded before. Of course, with the Recording Industry being so young-'n-all, it was no wonder he'd never considered it, until now. But now that he had, it most certainly was going to be his main concentration! At least, until it had been achieved. And he didn't waste a minute at it either!

Despite Jack's over-anxious whistling on the porch, when the Monsieur La 'Belle finally made his way inside of the living room of the cottage (leaving the door wide-open behind him) you could still hear him audibly-enough, calling to his family (somewhere in the out-of-view back rooms). With the over-load still in his arms.. standing in the off-room's doorway (as if not to lose sight, nor sound of Jack's whistle), he continued to stirringly beckon them…

"COME HERE EVERYBODY.. COME!.. QUICK!.. LISTEN TO THIS!…

LYDIA, MON CHERI!.. ADLIN!.. CLAUDE!.. MICHEL!.. DAVID!.. YOU WON'T BELIEVE THIS.. IT'S THE WIND.. WHISTLING A MELODY!.. YES, THE WIND.. WHISTLING A VERY, BEAUTIFUL WINTER MELODY!.. COME.. PLEASE.. HURRY!.."

And so they came.. the entire family.. appearing in, but a matter of minutes. The children (All being of young adult age; except Michel, the pre-teenage boy), together with the Monsieur and his beautiful wife stood staring eye-wide and listening attentively. We gawked back in at them, through the screen door.. seeing what-looked-exactly-like a family-picture, greeting card. Yes, like the kind that people send to their friends and relatives on Christmas (as a combination 'Portrait', 'Gift' and 'Holiday Wish'). That's the best way I can explain their appearance. For.. with all of them in a frozen-in-motion position as they were.. and with all of the parlor's Christmas decorations (not to forget, the glowing-little tree, so touchingly trimmed!) surrounding them.. there could be no better description I could find! The loving-warmth (that radiated from them) was not, in the slightest, affected by Jack's freezing bitterness. To the contrary, their happy and charming smiles remained steadfast, as they (without a murmur) listened very seriously for the longest time. They, being undoubtedly the most un-distracted, unfaltering audience Jack ever had!

Realizing that he had won them with his Carol, Jack plowed on and on.. in hopes that somehow-or-another the Monsieur La 'Belle would (as far-fetched as it might sound) get the brain-storming idea of recording it. Jack (being a firm believer in the 'power of suggestion') concentrated deeply on the thought, as he (without let-up) whistled away. Although a little off-target, Jack's meditating was not in vain. For soon after the Monsieur's wife, Lydia, interrupted their long silence with...

"Jean.. I just had the most wonderful idea!.." She paused to further think on it herself, causing a momentary suspense.

"Well?.."

"Well, Jean.. it came to me for some strange reason, that.. that it might be a good idea to.. Well, why don't you record that with your machinery?.. Yes.. so that we might be able to listen to it again on evenings when it will no longer be here to enjoy!..

It is such a beautiful winter melody.. I agree!..

Why don't you?..."

Jack was getting through.. but, not enough. He had to concentrate even deeper...'records.. phonograph records.. records.. phonogr..'

"You know.. I've got an even better idea, Jean...

Why don't you record it for a phonograph record!...

Yes.. I'm sure the public would enjoy it as much as we do!... Yes, you should, Jean!.. You never know, it might become very popular! I'm sure it would appeal to everyone, no matter what country they lived in!.. or what language they spoke!.. they'd be able to relate to it regardless!...

And it is such a pretty tune!.."

"Yes.." interrupted Michel (the youngest).. "That's Jack Frost!.."

The sound of his own name made Jack's jaw drop instantaneously to a locked-open position. He couldn't believe his ears! 'How, in the.. ???.. He was hearing things!.. He had to be!.. How could the boy have known his name? ' He stared in.. absolutely dumbfounded.. with a pale, almost-frightened-looking face.. waiting for the child to resume, that he might verify what he'd believed he'd heard..

"Yes, that's Jack Frost.. Really.. it is!.." adding more forcefully.. " It really, really is!.." as all of the older, remaining members of the family began to good-humoringly chuckle over the boy's suggestion. Jack himself (despite his momentary paralysis) didn't look at all too happy over their light-hearted disbelief. And I honestly believe that, had he not been so curious over 'what was going to be said next', he surely would have exploded into one of the worst winter-storms Northern France had ever seen! Yet, he contained himself.

Adlin (Michel's forever-sympathetic-older sister.. to protectingly spare the boy of any further discomfort..) interrupted abruptly with…

"Yes, I think you're probably right, Michel.. I bet it 'is' Jack Frost!.."

Jack still couldn't believe it.. How did they know his name?

"Yes, I bet you're right, Michel.. I bet it IS him, out there!.."

Turning her conversation towards her parents, she pleadingly continued…

"You know.. it really might not be such a bad idea to record that whistling.. and put it out on a record.. Really, Papa!.. The public might really enjoy it!.. It is a very pretty and catchy little melody!…

If you do, I could draw a picture of what Jack Frost might look like.. and we could put it on the record sleeve!.. And we could also put it on posters and advertisements in the record stores everywhere!…

Really.. I'd love to make an imaginary sketch of what he might look like.. It would be fun!… Okay, Papa.. Please?.."

David (the oldest) teasingly interrupted her and poked…

"Yes, maybe then, all of those years that you spent down in the Parisian Art College will not have been wasted!.. Yes, maybe then all of Papa's money will not have been spent in vain!.."

"Oh, be quiet, you big tease!.." she retaliated, as they both gave 'way to laughing.

"You know.. Really.. that would be such an interesting 'holiday project' for all of us to work on and be involved in!.." re-entered the Monsieur's wife.. "Really, Jean.. please.. please would you record it for a phonograph record?.. Please?.. It would make the children and I so happy!.. Please?.."

"Okay!.. Okay!.. I agree!.. Let me set up my equipment.."

Jack almost passed out for the excitement. He began jumping and dancing all about the porch, whistling crazy-'n-ridiculously!

Impatiently darting back-'n-forth.. from the living room windows at his left.. then back to the screen door for different-angled 'peeks', he waited nervously for the Monsieur to prepare the disc-cutter for his first, real-major debut to the un-expecting, un-knowing and uncaring world.

As Adlin took a seat on the sofa (that was conveniently-enough for our view-ing, propped with its back facing the living-room's windows.. and..) with Michel right beside and over-her-shoulders to watch her begin the visual-interpretation of Jack Frost, the Monsieur (at the same time) began what-would-be the audio-interpretation with…

"Okay, everybody.. you're going to have to be quiet now.. Okay?.. Let's get settled.."

When the commotion of the room finally died, he concluded with…

"Okay, I'm recording.." and started the machine.

Jack (in all of his nervousness) began his Carol. My heart was pounding! I had to have been, at least, as tense as he.. For it wasn't until quite a number of bars into the tune, that I realized.. that it was sounding awful! Just awful! It was wheezy..

pitiful.. and just-plain terrible! Jack was just too tense! He'd gotten so worked-up over the situation, he was.. for a lack of better words.. Blowing it! Man.. his 'one big chance'.. and he was messin' it all up!

He desperately fought with himself to regain his 'so-easy-every-other-time' Carol. What would he do, if the Monsieur was to change his mind?

Lydia began pacing the living room floor, appearing very nervous and a bit 'guilt-ridden'. The latter, in that it had been 'she' that had pressed the issue of recording it to her husband.. and now, it was beginning to look like she'd made a terrible mistake.

Jack closed his eyes, to momentarily escape the turmoil. He began trying (with all of his might) to think of something else to ease the strain. His thoughts drifted back to.. Angel Jane and the happier times he'd spent with her in Heaven. Oh, how he missed her.. and wished so, that he could end this quest and return home! If he could only make things right! Everything could be so different! He had to be strong! He had to! He would!

Instantaneously, the on-the-spot, winter's-early-evening recording session did a musical about-face. Jack's nerve-twisted whistle unraveled into a more-than-ever melodious Carol.. even more captivating than it had ever been in the past! Yes, it was just so beautiful! And refreshing! Smiles re-appeared on the inside-of-the-window faces. I sighed a breath of relief, as Jack gloriously 'went to town' on his tune. The show was definitely.. Thank God-fully.. on the road! Christmas would soon be coming. The record would be out. Yes, things were finally coming to-gether! The long-awaited, final horizon was, at last, in sight!

During the period of time immediately-proceeding his on-location recording session, Jack held ground.. basing all of his operations out of the small French vil-lage.. not budging any more than he had to. He was just too excited to risk being anywhere else.. in that, he might miss even the slightest bit of news concerning his 'Caroling Record'. He couldn't bear the thought of not being there, when it was issued.. to have one of the first hearings of it. Not only that, but what better place could he be, than right where he was? For the La 'Belle's continually listened for him, night after night.. and Jack, in turn, was beginning to (as far-fetched as it might seem, considering 'his nature'!) grow very fond of them and their glad-to-have-him company.

On occasions though, Jack did stray and wander about the village for a change of scenery. Not to mention, to practice 'his antics'! But in short time, he'd always be right back at their doorstep like some orphan child in search of a home. Yes, it was more than evident that he was becoming very emotionally attached to them as time progressed. Very, very! And I think.. as strange as it might sound.. that the feeling was a mutual one on the part of the La 'Belle's. For on many occasions, different members of the family would individually (or sometimes, several at a time) come to the windows and peer-out, as if they were hoping to maybe some-how catch a quick glimpse of their invisible friend.

The closer Christmas came, the more nerve-racked Jack became. Nevertheless he did remain a bit more stable than what-normally-would-have-been expected of him, under the circumstances. This.. due to, I'm sure, the 'family-like' conditions that he was simultaneously enjoying.

On and on, the days seemed to go. And as they went.. Jack, all the while, be-coming increasingly.. inflammably… you-name-it-ly.. more and more uptight! For there was still no sign of his record.. and the big day was getting awful close! Too-close-for-comfort! There wouldn't be time for his Carol to be heard and appreci-ated (Let alone.. be sung by the people) if the records weren't out and available as soon as at-all possible!

And, when at last, Christmas Eve and Day had passed, Jack was to-the-utmost.. depressingly bewildered at the still-no-sign of them. What had happened? Did the La 'Belle's plan to release it the following Christmas instead? Did it take that long to put out a record? Was this just normal procedure?

The frustrating 'perplexities' needled Jack for weeks and weeks after the now-already-upon-him new year. Up and down the snow-mounded roads of the little French mountain-town he'd pace.. abjectly lost.. returning on many occasions to the cottage, in hopes that.. maybe.. just maybe he'd been wrong. As much as he hated to wait another year for its release, maybe it would be 'for the best' some-how? Yes, maybe that had been the La 'Belle's reasoning? For after all, what did Jack know about the recording music industry? Yes, maybe it was just.. What was best!

Early on one Saturday morning.. into the middle of February.. while on an about-the-village-square stroll, Jack and I (at last) came upon the un-wanted sad-truth that we had so-needingly searched for.

Along the snow-crested sidewalk of the main street, we walked. Ahead of us, I could see the store-front-door of a small steamy-windowed restaurant swing open. A young boy (in a white apron) was propping it wide, so that he might more-conveniently sweep out the inside floor dust. Jack was much-too-involved with his depression to even notice, still pouting over his recording-industry disaster. But I (to the contrary) found myself very interested and attentive to the youth's clumsy (yet, still effective) antics at prying it wide and secure.

When steadily we neared-even-closer, I couldn't help but notice that the young man was whistling Jack's Carol, as he unthinkingly carried on with his toil. Jack (upon hearing it too) immediately re-surfaced from his inner grief.. and likewise excitedly 'perked' as we, in curiosity, more-readily approached.

When right upon him, we came to realize.. and better hear.. that the lad was (in all actuality) whistling 'along' with an inside-of-the-restaurant, wooden-cased radio. One.. being propped on a behind-the-register shelf, that was (with a fair amount of volume) entertaining the dining customers. Jack dartingly squirmed his way around the boy into the entranceway, to poke his head in for a better listen. Was it his Caroling Record? It was! It was?

To the background sounds of the restaurant's patrons enragingly yelling at the boy to "SHUT THE DOOR!", Jack whizzed off down the street in the direction of the La 'Belle's cottage.

Not even halfway down the same block, he screechingly came to a dead-stop, right outside the pane-glass-window of a large Phonograph Record Store. For right there.. taped-up in the window.. for all to see.. was a poster. One with Jack's facial image on it! I mean, it didn't look exactly like him, but it was definitely close-enough-a-resemblance for us to tell 'who it was'! Jack knucklingly cleared his reality-blurred eyes. He re-focussed. It was just so remarkable how Adlin (without ever even seeing him) had captured that much of a like-ness! It was almost as-if 'someone had helped her'! It even depicted his very hat and scarf.. and, well.. it was just an 'unbelievable' replica! Only thing missing was the fear-filled hurt and bitterness of his eyes and face. It.. reminding me a lot more of how he had appeared back in Heaven, when he was first created.. before all of the pains. Yes, my very first sight of him! Then again (now that I think of it) he did, as well, appear a whole lot more scuffier in real life than Adlin had interpreted him. But then.. how could she have known of all he'd been through.. physically, as well as emotionally! In her eyes, she (no doubt) envisioned him as being just a sort-of

'sad-little, in-need-of-attention-type' being. Little did she know just how serious the whole situation really was! Still, considering what it was being used for (to advertise the record), it was far-more-than sufficient. Quite honestly (in my opinion), it was 'as fine an artistic piece' as any others I'd ever seen!

Jack (confused and awe-stricken to head-spinnin'..) began reading aloud the bold-type printed words on the placard...

"The Winter Melody.. by Jack Frost..."

He went cold-silent.

Then...

".The Winter Melody?.."

A simultaneous 'flash-back' came to the both of us.. of that first and early-winter day at the La 'Belle's.. when they initially took note of Jack's Carol. The Monsieur's beckoning words replayed in our minds...

'.. "YOU WON'T BELIEVE THIS.. IT'S THE WIND.. WHISTLING A MELODY!.. YES, THE WIND.. WHISTLING A VERY, BEAUTIFUL WINTER MELODY!..".. '

'WINTER MELODY' echoed repetitively at the end of the Monsieur's re-played sentence.

Jack (still dazed) whisperingly repeated...

"Winter Melody..."

Again.. more audibly and articulate...

"Winter Melody?..."

Then at last recovering from the memory, he glanced up and down the poster.. finding and reading again the song title...

"Winter Melody?.."

In mounting tone, he resumed...

"Winter Melody?.. Winter MELODY?.. WINTER MELODY?.. IT AIN'T NO.. WINTER MELODY!.. IT'S A CHRISTMAS CAROL.. A CHRISTMAS CAROL!...

OH, MAN.. IT'S A CHRISTMAS CAROL!..."

It was too late. No wonder it hadn't appeared on time. The La 'Belle's hadn't understood. As kind and as loving as they were, they'd simply mis-took Jack's intentions! Jack had just worked-himself-up to 'believe' that they'd understood. He'd never even considered that they might not have totally comprehended his whistle as that-of being 'A Carol'! It had just never crossed his mind! He just automatically assumed they knew! It was far from being their fault that this had happened. No, Jack (when he finally started recovering from the disheartening-'disc'-overy) was the first to realize that, as well as anyone would have. For anyways.. by now he'd become completely lost in his affection for them. No, there was just no way he could become angered at them for the mishap. He'd become just too close to them to hold any ill-feelings.. especially over something that they themselves were totally unaware of! And.. after all.. they had tried.. and meant well, for sure! No, it's just that it was.. as usual.. just Jack's luck! He should've known all along that something would go wrong. It always did! Why should this time have been any different!

Throughout the remainder of that winter season, Jack continued to return re-petitively to the La 'Belle cottage. For something always seemed to be calling him back. He wasn't quite sure what it was.. their warm-family loving-ness? .. the attention that they always paid his Carol? .. their special-ness? .. he just really didn't know! But whatever it was.. many, many hours were spent there as a result.

Towards the conclusion of that winter (when his far-away Antarctica Home was again beckoning him) and after a number of 'rounds', we returned to the cottage, one night. On this particular evening, (for some reason or another?) the La 'Belle's were not, per usual, gathered-about in the Living Room. Jack whistled-up a tre-mendous storm.. while nose-pressingly he spied through the front porch windows.. hoping for their normally-cheerful, always-welcoming faces to soon appear. But not a one did!

After a good-fifteen-minute-or-so wait.. at last.. Lydia (the Monsieur's wife) appeared alone, standing in the doorway of the inside-directly-opposing-us room. There seemed to be something on her mind.. Something that had her very ab-sorbed in serious, troubled thought. Something likewise giving her an aura of melancholy-and-sad.

Jack (to try to cheer her.. and likewise in hopes of not losing her again to the cottage's back rooms) began whistling as loudly as he possibly could. It bringing her to her senses momentarily.. and in the same, to a right-in-front-of-our window, sitting position on the couch. Peacefully, yet drearily she listened. We still couldn't understand the absence of the other La 'Belle's, but regardless found comfort in her company. For despite her 'whatever?'-grief, she (as always before) remained a sincere and good listener. Yes, taking the time to, even in her most busiest of day-time hours! We assumed that the others had retired earlier, this night.. For with the chapel bells (from the near-distant village) tolling their eight-o'-clock melody through the darkness, it confirmed our uncertainty that we had not arrived any later than usual.

As she listened, again the thought-filled-look overtook her features.. and (seeming internally alarmed-and-discomforted) she arose.. and in so, began in the direction of the front door. We wondered what she planned to do!

After making her exit out onto the porch, she stood alone in the cold darkness, staring out-and-into the night-time's stillness.

Jack resumed his caroling to re-capture her attention.. immediately ceasing it, when all-of-a-sudden out of her deep thought she began softly speaking aloud…

"I believe in you, Jack Frost.. I do.. I believe that it is really you…

Yes, I believe that you truly exist.. and are here.. Sincerely I do!…

I'm sure that it has been you that has been visiting and serenading us, these last, past winter's evenings!…

I don't know exactly what to say to you, other than.. I sincerely believe that it has been you.. and hope that what-ever-it-is that you've been trying to tell us.. as little as we can comprehend it.. we do wish you the very best with it!.. And we pray that it all works out for you.. because we really care!…

Always remember that, of everything I tell you now!.. Have faith that it will all work out!.. Somehow or another.. Someday.. Somewhere.. it will!.. Yes, I'm sure it will!…

The main thing in life.. is doing what you must do to satisfy your deepest soul!.. To find more than just an existence!.. To fulfill your dreams and goals!.. And 'you' will!.. Yes, I'm sure you will!.. if you just keep trying!.. Don't quit!…

Because.. like I told you, I believe in you!.. You remember that, Jack Frost!.. Yes, you remember that!…"

There was a dead silence, as Lydia made her way inside the cottage.

Even after she bolted the door and left the room.. switching off the parlor light as she went, we stood in hush.. with tears rising in our eyes, staring in at her fading image.

Jack painfully gulped down the sensitive speech (that his eyes wouldn't freeze). But I just simply couldn't control it as well as he.

With Jack (a good head-start in front of me) sadly trudging away into the dark, street-lit and chilling night, I followed; fighting the continually erupting and over-powering sadness that was aching inside of me. A sadness that I couldn't quite put-my-finger-on. Yes, a mood of-the-sort that.. although we don't fully comprehend its deeper meaning at the time.. its intensifying and mysterious anguish lingers with us, despite all-or-any immediate reasoning for its existence. Not to mention, its 'true source'!

On the next-of-nights (which was likewise to be our final there in the little Lorraine Village), Jack began on his way to the La 'Belle cottage for his 'one-more-last-visit', before the departure south.

Along the way.. and upon the road there-going, we dartingly passed by three silhouette-and-veiled gentlemen (Who were walking and conversing on the op-posite side of the hazed and darkening through-fare), over-hearing in a fleeting instance..

"Yes, I heard that too.. and that her youngest of sons took her life!.. What an awful thing!.. Such an unbelievable tragedy!.."

Thinking it 'a very chilling and odd thing to hear' (.. yet, reasonably expected in a world gone totally mad!), we 'brushed it off' and trudged-on-further towards our destination. For, with things of that nature.. sadly enough, we simply become 'immune' to them, when we have no personal attachment to the victims involved. Whatever!..

Strangely-enough, when we arrived at the cottage.. all of the usually-on lights were now off. There was a pitch-black, dark-coldness about the sight of the dwell-ing as we neared. And I felt an odd-shivering sensation come over me, as we for-wardingly (and very cautiously) trudged through the now-beginning-to-melt snow.

What had happened here? Something wasn't right! No, not at all right! For what had (even on the most bitter of winter nights) seemed warm and homey; now had a completely different eiree-ness about it, that was very un-suiting for the place!

The fury of the night's wind-storm wasn't in-the-least making things any-the-more comfortable either! For the trees quivered and trembled, filling the dark silence with an extremely-uncanny hiss from the leaves against the increasing wind friction.. Bringing to mind, the sound-effects of a late-night horror movie.. Only this was the real thing! I shook pitifully, as we forced our way up the front porch stairs. Something awful had happened here.. you could just feel it!

After our brief ascent of the few stairs, we simultaneously came to a dead-in-our-tracks stop at the screen door. This.. for the sight of a white-flowered, small wreath that was suspended on-and-from its wire grill. A little paper note was attached to its center…

"Not Home.. Due to the Death of Madame Lydia La 'Belle.."

Jack (in instant reflex) clutched his forehead and face. Staggering his way back to the step's ledge, he dropped to a sitting position upon them. His frost-bit, trembling hands fell to his bent-and-waiting knees. In sheer agony, his eyes closed.. and his face gravitatingly came to descend down onto his dirty trousers. His arms, at last, circled to tight-fully encase it…

'… "The main thing in life.. is doing what you must do to satisfy your deepest

soul!.. To find more than just an existence!.. To fulfill your dreams and goals!.. And 'you' will!.. Yes, I'm sure you will!.. if you just keep trying!.. Don't quit!…

Because.. like I told you, I believe in you!.. You remember that, Jack Frost!.. Yes, you remember that!…"…'

After a long, chilling.. ear-hissing.. nausea-creating silence, Jack at last rose to his feet and darted-off into the further-raging, storm-filled night. I tried desperately to collect my breath and self, as I likewise pursued.

THE EIGHTH CHAPTER

- WORDLESS DIRGE FOR MICHELLE -

In the years immediately following Jack's Recording Fiasco, the wheels of progress (once again) began grinding slower. Despite the tremendous depression that his 'Winter Melody- Carol Catastrophe' should have caused him, he (the ultimate justifier!) saw it as a sort-of premonition of much better things to come. Yes, there was just no other way about it! The next step forward (he was sure..) was going to be an even bigger and better one than any previous! Just like the changing-of-the-seasons being an always-gradual process, so too was it with luck. Slowly but surely it would come around. That's how he saw it! It would start to shine like the sun in springtime.. and only get brighter! Some times to (for shorter and shorter spells) disappear.. Only to return all-the-more radiant and long-lasting! Yes, his enthusiasm steadily increased, in spite of the all-about-him, falling-to-pieces truth. While I (seeing things in their more realistic light) began growing more and more pessimistic and generally-'tired of the whole unfruitful trip', by the day. There just never seemed to be an end to it all!

From the 30's (of the Twentieth Century), right through to the 70's, there was a definite (if not 'a remarkable'!..) 'drop-off' in really-worth-while breakthroughs. There were several events that I'll briefly note here, but (for the most part) they were hardly worth mentioning. Of course, my at-the-time poor attitude might have made them seem all-the-more-exaggeratedly 'trivial and unproductive'.. But, in all fairness to Jack, they did mean something! At least, to him! So it is with disregard for my own feelings that I will quickly run through a few here. For the record…

On one particular crusade in the mid-30's, Jack encountered a vaudeville whistler in the Great Lakes Region of the North American Continent.

Whistling itself (by this time in history) had become quite a popular and accepted form of 'folk art' in all the nations of the world. And it was (with little wonder) that this above-mentioned 'vaudeville entertainer' was making a respectable living with it. Jack obviously was totally unconcerned with financial gains. To him, there was only 'The Quest'! And when the whistler, at last, discovered his melody and began using it in his stage act.. in Jack's eyes, the only way was 'up'! For not only did the vaudevillian imitate his Carol with the most-tasteful-of-an-approach; but also his above-average-amount-of-audience-response with it, had Jack convinced that (as they term it in the music business..) he had a 'Super Hit on his hands'! Yes, a surefire monster! The people loved it! Jack was in his glory! All he had to do now, was to convince the tent-show-minstrel that what he was performing was not a "Winter Serenade".. but, in all actuality, 'a Christmas Carol'. Yes, once again, the same problem.. Misinterpretation!

Jack followed the tour on every northern crusade, right into the late 1940's.. never succeeding!

Likewise I will note that, throughout the same 'frost', Jack simultaneously 'tagged' a country (or 'hillbilly', as they called it then..) singer, who was ironically enough dubbing himself as 'Jack Frost' (Whether or not this was a 'stage' or 'real' name, we never really knew). Yes, this songster.. traveling in the company of (among others) an actor who was to later go on to world recognition. (I will leave this actor's identity to your own researching efforts. For rather than to drop the slightest-of-hints, I would hope that this will 'gear you up' for some interesting 'trivia pursuit'!). As for the fore-mentioned singer though, all I will say is.. he (regrettably enough) never made it through. As likewise to this very fellow did Jack! No, just like the 'vaudeville whistler' before-mentioned.. it was all 'a waste of good wind'! And 'good time'! Not to mention.. 'good, but in vain, energy'!

The 50's and 60's brought zero! At least, nothing I can even vaguely bring to mind as being of 'considerable merit'. Of course, in these times I was more-than-ever becoming very bored and cynical. I was even (you might say) becoming 'very jaded' and turning into a bit of a 'misanthrope' myself! Maybe Jack's likewise-bitterness-towards-everything had, at last, taken its engrossing toll? I really can't say why I was becoming so scornful and apathetic.. But whatever the cause, the outcome was ever-blatantly evident. I was beginning to find myself tagging-along behind him more and more on our seasonal journeys. Even, at times, letting him stray far out of eye's reach.. and almost forever-off into the unaccountable, lost horizon.   I just couldn't rejuvenate my spirits towards his seeming-so-desolate quest. No matter how I tried! And on one particular occasion, in the late 70's (1978 to the Southern Hemisphere to be exact), I did completely lose track of him.. returning to the South Pole, alone and fearful of God's wrath, to await Jack's 'whenever' re-appearance.

It all took place in a public park, just outside of a small museum.. near the center meridian of the Earth. On his way to the more-southern parts of the Americas, Jack (on a sudden curious impulse) stopped at the building for an investigation. This (I believe).. resulting from the odd notice of a parked-beside-it-on-the-grass, full scale old train's engine and its coal car. This.. chain-link-fenced-in and resting aside.   And in so, confounding him, for its seeming totally 'out of place'-ness!

Through the glass windows (in the dead-center of the tiny-and-narrow building) Jack could see several middle-aged ladies congregating-about and inside. And with our nearing, he decided to (for the fun of it) serenade them with his whistle. With the new season at-hand, a 'brief rehearsal' might do him good, he thought.

It definitely couldn't hurt, regardless of whether-or-not they caught on! Jack was always one to believe in as-often-as-possible rehearsing. It was 'the only way to get good'. Yes, practice positively makes perfect! So on with it, he went.. coming (in seconds) to a dead-stop at the sight of an even-further-set young man, who was seated beside a desk within, singing and playing a guitar. Gawking at him (through the steaming glass) he startledly jolted his head about for a better look.

Stunned by his likeness (to someone

that I couldn't for-the-life-of-me put my finger on, at the time!) I, as well, found myself edging-in-closer for a better view. He (this young musician), all the while, successfully captivating the interests of the on-looking ladies. Singing a song (to his self-accompaniment) that rang a very deep-inside and unclear bell. I (in puzzled anguish) searched myself for 'what it was about him and the song' that made it all seem so distantly-familiar to me. Yes, I knew the song! I knew him.. the young man singing!.. From sometime before! Yes.. from some other time, in the past? I knew.. the incident! Yes.. this very moment that was unfolding right before my eyes! I somehow just 'knew it'.. But I couldn't grasp it all, clearly enough? Still.. I was certain of it! For that matter, I was absolutely positive! Yes.. to the utmost

convinced that I knew him.. and these very happenings that were taking place right before us now!

Studyingly I stared. It started to become clearer. Yes, it started coming to me! I turned unconsciously in the excitement to Jack. He wasn't there. He wasn't there?

I did an immediate about-face. He was gone! Long-gone! I frantically ran forward.. stopping lostly.. for there was nothing to follow. 'Oh, great! Now what am I gonna do?.. Just what am I gonna do?'

I'll tell you what I did. Confused, upset and terribly dismayed, I returned to the Antarctic.

Extremely on-edge throughout the remainder of that winter's season, I paced

back and forth, awaiting his return. All the while, expecting God to (at any given moment) show up and have my neck! But.. He never did. God, that is! Jack, at last, returned.. and not any-too-soon-enough for me either! Regardless, I prayed the mishap would be forgivingly over-looked. As sorry as I was though.. I still couldn't find it in me to rebuild even the slightest bit of enthusiasm towards any of the up-'n-coming quests, that I knew (fully well) Jack was again planning. I just couldn't help it! Something was lost.. and that's all there was to it! I knew I'd follow.. But unwillingly it would be, for sure!

During the off-season of that year, I must admit, Jack really started getting on my nerves. His whistle-rehearsals became (once again) as aggravating to me, as they had been back during the thirty-four ('three', I know!) year waiting period, in the beginning. And if it hadn't have been for the previous season's 'losing-him-episode', I'm sure that I would not have made half-the-effort-I-did in keeping-up-with-him on the Crusade of '78 (to the Northern Hemisphere) as I did when it, at last, un-welcomingly arrived. But determined not to have to re-live the former season's trauma, I trudged forcing-myself-ly on, as he (in so) began his northern sweep.

It took all of my effort (and more) to keep him in sight. He was just simply moving too fast for me, these days! I was sure he'd run me into the grave. Or maybe I should say, he 'would have', had I not already been amongst the deceased! He was either tremendously gaining something in his drive.. or I was drastically losing something in mine! The latter (of course) being much-more-likely the case!

During this particular, long-as-usual journey, I found myself (on many occasions throughout) falling behind.. overwhelmingly-lost in repetitive recollections of the many crusades that we had (more joyfully) shared together in the past. With an ever-strong feeling of melancholy, I'd repeatedly lose myself in the consuming thoughts of them.. Only to (in each instance) snap-out-of-it in the nick-of-time and re-locate Jack's up-ahead whereabouts. As staunch as I'd try to apply my concentration to his path, it was just no use! I'd still just keep drifting off!.. Thank God-fully, pulling out of it each time.. Almost as-if my eyes were, all the while, subconsciously completely-in-control of the at-hand situation.

The more the sceneries changed, the more I re-vamped our so-hurried pasts. And as the trip moved on, I began to find myself analyzing (in retrospect) our 'so-uniquely-and-oddly-entwined' relationship, more than simply dwelling on the eventful times we had collected. In so doing, I kept feeling a strange sensation come over me.. A certain kind of feeling that's hard to explain or relate to someone else. But the best way I can think of, to do so, is to say.. it was like some sort of 'distant voice inside of me', that seemed to be saying...

'.. These memories.. yes, the memories that you are recalling.. Don't they have a very definite symbolism to them?.. Don't they mean more to you, than just their surface appearances?..

And, Jack?.. What of Jack and his relationship to you?...'

There was something very deep and true in that. And it brought me to consider...

'... Boy, it is really strange how.. We are so alike.. Yet, at the same time, so...

Well, for instance.. When I was all gun-ho and raring-to-go on his Crusades 'n all.. Jack, all the while, was always totally depressed and ready to kick-it-all-in!.. Then when I was low-in-faith, he was always the one all-on-his-toes!.. Just like now, I'm failing and caring-less about the whole thing.. 'n look at him up ahead there.. going like crazy!...

It seems like, when he's up.. I'm down!.. 'n visa-versa!.. It's all just so ironic!.. Almost like-as-if, in some strange way.. we were one in the same persons.. Yet, both being at completely-different-ends of the same spectrum, if that makes sense?.. It's like..

We both have some sort of psychic bearing on each other!..

But then again.. Me.. What do I actually have to do with all of this?...

Why am I here?.. What's my purpose in being here?...

Ah, who knows.. None of this makes any sense to me anymore.. I don't even care!.. I just assume have God intervene 'n save me from this ridicu...'

It was a flash of deja vu! Even stronger and more definite than the one I'd experienced at the museum-site a Crusade before! Yes, paralyzing déjà vu! The sign on the roadside (just ahead of me) hit my dazed-consciousness like a ton of bricks, bringing me instantaneously back to reality!

Jack had whizzed right by it, without the slightest concern. But to me, it struck something in my mental reflexes that jolted my wits unmercifully to the utmost of attention. The sign.. I recognized it in the most strangest and compelling-a-way! Its shape.. its lettering.. its total setting.. rang a very beckoning-distant bell in the furthest-corners of my mind. The vision-of-it kept re-appearing in front of me, even long after I'd passed it in my determined-not-to-lose-track-again pursuit of Jack. I kept seeing it…

```
126
Walden  Pond
Framingham
```

That sign! What was it about that sign? I thought to return.. But, no.. there was just no way I could chance losing Jack again! No way!

Through the late afternoon, I (still confused) very unwillingly followed, fighting to keep my eyes and attention on the frozen-little-pathfinder ahead of me…

'… That sign?.. When was it?.. I know, for sure, I've seen that?.. Sometime.. yes.. someti… '

Then.. like double-deja vu.. my eyes impactually collided with.. yet, another even-more mind-shattering highway sign…

```
- Route 2 -
Arlington.. 2 miles
Cambridge.. 6 miles
```

Cambridge! My mind's verbal-pronunciation-of-the-word echoed unbearably inside of my head, as I forcing-onwardly fought my way through its mental-clouding-of-my-thoughts, not to further misplace my full-speed-ahead partner.

'... I've been here before!.. Sometime?.. I know I have!.. Cambridge!.. Cambridge?...

Cambridge?.. Cambridge?.. That name.. it means something?.. Yes, I know I've been here before!.. I just know I have!... '

Off the road.. down a slight cliff.. then along a line of night-beginning-to-fall-on-them railroad tracks, we sped.

In spite of the extreme difficulty and awkward-ness of keeping-my-footing on the wooden ties (while remaining at the without-let-up rate of speed), I regardless still found myself dwelling-anguishedly on the seeming-so-familiar, surrounding landmarks...

'... That Bowling Alley.. back on the highway.. I know it!.. I'm sure I recognize it!.. When was it though?...

These railroad tracks, for that matter.. What is it about this place?... '

Under a bridge, we sped.. and quickly-there-after past a very large (then, an-other smaller..) series of red brick apartment-house complexes on our left.

I was so confused.. yet slipping and sliding everywhere along the cold-metal tracks and frost-glazed wooden planks of the deserted railway, I held ground.

A city dump flanked our right.

A chain-linked fence on our upcoming left.. with a conveniently-opened, van-dalized hole in one lower-cornered section of it.

Jack darted under and through it with non-stop ease. I followed, likewise enter-ing what-was a medium-sized graveyard.. that had the dusk's gray and uncanny silence very-uncomfortably settled upon it.

Still puzzled and awe-struck by the unfamiliar (yet, too familiar!..) surround-ings about me (Not to mention, the creepy-ness of our at-present location), I shak-ingly came to a gradual stop, as I neared the opposing-end of the yard and the stabled image of Jack.

He had (for some strange reason?) finally concluded his Crusade's long-chase just-up-ahead at the near-end of the burial grounds.. and was (oddly-enough) standing there staring down at something I couldn't yet see.

As I further approached, the wind began to howl and whistlingly hiss with increasing power.. and in the cyclonic-rotating fury ahead, I could see and hear Jack's clothing and long scarf flapping all about his in-spite-of-it, sturdy stance.

What was he looking at?

I forced in closer.

It was a gravestone! A half-sized, gray marker.. surrounded at the base with freshly-formed snow and ice.

I crept inward, even more.. to (over-his-shoulders) get a better look at it.. for my curiosity was mounting beyond control. What was he so-taken-in-with about it? Why this particular stone of all the others in the lot? What was it about it? I couldn't stand it any longer! What was going on?

Jack dropped to his knees.. I believed to better study the engraved inscription on its misty-like, frozen face. He was so lost and absorbed in it, that it scared me! And the beginning-to-screech-about-us wind wasn't, in the slightest, helping matters!

Bending forward (like as-if he were in a trance), he cleared the lower-section's build-up of ice on the bottom-right-hand side of it.. For it was concealing the end of a particular sentence that he seemed compelled to read. I apprehensively gambled an even-closer move, to likewise read it...

' ..Here Comes the Sun.. '

'..Here Comes the Sun?.. '

I couldn't understand it! What did it mean? He just knelt there for the longest time, staring at it! What did it mean to him? I became so curious, I attempted a mind-reading of him. But I couldn't get through! There was like a blizzard-blasting 'atomic war' going on inside his mind! Absolute turmoil! Complete chaos! I became very scared! What was going on here? What was wrong? What was he thinking? All I kept on getting was the vision of an infant's face.. embedded in a fury so thick.. and with a perception so-static-filled, it just didn't make the slightest bit of sense to me. So unrelated to anything at hand! Maybe.. maybe, it was the word 'Sun'? Yeah, it had to be! Maybe he wanted to be warm again.. like the Sun?.. Yeah, that made sense! At least, some sort of sense. Sure!.. He wanted to go back to Heaven.. and be warm like the Sun!

Then (to shockingly snap me out of my contemplation) he began violently (and like a mad man!) punching the snow-patched Earth atop of the grave! What was he doing?   I became all-the-more scared and confused. What,-in-the-name-of-Heaven, was the matter with him?

All of a sudden (to further kindle my perplexity), he jumped to his feet.. and, in a rage, took off in the direction of the graveyard's arch-covered entranceway.. faster than I'd ever seen him go! What-on-Earth was the matter with him?

Jolting a very quick and baffled look at the stone, I took off after him. Out the main-front-entrance, I tailed.. following only the mist of his up-ahead advances.

Taking an immediate right turn down the main avenue, I (with all my might) ran. It was pitifully hard to see.. even a foot or two in front of me. So hard, that after three blocks of ridiculous effort, I had to stop to await the storm to clear.

When (in several minutes) it at-last settled, I found myself standing alone in front of a bakery shop's window, that was located (among several other shops) at a five-street intersection.

I jerkingly looked all about.. but there was not a soul in sight. Not a single, solitary 'living being' within eye's reach!

I turned back to read a masking-taped-to-the-glass sign, that was posted inside of the Bakery's display window…

'Closed Tomorrow.. Christmas Day'

Everything was so still! And, Dead!

I knew, fully well, that night was falling.. but it was surely not that late into the evening for it to be this deserted! Even if it was Christmas Eve.. Still.. there should have been someone out-and-about on the streets! Something wasn't right here! And, Jack.. Well, he was long-gone!

I felt so terribly lost and confused! Now what was I going to do? Where would I begin to search for him? And not only that.. but to top it all off, I was (once again) beginning to feel that strange sensation inside of me, coming from my odd-familiarity to the 'where-ever-I-was?' surroundings.. Making me feel just all-the-more uncomfortably displaced! No matter how hard I tried.. for the life of me.. I just couldn't organize any of the vague-reminicsents that were scatteringly drifting about my subconscious. Yet, they persisted.. only making my at-hand dilemma seem all-the-worse!

Realizing that I would have to begin my search for Jack somewhere, I started back-tracking in the direction of the graveyard. Maybe I had passed him along the way?

Re-considering the total improbability (and absurdity) of the suggestion (that I could have possibly out-run him!), I instead (when I reached the corner of the im-mediate side-street) decided to stop and re-organize my strategy.

Glancing about at the surrounding stores in the intersection, I (once again) couldn't help but marvel at the deathly-silent-stillness, that had even-further set-

tled upon the eve. The entire view-able area just seemed so bare and abandoned! It was like the Earth was stuck in motionless, mid-air.. with only I still moving! There were no sounds! The trees.. the wind.. Nothing! It sent a shiver up my be-ing! What was going on?

To my immediate front-left across the small street, my eyes came to scan a very large church and its welcoming, front-lawn sign ('Our Lady of Pity'?). As I followed its enormous length back, I could see (in its more-hidden-by-trees rear-setting) that there was a very tiny-little chapel neatly attached to its side. Intrigued by it (and figuring it to be as-appropriate-as-any-a-place to begin my search), I crossed the street at a leftward slant and began down along the churchyard's chain-linked fence in its direction.

After making my way down the snow-crested sidewalk (in a most hurried and clumsy fashion) to the fence's opening (leading into the chapel's front), I made a slippery-right and continued awkwardly up the curved-and-icy walkway.

Reaching the tiny shrine's limited-stone-stairways, I (in renewed disgust of having lost Jack again) plopped to a sitting position upon them.. looking back outward, towards the still-motionless night. Instantaneously as my backside made chilling-contact with the frosty seat behind me, it struck me (with an unexplainable feeling), that simultaneously the world had, once again, resumed its movement. It's hard to describe in words, but I just could sense that it had! Maybe it was the returning-sounds that came to again enhance the night.. But 'whatever?'.. there was definitely a 'coming-back-to-life' in the air, that I immediately took startling notice of.

Feeling about as helpless as a lost child without the slightest inclination of where-to-begin-looking, I instead surrenderingly remained there on the steps.. hoping somehow-or-another Jack would find me! For as much as I dreaded the penalties (Whatever they were?) for losing track of him, I just couldn't help it any-more.. I was through! I just sincerely couldn't take it anymore! I was simply too tired and weary to go on! Lowering my head to rest it on my knees and wrapped-around-them-arms, I drifted off into a peaceful silence, in attempt to escape my all-tangled-in-knots situation.

When (after a time) I felt more at-ease, I slowly began to re-surface from my self-comforting huddle. As I did, I came to hear the sounds of approaching foot-steps. In an alarmed way, I raised my head.. and blurring through the remnants of tears, I saw (in the nearing distance) a young man coming in my direction, down the very same sidewalk I'd (only a short time before) entered on. Aiming head-on, the closer he came, the more he appeared to me to be.. Jack! I'd have sworn it was him! The similarity was striking, to say the least! Only difference was.. he was taller. And most definitely.. Human! Bundled-up heavily in winter clothing (that he was forcing his chin down into in retreat of the cold), it made it harder for me to get an accurate appraisal. But I was almost convinced that it was Jack! Then again.. How could it be?.. Unless he'd somehow come to life!.. Human life, that is! It was him.. it had to be! It.. couldn't be!

The nearer he got (as well as I could see), the more I confirmed that.. It was him! It wasn't him? I couldn't make up my mind!

Excitedly I jumped to my feet. Through the hint-of-night, I squinted. Could it be? If he'd only raise his hat brim! Ironically enough (and not a split-second after my wish), he did so! And even-all-the-better.. pulled the entire hat itself free from his head.. exposing (in so) a mass of matted-shaggy-tangled, dark locks. With all

of the help he was giving me (Not to mention, his coming straight in my direction and right at me), I still couldn't tell!

When (at last) he closed-in on me and the chapel's stairway, I still stood there in 'gawking-awe' over his unbelievable facial like-ness. Even as camouflaged as his still-pointing-downward face was, I still felt certain it was Jack!

Very hurriedly, the young man began his way up the steps, clustered tightly into his winter coat's scarfed-collar, appearing pale and frozen-to-the-bone. I stood (awkwardly and nervously-uncertain of 'what to do') directly in-line of him and his coming-right-at-me way. Before I could move aside, he ran right into.. and right through me! It striking me very weirdly! For never (in all of my ghostly travels) had that happened to me. I had (at other times) passed through material objects.. But never had it happened with a human being! That is not to say, it couldn't have happened easily-enough in the past.. it's just that it never had! There was also a strange sensation about it, when it happened. Something like an electrical shock that occurred.. that violently stunned me!

I froze in the astonishment of it, as he continuingly made his way to the door.. stopping briefly to contemplate something-or-other that was on his mind. Then continuing further, he made his way through and into the chapel's entrance.

' Right through me!.. He actually went.. right through me!'

With the in-back-of-me clicking of the slow-closing, wooden door.. I (at last) pulled myself together enough to follow. I had to know.. if it, in fact, was Jack?

Once inside the nearly-pitch-black chapel lobby, I sneakingly made a quick surveillance of it. Being (as well as I could see in the solemn dark) completely un-inhabited, I resumed in the direction of the main-assembly-hall part of the chapel.

When (in moments) I reached the secondary doorway-entrance, I could see (regardless of the very-scarce lighting from the front altar's flickering devotion candles) that the entire chapel's inners were completely bare-of-life. Yes, not a soul was to be seen! I shook my wits in disbelief, for I was sure that I'd just seen him come in! He was here.. somewhere!.. He had to be?

I began down the main aisle, very slowly.. as to check, on both sides of me, the each-and-every-individual pews.. in that, he might possibly be hidden down inside of one of them.

Accompanied only by the sounds of my crackling, apprehensive foot-steps, I worked my way forward.. until, at last, I reached the final (or should I say, 'first') pew, in front of the altar. Where could he have gone to? He had to be here!

In desperation, I studied the altar and its surroundings.. coming in eye-contact with an adjacent-side-door entrance to my immediate right. There's where he went! It's got to be! I ran to it. It was locked with a bolt.. on 'my side of the door'! Impossible!.. He couldn't have!

Making my baffled-way back to the center of the chapel, I turned right and took a seat in one of the pews.. halfway in.. that I might 'wait-out' the young man's hidden whereabouts. Being conveniently located sort-of dead-center of the hall, I figured that if even the slightest sound occurred in any direction, then I would be more-than-likely able to detect its origin. For I was sure that he was there.. or somewhere very close-and-about. Yes, he most-definitely was!

As time draggingly elapsed on.. and my mind began wandering away from the young man's puzzling disappearance, I gradually came to notice just how eerie the about-me chapel seemed. Being (only a short time before) totally wrapped-up in my search for him, I hadn't even been aware of the dark-and-scary atmosphere of it. And the deathly silence made me feel all-the-more alone and un-consoled! I began (in turn) nervously jolting and twitching my head about, chasing false movements created by the jiggling of the lambent candles. My mounting tension found me reaching for the support of the below-me wooden pew-seat, as I (on-its-edge) sat. And on one occasion of my doing so, my trembling hand came in startling contact with a child's miniature wristwatch, that had (all along) been resting there. Amazed by the discovery of it, I raised it to read its ticking-away face...

"Five past Seven.. "

A very young girl's face flashed on the screen of my mind and disappeared before I could identify it. I fought to replay the image.. all the while, nervously clutching the time-piece. I knew that face!.. Who was it? It was someone very dear and important to me! Someone (I felt sure) I should've remembered? It was no use.. I couldn't bring it back!

Then, a sound in the rear of the chapel interrupted my concentration.

It was whistling! I turned to locate it. It was Jack!.. his tune was coming from somewhere outside, through a slight-opening in an-above-and-in-back-of-me, stained-glass window!

I started (without any ado) up and off of my seat to catch-up with him.. coming to a paralyzing stop with the echoing-the-chapel sound of a solemn, yet soft, voice commanding my restraint...

"STAY, MY CHILD..."

I knew immediately that it was God.

"I am fully aware of your growing disinterest in following Jack and his seemingly never-ending Quest.. So don't!.. Stay here and discuss it with me..

He won't go far.. I promise you.."

Still awed by His all-of-a-sudden and out-of-nowhere voice, I stared dumbfoundedly forward, spellbound and speechless.. Until I came to my senses enough to realize that (in the cold silence) He was awaiting my reply. Snapping-out-of-it, I timidly returned (in the direction of the altar and His nowhere-to-be-seen presence)...

"Well, Sir.. Father, Sir.. It's just that.. that.. " fumbling over my words...

"Sir.. I really don't know what it is?...

I guess, it just seems like.. this thing is going to go on forever!...

I mean.. he still doesn't have a single soul singing it.. At least, not as a Christmas Carol.. and it's 1978 and.. it's.. it's still... still just as... as... as..."

1978.. I tripped over it flat-on-my-face! 1978?.. What was it about '1978'? I glanced down at the little watch in my hand.. and then about the inners of the oddly-enough, seeming-somehow-more-familiar-now chapel.

"AS YOU WERE SAYING..."

"Oh, yeah.. yeah, it's.. it's.. yeah, it's still just as obscure, in that respect, as it ever was!.. People just don't understand what he's trying to tell them.. Let alone, his wild idea of getting them to sing it as a Carol, each year!.. And to tell the truth.. I'm just really beginning to doubt he ever will!.. I mean.. Well, if he's suppose to.. Y' know.. if it's part of your Master Plan that he does 'n all.. then, why can't you…"

I stopped short.

He immediately returned…

"Out with it, son.. Say what's on your mind…"

"Well… Why can't you help him?…"

"Help him!.. I have!.. Why, I've given him a lot of help!.."

Pausing to collect Himself, He continued (more subduedly) with…

"Child.. I have helped him.. in just.. just so many ways!… Ways that, I'm sure, you'll never even know!…

I gave him everything!.. Gifts such as.. the Will-and-Power that only the Great Wind itself has!.. I made him one-with-it!.. Yes, he controls it!…

What about his ability to create new and unique musical ideas?.. I blessed him with that!…

And, Love.. I gave him 'True Love'.. the sincere and real kind!   And a family!.."

A doubt-filled cringe tightened my face with the word 'family'.

"Yes.. A Family!.. At this very moment there are two father-less children that sadly await his return.. his and Angel Jane's two girls!.. Yes, a family!…"

Quickly I tried to mentally re-account that first night in Heaven… 'Children?.. Two Girls?.. How, in the…'

"So you see.. I have already given him a lot!…

And you think that I should give him more!.. Yes, you think I should intervene and make things go more his way…

When I call the souls of the world back to me, that's when I become involved in the decisions that they have made. Other than that, they.. each and every one of them.. have their own 'Free Will' to do as they please.   Jack, being all-the-more blessed in that respect!…

If someone asks me for help.. I'll give it.. if it's in their best interests. But Jack.. he thinks that I.. and all of mine in Heaven.. have rejected him! Unforgivingly he has turned his back on us, without the slightest of mercy. It's his own fault! He's so stubborn and self-centered about everything, it's really hard for me to sympathize with him…"

"But, Sir.." holding my tongue and realizing I'd interrupted. I waited, until He okay-ed my return. When He had, I very-respectfully and word-for-word-fully resumed…

"But, Sir.. What about what happened in Heaven?.. Jack was just treated like…"

"With every blessing, comes its curse!…

Yes, I allowed that to happen.. for many reasons!.. You, being one of them!.."

"Me?.."

"Yes, you!…"

"I don't understand?.."

"You will…

Among other things.. you needed to learn that.. No Road is an Easy Road!.. And that success is earned.. Not given!.. Nor does it always appear as one might think it should appear!…

Yourself.. Jack.. and every other being that I created.. has the ability to achieve whatever goals that they set out for.. Those, of course, within reason!.. But being bitter or pouting over failures and hardships, only makes the wait and road-to-success that much more uncomfortable!…

Jack will learn in time, that his rejection of all-and-everything.. and his spiteful attitude.. will only hurt 'he himself' and no one else! It is he.. that suffers with loneliness and inner torment over his self-chosen exile! It is he.. that has decided 'his road'.. not I! Yes, one day.. he'll come around!.."

I (feeling quite akin to Jack) lowered my head from a mixed weight of sadness and shame. He (of course) was right.. and I knew all-too-well He was! Yet, still.. I wished that He would only somehow..

"Regardless.. I will help!.. Even though I really don't know why I should!.. Still.. I will!…

Being that you are one of the gifts that I imparted on him, I will send you back.. to help him!.. Not to follow, any longer.. But this time.. to help!…

For deep inside.. with all he's put me through.. I still love him!.. and will forever, regardless!.."

Before He could say another word, the beckoning sound of Jack's whistle (once again) squealed through the still-opened, in-back-of-me window. I snappingly turned to see it, making a quick about-face back towards the altar and God's voice to await impatiently His permission to pursue it. I wanted so to run to him, regardless of the way I had been feeling about his fruitless Quest.. For, now.. at last.. Help was on the way! I didn't really know just what kind of help I'd be to him?.. But, still.. Help was on the way.. and that's all that mattered! Twitchingly, I sat on the edge of my seat.. Until…

"I think I hear your friend calling.. Why don't you go-ahead-on now.."

With that, I shot…

"Yes, Sir!.." and took off, making a mad dash for the chapel doors.

Just as I made my way out into the main aisle-way and down a handful of pews.. with a curious feeling still itching in my mind, I stopped and turned back, inquiring…

"Sir.. Could I just ask You one more thing?…"

With His consent, I continued with…

"What did You mean by.. I was one of the gifts that You gave him?… I just really still don't see what You meant by that?…"

"You will.. Don't worry!.. Now, go and help him.. he needs you.. And just do the best that you can…"

Accepting His still un-specific reply, I took off again through the first set of doors, yelling back as I did… "THANKS, GOD!…". Continuing then through the outer entrance, I zoomed into the now-pitch-black, waiting night.

Halfway through the churchyard, I came to notice (in all of my hurry), that still in my hand's grip.. was the child's wristwatch that I had nervously acquired and forgotten to leave, back on the chapel's pew. 'Seven-thirty.. 'n still ticking away'.. at least, I hadn't squeezed the life out of it! Coming to a more gradual stop, I thought to return it.. For surely it belonged to someone.. and sooner or later, they'd be coming back for it.

Then (to immediately distract my thoughts), came the nearby, in-front-of-me whistle of Jack.. beckoning me further into the dark-frozen night.

Not to lose track of his somewhere-close whereabouts again, I decided to continue on across the main avenue.. with hopes of possibly (somehow or another) returning later to replace the watch. There was just no way I could risk letting him get away now!

So resuming my speed, in a matter of minutes I reached the avenue.. only to

come to a screeching halt at the all-too-familiar-sight of a small, gray-ish blue house, that was situated directly-opposite from my frozen-in-motion stance. I recognized it.. but, yet.. didn't! Or maybe I should say, only in some vague and distant sense. That danged Déjà vu feeling again! Faces (a small collage of them) flashed my inner screen. Faces.. that I could now squintingly see in reality, exiting (in a sort of unison) from the small-framed house's porch-doorway. These faces.. very forlornly gathering-about inside of the tiny-fenced-in yard.. and all crying and greatly-upset by something that had obviously taken place inside of the homey-little dwelling. Yes, something had happened there.. Something very grave and traumatic! I suddenly felt pressed to discover what it was! I was also compelled to find out just who they were.. For I felt sure that I somehow 'knew them'!

Filled-to-the-brim with curiosity (So much so, that I'd completely forgotten Jack!), I began across the through-fare in their direction. It struck me, very oddly, that as I did, I found myself (on impulse) stopping to check for on-coming cars.. Something I'd never done before! Not letting the strange-notice-of-it deter me from my more-pressing investigation, I simply pushed it aside from my mind and plowed onward. Who were these people?.. I just had to know! What was going on inside of the house? Whatever it was, I was sure that it was serious! Real serious! Feeling a sort-of 'odd' kinship to them and their 'whatever?'-plight, I neared in even-greater hurry now.

Just as I touched-toe on the opposing sidewalk's curb, it came to me (in a very alarming and breath-stealing way!) that the sound of Jack's whistle was coming from the inners of this little house. Yes, this very house that I was encountering! With an odd and very distant-sounding 'eerie-ness' (as if it were coming from a very depthly cave), it caught my immediate attention. Before I could verify its exact source (or anything else about it, for that matter), it dispersed instantaneously into what-seemed-like an audio-vacuum effect; leaving a strange, echo-less silence in my ears. I gulped in reflex, expecting my ears to pop from its pressure.. But, they didn't!

Feeling extremely light-headed, in through the chain-linked fence I proceeded.. continuing (completely un-noticed) through the sad faces. Up the few, front-porch stairs and inside I went.

I couldn't place when it had been, but immediately I sensed having been there before. For even prior to my entrance, I was certain that there would be a looking-exactly-as-it-did living room right beyond the doorway that I'd (feeling-very-much-at-home-ly) just passed through.

Now inside, I came to see a young man stretched-out across a sofa, on the opposing-side of the room.. with (what-I-immediately-took-as-being..) his mother kneeling close beside him. His father (I likewise assumed), over-her-shoulders, stood looking on. Both appeared heart-broken and shattered. My feelings immediately went out to them. The children (his brothers and sisters I also deducted) were entering and leaving the house, as if someone were expected. And they (in all of their emotional desperation) were trying to do-their-part and keep vigil for the arrival. Their general behavior.. mixed with the intensity of the mood that prevailed, led me to quite-naturally reason that 'the young man on the sofa' was sadly-enough dead. The stillness and lifelessness in his facial repose was (without a doubt) only further proof. Yes, there was no question that my notion was fact!

With further study of this young man's face, it came to me that he was, in fact (and most definitely had been), the very same young fellow I had just-briefly-encountered back at the chapel. So here is where he was! It baffled me how he'd slipped past me.. But, still.. at least, now I knew where he'd wound up. Poor fellow! No wonder everyone was so upset. How tragic! How awfully sad!

Becoming as spellbound as a child attending its first wake, I found myself (at last) very fixedly staring at the all-too-familiar corpse before me. I couldn't pull my eyes from him! And it only seemed to get worse with each passing second! For I knew him! From somewhere? Yes, I knew him! I could more-readily see now, that it wasn't Jack. Although the facial characteristics were still strikingly identical! No, it wasn't he. But, who was it? It persisted in my mind, that this young man had been someone I had been very close to, at one time. Extremely close to! I felt embarrassed at my so-poor recall.

Interrupting my further study of him.. and distracting me enough to make me momentarily turn away, it came that (although I was right there in the very same room with everyone) their voices seemed distant and blurred. Or 'shielded' somehow? And it frightened me! So to try to mentally dodge it, I jolted back to the corpse. This, of which, being no relief at all!

With the fire of fear now being lit, I felt the pumping of my adrenalin.. like gasoline.. spreading and surging through my being, only further fueling and complicating the matters-at-hand. Despite all, I painfully forced myself to try to re-member the young man's identity. For somehow I couldn't help but feel it urgent! Extremely pressing! I had to remember! Who was he?

After strenuous concentrated thought, I felt it begin to surface. Yes, his identity started coming to light! But the anxiety that accompanied its still-distant surfacing (compounded by the already-fear that was gripping me) put my entire frame-work into a spastic-like trembling state. I shook uncontrollably! Something very deep inside of me so desperately wanted to turn and run away from its realization. For it seemed like, the more his identity shown itself, the more I didn't want to see it! It just seemed too painful for some reason. No, now I didn't want to know! And the less I grasped for it, the more it came!

Then, to make matters worse.. all of a sudden, I felt the most strangely-compel-ling sensation come over me. It was as-though I was being pulled-in towards his lying-there body! Yes, like-as-if a huge vacuum cleaner (of some sort) had been turned on.. and its over-powering suction was un-mercifully tugging at my soul! I fought with all my might to resist, while some inner voice (all the while) kept urging me to give-in and surrender to it!

With all the confusion and mental-mania I was feeling.. to make matters even all-the-worse, the sound of Jack's whistle came to my ears. 'Oh, yeah.. Jack!.. I'd forgotten all about him'! I attempted even more forcefully to pull free from its increasing cyclone. But it was just no use! It had me! I twistingly turned my head to look back in its 'high-pitched', somewhere-out-of-the-house-now direc-tion. It was calling me! As likewise seemed to be, the mirage-like images of the people in the room. Calling and beggingly reaching out towards me! The further I was pulled into the vacuum, the more forcefully-persistent the whistle became. Louder and louder it beckoned.. with a very-pleading-'I need you'- tone to it! It reminding me of the whistle that he had sent out to Angel Jane, that first night in Heaven (when she had unwillingly left him at the lagoon). Yes, it was a very similar and desperate one with a 'don't-leave-me'- sound to it! I fought to some-how answer it, as my consciousness rapidly weakened from the tremendous strain. Only God knows how unbearable the pressure was! A violent tug-o-war between two worlds! I felt absolutely helpless! 'Turmoiled'.. being hardly the proper description of my mental state!

The whistle.. louder.. louDER.. LOUDER.. LOUDER! The voices.. pleading.. pleading.. PLEADING! The vacuum.. pulling.. pulling.. PULLING.. AND PULLING! The anxiety and pressure.. mounting.. AND MOUNTING! My mind.. spinning.. and dizzy-ed.. and POUNDING! I.. whimpering, painfully...

"Please, God.. Please.. Please.. PLEASE!...."

I couldn't stand it any longer! I grabbed my ears to restrain the blasting volume of everything.. as I, through the darkness, kept falling forward.. At last, climaxing somewhere into a total unconsciousness!

THE NINTH CHAPTER

~ THE CAROL ~

"My Dear Lord in Heaven!.. I don't believe it.. He's coming out of it!.. It's.. It's.. It's a miracle!.. He's.. He's coming out of it!…"

I could hear the voice gaining audibility increasingly, as my eyes slowly blurred through the oblivious nothingness. It sounded like.. the voice of.. the voice of?.. of.. It was!.. the voice of my Mother! My Mother? I came to, very distinctly, recognize it as being hers.. even as faint as it was!.. and as far-placed as I felt! I'd forgotten all about her and.. and..?

The more conscious I became, the more I likewise became painfully aware of an intense sore-ness in the right-top-section of my head. I agonizingly reached for it, the further I surfaced.

Still feeling very much in-between-worlds and overwhelmingly confused and frightened, I began searchingly-calling into the coming-to-view-ness ahead of me…

"JACK.. JACK.. I'M COMING!…

JACK.. IT'S GONNA BE ALL RIGHT!.. I GOT HELP.. I GOT SOME HELP FOR US!.. JACK!.. JACK!.."

Over-anxiously I started up-and-out of my lying position.

"Hold on!.. Just.. hold-on-there now!.." physically resisted my mother, before I could reach a sitting position on the sofa's edge.

I surrendered, very willingly.. due to the spinning dizziness and bolting pain that my all-too-sudden rising up had inflicted.

In a mind-blanked daze, I looked back up at her and pleaded tearfully…

"But I've got to get to him.. He needs me!.. God sent me to help him!.. He needs me.. Don't you understand?.. I've got to get to him!.."

By now, the parlor had filled-up with all of my not-believing-their-eyes and absolutely-shocked brothers and sisters. As they awe-strickened-ly peered on, my Father (trying to calm me) assuringly offered…

"Relax… Relax.. You can help later!.. Just relax!.."

When I had, at last, settled back down enough to meet their approval, I began desperately trying to explain to them my losing-him-again dilemma.. and the severe reprimanding that it could (in turn) cost me. But it seemed useless! For in all of the joy of the moment, all they were concerned with was my astonishing recovery…

"The ambulance.. the ambulance was here.. and they'd.. they'd pronounced you.. They'd pronounced you .. Dead!.." my mother breaking down here.. Then in retrieving..

"They had another emergency.. and they just left, not even… Well..

The Funeral Home.. we called them.. and.. they're on their way, right now.. We were just waiting for them to get here and… and..

Well, it's just.. just.. unbelievable!.. Unbelievable!.. You were gone!.. Gone for, at least, fifteen minutes!.. At least, that!.. Maybe more!.."

'Fifteen minutes', I thought.. remembering the little wristwatch I'd picked up in the chapel and lost-track-of in my pursuit of Jack. The feel of it came to my left palm.. and I lifted it, shakingly, to see that it was still there, ticking away! I read it…

"Twenty minutes to Eight…it's Twenty minutes to Eight!.."

"Yes.. and it's Christmas Eve.. Don't you remember?.. " offered one of my over-looking sisters.. "We'd thought we'd lost you.. and on Christmas Eve, to top it all off!…

We were all in the kitchen.. and we heard the screech of the car's brakes.. and, well.. we thought we'd lost you!.. Oh, thank God!.."

With the mention of the accident, it replayed in my mind. It.. bringing back.. a world I'd totally forgotten! Things started making a 'strange sense' to me. But smeared-together with my more-recent recalls (of 'Jack' and the 'Quests and all').. well.. I was to-the-utmost confused! Where had I been? Yes, where had I been, all of this time?

"What year is this?.. " I asked in absolute earnest.

"1978, of course!.. Don't you remember?.." answered one of my brothers. Then, with a change in countenance.. "Are you sure you're all right?.."

"Yes.. it's.. it's just that…

Well, it's just that.. Well.. I've been…"

In a thoroughly-bewildered (and even a bit 'self-doubting', I'll admit..) frame of mind, I began my story.

Long into that Christmas Eve's early-morning-hours, I held their (no doubt, 'sympathetic'-) attention.. as I insistently persisted with the tales of my travels with Jack. As understanding and attentive as they all tried to be, none could truly find it in them to believe me though. So on and on, I went. But the more I pursued it, the less it seemed that they accepted it.. passing it all off (in a very kind and patient way) as being just 'some sort of very-depthly-dream I had had'! A wild fantasy that my mind had become lost in, during my fifteen-or-so minute death state! I tried (in every imaginable way) to convince them of the factuality of the events that had taken place. I even offered for evidence 'the wristwatch'.. and explained how, if I hadn't actually experienced it and lived it, then how could I possibly have it now in my possession. But still, it was no use! I further pointed out that I had left it there (in the chapel) by accident, before my unexpected traffic mishap. And if, in fact, then.. I had died.. then how could I have (in all likelihood) returned to get it and have it with me now? There's just no possible way I could have! Unless I had 'sometime in between' been back to retrieve it! Otherwise it would still be laying there on the pew bench, as it was when I had left it there, before my proving-fatal accident. It all made perfect sense, didn't it? Not to them!

With all the sincerity I could muster (considering my weak condition, to begin with), through the wee hours of the early morn, I (in vainly) sought their belief. Finally holding my peace. And accepting that it was all to no avail. For, yes.. they believed in 'my belief that it had happened', but that was the extent of it! And what good is that, I ask you? For still.. in their minds.. it was 'a dream'.. a dream as-real-as-life!.. But still, only a dream! So I surrendered. Deep down, I couldn't rightfully blame them.. for it did all seem kind of far-fetched, I know. Sincerely I could understand their doubt.. For had I not lived it myself, I too would have thought the whole thing ridiculously insane!

In the days of my recovery that draggingly followed, I seemed (in my sofa-ridden boredom) to constantly dwell on the events that had taken place in my former life with Jack.. hearing his melody repetitively resounding through the scenic reminiscents of my mind. At different times through-out my trying-to-keep-my-mind-occupied days, I found myself subconsciously humming it. Even in the dark middle-of-the-night sleeping hours, I would (cold-sweatingly and very abruptly) come to a dream's end with it still echoing-away in my ears. It seemed to be haunting me! Yes, it was like Jack was still trying desperately to enlist me in his yet-successful quest. Like he had all along known I had been with him. Or somehow sensed it! And now that I was no longer there, he missed and needed my companionship. I felt sure that he was trying to tell me something! Something he needed me to know! Something important! He was beckoning my help.. I was sure he was! But 'how-in-the-world' could I possibly be of service to him now? There was just nothing I could do for him in my present state.. for we were 'worlds apart'!

Then one morning (when my recovery had neared its end).. feeling quite-the-mood for being up-and-about from my confining bed-quarters, I did so.. slowly, but as-steadily-as-possible, making my weak-way across the room. There (stored in the parlor corner) was my guitar case. Strummin'-a-few in the morning always did seem to begin my days in a nice-enough way. So with that, it seemed the most-appropriate way to begin this particular one at hand!

Oh, how I loved to play my guitar! It felt so good to, once more, have it cradled in my arms, singing away at me in its brisk-'n-jingling way!

Running through a good handful of melodies and riffs, I soon was lost in the suspended moments of its forever-captivating-me air.

Then all-of-a-sudden (as if to purposely distract me), came the beckoning of Jack's whistle! I stopped cold to verify it. The front window had been cracked-open-a-bit (no doubt by my mother, while I was sleeping).. This, allowing its sounding-close-by entry. Wanting rather to return to the enlightening joy of my guitar playing (and not be bothered with fighting-my-way-towards-it.. Nor, being further reminded of the sadness I felt for Jack, each time I heard him), I began desperately trying to ignore it and concentrate on my rehearsing. But like every other time in the past, it was just no use! The whistle persisted stubbornly!

Half concentrating on my playing and half on the whistle, I amazingly-enough caught myself chording and accompanying its very basic melody line. The more I strummed along with it, the more I found myself amused by doing so. I assumed it pleased Jack also, for soon the sadness of his delivery transformed into a seeming 'much more happier and excited one', by far!

On and on, we went.. until.. like a brainstorm, it struck me that...

'.. I'm a writer!.. Why don't I write a song about Jack!.. All about his Quest.. and how people have been overlooking him and his Carol, for all of these years!...

Maybe.. Yes, maybe that's what Jack has been trying to tell me, all this time?.. Sure!.. And maybe.. maybe that's why... why God sent me back!.. To help him!...

Yes, that's what He said, back in the chapel!.. That must've been what He meant by.. "I will send you back.. to help him".. Sure!.. Back to Life!..Wow!.. It had to be!...

Maybe that's what He'd meant by.. Me, being one of the gifts that He'd given Jack!.. He'd planned it from the very beginning, when He'd brought me there to Heaven.. To witness it all and bring it back!...

That, no doubt, was the reason that.. when He first spoke to me, on that first Christmas Eve, He said.. "You will follow him, never letting him stray from your sight.. Until.. When the time comes, I will call upon you again for a more ultimate purpose".. Sure!.. That's what He meant!.. It all makes sense to me now!.. That's why He sent me back.. to communicate Jack's message to the world for him!.. What better voice could he ever have, to tell the still-unknowing world, than mine!...'

After stumble-hurrying my way over to shut-out the chilling-me-now window-draft, I struggled awkwardly back to begin my job. Yes, that of putting-words-to Jack's Caroling Melody. And in so, it all seemed to come to me so naturally!

When (at last) I had jotted-down my last lyric, I sat back to review it.. making sure that each line said exactly what I (and Jack would have..) wanted it to say.

Yes, it definitely seemed to specify everything that needed so desperately to be said. Telling the world, right from the start.. that Jack's whistle was not a 'Winter Melody' or whatever.. But, in fact, A Christmas Carol! I felt sure that Jack would have approved, so (before anything under-handed could happen to it!) I had it 'lead-sheeted'.. and soon there-after, shipped off to the Copyright Office in Washington, D.C.

Being that Jack, in all actuality, had written (or 'whistled', I should say) the identical melody, way back on that first Christmas Eve, I (of course) gave him the proper credit due. What a stir that created with the Copyright Office! Letters came

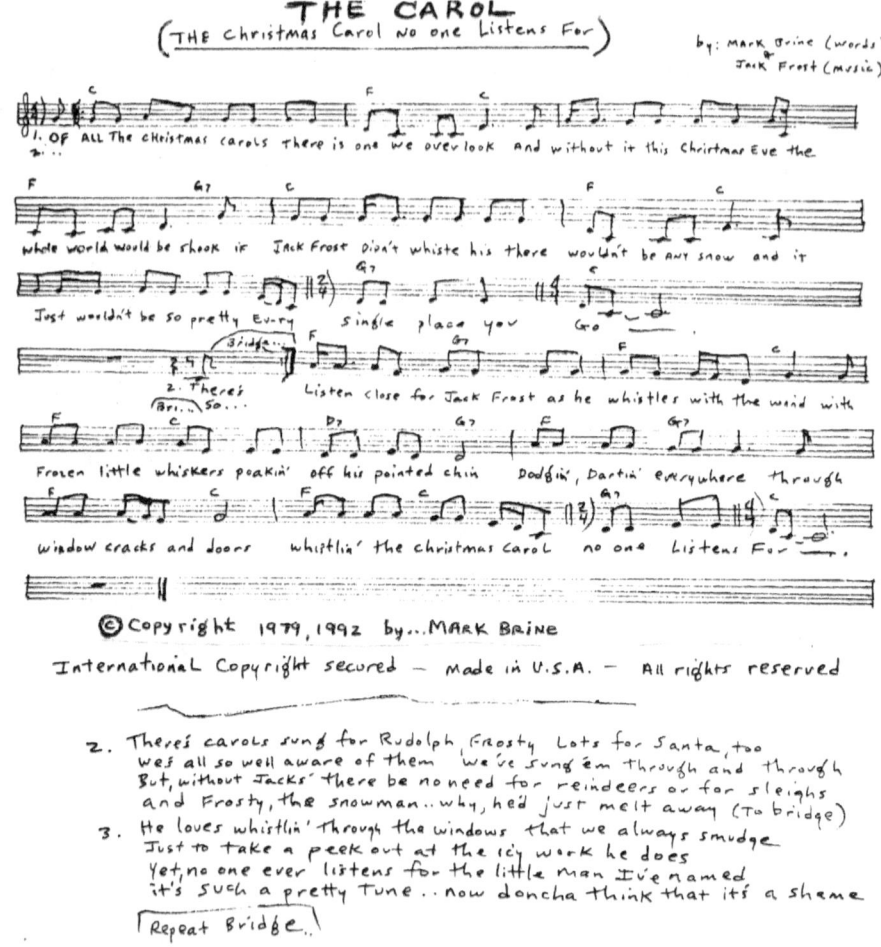

2. There's carols sung for Rudolph, Frosty, Lots for Santa, too
   We's all so well aware of them, we've sung em through and through
   But, without Jacks' there be no need for reindeers or for sleighs
   and Frosty, the snowman.. why, he'd just melt away (To bridge)

3. He loves whistlin' through the windows that we always smudge
   Just to take a peek out at the icy work he does
   Yet, no one ever listens for the little man I've named
   it's such a pretty Tune.. now doncha think that it's a shame

   [Repeat Bridge..]

back like crazy! 'You can't do that!.. Jack Frost ain't a real person!..' Yeah, sure!

Well, anyway.. after much red tape and too-numerous-to-mention correspond-ence (not to forget, a good bit of finagling!), it was done. Jack got his well-deserved billing!

Taking proper-charge of my duties as his emissary-on-Earth.. during the year of 1979, I made immediate plans for recording our song for a phonograph record.. to be pressed and released that coming Christmas Season.

When (at last) the holiday season of '79 arrived, I had (out of my own, more-of-ten-than-not 'empty' pockets) financed and accomplished our (.. excuse me, my..) project. The record was released and shipped to the radio stations (etc.). But, due to my very 'un-well-off' money supplies (Not having the proper funds to under-take such an endeavor as this.. and be able to afford promotion and so forth, which is always a must in these type situations!), the record did not 'hit' (.. as they would say, in the business). Still, regardless.. it did receive a fair amount of airplay. And 'great reviews', as well, from the trade publications and newspapers, etc. Yes, I was on the right track! And with my own promoting and selling of the discs, at least the 'word' was out. People (as limited as their numbers might have been) were hearing Jack's message! Besides, for me (as with him), it would be a lifetime Quest. So, even though it wasn't an immediate 'commercial' success, there would always be other Christmas's. I'd just keep pushing and performing (etc.) the song each Yuletide Season, until it was accepted!

Yes, once again, Jack's Quest became mine, as well.. Only now, there was something I could do, instead of just follow! Now I could put my knowledge of-and-from his Crusades to good use!

His strategical and scheming influence had me (his well-schooled disciple..) constantly analyzing the at-hand, earthly battlegrounds, for yet another of ways to further our ends. Something more impactual had to be done.. to greater clarify the still-so-obscure facts of Jack's story and at-present journey. And likewise.. something more monumental! The song was simple and touching-on-the-sub-ject-briefly-enough.. but people had to know the whole story! Something was needed to, at least, outline the Quest, the Crusades.. and the Why's and How's, etc.! For after all.. this (in every sense of the word) was 'history'! Whether or not anyone would actually believe it! These were facts that (at last) put into proper focus.. the third-and-final, missing part of the Original Christmas Story. It was (and is!) the connecting link between the 'Santa Claus-part-of-Christmas' and the 'Bethlehem part-of-it-all'. Yes, these were very crucial and vital facts that the world needed to know! Facts that hadn't yet been revealed! Hidden facts! Facts that I knew and witnessed first hand! There was no other way about it.. A Book would have to be written.. A Book that shed light on the truth! Yes, A Book!

"A Book?...

I can't write a Book!.. I don't know the first thing about Book writin', proper English and all 'a that good stuff!.. I never been t' school or anything for that sort 'a thing!.. There's no way!.. No.. Just.. No way!...

Maybe I could try?...

Nope.. Just no way!...

Just sorta tell it in my own words 'n all?.. Nothin' too fancy?.. Just.. y' know.. do the best I can?.. Y' think maybe?...

Nah, I can't do that!.. I just .. won't!.."

I did. I had to! If I hadn't, who'd ever have known the truth? Jack might have to go on forever, if I hadn't at least tried! No one would have ever been able to sympathize with him and his victim-of-historical-circumstance situation. Who would have ever been able to relate to his bitterness in an understanding and caring way? Even if somehow-or-another they 'had' comprehended what he was trying to tell them? Who would have ever known how hard he's tried.. And, for all of these years, to top it all off! Who would have ever known.. just how much he gave up for his Quest, that it might be acknowledged.. Angel Jane, his children, etc., etc.! Who would have ever known.. the hurt, inner agony and repetitive failings he had experienced.. and survived.. to get to where he is today.. Nowhere! And then (in spite of it all) to only become all-the-more persistent and determined to succeed. Yes, who would have ever known, if there hadn't have been.. The Book!

THE CONCLUDING STATEMENT

My underlying intentions in putting forth to you the preceding chain-of-events.. was to help a little man in his crusade to make a song, his personal form of expression and ultimately his life's quest known to mankind. I mean and say this in all sincerity. It is completely true. Just as sincere and true as reads the sub-title of this work "The True Folk Legend of Jack Frost". Yes, I realize the juxtaposition there.. This book is full of them! Most that I won't (and can never) go into again here! It would be impossible for me to point them all out. Besides, some are better-off left evasive and buried!

Upon publication of this work, I will have brought forth one of his many ideas and quests to the public. Yes, one.. as he had others. Many others! Some that could easily have been whole other books in themselves! For after all.. don't you think that it was originally (and always has been, for that matter!) his idea to put the light-bulbs in the refrigerator? Sure! So's he can take them out, whenever he needs them!

Many thanks to you, my little friend…

Jack Frost

"THE FINAL PAGES OF THE CAROL"

~or~

"Easter Everlasting"

~by~

Mark Brine c1992, 2011

~ THE SECOND BOOK ~

For Our Almighty Father…

Our Very Blessed Brother and Redeemer…

And the Giver of Eternal Breath.

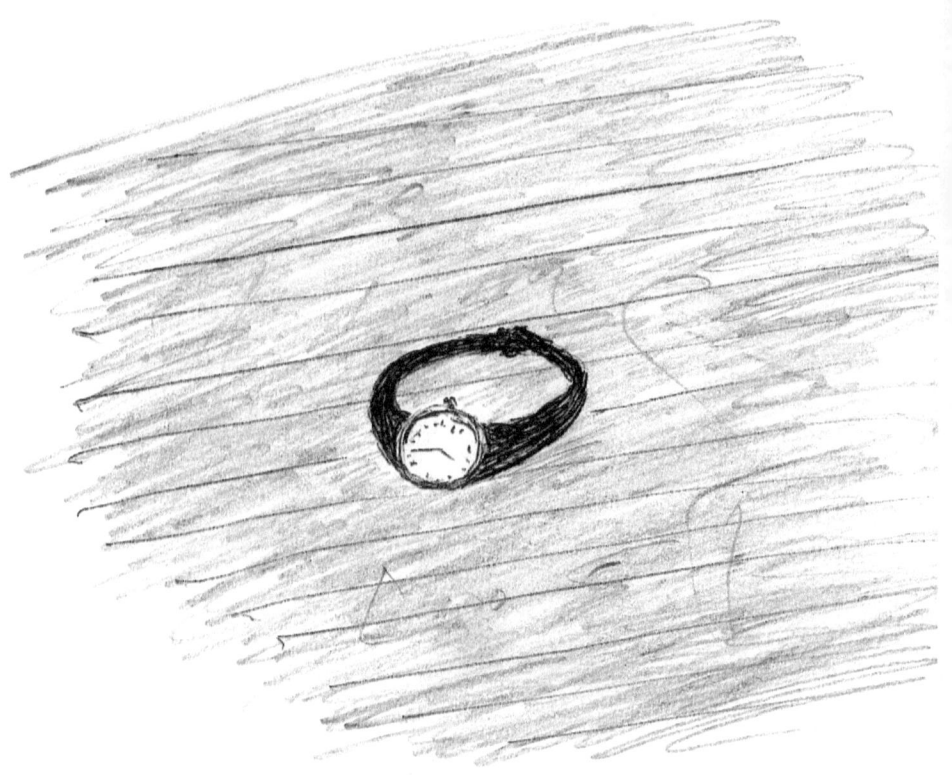

AUTHOR'S IMPORTANT AND "CRUCIAL" INTRODUCTION

~ VOICES IN THE WIND (INTO BACKWARDS) ~

It was not done. There was more to it and I knew, too well! Yes, the story had not been completed. I could just 'feel' it!

The years had passed considerably and the original manuscript (Book One) had yet-to-be published in print. Regardless, there was more. And needed telling! I slid its still-only-typed text onto the sofa seat beside me, finishing a long-since re-reading of it. The return of another-of-Christmas-Eve's (at my parent's house) had prompted me. And in so, I had undertaken the entire task of it this very day.. And as well, upon the very same couch that I had (seeming-centuries-ago) once 'lay dead on'.. and (in the same) 'returned-to-life- upon' thereafter. Yes, I sat on it now.. alone (the house empty).. rubbing my wearied eyes and re-scanning the room and the recall of it all.

So much had changed since then. I had re-married. Had a new son. My music and life (in general) had transformed beyond belief. Yet, still.. and somehow (?).. something of 'then' and 'it' remained.. and seemed incomplete. I knew it! But, what?

The sound of the Our Lady of Pity Church bells aroused me from my meditation and seat.. and I walked across the dim-lit (for late-day dusk) parlor, stopping at the cornered-and-hanging nick-knack shelf adjacent. Upon it now (among other things) rested the miniature wrist-watch. Yes, the very one! Now.. discarded with my baby-girl's early-youth and only a souvenir. It was silent for non-use.. and I picked it up to reset it to my own.. and in so, rewind it. Again it came to life with tick and I raised it to my ear. It sounded so peaceful and relaxed me into only-deeper thought.

As I listened-on with intent, it came to me, that.. ironically-enough, the time I'd set it to, coincided 'perfectly' with the very moments I'd been dead, so many years prior. Or, better yet.. the near-center of that fifteen-or-so minute time-frame. I thought it strange; but at last shrugged it off, as my mind drifted freely and peacefully back. This, until rudely-enough, I was alarmed and startled by the outside-somewhere-close pierce of.. of.. yes.. Jack's whistle! Yes, after all of these years of its silence.. returning! It.. entering and swirling inward from just-beyond the nightfall. And this, for some unexplainable reason now, scaring me! Yes, very, very much frightening me! It never had, in the past? I turned for it, like-as-if, in search.. though I knew it to be beyond my immediate confines. I waited. Holding my breath. As terrified as I was, something inside of me knew I must go! Yes, something was calling me.. back to the little chapel...

THE TENTH CHAPTER
~ IF I EVER MAKE IT BACK TO HEAVEN ~

Early 1979

Something was lost? Gone? Somewhere along the line? Poof! Jack sat on the iceberg, staring-out.. wondering.. and trying desperately to figure. Absolutely thought-tied!

It was late winter. At least, late winter for the Northern Hemisphere! Or even-more-precisely, it should've and would've been, had Jack not surrendered it (The Quest) for his at-present stance and meditation. But he had found it impossible to work! Yes, the further that he ran into the start of the new year, the more distracted he'd become with this feeling. At last, returning to Antarctica in a haze. And where he sat, time-being, was the very spot he had landed. Hadn't budged an inch neither! Not even attempting the normal Trans-Antarctic-Mountain-Way to his shack. The shoreline of 'home' had seemed sufficient-enough. And here he sat 'still' (In both meanings of the word).. Looking out. In extremely deep-'n-confused thought!

Now it's one thing to remember where something (that you've lost) has been misplaced.. But it's a whole different story (for sure!), when you don't even know what that 'something is (?)' to begin with. Puzzles of Puzzles! And that being his dilemma. Making his soul-search all-the-more frustrating! All he knew was.. Whatever-it-was(?), it was gone! And its absence being very heavily felt! A sort of 'withdrawal' ached in his spirit. It was a very painful (..as well as, a very strange..) feeling too! For at times, he'd even caught himself 'whistling out and at' this whatever! Yes, like-as-if 'to' it.. whatever this it was? For he didn't have a clue! Still it was there, this feeling of missing something? Yes, it was just mind-boggling him!

Where (along the way) had he first noticed its disappearance? He had studied on that, so ardently.. and for so long now! He felt so depleted and drawn-out from it all! At last, in a moment of total despair, he broke his concentration for a pause to scan-out at the ocean view. In so, gasping a hearty sigh of disgust.

Achingly lifting himself from his ice-ledge seat, he half-turned-back (in so) at the sound of his britches 'cracking free'. Erecting his small and thinly frame, he creakingly stretched. Rubbing his dirty-numb, little hands to awake the sleep in them, he there-after raised them to awkwardly 'comb-through' his icicle/snow-matted hair. Tangling it worse (If that were possible!). Then, with a heavy sniffle before-hand, he polished his nose-run (In so, further-smearing the accumulated dark-'n-dirtiness there and encircling) and searched-about for his way-laid hat. Discovering it near at-hand (Though pretty-nearly snowbound now), he raised it and banged it on his upper leg. This, setting-off a mini-blizzard that descended gracefully down and onto his ripped-'n-battered-ridiculously, toe-revealing tennies.

Penguins (in great multitude) were gathered-about and below-him on the lower shoreline.. and still-absorbed-in-thought, he began descent in their direction.

Upon reaching (what would have been..) 'beach-level' (in his trance-like state), he started through them, oblivious to their existence. They.. wobbling and scatting in-'n-out about him without his notice. Until, at last (and as surely as would've been expected, under the circumstances) one of them (And a big one at that!) bumped hard-'n-head-on into him. This.. startling Jack into stark reality. And in so, absolutely awing him at his feathered surroundings. Snapping his head back-'n-forth in all aims, he made a hasty mental account. Then spinning back at his aggressor (Who was, by now, unconcernedly puttering-away), he sputtering-'n-stutteringly shot…

"Hey, you… you… you… PPPPenguin.. " (Popping his 'p' terribly in fluster!) "Why don't.. cha.. LOOK where ya goin'?… PPPPAY ATTENTION, PPPPP-PENGUINNNNN!…"

But it was truly to no avail. For he wasn't paying Jack a single bit of mind now. Just teeterin' off, lost in his 'whatever?'-business. Despite.. it was the one 'last-straw-on-the-camel's-back' that Jack didn't need, at the moment.. and it sent him into a very lashing stir. Luckily though (for the surroundings, etc.), it only being a 'inner-fuming' stir! Irate to the absolute max, he snarlingly stared about himself at their flock. His vented-up anger and frustration ready to explode. Something mean-'n-nasty had to be said. But as wired as he was, he couldn't find any proper-'n-fitting words. Still, it mounted like a whirling tornado inside of him. But all he could think of, was.. was.. 'Nuns'! Yes.. little, fluttering-about-him Nuns! That's what they looked like. He couldn't help himself. The explosion grew nearer! And nearer! He was fixin' to scream it, full blast.. and scare the ever-lovin'- Antarctica out 'a them! He breathed in (in his trembling fervor) to get the proper wind he'd need for it. But just as he was on-the-verge, he.. stopped? Yes.. Dead-stopped! It'd hit him! Yes, the 'where' that he'd lost it (The whatever-it-was?). Yes.. it was.. was.. at.. at that.. that… Church! What was the name of it now? Yes, it had been when he'd ran by that.. Church! The sign that had been standing outside the front of it.. just beyond the sidewalk, inside of the fenced lawn.. What had it said? He mentally backed himself up to it, in the recall. He must remember! He must!

Collapsing to his knees on the ice, he strained his thoughts.. back.. back.. back to that church. A few penguins nudged-in on him.. and he (in unthinking retaliation) pushed them away.

'That Church.. it was a big one!.. In.. in.. in…'

"CAMBRIDGE!.."

Yes.. "CAMBRIDGE.. M.. M.. MASSACHUSETTS!.." He'd voiced it aloud (again and in full) that he wouldn't forget it with his resuming thoughts.

'Now.. the name.. What was the name?..' He closed his eyes in tight squint.. to focus the sign. In reverse, he saw his motions (like on a film).. and there.. yes, there it was! He could see it! Its sign-painted lettering, as clear as day. He screamingly read-it-aloud, as it echoed-out (in the process) across the vast Antarctic waters…

"THE OUR LADY OF PITY CHURCH.. IN CAMBRIDGE, MASSACHU-SETTS!.."

Jack's cold-return totally 'snowed-out' any hopes of what-had-seemed-to-be an 'early Spring' for the residents of Cambridge (and as well, for all of New England, for that matter!).

With his early morning arrival at the Rindge Avenue Site, he paced back-'n-forth in front of the church for hours. Not finding 'anything out of the norm', other than exactly what he had been looking for. Yes, the structure itself and its surroundings! And they, exactly as he'd recallingly envisioned them! But, the 'what' he was in-search of.. Well, there was not a trace of 'it' to be seen! Then again though, he wasn't even really sure (to begin with) just what that 'what' was, in the first place! Boy, was he confused!

At last, taking an arm-folded-defiant stance at the adjacent corner (of Middlesex and Rindge), he contemplated his next-of-moves. Scanning the huge church, he noted (in so), in the backdrop, the little Our Lady of Pity Chapel. Feeling somehow-and-oddly-enough 'drawn to it', he began down the opposing sidewalk's chain-linked fence in its direction. It seeming (as well) as-good-a-place-as-any to begin his more-closer surveillance.

Near approaching, he moved-in to the chapel's few stairs. But, touching its first with his sneaker's tip, a 'smarting-zapping, lightning-bolt-snapping'-sensation went through him. And in so, he quick-'n-retreatingly pulled back to the level ground and away from it. Totally stunned by the feeling, he again back-tracked even-a-few-more-feet in the mental recall of it. Shivering, in so! He simply couldn't understand it. It absolutely boggled him! For he had been 'in buildings' before.. So, why.. and what was the problem here? Yes, why not now?.. or this one?

Short-winded, he studied on it for another moment. At last, surrendering it for a search of the grounds that led-up-to and in-front-of the larger church. Maybe the 'what' had been something he had dropped there in his hurried past?

Other than new snow and ice though, there was nothing to be found. And after a reasonable lot of time, he became frustrated in it. So, fumingly he removed himself from the grounds by-way-of-the (to-his-left) driveway (-curve) and across Rindge Avenue, that he might regain his temper and again view from a distance. And as well, from a different angle.

Plunking himself down on the cold, stone stair of Phil's Barber Shop, he glared on. Yes, head-on and sharply at the church's front. Being more to one side of the step (or 'sitting lop-sided', as you might say..), his right hand (without thought) began down-'n-along the cold side of its vertical edge, pushing free (and with it) the lightly-mounted snow over its edge. But when reaching the blunted-tip of its front corner, it gave his hand a very snapping-'n-painful shock! And in this, he pulled it free-'n-away in an anguished startle!

Glaring back down (in a flash) at the corner, he evil-eyeingly stared at it. Having slightly withdrawn his entire being away in his grief, it was now all-the-more focus-able. What was going on? It just didn't make sense! Had it been an electrical-type bite.. like the kind that people get, when having dragged their heels across a rug? Well, first-off.. he wasn't a people! And secondly, this sure wasn't no rug! No, sir.. Hard as a brick! And probably, a lot harder at that! And, too.. he'd never encountered anything like this, in all of his time or travels.. so, why now? It had him bewildered! Totally and frightenedly bewildered! Man.. this was a strange, strange place! He slowly-and-surrenderingly scanned about himself in the thought and nervousness of it.

Then, to interrupt his further study and concentration-on-it, it came. Yes, from somewhere's in the near area. Faint, but clear-enough (in the morning's silence) to detect it as being.. Music! He spun his head to locate it. It floating from his right. He stared in its direction.

Where there's music, there's usually to be.. yes, when pin-pointed.. a musician! And another of chances to get through (to the people) his message! Yes, there was ultimate 'gain' in it.. and on reflex-'n-impulse, he started up.

But then it hit him (And this, more powerful than ever, ever before) 'Why bother?.. It'll only turn-out to be like all of the many, many other-'n-previous attempts.. a failure! And a waste of time!' He sat back down. No, he just simply couldn't bear a-single-'nother-one! Despite-'n-still, it came.. persisting. He tried desperately to dodge it and to think of his more-immediate-situation and purpose-in-being-there. The church and the real reason he had come.

But it kept creeping in, seeming to be almost insistent! He fought to regain his mental focus even harder! But regardless, he kept losing it. At last, he sighed a dis-gust-'n-surrender and turned in its line-of-fire. In so, noting.. that something.. yes, something about it made him feel good. Or at least, better than he had prior. But then again, he really didn't want to feel 'good'! Nor, even 'better'! So he started to re-swing free again.. 'til knowing, that it would only be in vain. So feeling even more defeated, he resumed head-stance. In its direction. Only now.. defiantly!

Aggravatedly he rose and scuffingly began into its increase. It seemed as though it was originating in a house several down. When there (in front), he found himself to have been correct. Two houses exactly!

Now (with its near-ness), he could better-'n-more-easily distinguish it to be 'guitar music'. And coming from the first floor's front window. It being cracked-open just-enough to allow free flow. Jack's first impulse being to slam-shut it down. But as short as he was, he knew it to be beyond-his-means. As for the chain-linked fence (surrounding the little porch-engulfed yard).. Well, that would've been a cinch! Not the slightest problem! But, well.. the window pane itself.. Hmm, that was just too high!   So, with no way to retaliate, Jack threw up his hands and defeatedly sat himself down on the curb (at hand) to listen. Heaven knows, he could have left.. but, he didn't! For something about the sound-of-it held him. And this, in a very strange way! For he'd heard many-a-guitarist in his time (And many a lot more proficient, as well).. But this one seemed to touch him very deeply somehow. Maybe it was just 'the moment (?)', he justified. Yes, it sounded as though, the player (Whomever he was?) had, too (like Jack), just lost his best friend. Or at least, 'something as equally as important to him'!   Still.. maybe he was just 'reading into it?', Jack re-considered. No, he could definitely feel it!   It was there, 'in the notes'! Yes, he was sure that there was no way he could be mistaken!

The more he listened, the more he could no longer resist it. And before too long (without knowing), he was 'whistling along' (to himself). Oh, the temptation had just been too great! But, no (on noticing it of himself), he stopped. It'd only be another flop, if he were to try! Why bother? Mentally rewinding-and-reviewing the countless millions-of-his-past, he began feeling all-the-deeper dismayed. And wouldn't you know, it was as though the guitarist (beyond the pane) 'knew' this (Or somehow had drifted into a further-melancholy state himself?).. For his notes came to identically blend with Jack's and his mood! Yes, as if he'd heard Jack's to-himself whistling! And as well, could read his mind and feelings! In dirge-like style, he accompanyingly followed with a piece that Jack had never-before-then heard. But whatever it was (?), it (for sure!) felt more than appropriate! It bringing tears to his eyes, that froze in-stuck on his cheeks. Visions of things-past rushed, collage-like, through his mind. Things almost un-related-like.. yet still-'n-some-how, very related in an odd way! He felt (in all of his confusion) to turn and call to this being, behind the glass.. For he just needed someone so desperately now! Yes, more than ever, ever before! Someone who he felt could truly understand and relate to his desperation! His failures! His agony! Anyone! Oh, please.. Anyone! Can you hear me? I need help!

The scene from when he'd discovered his whistle flashed into his mind.. and, on impulse, he repeated the identical way he'd executed it, that first Christmas Eve.

He, not realizing that he'd done it in actuality now, for all of his blurring grief.

Again he repeated it.. whistling in the passionate tone he'd used, when showing Angel Jane his hymn. To himself.. but this, only in his thoughts. For he didn't realize its true-and-real volume. Yet, all the while, it echoed and swirled-like-a-whirlwind about the Rindge Ave. morning in wild fury. Moving and lifting the new mounting snow in its power from off of the roofs. Creating blinding sprays aground. And this, being the very way he felt inside. His entire soul, groping through the darkening, lashing pain internal!

Then (all of a sudden) into the cyclonic hysteria and confusion, it poked. Like a finger, tapping on the back of his thoughts. It was.. was.. the melody! Or, at least, the 'perfectly-accompanying'-chords to it! Yes, to his.. his Carol! The guitarist was playing it! Had he been whistling it? He felt sure he hadn't! His mind cleared instantly, in amazement. Emptied-out in a flash! He hopped to his feet baffled-like. Had he been whistling? He honestly couldn't remember.. Though he felt safe 'not'! Regardless, he knew that he wasn't now.. and still, the player was jingling it head-strong. He listened for a moment ardently.. at last, joining in and (in the process) it changing his (as well as his music's..) mood 'liltingly' to the other end of the pendulum.

Working his way into the tiny yard, he slid his way up the first few stairs.. reaching-for and trying to peek-in the window. But it was no use, for it was simply (and still..) too high! With this, though, came its crashing close! Someone inside had shut it! But, who? Must've been the musician, for the playing had stopped, as well!

Just as Jack's face began its drop, again came the tune. Only now, muted. The guitarist had re-seated himself (Jack assumed) and, in so, resumed. But, yes, now it was more difficult to hear. Still it was there! And a smile returned.

When Jack attempted to 'whistle along' though, he could no longer tell if it was being played or not. So this forced him into quiet. But as he listened, he heard the musician toying with it, over and over.

Jack grew so anxious to see inside, that he made a leap from the stairs for the sill. And in it, he did get an awkward grip a-hold, affording him a very brief glance (before he slid off) of the inner room. But in that blink-of-an-eye look, all he had seen (through the slightly-cracked window blinds) was the bottom of a guitar.. the player's bare, supporting-it legs.. and a coffee table with a sheet of paper atop (that this same person was writing something on). Nothing important, he figured. Then again, what had he expected to see? He really wasn't sure! Judging from 'what he had seen' though, he deducted the player to be of 'reasonably, young-adult'-age. And male. And, as well, one with dark, brownish-t'-black hair.. to match that on his legs. Other than that though, it was all still a mystery. And one that would make him 'hang-around-awhile' to try and solve.

And that, he did! For a number of weeks. 'Til, at last, he could no longer linger. For the natural progression of the seasons would not allow it. So back to Antarctica he knew he would have to go, with only 'plans of returning again at a future date-'n-season to search it all out' to take along with him in his flight. This, for the cold-hard fact that.. the young man had never once 'surfaced' from the premises. Not once! This (as well as everything) confounding Jack intensely. But there was just nothing he could do for it! Short-of 'wait'.. and that he'd surely done! Fruitlessly (Per usual)! Yet somehow, the whole ordeal had brought him a 'token of enlightenment'. At least, 'somehow' he had felt that it had. Somehow? Yes, that (and only that) he would carry-away with him in his return home.

~ PREPARIN' THE WAY (FOR THE COMING OF THE SUN) ~

On the late day of his planned departure, he had hoped so that his 'wish' would be fulfilled. And that of, the young man's appearance. But with gradual loss of his faith in that eventuality (and the increasing fall of dark..), Jack at last began away. With his head hung in full droop. Despairingly dragging-and-pulling-himself-free from the scene, he (imprisoned in his thoughts-of-it) scuffled along Rindge in a westward (left-hand sidewalk-ed..) movement. This, leaving the huge church to his over-the-shoulders rear-left.. and the musician's abode to his behind-right.

As if to further deject him, came a passing bus on his-side-of-the-street.. bringing (with its hurried, unconcerned-like motion) a wet-sloppy-'n-slushy, heavy-hittin'-him-in-the-face puddle. Whew! Mushing-up his scarf, as well, in its 'high hit'. Dead-stopping him in his trance-like tracks. This seeming as if (and almost-like) the entering Spring Season 'spiting'-him for its onset victory. Totally disgusted, he scraped it and cleaned himself off.. feeling, all the while, the heavy-mounting lump-in-his-throat beginning its aching ascent. His eyes, as well, reddening-'n-steamingly burning in blur. Oh, everything just.. just always.. seems t' work out so.. so.. so bad! Why him? Why him?

At last, recovering enough to glance upward (out of his turmoil), he noted (before him) a graveyard's entrance. Yes, at his direct-'n-immediate left. It.. an old-style-type, large-'n-gothic-like-designed gateway.. With a paved driveway below and through it (from the at-hand street) for car entry.

Still wiping himself some, he straggled-in closer and peeked through study-ingly. Then it hit him.. that on his previous-of-visits-there (Christmas Eve of '78), he had (in fact.. though unnoticingly at the time) passed through it! Yes, this very gate! In exit. Yes.. and beyond it (and inside, as he recalled..) had been the very location where he'd seen.. yes.. that grave-marker!

Needless to say, in he began. Curiously. Beyond the archway, he scanned about himself at the many, many head-stones. These, separated by the centering drive-way that continued straight-on through them.

In the silence and solitude, he remembered.. "It was to.. the.. right!.. Yes!.." and, in so, started up and over the slight grade near at-hand in its direction.

After a short walk (and equivalent search), he spotted it.. despite the darkening-quickly-now day.. and moved-in accordingly.

Kneeling slowly in awe, he brushed-clean the lower face of it. And there.. again.. he saw and, in so, read aloud (though softly-like in whisper to himself)...

"Here Comes the Sun.."

In the grey and following silence, he stared at it. Studying its type sharply. This, as he had once done before (unknowingly-'why?', even then to himself!).

Then.. all of a sudden.. there was a strange shift-'n-movement in the air, out-of-nowhere.. and (in the same) he noted that.. one of the letters (in its sentence) began transforming! Yes, re-shaping itself into a totally different one! Ultimately and in-the-process, altering the entire meaning (to him) of the phrase. And very con-siderably, as well! He (in the moment) shook his head to try 'n rid the delusion (or at least, what he initially thought-to-be 'a delusion'!). For he felt sure that it was all being caused by/ and as a result of himself and his too-hard stare! And this (and only this..) creating the illusion! But with so doing, came a far-off and entering-even-stronger wind!.. From the distant-end of the graveyard's rear-bordering. A howling and violently-stirring one! And this, he knew (beyond-a-doubt and imme-diately..) to be (in his fear-filled head-turn for it) not of his own making! Its ap-pearance (at first) confounding him for that. But in regain, it came to him of who.. yes, 'who' was the only other 'being' (in all of the Universe!) capable of executing such a feat (Other than he himself, of course)! Yes, he knew (beyond any question) who it was! But.. but.. but.. Why? For He'd never done that before? 'Least, not in all 'a Jack's existence! So.. Why now? He very-nervously first-fingered his forehead. Shooting his eyes about him. Slowly dropping his head (in so) to his still-smushed scarf to twiddle it in the anxiety.

Then (with its unrelenting entry), he flashingly returned back to the stone. The 're-writing of its sentence' still stood. And now, not waveringly-blurring back-'n-forth as it had prior. Jack blinked and squinted to re-clarify. Bending in closer, he ran his trembling frozen fingers across-and-into the new letters' U-now-an-O empty arch-topped crevice. Yes, it was engraved! In a shuddering whisper, he read aloud…

"Here Comes the Son?.."

Yes, it definitely was there! But.. what.. what did it mean.. exactly? A quick, fleeting recall shot through his mind.. of Jerusalem.. and that happening he had witnessed on the hill. Yes.. I mean, he had a strange 'sense' of what it might mean.. but still, it was all very confusing! There was just too much, regarding all 'a that that he didn't understand! And what was even more confusing was.. Why?.. Why was he seeing it? I mean, why him? It just didn't seem right! No, not at all right! For he had been away from Heaven 'n all 'a that for so long now.. and.. and.. well, Why?.. Why him of any? He knew what he was! And well, so did He! So.. Why? He just couldn't accept it. No, this message couldn't apply to him. Not Jack! For what had all 'a that to do with him and his quest? It.. it.. just seemed.. so.. unrelated and apart-from him and all 'a his plans for his Carol! Yes, Why him? He wouldn't have it! For.. What could he possibly do, in regards t' all 'a that anyways? What part could he possibly play in all 'a that? No.. That was all.. just.. so 'out of his realm' to begin with! Not that he was, in any way, against it.. Or that he didn't want to see it happen!.. Quite the opposite!.. But him and his personal business-on-Earth.. Well, he just couldn't see (for the Herald-Angel-of-him) what that could have to do with 'his work'? And his goals! Nah, the mere thought was absurdity! No, it just couldn't be right! He was imagining it. Surely! He shook himself inwardly (as well as 'outwardly') in the fathoming of it, trying desperately to free himself of its grasp. But it wouldn't let him go, no matter what!

Quickly lifting himself to his feet (And this, a true task for the tremendous force of the still-increasing winds!), he held tight his head (and hat) in great upset. At last (in all of the inner-'n-outer commotion) screaming out at the top of his lungs...

"NO!.. NO!.. I HAVE NUTHIN' T' DO WITH ALL'A THAT!.." This.. as if, towards the source... "YOU DON'T UNDERSTAND.. I STILL WANT CONTROL!.. IT'D JUST.. INTERRUPT EVERYTHING I PLANNED T' DO!...

BESIDES.. YOU DON'T UNDERSTAND.. I CAN'T!.. ALL 'A THAT.. JUST.. FRIGHTENS ME!...

WHY ME OF ALL THE OTHERS ANYWAYS?.." beginning to breakdown into a whimper tone...

"I'M YOUR.. WORSE BET!.. Y' KNOW THAT!.. I JUST.. JUST.. CAN'T!.. DON'TCHA SEE?...

PLEASE?.. PLEASE?.. NOT ME!.. I'M JUST NOT.. NOT.." becoming so flustered and overtaken by mental confusion, that he lost his further wordings and train-of-thought.

In absolute terror and perplexity, he snappingly jolted into a run. Yes, away from it and the stone's site.

Through the chain-linked-fence opening (of former note), he went. Awkwardly, for the speed. Continuing out and down the railroad tracks. Under the bridge. Passed the Bowling Alley.. and.. gone.

Now home in Antarctica (and somehow feeling a bit more safer-'n-away from it all), he contemplated 'the message'. Studying it over-'n-over in his mind. This (coupled with his already-and-still 'feeling of loss') was just completely overwhelming. And in the traumatic discomfort of it all, he sat in the very spot now (overlooking the Antarctic Sea-line) as where he'd originated from, when he'd begun this same journey. Yes.. and in the very identical-'n-exact stance, as well! Only difference being.. his hat.. still plunked on his head. Arched back-'n-off his brow, yet stuck firm! For in all of his mental turmoil, he'd totally overlooked its removal. Only nudging it back for quick relief.

The wind howled constant, out and over the due-to-it rough waters. Not even nearly as powerfully as it had back at the grave-site, yet still.. there! And, too.. a very, very dark gloom hung creepingly in the air, all about him! In extreme heavy haze! And he wondered if it were only a result of 'himself' and 'his deep inner depression' that it existed.. Or if, in fact, the day itself were not truly like that? And impending smell of doom was settled thick into it. And shivering in a fearful-ness (like he'd never before this known!), he peered about himself in his very-troubled thoughts. This, as though, awaiting some tremendous-'n-terrible tragedy to soon appear and overtake him. It was a very awful feeling! Awful.. Awful.. Yes, just really.. awfully awful!

Despite everything, he tried desperately to concentrate. Dodging the 'message' as best as he could (Though, quite honestly, it kept constantly 'seeping' into all of his thoughts and, in so, distorting every other!), he tried to think only of his former problem. Yes, the 'loss'! And what he would do about that. With all the mass-confusion/ inner-hysteria he was experiencing, he wondered, at times, if 'it' were not (in fact) his mind that had been 'lost'? Yes, it surely seemed so! But, no.. he wouldn't have it! Nor, couldn't! For there was just still so much to do! But, then.. What? For if he couldn't re-organize himself and make some sort of decision about it all, then.. well.. who knows what might become of him! He must think! And make a plan! Or, at least, do something! Anything! Sitting here was going nowhere! And real fast, at that!

'The Loss?'.. 'The Loss?'.. he fought to think on it. It was hard.. but.. 'oh, yes.. that something missing feeling!.. Where.. from here with it?.. The Southern Hemisphere's Quest?.. Yes, he must!' Yet, somehow (in all of his forced enthu-siasm) all he truly felt to do, was to return to 'the places of the past'. Well, that seemed okay.. for how-else would someone search-out 'something lost', if not in so? Then again, on second thought, what of his Quest?.. It should be going forward, not backwards! Still, he needed to find it!.. Whatever it was? It seemed the only logical thing to do now. Okay, then.. where to first? He removed his hat, putting it (as before) on the aside ledge. Bringing forth his right hand, he pressed it forcefully on his aching forehead. Where to.. from here? Yes, Where to?

The Southern Hemisphere's Museum was re-located. Yes, Jack finding it (near the center meridian) with its middle-aged ladies there and within, as hoped. Everything.. identical to the past! Only, the young man (that he'd 'window-viewed' on his first trip there) was now absent. And in so, general silence prevailed there-in. Yes, this.. short of the ladies' light-'n-occasional chatter. Jack's 'scarf-flapping' interrupted his study, making him frustrated (in trying to eavesdrop) and with a violent grasp, he snatched it and jerked it affront. In follow, fuming and re-focussing again. But nothing changed in his continuing-'n-lengthy observation. Until at last, he surrendered it all for 'roads ahead'. 'The Loss' was not there and he knew it now! Satisfied, he'd move on.

In days there-after, the vaudeville whistler was sought out. But to no avail. For all the fields and town-squares that once bustled with happy, cheering crowds (Listening to the entertainer and his traveling companions) were now empty and silent. And Jack had hit them all, one by one. But it seemed, as though, 'vaudeville itself' had vanished from the face of the Earth. Gone forever! And replaced with nothing even near reminiscent. Buried somewhere without even a grave-marker for respects! It was all so disheartening. For Jack had loved and enjoyed it so! This.. along with his 'already gloom' was an almost-unbearable-realization to survive!

But at last, when Jack finally did come-to-terms and accept it, he likewise (in so) surrendered his 'any hopes' of ever finding the hillbilly singer. Yes, the one who (as you might recall?) had even once traveled in the same-of-situations.. using 'Jack Frost' as his name! Yes, with 'vaudeville no more', he (too) would be lost forever!

The moon (though, full) barely lit the snow-covered slopes of Lorraine. Having spent the greater part of the earlier-evening 'goose-stepping' through the white, waist-high mounds, Jack (exhausted-to-the-hilt) fell with a twist onto his back. In this, peering up at the huge, glowing ball. Yes, the Great Night-Light! That of which (in his notice of it now) seemed to contain a face, that was staring-back-'n-

down at him. But this, though.. not a smiling-'n-friendly-like one! And for that, Jack turned away towards the horizon's darker skyline-'n-end. The mountains (below it) appeared endless from his (as well) elevated stance. This, disgusting him further for the 'road ahead'. He felt to sleep, so badly! But he knew he couldn't. There was just 'too much more' to journey. And he wouldn't put it off. The village was still miles yet!

In his following frustration, he turned back to above.. though not directly at the moon. Dodging it. No, instead.. at a single, sparkling star specked on the very distant and black sky. It flickering on and off. Blurry-eyed, he lost himself in it. This, with hard stare. In time, hearing (in and coming-out-of his subconscious) a once-familiar voice, echoing-like from the past. He concentrated-in-on-it, trying to make it more-audible to himself in his mind. And for this, it did.. increasing gradually in volume! At least, enough to distinguish and hear. It was?.. was?.. Lydia! Yes, Madame Lydia La' Belle! He listened on ardently now, focussing (in so) as sharply as possible (for his dreariness) on the star, as well (as though 'it' were 'this' that was instead sending forth the voice).

'.. "The main thing in life.. is doing what you must do, to satisfy your deepest soul!.. To find more than just an existence!.. To fulfill your dreams and goals!.. And you will!.. Yes, I'm sure you will!.. if you just keep trying!.. Don't quit!...

Because like I told you, I believe in you!.. You remember that, Jack Frost!.. Yes, you remember that!..."..'

The final sentence.. echoing louder.. and louder.. and LOUDER.. AND LOUD-ER!.. in his mind.. and violently waking him out of his dozing-off sleep. Or had it been 'out of his trance'? He really didn't know! Now.. in the aftermath of his bolting-up-to-sitting-position stance, he wondered. Quickly-'n-fearfully, he spun a search about himself, thinking 'maybe the voice had come from somewhere more close-at-hand'? But other than a handful of tall-enough-and-still-protrud-ing-shrubbery surrounding, there was only sparkling white! This, almost blinding for his 'high-inner-tensity'!

He snapped back up towards the star, only to witness it flicker-out and disap-pear. He gulped in it. He must calm himself.. and the storm that was now build-ing-up-about-him as a result! It rustling the shrubs and lifting the snow-surface.. and disrupting the moment's-before peacefulness. And that, of which, he more needed! Yes, the latter! So shaking his head, he tried to recover. But nothing

settled. Maybe he should leave.. and burn-it-off in miles? Jumping up, he did so
without further thought. Its powerful flurry, clearing a way.. and he, using it!

With dusk of the following day, Jack had (at last) reached the La' Belle's cottage. It.. structurally identical to how he'd left it. Only a tad worn.

Standing on the roadway, he studied it, feeling almost (and somehow?) afraid

to take another step closer. For something about it seemed very 'different' now!
Yes.. and for this, a gradual (but quickly-increasing..) anxiety mounted in him.
Darkening (in steady process) his total 'inners', as was (in similar way) the fall of
night engulfing his complete 'outers'.

No sooner did he (at last) work-up his courage enough to take the first of steps, when out-of-nowhere (and into his quite-constant-surrounding wind flurry) came a discarded piece of paper. It.. crumbled up some.. and swirling (as though, from the roof and..) down towards him attackingly. He watched it (as if, in slow motion..) approach.

Sure enough (as his luck would always seem to have it!), it hit him smack-dab right in the face! Smartingly blinding him, in so.. and clinging there unmercifully! Almost, like-as-if, rubbing his nose in its dirt!

Aggravatingly snapping it from his pucker, Jack pulled it down-'n-free (in all the flurry) and was just about to discard it, when he noticed on it (Despite its folds-'n-crumbles) something-of-interest to him. In so (with the wind still flapping it), he un-accordion-ed it (as best as he could, under the circumstances). This.. revealing what-had-been one of the old leaflets that the La' Belle's had made to promote his recording, years past! Yes, one of the smaller versions (handbills) of the very poster that he had once seen 'taped' in the Record Shop's window (in town).. With the very drawing of Adlin's on it of his 'like-ness', along with its print!

In quick-'n-further study of it (despite the extreme awkwardness of its rustling), Jack noted that 'something hand-written' was showing through it and coming from the reverse side of the sheet. This, very lightly distorting the set-type (though, only barely) on the poster side.

Regardless of its vague-ness, it seemed to be that-of a child's hand-write. And (when, at the time written..) had been pressed down-'n-through, quite harshly! Almost scribbled-ly, as well! So curiously, Jack flipped it over to read it. But it was now gone. Yes, the ink somehow 'faded clear' from moisture and time. Only the 'damp-stains' still viewable (Though not read-able). So re-flipping it, Jack (squintingly and very-confusedly) read aloud its only remaining (legible-ity and..) trace...

"Li.. ?...?.."

The wind about him, circling-in and fluttering the entire sheet almost free-of-his-hands. He.. grasping it again to stretch-it-forth for further read. But it was just so hard to see.. and he continued to fight with the individual letters that followed...

"V.. looks like a V?.. Yeah!.. Ah, let's see.. an E.. Yeah!...

and a D.. Okay!.. and a G.. yeah, that's it!.. and.. hmm.. an I!.. and a 3?.. No, no.. an 8?.. Nah, that's not an 8, it's a.. " Before he could speak it though, it pulled free.. blowing up and away into the surrounding swirl. Jack dumbfounded-ly watching it escape-'n-disappear down-'n-through the snow-mounded driveway aside the cottage. And it was gone!

Jack tried to figure what he'd read. But it really didn't seem to make much sense. Whispering aloud, but to himself...

"Livedgib?.. Hmmm.. maybe it's Lived Gib!... Nah!.. Must be in some foreign language or somethin'!.." Surrendering it with.. "Oh, well!.."

Turning now to the cottage, he re-noted his earlier observation. Yes, something.. something?.. seemed 'different' and 'strange' about it all now!.. But, what?

The night's deeper-darkness was consuming the Earth. Feeling double-per-plexed and confused by the 'all about him' and 'what had occurred' (on top of his already dilemmas), he decided to wait 'til daybreak to further pursue the building's immediate grounds and whatever-inhabitants. This all had been 'more-than-enough' for one night! He must rest from the travel, as well. This.. if, at all, possible! So, to town it would be.. to retire somewhere's there. For somehow he truly feared staying here! In the morning, he would re-search out the Monsieur.

Christmas had totally slipped his mind. What, with all that he'd had on it.. Well, it was understandable! But in the village, the sights-and-sounds-of-it were everywhere! Bringing it all to recall.

Down and along the main-thoroughfare, he proceeded. At last, reaching the little restaurant (of old!), he stopped to watch and hear a bundled-up, heavy-set gentleman (Who was entering the doorway) say.. to a similar-dressed-and-like fellow (Who was simultaneously in-the-process of exiting the establishment)...

"Well, hello, Monsieur De Robillard!.. And how are you, this fine Christmas Eve, sir?.."

In the continuing of their brief conversation, Jack contemplating to himself.. 'and it's Christmas Eve, t' boot!.. Where have I been?..'.

Becoming lost in further thoughts of it, he walked on (Though, totally 'to himself' in this), passing a little street-cornered band of minstrels. They.. armed with a cello, violin, guitar and mandolin.. and playing, full force, "Joy to the World". It sounding almost gypsy-like in its execution. Though Jack, barely (if at all) hearing it!.. 'Where have I been to have not remembered?' Yes, this.. bothering him greatly!

Several blocks later, coming to a river and its steeply ledge, he sat (on the latter, of course), still contemplating (and mumbling to himself in it).. ".. 'n Christmas Eve t' boot.. I just can't believe it!.. What's wrong with me?.."

Becoming more inwardly engrossed, he wondered (as well) if he should just return to his Quest and forget this 'back-tracking'? Yet, still.. in another way, he felt somehow 'so displaced' from all 'a that anymore! Yes, he had been so involved in 'the loss' and 'what it had been', that he'd hardly even considered 'further pursuit' of his Crusades. Really.. somehow now (and he truly didn't know why?).. Well.. it all just didn't seem to matter anymore. I mean.. it did!.. but, well.. he just really couldn't figure anymore what to do with it. And as for 'the message' (that he'd received in the graveyard).. Well.. that might be a direction? That's if, in fact, he was understanding it right? I mean, he really wasn't sure! Not only that.. but.. well, the thoughts of it alone, frightened him even worse than anything! No, he would continue in his way.. Even as 'confused' as it seemed to be making him, in the process!

Rubbing through his now-matted-wet bangs (due to the removal of his hat), he surrendered his thinking momentarily to study-out at the winding river affront. It.. with its sparkling-cold, shoreline lights opposing. Some of red and green for the season. Its initial beauty, fading quick in his further inner-retreat of grief. 'If only I knew what I was looking for.. But, t' tell the truth, I don't even really know anymore!'

Hours passed.. and, at last, ice-bottomed, Jack cracked-free and began back for village center.

The earlier musicians were now gone.. Dispersed to their 'where-evers'!

The restaurant was still open. Its off-white-ish glow, centered into the dark-shadowed-like images of its surrounding peers. Jack (on the opposing side of the avenue now) didn't even bother to cross for it.. Simply leftwardly scanning it in his passing.

In further-'n-gradual progression (soon after), he encountered (in the same fashion) the old record store, peering across at it in his continuation. It.. closed and hazed-in-dark. A drunkard was sitting and leaning up against its doorway, singing "Hark, the Herald Angels Sing".. and Jack (in noting) just sort-of smirked in it to himself. But somehow (in his further movement), the song's words started penetratingly 'hitting home'.. and with this, he began recalling that First-of-Christmas-Eve's. This, frustrating him.. and, in short time, upsetting him ever-greatly, for its mounting-'n-pounding internal increase.. Multiplying steadily, with each further-away footstep!

Still hearing the drunk singing (If that's what you would've called it!) behind him, he tried to move faster to escape it. But ironically-enough, in so doing, it only seemed to get louder!.. Echoing and ringing violently in his mind! He began a trot. At last, breaking into a full run. But it only pursued him louder and louder!

Jerking free his hat (as though it were that, that was causing his rapidly-increasing 'head-aching'.. and this, as well, that he wouldn't 'lose it' in both meanings of the term!), he (at last) came to an out-of-breath stop. In this, grasping his forehead with his free hand. Totally agonized, he dropped to his knees, crying and whimpering in the same.. like as-if the voice were driving him insane. It wouldn't stop!

It.. with its grotesque slobbering-'n-slurring.. sounding almost defiant in its execution! With all of his remaining might, he screamed out (as though, to exorcise the inner hysteria-and-pain that it was causing him)…

"JESUS!.. LORD!.. I CAN'T TAKE IT ALL ANYMORE!.. PLEASE!.. PLEASE!..

WHAT AM I SUPPOSE TO BE DOING?.. PLEASE.. TELL ME!.. 'CAUSE I JUST REALLY DON'T KNOW ANYMORE!.. HELP ME!.. PLEASE!.."

In the dead-silent aftermath, Jack waited.. hoping to hear a return. Looking (nervously and tear-filled-ly) all about himself, as if expecting.. a Voice?.. an Image?.. An Anything?.. But nothing!.. No, nothing came!

Finally and very faintly, he heard it. No, not a 'voice'.. but, instead.. many! Yes, a soft, calming.. very sedating Choir! It, though.. distant. Or at least, seeming so! He listened in the settling. Ardently. Was it coming from within (himself).. or from outside? Either way, it was soothing! It was like his 'first time' hearing (or should I say, truly hearing..) a Choir! And appreciating it! Understanding its beauty! Slowly, but surely.. it increased (in its volume), due to his mental focusing. And he realized that it was, in fact, coming from outside and into his ears! A choir.. with its hallowing and solemn-majestic-ness. Transcending down and upon him from atop of the ahead-of-him hill. Yes, a midnight Mass (in the crowning-it church) was in-process!

Arching himself forward on his dried-tight-'n-sore knuckles, he (wide eyedly.. and eared-ly, as well..) aimed closer in its direction. Seeing (in better focus through the haze) what was a giant-steepled church (very gothic-appearing with its black, white-cement-lined bricks) on the moonlit crest.

And the song?.. with closer listen, it seemed to be.. Yes.. it was "Hark, The Herald Angels Sing"! Only now, being delivered with beauty and perfection. And this, bringing a very deep and inner peace!

Jack hopped to his feet, moving hastily towards it.. Trying desperately (in so) to be light-footed, for the 'snow-crunching' was interfering. When closer though, it didn't matter.. and he gave up the worry of it.

Outside the building, it was much more audible. And Jack began up the stairs in the awe of it. Yes, he'd never heard choir music to sound 'so uplifting' before now! It was just so captivating! And somehow, it seemed to be 'calling to him' for some strange reason now. He wanted to go in. But, couldn't. Feeling certain that he'd 'run-all-out' with his cold.

So when top-platform-ed, he instead took a seat behind one of the large, supporting columns (against the wall) to listen further. Content in that.

Snuggled-in, he hand-warmed his tears (just enough to wipe-'n-crack them clear).. pinched away his nose-run.. and settled back, grasping his knees for circular-like support. There was 'true comfort' in being here. Somehow, with all of the changes that he'd been experiencing and so forth, he couldn't understand 'why?'.. but he did know it to be true! Yes, there was a feeling here that he needed. Desperately needed! And it really didn't need to make sense! 'Cause, for that matter, nothing did anymore anyhow! No, all he knew was it did.. and that was enough! This was where he would spend his night.. and not move an inch from it either! He shivered in the mere thought of otherwise! Pulling down his hat further onto his skull and twisting more-securely his scarf to his neck, he closed his eyes in a saddened surrender. His ears 'still awake' though, for the choir's sedation.

Christmas morn, Jack awoke momentarily 'in wonder' over how he'd arrived there. But with the gradual focussing of his eyes (onto his lower self), it came to him. And he remembered.

Still, in the yawning of it, another question quickly replaced the former. And this.. as a result of his self-scanning notice and the (in so) detection of his scarf's initials. For now, they were.. were changed? Somehow or another, during the night in his sleep(?), they had been miraculously transformed! Yes, for one.. the spacing between the cursive-lobes of the J and the F were much more circular and further apart now. Bloomed-like! And as well, there were two newly-added markings! The first.. a sort of candle's-flame-shaped stroke atop of the left-side's up-'n-out-swung tail.. And, secondly.. a doubling-split in the down-cline of the right side's! And to even greater-ly top it all off, the thread was new! Yes, pure-'n-clean Gold.. and appearing freshly sewn! It all.. looking like this…

Jack marveled at it. Totally! Where had it come from? What did it mean? He studied it astonishedly, through his sleep-crusted eyes.

Finally surrendering further thoughts on it for the waiting-and-below main thoroughfare, he began out. This, in creaky, bone-stretching fashion. The light of day-break made him dizzy and a bit nauseous. His eyes, head and entire-wirey-frame seemed to crackle (each in their own way..) with the slightest of movements. His skull felt warped to one side. Oblong-like. Disfigured. Sleep (after a great 'lack of sleep') can be a true killer! Almost seeming to do 'worse' than having gone without totally!

In his awkward and slow descent of the stairs, he noticed the abandoned-ness of souls. Yes, the morn was ever quiet. And absolutely still! And likewise, there was a sort-of 'odd-ness' settled into it! This.. possibly due to the gloomy-'n-hovering snow-clouds above(?).. He really didn't know? But whatever was causing it, was neither here-nor-there. For it was so.. and would be, regardless of 'why'. And 'that'.. was all he 'did' know!

Listening-'n-hearing solely his sneaker crunches below him, he began in the direction of the La' Belle's. It would be a hike. This, for sure! But with the moment, it seemed there would be nothing-else-better in the world to do. Besides, it might help him sweat-out some of this inner agony!

Up and over the hills of the street-spoke leading out-and-away from town, Jack tramped. On several occasions, seeing a human or two. But they.. hurrying off to somewhere.. and wrapped-up ever-tight in their 'winter-garb' and 'private-affairs'. No one loitering.

When at last there at the cottage, Jack (no longer anxious) moved-in right away. Scatting through the slight yard and up-and-unto the porch in a breath.

Excitedly peeking in through the window, he noted the parlor couch to be set in its same-'n-exact place.. Directly beyond the glass, with its back resting up against the window frame. Other than that (and the fireplace to his left, which was stationary to begin with), the room and its décor were totally different. Changed with time.

After a fair wait (in his further study), there entered a woman. But one that he'd never seen before. She (after her little cleaning duties about-the-room) sitting herself down on the sofa.

At first, Jack assumed her to be 'just that'.. a cleaning lady. Possibly hired by the Monsieur? But with Jean's likewise-'n-soon-after entry (That, of which, sending a shiver through Jack), this notion was dispelled. For directly to the couch he came, sliding himself in and to her with a kiss and embrace. Yes, it was obvious now, that she was hardly an employee! Instead, the Monsieur's wife. Yes, things had changed! And greatly! Times move on. Jack watched them in mounting dismay. And this, not for 'their situation or happiness'.. No.. But for the simple realization of that forever truth!.. Yes, how things (and even people) come and go. The good.. as well as the bad! And this, impartially! But, oh.. what times he had had there, when Lydia was alive! The memories. Yes, that's all they were now. Or, all they would ever be, forever more! Memories! Gone for good! Just like Lydia herself.. never to return! It was this and only this, that saddened him. And very deeply and greatly at that! All of those nights, spent whistling for her and Jean.. and the children.

The children! It hit him! Where were the children? Jack quicked his eyes in the direction of the inside-and-beyond doorway, in search of them. Waiting and hoping desperately in the aftermath for their appearances. These, of-which, were never to come. Even long after the Monsieur and his new Mrs. were to leave the room. Yes, night fell with Jack still 'in wait'. But as I said.. to no avail.

Jack simply could not find it in himself to leave the Lorraine town. And for this, several days later, Adlin was spotted.. In the square, shopping, with her.. her children? Yes, children! Time had most certainly moved on!

Jack (in his discovery) being parking-metered and leaning.. When, out of the corner of his eye, he spotted her (and her little elves) exiting a store on the block's end of the main street.

By the time he reached them though (in his prompt scurry), they were already shopping-bag-packed into their vehicle and starting off. Jack, in desperation, whistling at them. And, in a flash of this, he noting Adlin glancing-back-over-her-shoulder (as though she might have heard it). And as well, her curious-faced look in it. But in this, she seeming uncertain. And as a result, she returned and continued her exit.. Leaving Jack in the cold!

He thought to run after her (For she had always been so interested and compassionate towards his Quest).. and did for a brief minute. Until it proved to be totally in vain. For somehow she had disappeared much too fast.. like a bullet's ricochet.. whizzing a sharp turn-off of the main-way and up into an obstructed-by-buildings road. It was lost! And all in a split second too!

Jack hung his arms defeatedly. Everything just seemed so 'out-of-reach' for him here anymore! Why was he hanging-in and wasting his time? He just really didn't know!

Claude and David were gone. Or at least, never found! And where was Michel now, he wondered. This (the lattermost), at times, haunting his mind. And following Jack in all-of-his-days (there and otherwise); for the lad had been so intense and intelligent. Many of the things Jack remembered of him, in recall now, seemed to be 'so much older' than that of his actual age. Words he had heard him say. Things he had seen him do. The boy's logic. And reasoning. Yes, the list was numbered! And in retrospect, it all confounded and perplexed Jack greatly! What was he 'up to', these days?   For he had been the youngest, as well.. and Jack couldn't help but worry over him. Yes, if he only knew!

After much detainment about the town, Jack (at last) made up his mind to return to the cottage and try his whistle (and 'luck') one more time.   Maybe the thought of 'another recording' had been what had led him back in the first place?   He really didn't know?   But with it (at present) crossing his mind, he figured 'why not?'.   The idea beat anything else he'd been able to logic out of it all, to this point!   Yes,

maybe.. deep down.. this had been what he'd been truly hoping for in returning? He sincerely didn't know? But either way, it was worth a shot! For absolutely nothing else was happening here for him! And that was for-utmost-sure!

So late into a darkening night, he made for the La' Belle's.. head-strong-atti-tude-'n-all.. planning the 'Best of Shows' for his whistle. Practicing all the way there, up the hilly-'n-curvy road. Talking to himself, as well, in the ascents-'n-descents. And trying desperately to stay 'as positive as possible' through-out.

Trudging up the last of mounts in his journey and in through a small center of

commercial shop-fronts (Just before the cottage), it began!.. A quick-'n-increasing stir in the night's air. One bringing with it (and to Jack) an odd, inner discomfort! A 'threatened' feeling, as like he'd never-ever-before experienced! Short of maybe at the grave-site in North Cambridge. Only this, being worse! Unquestionably worse! It inwardly shaking him, as was the gush of harsh-cold wind spankingly hitting him now, externally and head-on from over the slight-of-ledge. And displacing him, as equally! Yes, it was as though 'he, himself' were up ahead (at the cottage) and blowing (back at himself) one of his worst-of, smarting-'n-painful-like hurricane-cutting winds. It was awful! And ferocious! It penetrating so deep, that Jack (in actuality) fell to his knees now. Yes, from its horrendous impact! In so, snappingly grasping his hat (in all the frenzy), that it would not be lost. His scarf almost strangling him in its initial flap! This, as well, 'backwards-ing' his all-other loose-ends-'n-apparel! Like flags in a cyclone! In all reverse directions!

Why was this happening? Jack cringed and fretted terribly! Was it the end of the world? The night-about-him swirled.. carry with it his visions, fears and thoughts, like-as-if tiny fragments in a bomb explosion!

He fought desperately to regain his own senses.. let alone, to try and deal with the blowing-t'-bits reality of the 'all-about-him'! That of which, he knew too well to be beyond his control anyway! All of the events of this visit to the village.. blurred together with 'the same' of his first experiences there past.. came together into a new picture now.. But, a disfigured one. Very ugly! Yes, jumbled-'n-jelled into a 'new sense'! It (all together) appearing (to him) as would a jigsaw puzzle, that had identically-matching-and-cut pieces.. that, when re-assembled (in any of its innumerable ways) made an entirely different picture. Yes, everything in this windy turmoil (that now 'out of nowhere' came to an abrupt end.. and in so, totally catching Jack off-guard and marveling at it!) dropped its pieces mix-matched. But ironically enough, not seeming so! Yes, it all appeared 'too real' to be wrong! Yes, it made too much sense to not be correct! Yet, sadly enough, if this 'new picture' was right?.. Well, it's reality was horrifying! Jack shook his head in the now-stillness, hoping to somehow re-shake the picture back to its before. But it just wouldn't go!

Slowly rising to his feet and feeling extremely weak-'n-light-headed in so, he tried a step forward. Having to stop in it for multiplying dizziness. Squatting again momentarily, he squeezed his upper nose and eyes for relief. It helping a bit, so up and another was taken. Then a slow 'nother.. and he was moving. Yet slowly.. as with and as-was in the same way, his inner regain.

After a time.. reaching the cottage, he stood shakingly staring at it from the roadway. Engulfed in the heavy darkness and the weird-about-him feeling night, it (the cottage) seemed very 'alien' now and un-welcoming. And somehow scary! For with this new inner picture of Jack's (concerning it and all that had happened there prior), it appeared very distorted-like. Yet, in its disfigurement, 'more clear'! This being equated with (for an example) the way one views another person, when we have learned of some 'deep-dark, profound secret' of their life.. And in so, now see them in a totally different light! And as well, once 'known', nothing can ever be as was before. Yes, somehow now, the cottage seemed only a structural symbol and reminder of all that had occurred. And whether wrong or right (in his analysis), to Jack now, it all appeared that way! And he just couldn't find his way around that 'new view', no matter how hard he tried. For it all made complete sense! At least, he felt sure so! Yes, all the mystery solved! And being known, how could he pretend otherwise?

He wondered if he should even bother anymore with his 'original plan' in returning there, this night.. The whistle and trying to reach the Monsieur. The latter of whom he wasn't even sure was inside to begin with! For everything seemed so still and lifeless! There was no light within. At least, none that Jack could see from his stance. Un-nerved he stood, fumbling with himself.. trying to decide on his 'next of moves'. Wanting in truth, to just run away and escape from it. For it was causing such great discomfort! But for some reason, he couldn't budge? Then, the decision was made for him.

Up from the structure's side-drive, it came (along with the again-returning windy turmoil of the night). Yes, like-as-if at one hundred-miles-an-hour, it struck him face-on! The very same discarded, dirty sheet of paper that had greeted him originally on his return there, this visit. The crumbled poster! Its impact even stronger now than before.. feeling equivalent to that of the power of a muscle-man's hand (at full force) slapping him dead-center face! Jack falling back in it. Fearfully grasping and tugging it free. This.. long enough to verify it, in fact, as being the one-'n-same leaflet! And as well, in it.. to see-through-it clearer at its added hand-write. And make greater sense of it (too and as well) now, in his 'new picture' focus. Yes, now it made perfect sense! But then.. like a 'live' electrical wire in his grip, it (wiggling ferociously-free) snapped up, paper-slashing his right cheek! And in a blood-splitting second, it flew up-'n-away behind him and out-of-sight!

Gasping now, Jack held his wounded face and thought on it (Despite the continuing mania!). Re-analyzing its contents in his grief and terror. Yes, in the 'now' picture, it did make a strange, but perfect sense! But, "No.." he argued with himself.. "that's crazy!.. Absolute absurdity!" He rebutted.. "Still, it does make perfect sense!". He gulped in it sharply. For it truly, truly did! As much as he didn't want it to!

The wind was still coming.. as though, originated from-below and heading-up the drive. Poundingly it smashed him. It was nearly impossible now, for him to stand in it.. What, with his earlier-stated light-headed-ness! Who was controlling this wind? Was he doing this to himself? It didn't seem so? It felt totally out-of-his-hands!

A howl came with its multiplication. A loud and low-toned one (unlike his 'high' own). A ghost-type 'Whoo-u-u-u-w-w'!

Then, from behind it (and passing him in a sort-of 'whooshing'-flash) came screams! Yes, wild and hell-ish-like screams! Terrifying and agonized-sounding screams! Whizzing at and by him in machine-gun-like fire! What was going on? He fell to his knees again, to try and dodge them and its lashing fury. It was un-merciful! Stinging! How could he whistle back at this? Even if he had been 'as strong as usual'? It was literally blowing him away!

He spun around, using his back for defense. But it only grew stronger! Almost knocking him aground! The only escape seemed to be to run with it. He arose and did so. Running.. Running.. Running.. with its squealing voices, biting and snipping at his ears. Its static-like chilly-'n-creepy hands.. feeling and pinching at his body!.. As though, right through and under his clothing!.. Gliding, in so.. and painfully-tickling across his trembling-heavy flesh! He felt in absolute anguish and terror! Running with all his might. This.. to where?.. He didn't know?.. Nor even care!.. Just.. away!.. Anywhere away!

Back and through the village and down its main-way, he fled. Whizzing passed the earlier-mentioned church.. And down towards the Record Store and Restaurant. Now, on their side of the street. Descendingly he saw.. there (in all of his confusion) in the doorway of the former (again), the same drunkard. Or at least, he 'looked to be the same' (For in his former view of him, it had only been from afar to begin with!). But, yes.. he.. lying and leaning-as-before in the coming-clearer-'n-closer front of him. The drunk (in his stupor) glaring up at Jack (in his approach) with a guile-like smile. Or better yet, this.. a sort-of 'smirk'! An evil-ish-type one! His face (in Jack's amazing discovery) being that of.. of.. The Angel of Musical Dis-chord! Yes, the Herald Angel! The very one created right before him (This, of course, known to Jack by the latter lining-up and nicknaming of the crew). Yes, at least.. well, it sure 'seemed to be' him (jogging his memory in the flash of seconds)! Yes, he'd almost swear to it! It sure looked exactly like him! Though the clothes were deceiving. In an instant-'n-vague recall, Jack inwardly returned to that first-of Christmas Eve's. He couldn't put his finger on the Angel's nickname.. but remembered him as being the one who'd ultimately steered Leah away, when they'd been sent on their 'two-hour-hymn-creating mission'. Yes!.. and as well, hadn't it been he that had been behind him (on the cathedral stairs), when Jack had been bumped-out into the light?.. from behind the pillar?.. directly following their creation?.. Why, yes... it had! Jack wondered in this now, if (in fact) it had been an accident after all!

The only difference now though, was.. his face! Yes, it was somehow blended-together with 'another's' of Jack more-recent, earthly past. And in so, it seemed different. Meshed! And confusing! For it now, as well, looked like..(A simultaneous flash-back came.. "Yes, that's Jack Frost.. Really.. it is!").. No, it.. it couldn't be! Yes, in another thought, the characteristics did seem very similar! He wondered why he'd never noticed that, in the past, there! Was he hallucinating? He grabbed his face-sides momentarily in his further run. Now, though.. directing himself and swerving left and away into the street to dodge him.

Out further and towards the opposing side of the avenue in his continuing crazed-flight, he shot. Hearing in-so and behind-him laughter. Hard and heavy, mocking-like laughter! This.. mixed with a few sick-offerings of "Hark, The Herald Angels Sing"! Trying desperately to push it from his ears, he sped even-greater away.. Never turning back once at the village through-out it all.

Into the night and mountainsides-awaiting, he went. In fear-filled confusion. And almost total hysteria! Not even steering himself in the slightest! His mind lost in terrible, terrible thoughts! Visions of a world in the most awful-est of states! This.. without law, love or any order! A world where there would no longer be any comforts at all! Total chaos prevailing! A world, too, where the Sun no longer shined! Always dark and crime-filled! Where evil thrived unchallenged! Ugly and terrifying scenes plagued his mind.. Of unending agony and absolute hopelessness! Of sick and perverse violence! Atrocities! It was terrible! Sheer Hell! He uncontrollably shook in it, in his further-and-fumbling retreat.. But he must go on! And get away! From it and that village! Going?.. Going?.. Anywhere!

- THE CAROL RAG (RETURN) -

There, on the high grade, it still sat. The old timer's Hansel-'n-Gretel-like cottage. Jack eyed it (between a-feared 'back glances') from inside of the immediate-area's likewise-descending-tree-line, as his 'appearance' brought forth its snow-lifting flurry. This, causing a mist to climb the open-area's hillside in a gusty whoosh. Jack studying its attack and break-around the cabin's porch and front. Otherwise, all else was extremely still-for-winter and quiet-for-daybreak.

The frozen misty-dew across the morning gave it a strange appearance. One of heaven-like glory. It almost appeared as if a 'new world' had arrived. Such a tremendous contrast to his night-before visions. And gradually (with time), feeling a bit more at-ease (for this and the daylight).. and secured (in that nothing or no one had seemed to have followed him in his previous night's episode-and-flight), he breathed a slight easier. Though still not normally.

Staring onward (Though not totally concentrating on the cabin and its landscape), he re-vamped the events of the Lorraine Village. Sporadically and still (on occasions, though not as often now..) sneaking peeks behind him. For now, even though 'away from the town', the 'new picture' still held. And only seemed to

'develop'-further in his mind. It all.. chilling and sending bolts through his nervous system, at times. He (in retaliation) trying to ignore them and think otherwise.
Though, this.. seeming useless for the most part; for everything just kept drifting-
back mentally to then and it! Yes, the 'shock' still had its grip on him.. and very
firmly, at that! He was obsessed with it! Yet, still he tried.. hoping he'd make
some better sense of it all, at a later-'n-healthier time. But for now, he must try to
get out from under it to be more objective. And this, seemed the only 'surviving'-
way at the moment. For he had never dealt with anything like this before! His
thoughts felt absolutely clotted. Stuck in its traumatized mode. And in this, distorted beyond belief! Yet, really.. in another thought, he wondered if (in fact) it
was 'distorted' or simply 'better insight'? He really wasn't sure? Still, there was
one thing.. yes, one thing for sure.. and that being.. that he knew himself to be in
dire need of healing. This.. and only this, was.. for sure! And the old timer's fid-
dling might be the very medicine he sought (?).. He wasn't totally convinced.. But
he did know it to be the main reason for his returning now! This and its geographic
close-at-hand-ness. Yes, he hoped to 'listen' again. For maybe 'hearing him' would
be helpful? Sentiment-a-cillin! Actually and really, he honestly didn't know 'why
he was here'! Or 'what he needed'! But the formers, at least, made some sort of
sense in all the craziness! Maybe there was a 'deeper reason' for his being here?
He truly didn't know! But either way, it all didn't seem to matter at this point. He
was just so confused! And what better or more logical (..or whatever?) was there
that he could do than this?

Sadly enough now (after all of his travel and anticipation), the old man was not
appearing. This distressing Jack greatly. For in his at-present state, each minute
seemed like hours in his wait. But despite, he did.. though nervously pacing
through-out.

After a time, growing increasingly anxious, Jack began closer towards the cabin's side.. along and through the ascending tree-line. In the process, passing a
deep and imbedded massive-boulder on his left (Though all-the-while peering
steadily to his right, through the shrubbery at his up-'n-coming destination), it hit
him!.. Coming from out-of-nowhere and literally knocking him (from his left side)

off of his feet and to the ground. Jack (in his already terrorized frame of mind) was now panic-stricken-to-the-max in his jostle through the near-bordering shrubbery. In his hurry-scurry to escape it (and return to his feet), he let out a sort-of 'squeal' there-tumbling! But, afoot.. and seeing his attacker, he gaspingly stuttered out…

"Y… Y… Ya.. Ya... You're Leah!.. I remember you!.. Y.. y.. you're the.. Angel of All Basics 'n Beginnings!.. W.. W.. Why.. Why'd y' do that?.."

She (still leveled from the collision and trying to tidyingly 'fix herself', despite it..) shooting back…

"Why did I do that?.. You.. You.. You got in 'my' way, Jack Frost!.. 'n just look at what you did!.." pointing (in tremble) to her instrument, now 'stuck' (arrow-fashion) in the ahead-snow-mound.. " my violin 'n bow! …'n my.. my brand-new Bible!.." (This, as well, lying right beside it.. Though fortunately sealed tight with a leather-like band surrounding) "They better not be messed up!.. in any way, nei-ther!.. or I swear.. I'm gonna.. gonna…"

This outburst, pulling Jack immediately-back and out-of-his-anger. Realizing it all had been as much 'a shock' to her, as it had been for he himself. Trying to calm her…

"Ah.. It'll be okay.. They don't look damaged none!.."

"Better not be!.." She, at last, to her feet and retrieving them.

When in her hands and being snow-brushed, Jack asked guilty-like…

"Well, they're okay.. right?.."

"I guess.." She.. still looking down at them and upset (Though slightly cooling).

"What 're you doing here?.." Jack trying to change the subject and make con-versation (Though truly curious).

She responding…

"What are 'you' doing here?.."

"Well.. I.. I.. " He fumbling.. "I'm.. I'm here t'.. t'.. " having to stop momen-tarily to remember.. ".. t'.. hear the fiddler!.." motioning in the cabin's direction.

"Well.. me, too!.." She, a bit arrogantly.. for still in a fume. And to sound 'more-in-the-right'.. "I'm studying him!.."

"Listen.." Jack (in no mood for this) pleading.. "I'm.. I'm sorry about that!.."

Pointing to the near-hand site of their mishap.. "Really.. It caught me off-guard too!.. Y' know, it wasn't on purpose, f' sure!.."

"Well.." She conceding.. " Yeah, I know.."

"Besides, we're both Herald Angels.. 'n we shouldn't be gettin' upset at each other!.. No ways!.. " Jack remindingly.. "We're suppose t' be comrads! " (When, in truth, he had always felt so 'alienated' from the others! But now, he felt this 'strange attraction' coming-to-life inside of him for her.. And, as well, a true need to 'not be alone' at this present 'worst of times'! Yes, it seemed the most appropriate thing to say!).

"Yeah.. I know.." She, as well, seeming to share this attraction. And now taking an about-face in her temperament.

He moving closer to her to put forth his cold, cracked hand for a shake.

When near grip...

"Jack.. What happened to you?.. " She peering sadly at him and his hand, asking soft-like and in true compassion. This, making him almost break into tears at the sound of it. For no one had even given him the least bit of concern, throughout all of his long days on Earth. Yes, since Angel Jane 'n all 'a that!.. And, well.. that had just been so, so long ago! He'd hardly remembered the feeling! And now.. yes, now of all times, it was just so badly needed! So it was with little wonder that, hearing it, his forced-smile was cracked into falling-to-bits-now pieces. And with her gentle touch to his hand, he could absolutely no longer contain it. For she was feeling them with such sympathy and care! Bursting him into a shower of agonized tears! She alarmed by it...

"Oh, I didn't mean to hurt your feelings, Jack.. I was just.."

"No.. No, you didn't!.. It's just that.. " he, trying desperately to regain himself.

"I only meant.. Geez, Jack.. What happened to you, to have.. Well, you know.." She meaning exactly as he'd perceived it (How he looked now, as opposed to when-in-Heaven). Understood without words.

"Well, Leah.. it's.. it's been.. well, it's been a long, long journey.. 'n well, now.. somehow.. somethin' ain't right, n' more!.. Somethin's happened.. 'n I.. I.."

She not truly comprehending.. but, trying to sound as though...

"Yes, I understand.. But why haven't you come back?.. Y' know, to Heaven?.. Where you could.." She truly not aware of his still-ignorance towards 'having been accepted' and so forth. But he cutting her short before she could elaborate (for still lost in his previous thought)…

"Somethin's happened, Leah.. 'n I can't figure it?.. I lost somethin' along the way.. 'n well, I'm tryin' t' find it!.. 'n.. 'n.." He slowly talking himself out of the tears.

"Well, it'll show up!.." She trying to be encouraging.. "Don't worry, Jack.. it'll be found!.. Everything happens for a reason.. So, don't worry.. God'll help you find it!.. Just trust in Him!.. No, don't worry!.."

Calmer now, he stared into her eyes. Listening to her every word. This, as well as for the strong feeling he had for her. But his feelings for Angel Jane remained and soon erupted.. And, in so, he found himself feeling guilty in it. Though somehow (and in spite of it all) it did make him feel good. It was strange! She staring back, at last, in the same tone. Noting this, he (to deny it) offered in a change-the-subject fashion…

"You said you're here t' study the fiddler?.."

"Oh, yes.." She snapping-to, as well.. "Yes.. and when my assignment's done, I'll be off to the Middle East to study, in greater depth, Hebrew Hymnody.. as well as the language!.. Yes, it's all in preparation for the work I'll have to do on the Greatest Hymn of All-time!.. Gabriel has given us instructions to be.."

He cutting in…

"Gabriel!.. Golly.. I ain't thought 'a him.. in.. well.. Man-o-man, a long time!.." This causing her to lose track of her words. And as well, her place in it all. Offering instead…

"Anyway.. the old fiddler.. Well, he was the first to have performed.. on the violin anyway.. the melody to…"

Jack interrupting again (still lost in Gabriel)…

"Man, he didn't seem t' care f' me, huh?.. Well, anyways, now that I got the chance.. well.. Thanks f' defendin' me at the nicknamin' ceremony!.. Y' know, I never did say that!.."

"Yes, I know.. it was.." She squeezing in. Though Jack hardly noting.. Only further blurting-out…

"He just.. Well, I dunno, Leah.. " ramblin' on.. "..'guess he just needed some-one t'.."

"No need to open old wounds, Jack.. Besides everything's totally different now!.."

"Yeah, y' rite!.. Still.. I always had wanted t' thank y' !.."

"Well, that's okay.. I knew how you felt about it, when you turned back then, anyway…

Listen, Jack.. I do have to get on.. Y' know, to the cabin. The old fiddler will be coming out soon, per usual.. and I must be there to play along with him.. It's my duty.. Understand?.."

He nodding his head, though not truly comprehending the reasons. But in desperate hope (to follow it), he asked…

"Will you.. I mean.." Then, shyly.. "Well.. will you be busy later?.. I mean.. Will you be able to come back 'n meet me here after?.."

"Well, no.. I won't.." Causing a facial decline that brightened upward with.. " But.. well.. tomorrow.. same time, I can.. When I return!.."

"Yeah.. Okay!.. It's a deal!.." starting to put forth his hand for a shake, but self-consciously pulling it back and hoping she hadn't noticed.. "I'll be here to-morrow.. same place.. 'k?.."

"Yes.." She looking at him a moment.. hugging him.. then running off in the direction of the cabin. Jack straggling behind to watch and listen.

Settled in (behind some shrubbery at the very-edge of the glade.. and she, di-rectly beneath the porch), Jack wiped his sniffle, crouched down and waited.

At last (after the sounds of much wind-whirlings and hissing-silences, non-respectively), the clack of the door bolt echoed-out across the valley. And then (as well), the cobblings of the old minstrel's shoes. The footsteps now, sounding terribly-terribly feeble and awkwardly-frail-like-and-shaky. Yes, time had greatly taken its toll! For even back then, he had been old.. Now (Which was miraculous to begin with), he was truly 'ancient'! Yet still, a fighting, ole trooper! A very coarse-'n-scraping cough rattled his frame. One that could be 'felt' even from afar. And his 'back-slump' was near completion. Jack immediately noting all-of-this, despite his fair distance.

When finally to the edge of the deck, he raised his violin and bow and began in. Slow-like. His playing a bit squeakier now, yet still resonate-'n-clean-enough. It (as with everything prior) rebounding in the distance.

Jack (in hearing) tried to place the tune. For he knew he recognized it. But, from where? Something about it was very familiar! Yet, something else of it was throwing him off? He tried to hum it in his head.. Being momentarily distracted by the in-harmony entrance of Leah's playing. Yes, she was accompanying him. And beautifully at that! The sound.. so sweet.. and lonesome-like together! Almost Classical! And with the natural reverb from the surroundings, it was all-the-more enhanced!

Back to his thoughts, he forced himself to place its title. Anxious (to return to his listening), he found himself (as a result) 'speeding up' the notes. This, ironically enough, bringing it to him. Yes, and with a startling realization! For it was his tune! Yes, only played a bit slower! He was flattered. To think, the old timer (after all of this time) was still playing it. Maybe 'age' had slowed it? He wondered in his amazement. He really didn't know? At last giving-it-up for the excitement, he joined in.. whistling it to their rendition.. all the while, ecstatic over its returning-sound from the lowland.

Somehow (in all of this), it seemed like the old minstrel came to life. As though, hearing Jack again had re-inspired him or something? But whatever?.. the tempo picked up. Gradual-like. And soon, it was as-it-had-been in the years passed. Yes, on his first-of-trips! Only now, it sounding all-the-prettier for the second violin part. Jack was in his glory! And he, not the only one.. for the old timer, as well, was smiling as-wide-as his mouth would allow. The spirit was moving, f' sure! There was a magic that was being re-lived and shared, in all of those present.

When it ended (after a good and fair time), the old man was totally 'tuckered-out'.

Yes, his return to the inside proved it. Jack was greatly disappointed at his exit (Need I say!).. But well, there would always be tomorrow. Or at least, he sure hoped so!

With the slam of his door, Leah was gone. Jack quickly focussing below the landing to see she'd disappeared. All in a flash too!

That night was a very alone one. But somehow Jack felt 'a bit' re-born. The earlier day replaying constantly in his mind. And almost totally wiping-out the earlier memory (and terror) of the Lorraine Village exit. But when 'this' (the latter) was recalled, he shivered violently in it.. feeling extremely uncomfortable and threatened. Especially considering his still-'reasonably-close-ness' to its location. And in so (with each reminder) he'd quickly search about his seated-'n-waiting self to verify his solitude. Through and into the dark-covered, surrounding shrubbery he'd peer. Yes, like I said.. it was a very, very alone night! The moon (with its muted power) reflecting off of the virgin snows below him. Lighting the cold. But not warming it. Would the morning ever come?

- IN THE LAND WHERE WE NEVER GROW OLD -

Dawn found Leah gently shaking him awake. She arriving earlier, that they might have greater time to talk. And this (as well) for a 'discovery' that she had anxiously wanted to share with Jack. A mysterious one, that (when finally his eyes and consciousness were 'opened-enough' for 'to make sense of"..), she disclosed...

"Jack.. Look here!.." She seating herself beside him (in the slight cave of the huge rock, where he'd settled himself for-the-night) and openingly flapping her Bible onto his un-awaiting lap...

"Look.." pointing.. "This mark was in my book!.. I discovered it, last night.. and well, it was brand-new.. so.. well, it shouldn't have been there!.. Must've happened in our little accident yesterday.. But.. but.. it's strange!.. Y' know.. Where it is!.. See?.. Verse 24.. Chapter 5 of Genesis!.."

Jack focussed through his awakening. And sure enough, there it was! A black mark! And one that looked very similar to the scribbling on the reverse of the poster, that he'd seen of-recent in the Lorraine Village. Yes, as though written by the same hand! This immediately stirring him up in earnest and fearful-like concern.

"..and.. what's even stranger is.." She, in anxious resume.. "Well, it was belted!.. Remember?.. I mean, even if a piece of dirt 'had' gotten in there.. well, it surely would've smeared the opposing page!.." Jack, in that, eye-flashing the near-hand-'clean' sheet, as he secured the book to himself...

"Let me see!.." pulling the Bible even-closer from her hand (Though, not rudely-like).. In so, reading it further and noting its place in the text. Then (in nervous flurry), flipping the page to see if it, as well, might be on the reverse's. But it wasn't!.. So back over.. Again noting its absence on the left (The verse and scar, being on the right-hand page). Leah offering (Though not intentionally-to-scare)...

"I think it might have something to do with death?.."

Jack not answering, but only reading it again. Somehow he felt it was 'telling him something'. Yes, intended especially for him! Personally! He could just tell!

After a time of silence (while Jack had mentally studied and contemplated on it)...

"Leah.. Would you be so kind as to let me borrow this?.. I mean, y' know, not f' good!.. Just f' while I'm here?.." Looking about himself.. "I'll leave it right here.. on the ledge.." pointing to a one that was deeper set into the earthly crevice from their position.. "No one'll take it.. 'n if y' ever wanted it back.. well, you'd know where it'd be!.. Y' know, if y' needed it.. well, it'd be right there.. I promise!.."

"Well, okay.. but.. just.. well.. take good care of it.. okay?"

"Promise.." raising his hand as if 'in oath'.. "I'd just like t' read some 'a this.. y' know, get more familiar with it 'n all!.."

"Sure, I understand.."

"Well, anyways.." to change the subject, he began.. "That was sure beautiful yesterday, wasn't it!.. I mean, the old fiddler.. he.." into a long and drawn-out conversation about the old-timer, they went. This (as with many of their to-be talks) becoming the main focus. Because, for one.. it seemed a 'perfect way' to dodge and disguise their true (and growing) feelings for each other. And, for an-other, their mutual love for him and music, in general. Yes, it was always 'com-mon ground'.

"Yes, Jack.. He is a true master!.. His feelings just pour out with each note!.."

"Leah, he is wonderful!.. 'n you, as well!.. I listened very close.. 'n you, too, have that pure touch!.. That real-ness!.. I could feel it!.. Boy, was I surprised when I discovered you were playin' my hymn!.. Why, I just.. just.. couldn't believe he'd remembered it, after all 'a this time!.."

"Remember it!.. Why, that.. and only a choice-few other melodies is all he ever plays anymore!.. And the others.. very rarely, at that!.. For yours is the.."

"Gosh, really!.. I dunno.. I just never would 'a.."

"Well, that's because.. something inside of him, Jack.. Yes, in his limited human-ness.. knows and senses that it is the very one that..."

"Leah.. what was that?.." He fearfully pointing quick at a sound approaching.. A crackling! And in this, gripping himself in his seated-position to prepare for hopping-up-and-running-away. She (alarmed at his over-reaction) turning in its direction and comforting...

"Why, Jack.. it's only a fawn!.. Yes, just a baby deer!.." jumping up, at that, to go for it. And it.. not retreating, in the least.. but only further nearing.

Patting it and hugging its neck...

"See.. there's nothing to fear!.." Then, continuing on with baby-talk to the animal. This, as lovingly as if it were her own child. And the creature.. soaking it in, as though she were, in fact, its own-'n-very mother.

To interrupt it, came the old fiddler's playing. Startling her into reality and away from the fawn...

"Oh, Jack, I'm late!.." coming forth in her bustle and grasping her instrument in a flash. Then, proceeding off.

"Will I see you tomorrow?.." Jack, in anxious.

She answering back in all of her hurry... "Yes.. Same time!.."

The day's-earlier events were replayed. The trio 'going-to-town' all over the surrounding mountains! Only difference being, when Jack's piece was completed, the old-timer began in (instead of leaving) with a new tune. Or at least, it was new to Jack's ears! A religious piece, that obviously had deep roots in the past. At least, musically, for sure! The old man singing it, as well, to his melody-line playing. Jack holding quiet-'n-still throughout to hear. For it was just so beautiful a piece...

"That Old Road.. Never we'll walk..

In the Land Where We Never Grow Old…

That Old Road.. Never we'll walk..

In the Land Where We Never Grow Old."

It touched Jack very deeply! Despite its shortness and simplicity. And as well, it rang in his ears all throughout the following and again 'alone' night. Something about its melody-line was intriguing. And habit-forming. It commanded constant re-singing. Internally, if not ex! And somehow, it was sedating. And that of-which, was a true necessity of Jack's throughout these particular hours. Especially feeling as 'threatened and scared' as he was! Yes, for somehow, when all alone like this, thoughts kept entering of 'being sought after'. An impending and grave feeling of doom persisted. As though, someone (?) were stalking him.. For the kill! Yes, it was a very odd and inner-trembling sensation. And no matter what, it held.. and only seemed to grow with each passing (after that..) day! Or might I better say, 'night'! For that's when it seemed its worse. Yes, alone in the dark-ness, he (at present) sat.. knees wrapped in his arms.. humming-constant the old-timer's tune. Studying pensive-'n-ardently about himself. Waiting. Yes, waiting so desperately the light!

Leah was so much like Jack. And this, not only in 'size' (their elfin stature and characteristics).. but, as well, in their natures. There were so many similari-ties! Almost to the point of being uncanny. The more he grew to know her, the

more he marveled in them. It was like-as-if they were 'soul mates' or something! And 'musical soul mates', as well! Yes, it was hardly a mystery why they found themselves attracted to each other. For they understood one another so well. Even 'thinking' alike. It was mind-boggling. But, true. Too true, at times! Their conversations (as a result) were so fruitful. And for many-a-day (throughout the remainder of that winter), they had them. The old-timer, as I said, though.. being the main focal point notwithstanding...

"Jack, he's very, very old!.. As much as I hate to tell you this.. for I know how deeply you love and care for him.. But, someday soon, he will die!.. It's inevitable!.. And when that time comes, I, no more, can.. For then my assignment here will be completed and I must move on to my next!.."

This much saddened Jack.. For it would mean losing two friend at once in the outcome. And he was just so desperately in need of them now for his recovery. The very thought of 'going-it-solo'-again absolutely terrified him! He tried pushing it from his mind. And instead, concentrating on 'the time' they had left.. However short it might be in the end! Still, the 'ghost of its eventuality' haunted. Along with all of his other 'threatening thoughts'.

"Tomorrow is Easter, Jack.. You've remained here for so long, that it hardly appears it, I know!.. But still, by the calendar it is!.."

He slipping in (in true naïve-ness)... "Easter?.."

"Yes, Easter!.." She, confused over his ignorance.

"What's Easter?.."

"Why, that's when Jesus returned.. You know, that's when all the Christians in the world celebrate Jesus' return from the dead!.. You.. You must know that?.. Well, on second thought, maybe you.. you...

Well, anyway.. on the third day after His crucifixion, He.."

"Well, yes.. I was there, at that!.. Yes, I was there when they crucified Him!.. I saw it!.. 'n just couldn't believe they.. they.. "

She aggravatedly nudging back in, before losing her point...

"Zipper it, Jack!.." He complied.

After a brief stare-down...

"Anyway, as I was saying.. on the third day after that, He arose out of the tomb and.."

"Really?.. Gosh, I.." He stopping at her re-affirming, cold and refusing-to-be-moved eye-lock…

".. walked on Earth.." She returning slow and word-for-word-ly.. "Then, later.. He ascended into Heaven!.. Where He is now.. with God, the Father and.."

"Oh, whew.." wiping his brow.. "that's great!.. I mean, that's truly wonderful!.. I.. I hadn't.. Well, I just.."

"Yes, and when He returns to Earth.." She trying to conclude.. "to claim His Kingdom, they will all be sing-"

"Geez, Leah!.." Jack hardly listening (for still astounded at Jesus' Resurrection) slicing-in on her word forcefully (Though innocently).. "That's all.. Well.. just.. mind-blowing!.. I mean, well.. I knew He wasn't here, no more.. on Earth, y' know.. as a person!.. But.. well, I.. just.. well.. I mean.." He, having another thought…

"Y' know, that's funny!.. 'cause, in a graveyard recently.. in Cambridge!.. y' know, Massachusetts?.. Well, somehow I sensed.. or, well.. Oh, I dunno.. I just somehow.."

She was totally flabbergasted, by now, shaking her head and mumbling-aloud (as though, to herself)…

"Jack.. If you'd only listen for once!.. I swear, you just don't listen to nothing without interrupting constantly!.."

Jack was still lost in his own words; continuing on despite all, right over her and into a jabbering blur.

Hours passed. When the old maestro appeared, Leah and Jack were already positioned and waiting-in-anxious. His entrance out and onto the porch, being very heavily distorted by coughing. This stronger and more-grating than ever! And constant, as well! Until he was finally able to regain himself at the ledge.

Tremblingly lifting his instrument and bow, he began in instead (as opposed to all of the other times previous) with "In the Land Where We Never Grow Old".

This catching Jack totally off-guard. And Leah, as well.. for the look on her face (as distant as it was to him) proved it so. The unexpected-ness of it, making the two listeners attend and study it even closer than before. And it (as stated) being the most touching version of the piece that he'd ever done! Despite the heavy coarse-ness of his vocal! That of which (the vocal crackings and lackings, etc.) only making it seem all-the-more sincere and heart-rendered!

It brought a lump to Jack's throat. A big one.. and very harsh one too! The echoing of it.. absolutely devastating! Jack actually 'watching' it return, out from across the open-ness of the large-'n-below gulf, for double-concentration. And that, as not to miss a single note!

Without even the slightest pause (after its conclusion), the old man 'bow-slid' into "The Carol". This in neat, smooth transition. Jack was so overwhelmed-'n-touched, that he had to clear his throat throughout the entire first part of it, before he could join in. Leah (already accompanying with the most tender of harmony lines) was so 'moved' by it all, that she'd impetuously taken to her feet.. and was, in an instant, giving it her all. Yes, the musical electricity was flowing! Out and forceful.. and sparkling the air! Like static, gold stars streaming and exploding from its source! Out across the bitter, in melodic combustion! And this (for some strange reason) happening greater than ever before. Yes, it was intense! And after a fair play of it, the excitement only grew. This causing the old timer to speed-up the tempo.. Almost to the point of playing it wildly! All accompaniment following suit. It becoming so fast.. that, on several occasions, Jack had to stop momentarily to catch his breath. But when inflated, returning with his whistle as quickly as he could, as to not miss-out on any of the 'en-crazed enjoyment' it was bringing. For he had never before heard his tune played in this way! It was truly innovative, how the old man had conceived of doing so!

At last (when the excitement was reaching its absolute max), the old fiddler dead-stopped. Yes, and without warning (in so).. grasping his heart in dizziness. Jack and Leah both halting accordingly and nervously waiting, watching his every move in the resulting 'deathly silence'.

Grasping the ledge's rail with his bow-holding hand, he waited.. as though desperately trying to regain himself internally. Jack prayed he wouldn't drop. Leah looking, as though, doing so herself. For what would they do?

The old timer breathed heavily and rapidly, as the two-some held theirs to hear. Was this it? The end?

Finally (and I mean finally!) his breathing slowed to almost normal. Or at least, what would have been 'almost normal' for him. He was all right! His audience breathing properly again, as well! Only now, the cough returned.. Echoing rasp-'n-cruelly out into the lowlands and ricocheting back like repetitive gunfire. Jack dodgingly jolting in each return of it.

Very, very fragile-ly, the old minstrel creaked his way back to the cabin's door-way. The cough following him with each slow-uncertain step. Jack and Leah 'on eggs' throughout.

Pausing at the entrance (for a moment), he (at last) turned.. caught his breath.. and there-after, called out (as though, at someone across the valley)…

"THANK YOU!.."

There was a goose-bumping, chilly pause. Hair-tingling! Then, again…

"THANK YOU!.." This (the latter) sounding choked and extremely emotion-al.. Causing Jack and Leah to gulp and shiver in its echo. And that, of which (the reverberation) being greeted in its 'boomerang' with the 'BAM!' of his door. This being the first time ever Jack had heard him speak! Short of in his singing. His voice was somehow so comforting to hear. Oh, how he loved the old man!

Through starting tears, Jack eye-darted down to Leah. But per usual, she had disappeared. Gone in a spark! If only he could've spoken with her about this! For it all had been so eventful and exciting! And as well, heart-discomforting in the same! And, in so, confusing! Now over and done with, his sadness was greater than ever! From an 'all-time high' to an 'all-time-low' in an instant. He needed someone to discuss this with! And who.. better than her?

In trembling desperation, he shot for the cave. For maybe.. just maybe.. she would be there. But (at last) at its location, he found it silent and void. Slow-ly (in his blurring scan) he noted.. the Bible! Yes, it was still shelved-'n-there. "Whew!.." She'd be back!

Springingly he took it (and, in the same fashion, a seat) to read. Splitting its mass at-randomly, he began in at the page's top…

"Daniel.."

Then letting his eyes drift down the text, he started at Chapter Five. In short time, becoming totally absorbed in it.

By the conclusion of this grouping, he felt very confused by it all.. and (in lifting his eyes from its finish) he noted that the dark (Which had fallen greatly, during his absorb-tion!) was heavily upon him. This making him shiver-sharply in both. Un-nerved, he flipped the pages to…

"Hosea?.."

This time beginning at the start (of the entire heading, as not to mis-interpret), he read all the way through Chapter Four, Verse Five, stopping there. For somehow, that (among other verses there-in) seemed to greatly apply to him personally. Yes, and to the events he'd witnessed in the Lorraine Village. Not literally or directly.. but still, 'somehow' related to it all! He wondered, was he (himself) making it so? Yes, reading 'into' it, with that (all the while) on his mind? And in so, strangely tying them together? Fear-warping the text? Or was he truly seeing something here? A connection? It sure seemed so! Was it 'a message' to him? I mean, had he really, in fact, witnessed something relevant to it all? In the vast scheme of things! He felt so unsure. Maybe he should continue?

This he did.. stopping at 9-11. The book was closed there. And he contemplated on it now, peering fearfully around himself. He must put it aside. For it was too dark now. He must try to relax.

That night was the worst-of-all that he'd spent there. Feeling terribly uncomfortable and restless, he found himself roaming and pacing the woods. Walking on eggshells throughout. Hearing sounds(in so and constantly) and anxiously head-darting at them in the bleak dark. Only to find nothing!

At last, wandering (in his nervousness) to the old-timer's cabin, he came to feel the 'odd-presence' of something (?) about him there. Yes, there in the immediate area and the night. It (?).. settling itself about and around the inhabitants. This..

sending a violent shiver through him in his initial notice of it, as he slow-'n-silently crept up to the rear window's beckoning-like light. That, of which (this glow).. being caused by a candlestick resting on the inner frame, that shone out slightly from (what he felt sure to be..) the old maestro's bedroom. Its dim, yellowing-like ray casting a moving sheen on the just-below and outside snow mound.

Having pretty much left the tree-line, he moved in closer, out of a morbid curiosity. At last, coming to a startling stop at its bordering-the-cabin surface. For now and at this near-ness, he could see it! Yes, perfectly at this angle! There (in the virgin-ness of its smooth..) on the mound, lay a strange symbol! This.. like 'finger-grooved'.. with no surrounding-it footprints, making it seem all-the-more mysterious for its existence. Appearing like a circle.. with two parallel lines running aside each other, cutting center and down through it…

What did it mean? Who had put it there? It absolutely confounded him! He quickly peered about, then back at it. It was intended for him.. he felt that! Knew that! Or at least, he felt sure he knew that! He was so scared! Wanting to run.

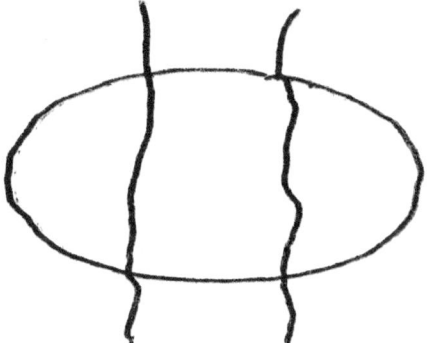

Turning to do so.. but instead holding himself, he spun back.. trying to figure it. Make some kind of 'sense' out of it! Had someone from the Lorraine Village put it there? Had.. God? Who?

Then, remembering the first-of-texts that he had read earlier, that night (in the Bible), he saw a strange similarity here. Yes, to it.. and this at-present experience. He must return to the cave-crest and re-read it!

So about-facing, he began off. Running with all of his might. Through the dark and winding pathways. And trembling terribly, throughout it all!

Finally reaching the earthly in-groove, he made in-a-flash for the ledge. But.. but.. but.. it was gone? Yes, Leah's Bible! Quick and uncertainly, he looked about. Then below to the ground, that it might've slipped-off somehow? But, no.. it was gone! In eye-return, he reached forward and felt the ledge's cold-bare surface with his shaking-awful hand.. as if it might better serve him than his sight. But still, it was gone.. and that was all there was to it! Now he felt all-the-more confused and upset! Quiverin'-'n-shiverin' like a hurricaned-leaf , he graspingly wrapped himself in his arms (as though to try 'n support his rib cage from its rattling.. and for that, the possibility of its ultimately-falling-apart!). Then in a sort of surrendering, he fell back against the hard, behind-him surface. At last, allowing his back to coarsely grade its way down the cave's wall to a sliding-seated stance. He felt so faint! And, weak! But, he must recover. He couldn't afford to be unconscious now! So, with deep breaths, he forced himself through.. peering around-and-about the area simultaneously in it. He couldn't leave. No matter what! No, first he must see Leah and the old fiddler, before doing a thing!

Day, at last, broke. Jack having not slept a wink. Throughout the entire A. M., he sat in exact stance. Waiting.

By afternoon though, he was up and pacing. For Leah had yet to show. 'Well, after all..' he justified.. 'she had said that today was Easter!.. Maybe there's a good reason for her delay?..'

But with steady progression of the P. M... and still 'no sign of her' (nor the old-timer), Jack began having serious doubts. Still, he would wait.

Late day and fall-of-dusk, it hit him. And at last, he understood. Yes, the old man had passed away! And as a result, that was why Leah had never come. Nor, would she ever again! That, as well, was the reason (he deciphered) for the disappearance of the Bible. It was over. Forever! He could hardly bear it, in the realization.. falling onto the cold, hard ground in agony. There, hanging his head between his all-fours. Where would he go now? Or even better.. 'how' would he go now?

He just couldn't take it anymore!

Then.. coming slowly-but-surely to him (in his noting of it through his anguish) began an increasing wind-stir. This.. from the direction of the Lorraine Village. In progressions, hitting and waking him out of his grief. Bringing him back to an even-harsher reality! Jack, at last, raising his blurry (yet, fearful..) eyes in its direction. Remembering!

With its tremendous-now howl and lash, Jack hopped afoot. His 'scare' finally overpowering his 'sadness'. In a jolt, he began off. And away. Picking up speed with each leaping bound. Never once (throughout) looking back at the monument of the old-timer. For he chose to remember him as he'd last seen him. Happy and smiling in his fervent execution of the Carol. That was memory-enough! True memory! For in his heart, the old fiddler was still (and would always be..) alive. And, Leah.. she too would remain there, as well. He knew he'd see her again. When?.. he didn't know! But someday.. somewhere.. in his travels! Yes, they'd always be 'the dearest of pals'!

Across the slopes, he sped.. slipping and sliding in every-which direction in his escape. Hearing in his mind (and all-the-while).. and trying desperately to sing it to himself, in so, for comfort...

"That Old Road.. Never We'll walk..

In the Land Where We Never Grow Old...

That Old Road.. Never We'll walk..

In the Land Where We Never Grow Old."

– ORCHID LADY ELEGY (REFRAIN) –

'So Dearly Loved.. The Orchid Lady'

Jack had scraped-clean the flat-to-the-ground, grey head-stone in several, quick hand-swipes.. and now stood above, reading it.

The Garden of Prayer was deathly dark and silent. For it was very late night. Jack's scarf moved freely.. though not flappingly, for his mediative state.

After his timely study, he slowly raised his head and scanned the about-grave-yard. Being that the site was on elevated ground, he (as well and in so) gazed about at the surrounding-and-bordering houses in the off-shoot. Then, further and beyond them at the lights and glow of the Musical City. This.. almost seeming to have tiny-electrical sparkles in it, from the extreme-bitter cold. These molecules.. ascending upward-ish within the outline of the jet-black night. The ever-harsh air making his eyes blur-'n-smear them. The steam of his breath, so full.. it being their only obstruction!

Back to the stone and his meditation, he went. Why had he returned, he wondered? For she was dead! He'd known that! Gone forever! So.. Why? He didn't have the faintest! Still, something (?) had brought him back again. Oh.. yes.. 'the Loss'! Maybe it had been misplaced here? That.. and, well.. he really just didn't know why-else exactly! But it seemed at least familiar-enough ground to re-trace. So, yes.. why not? At this point, nothing (quite honestly) made much sense anyhow! Yes.. and just everything was getting pretty messed-up anyways! So what did it really matter? Besides and as well.. at least, he somehow felt safer here. For the time bein', anyways!

Memories flooded his mind.. of the Goodwill Shrine.. Thomas (the harmonica player).. Sister Roberta and Mother Superior Elizabeth.. and so on. Would they all still be here? What would be different now? Yes, what would this trip bring?

Then (and very startling enough at that!).. from somewhere near and above him.. in the darkness.. came a.. a whispering voice! Stopping him instantly in his thoughts. For never, ever had he heard one like so!

Fearfully (in ready-to-split stance!), he listened further. It voicing again softly…
"Jack-Jack…"

Was it her? The Orchid Lady? He spun his head in search. But there was nothing! Or better yet, no one!

Gulping a sharp swallow, he (almost dizzy from the scare of it) listened harder.
"Jack-Jack.. Don't-be-frightened.. It-is-only-I.." This (the latter part especial-

ly..) executed extremely fast. And, in so, ringing a very distant, inner bell.

It couldn't be her.. for it was a male's voice! Shivering (Despite the speaker's comforting), he held tight for.. for? He didn't know what for, exactly!

Into the sounds of the 'whooshing winds' about and surrounding, came…

"Jack.. it-is-only-I.. Johnny!.. The-Angel-of-the-Musical-Spirit!.. Remember-me, Bud?.."

Jack answering in stutter and gulp…

"Y.. y.. yeah.. " eased slightly by the knowing.. "Y.. yeah.. Sure I do!.." Then (after a pause), truly inquisitive, he resumed.. " Yeah, I do!.. But.. but.. Why.. Why do y' speak t' me?.. I mean.. Well.. W.. Why have y' come?.." facing the direction and origin of the voice. For there was no image.

It coming again…

"I'm-here-t'-bring-you-good-cheer, this-new-season-'a-Christmas!… Y' know, like.. well.. 'Tis-the-season-that-you'll-find-out.. Fa-la-la-la-la.. la-la-la-la!.. Ha!.. Ha!.. Ha!.." (The ending laughs executed earnest and sincere-like).

Jack interrupting, but really-'n-more to himself…

"Oh, yeah.. it is Christmas-time, isn't it!.. I'd.. well.. I'd forgotten!.. Yes, it is Ch-.."

The Spirit slicing Jack's meditation…re-entering..

"See-man-I-was.. well, I-was.. Y' know, sent-t'.. well, t'.."

Jack re-interrupting..

"Why y' talkin' t' me anyways?.. I mean.. Well, after all 'a this time.. it just don't.."

"Well, it's-like-this, Jack.. Time-has-changed-'n-well, there's-been-some-changes-'n-well, you've-noticed-'em, right?.. I mean.. You-saw-Leah, right?.. 'n.."

"But, why now?.." Jack halting the machine gunner. Though only split-second-momentarily.

"Well, f'-one-thing.. you've-changed-Jack!.. I-mean, man-haven't-you-noticed-it?"

"Well?.. Well?.. " Truly uncertain. Jack looking down and over himself.. in so, re-noting the only 'showing' difference. His insignia! Grabbing up the scarf and pointing-it-like in his direction… " Do y' mean this?.."

"Well-that's-sorta-part-of-it, Jack.. but, well.. you-lost-somethin'-'n-gained-some-"

"D' you.." Jack cutting in again.. "Do you know what it was?.. " truly excited in the thought and chance that Johnny might.

The Musical Spirit (unsure now, if they were speaking about the same thing) stuttering back…

"Well.. it's.. well-it's.. I-don't-think-I.. Well?.. What-exactly-are-you.. Well.. Ah.. ah.."

Jack.. confounded now, as well.. cutting in to spare him any further babble…

"Ah.. forget it!.."

A silence followed. At last, broken by Johnny…

"Anyways.. my-time's-runnin'-out-here, Jack.. Let-me-tell-y'-what-I-came-t'.." momentarily losing track of himself (Still somewhat lost in the previous confusion).. But then catching… "Ah.. ah.. Well?.. Oh, yeah!.. Gabriel.. He-wanted-me-t'-tell-"

"Gabriel!.." Jack snapping.. "Y' know, that's the second time, 'a recent, that his.."

Johnny trying to fight through…

"Anyways-he-wanted-me-t'-tell-you-that.." stopping, for Jack was not listening, in the least. Instead, still ramblin' on to himself…

"name's come up!.. Y' know, I never could fig're that whole.. "

"Jack!.. He-wanted-me-t'-tell-you-that-very-soon.. God-is-gonna-put-it-in-your-heart-the-reason-that-that.."

He.. still not listening, for… "thing out!.. It just seemed like.."

"Jack!.. Jack!.." The Musical Spirit's voice starting to grow dimmer.

"Y' know.. like.. well.. it just seemed that.." Jack, still babbling.

"Jack!.. Jack!.." This vanishing rapidly-now in volume. Until it had disappeared. Jack noting that though! And in the realization of his error, calling…

"Johnny?.. Johnny?.. Where've y' gone?.. Ah, man.. I didn't mean t'.. Well, I.. I just…

Johnny?.. Johnny?.. Come back!.. 'n tell me!.. I want to know!.. I really want t' know!.. "   This.. 'til it was obviously to no use. In the aftermath, mumbling to himself.. "I wonder what it was that he had to tell me?.. from Gabriel?.. Gosh, why d' I always do that?.. Dang!.."

– EASTER EVERLASTING –

The Musical City was exactly as he'd left it. Or at least, it seemed so at first glance. It'd never change! The Lower Broad still having its more-than-fair-share of loitering vagrants, bag people and drunkards. Its nightspots, still blaring-out their music onto the evening's neon-lit streets. And in the same, thwarting any notions that Jack might've had of pursuing his own to the inside-audiences.

There were several newly-constructed buildings. Jack (walking endlessly through the district) noted them, on occasions, in his search. Thomas (the harmonicat!) was his first-of projects. But after several days and nights of fruitless endeavor, he gave it up for lost. For the lad was simply nowhere to be found! Time had absolutely erased him from the scene. Yes, totally! Gone forever.. somewhere? And as well, along with him, his friend Earl.   Yes, he too.. disappeared now without a trace!

The holiday's approach brought with it the sights and sounds of the season. Christmas lights in the shop-fronts.. Carolers.. and so on. And as Jack grew wearier and wearier in his search.. at last, on the late day of Christmas Eve, he did find enlightenment.

Having passed the Goodwill Shrine-and-Store throughout all of the previous in his travels, he had not though made much of 'pursuing it'. This, for obvious reasons. The Orchid Lady was gone now.. and really, why bother?   But with gradual-mounting-and-festering anxiety in him (due to all of the former mentioned dead-ends), he, at last, found himself returning to it. This.. as a sort of 'last resort', before moving on, for good and forever.

The earlier morning, that had reeked with drear.. now, whitened. With snow. Somewhat illuminating the still-smeared, blackened-cold sky.

The main thoroughfare was busy (and would have been, despite whatever the weather), due to the 'last minute' (as always!) Christmas shoppers. Jack, parking metered, watched them enter the daybreak in their yawning-hurried bustles. Heavily clothed and wrapped for his presence.

The Goodwill Shrine (his target) lay dead on. Eye-sighted and across the way. Still closed from the previous day, but 'in business'. This, known from having noted before-hand. He waited impatiently. Wondering if the nuns would work on Christmas Eve.. What, with all else they'd have to do church-wise.

But when, at last, Mother Superior Elizabeth wobbled her way into view (down

the opposing sidewalk), his uncertainties were relievingly squelched. Yes, they'd be open!

As Mother Superior began her tangle with the door's latch, Jack made-in for right behind her. This (in completion), bringing forth-'n-out of her…

"Dear Lord.. is it cold today!.. Brrr!.." And in the same, forcing her into a fumbling hurry.

Finally releasing the padlock, she pushed ever-forcefully on the door with her short, yet-stocky body.. squeezing herself in.. trying desperately (in so) not to allow (as well) the encompassing and surrounding draft. But this, to no avail! For above and around her, it came.. gushing-'n-gusting in.. and disruptly flapping all of the still-hanging-there wall decorations. She flabbergastedly hem-hawin' to herself in it, as she (in a second's-after recovery and flash) turned to pouncingly slam tight the wooden separator. Jack immediately putting his face to its glass, looking through, and seeing what-he-believed-to-be her melancholy recall of its 'similar happening', years before. Yes, when the Orchid Lady had been there, and she (with the other nuns) had ran to help her 'shut him out' then. It was there, in her face.. and he could read it as plain as day. Yes, he was sure it was this, that she was thinking of! And when her reddening-eyes-'n-tears came, he was double-certain! Things like that (Though simple and seeming-trite) will most-surely bring back such memories. After all, it had likewise brought the 'same' back to Jack! And he gulped in it, watching her now. Her face (in this) somehow 'momentarily-'n-miraculously' becoming the face of the Orchid Lady's! Then slowly, blurring back to that of Mother Superior's! And, hers.. seeming 'as ardently-a-stare (back at him)' as had been the previous's! Making him (as in days past) wonder if she might, in fact, see him through the glass? He nervously twitching his face in the thought. But her quick spin, back and away.. and hurrying-off, proved otherwise. And he, breathing freer in it.

Before he could re-swing his stance out and towards the main avenue, Sister Roberta bustled around-and-by him, tangling her way (as well) into the store. She being 'so involved in trying not to be late', that she had hardly noticed the extremely-bitter-cold wind pocket. Though Mother Superior yelling at her and bringing it to her attention, as she stood there now in the wide-opened entranceway…

"Sister Roberta.. Please!.. Shut that door!.." In fumbling compliance, she doing so as quickly as possible. And in this, she (as well) recalling the 'very moment' of the Orchid Lady. For Jack could again see it in her look. Only hers, not being as long-lived as was Mother Superior's. This, for the latter's disruption…

"Sister Roberta!.. Don't just stand there!.. " Though in fact, she wasn't!.. "We've got much to do to prepare for our day.. After all, it is Christmas Eve!.. You know that!.. So, come.. Let us begin!.." and the nun doing so, without enough time to dwell on the recall.

Jack watched them as they hurried about in their chores. It bringing back the recall of the penguins. In his homeland. And the earlier mishap of the one that had rammed into him at the time. And this, as a result, likewise-recalling the thoughts of the Our Lady of Pity Church.. How the penguins had helped him remember it! Maybe that's what this visit here might do for him now?.. Somehow help him remember 'the Loss'? Or even something closely related to it? Anything would be of-help, at this point! He wished (for a moment) that he had contained himself better to have 'heard out' the Angel of the Musical Spirit. Yes, on the night of his re-entrance to the Musical City. But it was too late now! He wondered if he might return again, and speak now? His eyes spinning about-himself in a flashing (and fleeting) hope. But of course, nothing! Things like that never happen, when you're hoping they will. Why did he always do that? Ramble on, rather than listen? It was the same, even with Leah.. and with all of the things she tried to tell him! He wondered now, if it was a result of his constant solitude.. and how, when finally an ear did appear.. Well, he just simply couldn't control himself any longer! Who knows? But whatever, he wished now that he'd listened. That, for sure!

Thinking on, he returned to the Our Lady of Pity Church and that graveyard. There was definitely something very strange and confusing about all 'a that! He wondered just what it might be though? For there was some sort of an 'eerie dichotomy' about it in his mind. Something about the place seemed to be forever calling him. At least, since, for sure! Yet, another part of him wanted to stay absolutely clear of it! It was weird! But he wouldn't be heading there now anyways.. so…

As the morn progressed, Jack grew tired of lingering about the Shrine. For nothing at all seemed to be happening. His caroling went unheard in their fury-of-business. Yes, they just seemed 'too caught up' in their affairs to even pay him the slightest bit of mind! So at last, he re-crossed the avenue, re-parking-metering himself in the same.. Listening to the cornered (-now) minstrels to his left, performing their carols to the passing peds.. With their tip can occasionally chiming from coin. The remainder of the unfruitful day being spent as so.

With fall of the night and the tremendous 'slowing' of traffic, Jack began wandering up the ascending (to his left) avenue aimlessly. This, for nothing better to do. In his initial efforts, recalling the two fur-coated-'n-toothless street minstrels; looking over his right shoulder (and across the street) at their once-spot.. and in the moment's after, re-turning to continue his uphill climb. Wonder where they are now? Gone.. like everyone else, pretty much! Oh, it seemed such a waste of time now! This trip. Why had he even bothered with it?

After nearly twenty blocks of straggling-along travel, ahead (in the night's descending-darker and silencing dusk) Jack caught sight of a church. One, that immediately reminded him of the 'Our Lady of Pity'. Yes, huge! Though different, in that it was fronted by the main street's sidewalk (and not by a lawn, fences, etc.).

In nearing surveillance, he (as well) noted that there was no little chapel tacked to its rear (as with the previously-mentioned assembly). Yet still, it was all so majestically reminiscent. At least, in its structure and protruding-out stature! Jack paused in the fore-ground of it, studying up at its royalty.

It emotionally moving him greatly. And in all of his melancholy and depression (Which the sight of this only seemed to be compounding in him), he momentarily glanced down upon his scarf. At the initials. They reminding him of Johnny.. and even greater, of the night of-recent that he'd spent in the Lorraine-Village-Church's outer vestibule. There had been something 'very special' about that night. And the events leading him to it. As well, that morning. Something mystical! He wasn't quite sure what all of it had meant?.. even now.. but, still.. it had been a 'monumental' event! He did know that! For somehow, he sensed it to have re-kindled a very 'old' (and 'seeming forgotten') feeling in him. Yet, totally new, if that seemed possible? Deep down in his soul! This.. oddly-enough, very comforting. And 'comfort' being something he had not known for the 'most' of his time! And as well, in this.. somehow 'everything else in his existence (even his Crusade)' seemed to pale. Yes, become over-shadowed by it! In the same, making all-else become secondary. I mean, it was all still there (in him).. but now, there was something greater! Something truly-and-always gratifying and fulfilling. Yes, something of greater grandeur. And importance. And he longed to experience it again. Yes, now! Only there was no outer (and opened-air) vestibule here. There were only doors leading directly inside!

He peered about quickly. There was no one. Might he attempt a brief 'step in'? Could he contain himself in it, in case there were people inside? He didn't know. But he could try!

Casually (but sneakingly) converging closer, he cracked-open the large door, peeking in. It was more silent inside than out! And from what he could see from his stance, uninhabited! Putting his first foot in, he waited to hear a reaction. But, nothing! Just the squish's echo and only more silence. So pushing his weight forward, in he slivered.. letting the door click soft behind him.

After a fair pause for listen, on he darted to the inner doors. They, propped open.. but, this.. to confirm his alone-ness. Yes, it was empty, just as he'd first suspected. And, dim. Very much so! And solemn, as well. You could've heard an ice drop!

Should he continue in? No, he downwardly shook his head to himself. In this, catching the sight (out of the corner of his eye..) of a beside-him doorway. This, no doubt, leading up to the above-him choir loft. Yes, in there he would go!.. And did so, accordingly.

Hand-supporting the door frame behind him (that its latch would only barely snap), up he began. The stairs, being narrow and curving-to-the-right at the very top. When there at the bend, he paused momentarily to survey-'in-a-peek' around it first, before resuming in his creep. No one was there! So continuing the turn, upward and in he went.

A slight vestibule greeted him.. Very dark and cluttered with old chairs (folding and regular). These, he felt (without touch) very dusty! Out and beyond all on the main landing, there was light (at least, reasonable light) and a welcoming opened-ness. So through the archway he crept, pulling his coldness inward. Checking ahead (in so) for persons. But thankfully, there was not a single one!

Onto the large landing, he squished. Creaking his way, as well. The latter, for the aged floorboards. In an instant, he unknowingly kicked a discarded pen across the planked and bumpy wooden slats. He hadn't seen it ahead of him in the drear. This.. adrenalin-filling-him into stopped and cringed stance. In a gulp, he watched it in its continuing-somersaulting flight. Breathing freer in its furthering disappearance. Whew! Lifting his head and re-focussing across the huge platform, he saw a large organ on the opposing side. Its non-painted (unfinished) backside facing him. Propped in this fashion to addressingly face the line of seats, just ahead of him. These.. aimed forward towards the main church and altar for the choir members.

Scanning to his right, he eyed-along the loft's high-standing fence. This, with its solid-bottom half. Topped with its fancy-'n-lathed-circular guard-rail (This.. perfect for 'peeking-out-'n-over's!). It.. stained dark-brown. These.. double-pur-posely-intended (he felt sure) to prevent the church body from looking up at and, in so, distracting the singers. To it he moved, hopping up on a chair and peering down at the empty pews below. And in the same, at the seeming-so-far-off and ahead-now altar. It all appearing 'high-enough-up' to momentarily jolt him into a sudden 'dizzy'. Pulling back, he regained himself and bracingly returned, holding (in so) the ledge for another viewing. It was beautiful! Truly breathtaking!

Absorbing himself, he stared ahead at the majestic-radiating altar. His hands gripping two of the circular-fence-pegs (looking like-as-if a prisoner behind bars). And in this, he withdrawingly noted his dirty-numbed fingers and nails respec-tively. This, making him feel all-the-more ashamed and unworthy of being there. Quickly in a re-scan of the altar, he whispered...

"God.. I'm sorry!.. Really!.. All I ever wanted t' do was please you.. 'n look what a mess its all become!.. I.. I didn't mean f' it t'...

Well, y' know what I.. I.. I am!.." his voice stutteringly cracking for the erupting emotion…

".. and, well.. as f' the New Work.. Well, I.. I just don't feel…

Well, f' one, I don't even really know exactly what.. Well, what y' want me t'.. t'.."

Before he could utter a word more, came a voice behind him…

"Jack?.."

This, freezing him into 'instant still'! His eyes, at last, shooting to his left. But, his head, not following.. nor allowing them to continue their search. There was a deathly silence. He knew he'd heard it?

"Jack?.."

Yes, he had! At least, this time, for sure! Slowly pivoting in his breathlessness.. he, at last, exhaled in a startled wind…

"Len?.. Wh.. What are you doing here?.." Yes, there in front of him now stood the Angel of a Chord! He returning in the exact tone…

"What are you doin' here?.."

Jack stuttering-out in his confounded amazement…

"Ah… ah… ah…"

"I'm here to study the choir!.." Len taking the reigns, as steadfast and as-stern-appearing as he had always been… "The choirmaster, Mr. Strubbel.. he's a wonder.. Yes, an absolute wonder!.. I come here often!.. But, you.. Jack.. What're you doing here?"

"Ah… ah… I… I dunno, t' tell the truth!.. I just.. just.."

"Well, anyways.. here y' are, right?.."

"Yeah.." Jack turning back with his face in a question-marked-like stare.

At that, Len moved away.. over to the organ to surround it and sit. Jack squeak-ingly tagging him (in wonder over his taken silence).

When comfortably seated, Len played a chord. Jack (shoulder-leaning on its edge to watch) listened. It.. ascending upward-like and sounding so beautiful, as it echoed throughout the entire inner sanctum. Then, to it, Len added several melody notes. These seeming vaguely familiar. And Jack (puzzling in-himself) tried to place them. Len, at last, looking up from his brief stop…

"I've been workin' on this.. What 'a y' think?.."

"Ah, well.. yeah, it's pretty.. but I don't…"

"Recognize it?.." Len finishing his sentence.

"Yeah.. I don't really.. Well, it does ring a bell, but.." Jack quite naturally expecting it to be one of Len's own. Yes, something he'd created.. either alone or with one of the other Herald Angels.

Len, cutting in.. "It's your tune.."

Jack hearing it then, with Len's resuming help on the keyboard…

"Yeah.. Yeah, it is!.. Ain't it!…"

Len adding.. "Just played a lot slower!.."

Jack nodding back. Then closing his eyes, he re-listened. In so, totally losing himself. For it just sounded so.. so moving now! So solemn and different-like! The church-sounding chord movements that Len was adding fitted so well. It was astounding! Jack was so ecstatic and jubilant, he felt to cry. He'd never conceived of 'how religious'-a-piece it could sound. Until now! And he floated with it. Ascending up-'n-away on its melodic-free-flow. And this 'blinding-of-himself' made his ears seem 'all-the-more'-attuned and aware. He was flying! On each note!

Then out of nowhere, he fell! Ka-plump! It ending in mid-note. Forcefully blurring through his watery-eyes, he came to focus on.. nothing! Or maybe I should say, no one! Len had disappeared! Gone in a split second! But, where? Jack (in his awakening) spun about. But, he was.. nowhere?

"Len?.."

Nothing.

"Len... Where are y' ?.."

Back towards the now-empty organ stool...

"Len?.." soft-like.

Had it only been a 'hallucination'? Or some sort of 'vision'? He grabbed his forehead. Feeling a bit faint. He'd have sworn that.. Well.. Yes, he was sure that he?.. How could this be happening?

Pivoting himself around and back towards the line of choir chairs, he voiced again..

"Len?.."

In this, hearing beyond them, the stairwell's below-door opening. Accompanied by soon-to-follow human voices. It was.. the.. Choir! Oh, no! No wonder Len had split!

In un-nerved confusion, he began a run towards the staircase (momentarily dropping his concern over Len).. stopping just before the little hallway. What was he doing? He must regain himself! Spinning around and about, in search for a place to hide (For the voices and footsteps were rapidly nearing the top landing now), he leftwardly noted an on-rollers blackboard that was angled out-and-at-him from the fencing. And in this, partitioning the main loft from its near-the-wall stance. It creating a conveniently-placed 'dark'. In behind it, he darted. Panting profusely (Though as 'quietly' as possible) in his 'stooping' stare-out. All, just in the nick-of-time too! For here they came. Trooping out. One of the choir girls (in her en-'lightening' entrance) complaining to another...

"Gol-ly.. is it cold up here!.. Huh?.."

Jack gulping in this.

"Yes, it is!.. " Her recipient agreeing.

"They've got to get some heat up here.. I swear!.." resumed the first. They, in further, taking their seats.. Tagged by the line of other converging men and women.

In his silence and dark, Jack wondered again over Len's disappearance. Was he (as well) still here?.. Somewhere's hid?.. Oh, well.. even if he was, there was hardly a thing he could do about it now anyways! For he was trapped. At least, for the time being.

After the general confusion and turmoil of their seating, the choir attended themselves in forward gaze.. listening.. as their leader began in with his 'uplifting' address…

"Well, hello everyone!.."

They.. "Hello, Mr. Strubbel!.."

He resuming, after his acknowledging nods…

"Well, here we are!.. And here it has come!.. Yes, Christmas Eve!.. What we've all been rehearsing for, for so long now!…

Yes, this Midnight Mass.. and of course, Easter's Celebration.. are our most important of the Liturgical Year!.. And we all know how hard we've prepared and toiled for this occasion!…

So let's all give it our bests!.. Okay?.."

This being met with (as would've been expected!)…

"Yes, Mr. Strubbel!.." in almost melodic/ harmonic-like unison. And as well, a scattering of applause following.

Down below in the lower church, people were entering.. and Jack caught sound of their disrupting noises. This pulling him deeper into the crevice to peer out-and-over the ledge. Coincidentally, a chair had been propped there, allowing him (in a hop) immediate-access to this end.

Now, up.. he could see perfectly down-and-on them, through the railing. Only problem was.. now (due to the main assembly's centering-and-massive ceiling posts and supports, that ran down both sides of the hall and middle-seating to the altar, separating it into quarter seating sections) he could only view the Fourth (1/4) section in front-and-straight-ahead of him. The right hand rows. No longer the main center aisles, podium or beyond. Instead now, directly ahead in the far-front receptacle, he could only see a huge, life-sized statue of Jesus on the Cross. And its figure.. flesh-toned.. making it all appear so real! In front of it, the devotion candles flickered on their roll-able stands.

After a fair study of it all, Jack crept back to the other end of the partition to peek around at the hushed-now choir. They.. still snuggling themselves in their coats and tremblingly leafing through their texts. Some talking in whisper amongst themselves. Though most, in silent and 'cold' wait.

Choirmaster Strubbel was re-positioned now to a stance by the organ, speaking (with his back to Jack) with the musician. Discussing the program. Though this, in assumption (on Jack's part), for it was all too far away for any audibility.

Then (returning Jack to the railing) came an announcement over the Public Address System (Though the speaker himself not viewable). This.. sounding to be from the altar of the church...

"We must apologize, folks, for the cold.. We can't understand it.. Our heating system is up to its absolute max!.. We assure you!...

But we have called-in for an Emergency Crew.. and they should be here, as soon as possible, to check it out for us!...

We appreciate your patience and understanding.. and hope that it will be in-order by Mid-Mass.. Thank you!..."

At this, Jack cringed and slightly blushed.. and tried harder to pull-in his cold. For he didn't want to leave. Not now. This was all just too interesting! And (as he had hoped), in the same, comforting! Yes, there was a strange.. but, good feeling in being here. Despite his 'not feeling worthy'-ness!

There was a cold (and I say that very 'literally') silence following, while more parishioners entered and seated themselves. After what-seemed-like five-to-ten minutes of this filing and filling, the entire lower level was jam-packed (or at least, it appeared to be, considering what Jack could see from his side). He felt somehow relieved in seeing it.. For he knew that the 'body heat' alone (Due to their great-

'n-squeezing masses) would afford an even-quicker warming of the building. Or at least, this he prayed! Though he couldn't help but notice (in this justification), how none-of-the-below were loosening-or-discarding their outer wear! Still, time might change that.

Then, with a sudden 'fall of hush' upon the crowd, it came. The announcer's proclamation…

"The Twenty-fifth day of December. In the Five Thousand, one hundred and ninety-ninth year of the Creation of the World, from the time when God in the beginning created the Heaven and the Earth; The Two Thousand nine hundred and fifty-seventh year after the flood; The Two Thousand and fifteenth year from the Birth of Abraham;" Etc., etc…

Jack listened pensively. Hanging on each line. It was so stirring, that he tingled and marveled in it. And by its conclusion, he found himself wobbling and trembling in spirit. It was beautiful! And touching!

Then, down the aisle (from beneath the choir loft in the vestibule) came the procession of altar boys and priests, carrying the golden cross, lit candles and the burning incense shakers. It all (in the dimming-now of the house lights) glowing brighter in its movement forward.

Towards the altar (and out-of-sight for Jack), they proceeded. He (blurry-eyed) watched them disappear, one by one. His entire being.. now, a strange-and-intense mixture of jubilance and fear. But regardless (in its paradox), he never would've chosen to have been anywhere else. This was pure rapture! And along with the choir's entry and accompaniment to it (of "Joy to the World"), it was so glorifying and exciting, that he had to support himself on the fencing (that, not to fall from his inner shaking). But in doing this.. again his eyes scanned down and upon his hands. This, making him feel all-the-worse! Heavy distress came over him.. Covering him (internally), as if and as-though, a large bucket of black paint had just been poured down and upon his head.. and was descending its way, slowly-but-syrup-ly, over his total being. Reverently he removed his hat, breathing heavily to try to recover himself.

Then, all of a sudden, it hit him! A revelation.. coming to relievingly distract and thwart his anguish. A mind-blowing revelation! Yes, a tremendous and over-powering idea! And a beautiful-a-beauty-of-a-one too! It was like there was a voice that was calling him. A message that only he could hear! And understand! This changing his entire consciousness and mood in a flash! He wondered if it had been inspired by Len's rendition of his 'Carol'? He really wasn't sure? Maybe it had been the result of things that Leah or Johnny had said? He truly didn't know now? But, whatever?.. or somehow?.. it was just there! And clear as a bell at that! Yes, telling him (through-out the unfolding of the Mass and its continuing cer-emony) 'tremendous things' concerning his 'Carol' and what its ultimate purpose and outcome would be! Yes.. and now seeing exactly what his new job was to be! Yes, his new work.. no longer vague and uncertain.. but absolutely clarified!

Then to momentarily baffle his jubilance in it all, came the thought that 'maybe this was just a result of he himself'? Yes, his imagination! He wondered. No, it surely didn't seem so. It was all just too intense for that! No, this felt, as though, 'inspired' from on High! Imparted down and into his heart. As a gift. But, Why him, he puzzled. Yes.. Why him? He was just so unworthy of such a vision! Yet, in spite and regardless, his soul floated in the ecstatic discovery of it. Yes, he could hear it in his mind. His Carol.. with words added to it.. and sung by choirs. Yes, entire choirs.. in harmony with each other! And he could envision it, as well, com-ing out of the sky and clouds.. and down upon the Earth.. In its hallowed beauty! The melody and tempo slowed tremendously.. like Len's execution earlier.. But instead, accompanied with the entry of a single singing voice (and this, backed by the solemn humming of others). It.. sung in Hebrew.. and in two-note-(for the syllable)-to-the-seven of his melody. This song continuing throughout, telling the story of the Deliverance of the Jewish People by its First-of-Prophets. And it (in progression) changing its numbering system to suit; Despite the simultane-ous entry (after the second verse) of an entirely different other hymn (by another choir). Yes, sort of as an extension or representation of it into Christianity. This.. sung in three-notes-to-the-seven.. and in Greek. The two choirs jelling together in a (despite their difference) 'unique-harmony-of-their-own'. And this (as well), the story of the very beginning of the church. Then, by the third part.. again enters a totally new choir.. Singing in four-to-the-seven.. and in Latin, now! And this, too.. blending with the 'two prior' beautifully!.. Into a massive-like sound! And continuing the history of the Christian Church in song. What a 'hymn of praise' to the Father, Most High!

Jack held his face and head in the overwhelming intensity of it all. Yes, it was just absolutely mind-blowing! The Mass and Choir (about him) moved on through its celebration. But Jack glided away still.. and only further into it. Hearing its 'continue' in his mind. All this, singing and praising the Infinite Glory of our Eternal Father.. and as well, of the Salvation through Christ Jesus! And in the same, to the Power of the Holy Spirit! And it, throughout in this.. building in tempo and speed. All heading towards a climaxing end. And Jack (upon hearing and sensing this) nervously sniveling and pinching at his under-nose for distraction. It was just all so intense! He could hardly stand it! He wondered if anyone else (present) was feeling this 'hysteria'?.. and momentarily and fidgetingly looked around and about him. But it seemed no one else was.

Then it hit! The Climax! The tremendous, tremendous 'Amen' .. with all of the voices pounding in one! With crushing-like power.. and reverberating for what-felt-like ten minutes! Jack gasped exceedingly through its pulsating-away, resonant drone. His mind exploding in ecstatic confusion.. and ultimately, relief!.. If that (the two together) were possible? Yes, the blend of these 'opposing feelings' creating 'Absolute Mental Pandemonium'!

With and in the dead-hush that followed its finale and 'grand rapture', came (into his mind) the words that exhaled themselves from his quivering lips…

"Easter Everlasting…" These.. in shocked whisper. And of which, Jack himself not really or fully understanding. He wondered (in the 'mind-ringing' seconds that followed)..'Why did I say that?'. Considering the 'mania' he had been experiencing.. well, it seemed 'the only fitting way' to describe it! Oh, what a glorious and beautiful gift that would be for God and Jesus.. And the Holy Spirit, as well! What a 'Great Hallowed Hymn of Praise'! It.. extending across the sky (in his mind), like the dispersing rays of the Sun. And coveringly 'warming it' in its pure tone. Heralding.. yes, Heralding.. the.. the…the…

No… Hold on!… for that could never be of Jack's Will to say! Nor, really even 'think'! Yet, somehow the thought had just dawned, so naturally! And he simply 'couldn't help, but think of it' in his momentary excitement. But, no.. he knew too well that, if this were to-be the hymn that would be used for this particular occasion, it would only be, if by God's Will!. And not of Jack's! Yes, this he knew 'all too well'! For 'All Wills' stem from His!.. And only His! For it was He that created 'All' of the roads-of-mankind (and Angel-kind too!).. and the Universe was His! And this, as with everything; could only be, if it were of 'His' choosing. Especially regarding something as 'Monumental-an-Event' as that! Certainly God would have 'His own plans' concerning the 'particularities' of that Colossal-of-a-happening! Yes, it would surely be in 'His Way'! No, there was no way around it. For all and all, 'all ways' were subject and subservient to His in the end! Otherwise, they were-and-are.. in absolute vain!

Yes.. and in consideration to all of this, Jack's Quest could no longer go on. At least, not as it had been, to this point (by and for Jack's Will!).. For this event and the hearing of this Great Hymn had changed everything! And it would.. and could.. never, ever be the same again! Though now, in knowing this, it could only be of 'Greater Purpose'! Yes, somehow.. everything made a 'Greater Sense' now! What had seemed 'Lost'.. now, miraculously-'n-somehow, seemed 'Recovered'! Or at least, it sure 'felt so', in the moment. Either way, a newer extension of 'The Quest' had been added.. And in so, a 'venue' to pursue. And this, for a much greater cause!.. And end! No, nothing would ever be the same again! But, how.. yes, how.. could he ever accomplish this 'artistic feat' alone? He felt 'so confounded' in the mere thought of it! For after all, think of how long he had been on Earth.. and how unfruitful all of the previous had been. Maybe.. just maybe though.. with help.. from, say.. the other Herald Angels, it might be accomplish-able! He didn't know? But, well.. they had been coming into his life, of late! Maybe.. yes, maybe they could (and would) help? But, then again, could they ever hear what he had heard?.. And understand it, as he had?.. in the same light? And even if so, would they 'love it' and 'feel for it' in the same way as he?.. And see what it could be?

And ultimately (if his feelings were right), what it could mean to the whole world? What kind of glory and peace it could (possibly) bring forth unto all-of-mankind! Whatever?.. he must try and reach them! It was his only chance! Besides, even if he could execute it himself, why do so? Why not share the glory and joy of it all with 'what he had always hoped would be' his friends and comrades. Maybe if he included them, then they would be! And in so, they might all become part of this 'Ultimate-of-Ends! For really, as well.. this was not the kind of thing for 'one' to undertake (in especially considering what its ultimate execution might bring about!).. or at least, by 'one' short-of the Holy One! But then again, maybe it had been He that had sent it forth? .. to Jack? Still, other minds should be consulted on this first! This was just 'all too big a deal'!

Without a minutes-more ado, Jack peeked-out from his hiding place. For he knew he must leave. Where to? Well, he wasn't exactly sure? Maybe.. Heaven? Well, for now though (and more immediately), he knew he must depart from the church and Mass. He would consider his options later and outside. He couldn't think-on-it-all here, any longer! He must get out from the vacuum of its intensity. Breath freer for a moment. Besides, he'd been pressing his luck, as was!

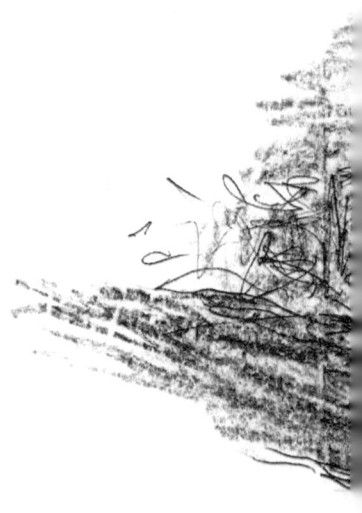

Noting that no one (the choir) was looking in his direction, he dartingly exited.. scurrying around and down the stairwell.

Fortunately (at this point), the Communion was in-process.. and a greater majority of the people were removed to the altar and the front of the assembly hall. So, sliding out of the choir booth door was a cinch. A few wall-leaning stragglers (in the vestibule) trembled in his passing. But it was nothing to be concerned over.. For there was so much more pressing on his mind now!

Tightening their collars (and such), he whizzed past them in a flash.. Practically un-noticed!   But before actually leaving.. and at the large door (as he pryingly opened it), he turned back (in so) and yelled… "THANKS GOD!.."

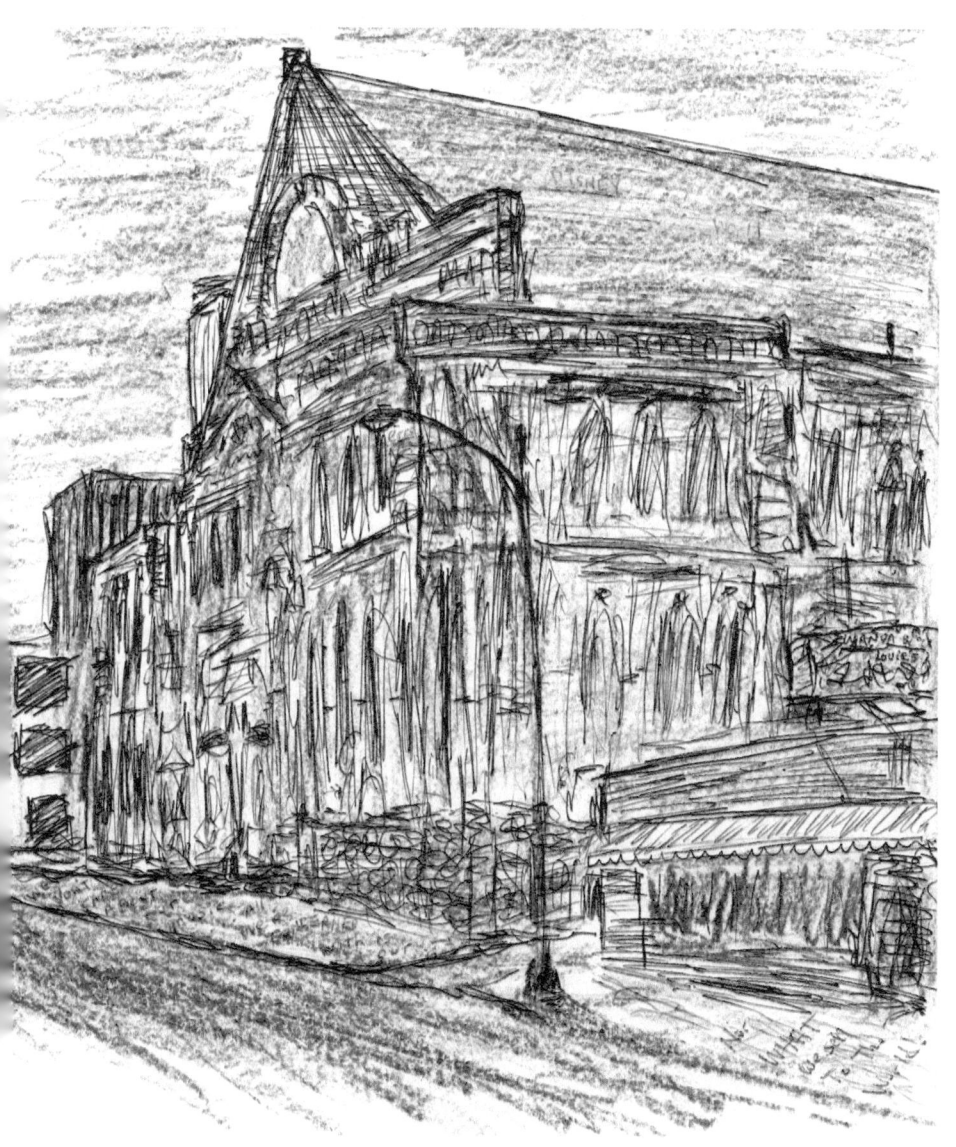

Up the narrow streets of gold, he swifted. And the nerve 'a him too; for it was only late day! Dark.. only starting to fall! But after much thought on his 'Carol' (and its new, more-ultimate purpose), he felt just too wound up to contain it, any longer.. and knew that (no matter what), he must speak with the others. And get some sort of 'feed-back' on whether-or-not they would approve or be interested in it? Or even see the 'same realization' as he? Whether positive or negative, he must know! The suspense was killing him! So 'as serious a chance as he was taking', it was in absolute necessity!

Fortunately there was 'slow traffic' this time of day. Pedestrian- (of course)-wise! Almost 'too slow' to seem right? And he wondered, in a brief, how much longer 'his luck' would hold-out, concerning these visits. And even greater.. Was it even 'luck' to begin with? Whatever.. it was.. and really that's all that counted anyways!

So, up the final-of- (abandoned now)- alleyways, he made.. coming to a para-lyzing stop at the sight of.. the Cathedral! Yes, the very one of 'Creation' (At least, concerning him)! Of course, he had been back, since then.. But still, every time he saw it, it brought something of 'awe' out-of and up-in him. Breath-taking! Not only for its enormous 'huge-ness'.. But, as well (as I said), for his personal attach-ment and memories of it. In the massive shadow-like-'n-dark of it, he stood now staring up in unflinching meditation. And with his 'newer knowledge', it somehow seemed all-the-more 'monumental' now in its standing. This, in retrospect.. as do all things when we've unveiled a deeper, more-hidden truth and juxtaposition in their purpose and make-up. Yes, it was absolutely mind-blowing to think of how God had always known and planned it to be, as so! Or, at least, if Jack was right in his feelings? But, this.. he couldn't help, but feel! Yes, what an 'Absolute Genius God was and is'! But, of course, who don't know that!

At last, into the immediate-street-area he proceeded.. Hearing 'the voices of the past' (the first of Christmas Eve's) resounding in his mind. They.. ringing so real and vivid.. that, at one point, he swung his head to follow.. "The Angel of the Wind" (God's proclamation) echo across and down the empty street in a ricochet-ing fade.

When recovered from this memory and his in-foot 'stop', he again resumed movement to and up the long stairs. But there (at the top of them) having another flash of his 'fall' on the landing (of that night), he heard the crowd's laughter (in so) and turned (in the reality now) to embarrassedly scan-out. But, of course, no one was there! And he shook his head free of it to continue further.

Inside, there was no one. His faint and careful "Hello?", echoing back outward and upon him with nothing following. "Oh, well.." and back-about-face-and-out he went.

At bottom step, it hit him.. that 'maybe Angel Jane might be of-help to him'? Despite her new situation. For after all, he felt certain they were and would-always-be 'friends', if not anything else. Yes, he would search her out! For he simply must discuss this with someone. And hopefully someone understanding-enough to (at least) allow him the courtesy of a 'fair hearing'. For he was just so confused now! Everything was building-up and near explosion. And that.. he knew for sure! This New Carol!.. The events in Lorraine!.. The Loss!.. Just everything was coming to a head! And he felt certain that his 'top' was soon to erupt, if some sort of 'relief' wasn't found.

So, along the alley-like thoroughfare, he went.. in near jaunt.. growing more and more fearful and anxious with each-'n-every little sound that came to his 'hiss-ing-away' ears. This, whether from near or afar! All, without favoritism, penetrat-ing inwardly with deeper and sharper-crisp volumes.

"ANGEL PETER?.." yelled a womanly voice from out of a second-story window, above and ahead-of-him.. and he (with its hair-raising execution) shooting into-and-behind a chimney-like protrusion that edged a near-at-hand building aside him.

His nerves-'n-thoughts on tingling end, he awaited its outcome in the following-it silence. Hardly breathing! The lad (at last) appearing.. and in so, scatting his little-self into the ahead-building's arched doorway. This, accompanied by his...
"I'm coming, Mother!.." –answerings.

"Whew!.."

With another quick-'n-nervous scan, Jack caught view of an opposing atrium entrance (that continued in a leftward direction and away).. and with discovery, shot for it. Walking close-'n-briskly passed its quiet, abandoned store-fronts (there-in), he wondered at the reason for the emptiness-of-souls and general-'shopping'-traffic. But whatever the reason (?), he was grateful for its being so!

Up to his left (Where center-court would be) were tunnel-shaped openings.. and he prayed (in a breath) that no one would be out-and-beyond them. And when temporarily out-of-the-sheltering-darkness and into the only-very-dim-now-daylight of their clearings, he saw the answering of his prayers. Not a soul!

When back into the veil of the drear, he inhaled again. In relief. But this, only for a quick second, for into the darker-end of the hallway-ahead came a sound unexpected. It instantly-forcing Jack into a near-at-hand doorway to hide.

With his body flat and pressed-to-the-nail-studded-door as snug as possible, he (at last) peered around the frame (Which took very little effort, for the door itself was hardly inset to begin with), only to see approaching a young girl-angel. She.. skipping along and bouncing a ball in play. She (despite the dim).. with long, blondish-like hair.. Wearing a typical (for Heaven!) white robe and sporting (as well) a to-herself smile of contentment. And a very precious smile it was, at that! Jack taking immediate-'special'-note of it, in his uncomfortable watch of her.

As she neared too close, Jack knew there was no escaping her discovery of him. He looked everywhere for a possible 'out', but it was inevitable now that he'd be seen. Absolutely cornered!

Stopping dead-in-her-tracks at initial sight of him and a-feared for the dark, she pleaded… "Hello.. Who's there?.."

Jack (not to frighten her anymore than he'd already done) answered promptly…

"Oh, it's just me.." coming forth, away from the door and into the dim-still (but clear-enough-to-see) light.

With closer surveillance, Jack noted her to look somehow very familiar. Yes, in a strange way! Her face having characteristics of someone that he knew! But as reminiscent and 'striking' as they were, he simply couldn't put his finger on 'whom it was'. Staring at her, he tried to figure it out. Until realizing that (in so) there was a cold silence (that was, in the same, making her appear cautious and still-scared), he caught himself and resumed with…

"I… I… I didn't mean to frighten you.. I was just.." momentarily looking back (as if, pointing..) to the doorway, that he'd just stepped from. Then back to her, nervously…

"Well, I was just…"

"Going into your shop?.." She finishing it for him.

"Well, I…I…" Jack, not to lie.

"I understand.. You're a merchant!… Though I must say, I've never seen you here before.. and well, I know most of the shop owners!.. I live just a short distance from here.." She.. loosening up some and becoming truly inquisitive over it all now.

"Well, you see.. I.. I.. travel much.. Hardly ever here!.." being as vague as he could be (And after all, it was true.. to some degree!).

She.. seeming satisfied-enough with that…

"Oh, well.. Hi!.." Then (for nothing better to say).. "Wha.. What's your name?.."

"Jack.. yeah, Jack!.." He tangling out.

"Well, hello Mr. Jack .. My name's Angel Juniper!.. Hey, how come you aren't wearing a robe?.."

"Ah.. never do.. when I.. I.. travel!.. Y' know?.. 'n I've got t' be leavin' soon, so.."

"Oh.. well.. anyway.. I live just a little ways from here.. with my Mother and Step-Dad.. 'n my sister!.."

"Oh, that's nice!.." uncomfortably looking about for other angels. Though trying desperately not to let on in it. The coast was clear! At least, momentarily!

A bench was placed affront-and-against the nearby shop's window, and she (obviously wanting to talk further with him) walked over (leading-like) and took a seat. He joining her, for it was more inset from the walkway and less-obvious-a-spot (Despite his better judgment to 'get-gone-'n-out 'a-there'.. and as-quickly-as-possible too!).

Then (like-as-if they had been talking along now for several hours and just plain 'good-ole-friends'..) she begins in with…

"You have the same name as my Daddy!.. He's not here though.. I haven't ever actually seen him, to tell the truth!.. But my Mother.. Well, she's told us all about him.. said he's far away.. in another land!..

She said he had this 'special' hymn.. that he'd made up for God.. and Jesus, when He was a baby, back on the first Christmas!.. Yes, he's one of the Herald An-gels!" This.. bringing Jack's undivided attention to her. Now.. Yes, now he knew why she'd looked so familiar! "Yes, she told us all about it.. and how his hymn meant more to him than anything!.. Yes, even more than her!.. And I guess.." with saddening in her eyes..

" even more than us!.." Her head slowly drooping.

Jack, in gasp, interrupting at this…

"Why.. is your Daddy's name 'Jack Frost'?"

"Yes.." She suddenly excited.. raising her face…" Do you know him?.."

"Sure.. yeah, sure.. I do!.. I've met him lots 'a times.. in my travels!"

"You have?…" She standing up. Then re-seating herself in sharp listen.

"Sure thing!.. 'n seems t' me like.. Well, he always spoke real highly 'a you kids of his!.. Yes, sir-ee!.." pausing to retrieve his thoughts and breath. For it was hardly the proper time for either to be coming-up short!

"Well.. What did he say?.."

"Said he loved ya's very, very much!.. 'n he wished, so bad, that he could be with ya's!.. He just.. well.. never realized that he.. he.. he.."

"What?.. that he what?.." She, terribly impatient and fidgeting in his pause.

"Well.. that he.. he'd be gone, f' so long!.." Jack forcefully recovering him-self.. "and as for him loving his hymn more than your Mommy or you kids.. Well, that just don't seem right at all t' me!.. Or even near true!.. For after all.. I know him.. 'n quite well at that!.. 'n well, I just know that isn't.. nor ever was, f' that matter.. the case!.. No, sir-ee!.. It's just that.. Well, you're kind 'a young now, t' really understand.. But, well.. when you're older you'll see that you can't always control the things that happen in your life.. Y' know, like the different situations and stuff that comes up!.. But, that don't mean that.. well, y' know.. that.. he don't love you 'n all!.. I mean.. like.. well, y' see.. that hymn 'a his.. well, it's.. it's more than just a hymn.. t' him!.. I mean.. oh, how do I explain it t' ya.." getting tangled and fumbled-in-himself over the word jum-ble.. "It's.. well.. it's.."

"That's okay, Mr. Jack.." She interrupting.. "I believe you!.. whatever you're saying!.. I mean, I don't exactly.. but I guess.. somehow.. I kind of do!.. Well, anyway, I think I understand!.."

"Well, t' tell the truth, I'm not really sure I do anymore!.. But, well.. if you do then.." Jack babbling on, more to himself than to her.

"Mr. Jack.. Did he ever say when he'll be coming back?.."

"Who?.." Jack (being pulled-out of his introspect), truly confounded.

"My Daddy!.. Who-else?…"

"Oh, yeah.." catching himself.. "Your Daddy!.. Right!.. Ah.. ah.. yes, it does seem t' me, he mentioned.." At this, her jumping up in excitement.. and simultaneously in the near distance, the 'old cathedral bell' tolling. The latter, bringing him nervously to his feet, for the recall of 'where he was'. Totally perplexed, he peered about quickly in the revelation. She grabbing his hand. This, sedating him some and bringing his attention back to her.

"Well, What?.." She, still trapped in what he had begun to say, and awaiting its finish.

"What.. What 'a y' mean 'What'?.." Jack, sincerely confused.

"What did he say.. you know, about when he was coming back?.. You were saying he.."

"Oh, yeah!.. Well.. he'll be.. yeah, he'll be comin' back.. someday!.. When.. when his.. his work is done!.. Yeah, someday!.. You'll see!.. But just 'cause he's gone.. well, that don't mean he don't love you!.. 'n think 'a you!.. No.. You remember that!.. and.. you tell your sister that too!… Okay?…

No.. don't you worry about all 'a that!.. Everything's gonna work out fine in the end.. you'll see!.. You just believe me!.. 'cause I know!.. 'n trust me.. he will be back!…

Now, listen, Juniper.. I've really, really got to go..":

"Oh, please stay, Mr. Jack?.. I like talking with you.. Please?.. " She, beggingly.

"I can't.. I really can't!.. Not yet!.. You don't understand!" His slip-up, going un-noticed. "But listen.. You.. you be a good, little girl.. 'k?.. for your Daddy.. 'n Mommy too!.. 'cause they both love you.. n' matter where they are!.. And don't worry.. 'cause everything's gonna work out fine!.. You'll see!.. 'k?.."

She sadly nodding to him.

Letting go of her hand, he began away. Then stopping, he came back, planting a soft kiss on her forehead.

"Are you crying?.." She asked, as he re-turned away. He.. never answering.. only pretending not to hear in his beginning trot.

Passing the brighter-inner court, he heard her call again. Breaking speed and almost stopping, he (about-facingly) resumed his walk in reverse-backwards fashion.. yet, still away.. listening to…

"Mr. Jack.. Would you please tell my Daddy I love him?.. and miss him?.."

With all he could muster to call back, he exhaled…

"Yes, Juniper.. But believe me, he already knows!…

Now you remember.." Through streaming tears, that she couldn't see. "Be a good girl!.. Always!.. 'n don't worry.. he'll be back.. You'll see!… Someday!.. Someday.. yes, someday he'll be back!…

In the meantime.. if y' need him.. he's in your heart!.. Just like you're forever in his!.. Don't forget that!.. Ever!…"

"Thanks, Mr. Jack… and Goodbye!.."

"Goodbye, Juniper!.." Then to himself in whisper, finishing it with… "..my Baby.. I love you!.. Forever 'n ever.. 'n ever!.."

- IF FOLLOWING MY DREAM -

Across the clouds, he flew. In a delirious mania!

Around the Crystal Lake, he plowed.. like a wild man! On and on, in a frenzied ricocheting; as if bouncing off of things not even there! This, short of, the misty clouds and haze. Whimpering and howling in the anguish; totally unconcerned over whether he was being watched. Too agonized to care! Fumbling and falling, on occasions, in choking pain! Not even looking where he was going. Gasping and tramping on in fervor.

At last (after much running), emotionally drained beyond belief, he fell.. face down.. on the top of what-was-like a cloud ledge. In so, surrounding his head with his terribly-trembling arms, he remained.. his mind pounding at him, inside of the self-caress…

'I never knew!.. Two daughters!.. That makes it all.. just everything, even worse-a-tragedy!.. God forgive me!.. I didn't realize!… Oh, what I've lost!.. And all 'a these years!.. The time!.. Oh.. Oh, what I've lost!..' his mind attacking him in accusation. The agony and tormenting, being totally overpowering! Paralyzing!

'Now I feel all-the-more unworthy of all you've imparted on me, Lord!.. Tell me.. Where has my will led me?.. Can you retrieve me from it?.. Oh, please?..'

It was absolutely painstaking. Yes, now he felt all-the-less deserving of the 'new hymn' that he'd conceived-of in the choir booth. How could he ever have considered himself 'creditable-enough' to be involved in something 'that hallowed' and important? It just all seemed so crazy and misappropriated now!

His conscience continued in its 'nuclear-bomb-like'-attack. Exploding in him and tearingly scattering his mind and thoughts into molecular bits! He shook violently in its tremors. Yet, all the while, somehow.. and like an all-the-more perplexing paradox.. 'the cause' still lived-and-burned in his heart. Yes, despite all.. something inside and way deep down.. was still believing in all that he had done! And as well, what he felt still-needed-being-done! It was all.. just so confusing! Extremely!

An endless time seemed to pass in this ferocious-inner war.. Hours? Days? Weeks? He wasn't sure? But at last, into it.. came… a.. a.. soft voice! A comforting voice! A concerned and caring voice! Yes, a real voice.. coming from beyond and outside of his self huddle…

THE TWELFTH CHAPTER

~ REAL SPECIAL FEELIN' (RETURN) ~

"Hello.. Are you alright?.. "

Jack (absolutely startled at its coming) cautious-'n-slowly raised his weary head and eyes. They (the latter), red-smeared and totally bloodshot. And in this, extremely blurry! Yet-'n-despite, at last through them, he saw (that somehow-or-another in his earlier 'run', he had ironically-enough fell directly-above and over-looking..) the lagoon! Yes, and as well, in lifting himself on his hands, he noted himself to-be in the very spot in which Angel Jane had originally stood, when she'd appeared to him there on that first-of Christmas Eve's! And even more odd-ly-enough in it all, below (in his very position of that long ago event) now stood a very beautiful girl-angel! She, in this, looking up at him with a very pleasant smile. And this smile.. an ever-warming one, as well! Jack initially noting this, above all! But (in all of the amazement and shock of it..) now, for the nervousness of the moment, he hopped-up to attention.. and in the same, better-secured his hat onto his head. Tidying-himself-up some in the hurried process! And all of this.. in great awkwardness, I must say!

When in reasonable order and control, Jack took another look down upon her. She.. blondish-brown, fine hair.. and a figure 'sleekly thin'. In a white robe, so elegant! Fragile-looking! And she (throughout all of his antics and observations) still smiling away and patiently awaiting his reply.

"Ah.. ah.. Yeah.. I'm.. I'm alright.." nervously brushing off his britches (forgetting that he had been lying on clouds and not dirt!).. and rubbing at his still-running sniffle. She was so beautiful, he just couldn't help but feel like an absolute clux!

Raising her hand to him, he began down towards her. The closer he got, the more radiant and appealing she looked. And by the touch, it was all over! Yes, it was love.. and he knew it! And she, as well! It was so obvious! Though never spoken! Instead, she searched-out a seat (near the water's edge) and he followed.

In it all, Jack looked about himself.. wondering if 'this particular spot and place' were not, in fact, 'magical'.. or 'mystical'.. or 'what have ya?'! It just seemed so odd-a-site, concerning 'matters of the heart'!

"My name is Kare-Angel.." She seated-now and smilingly staring.

"Mine's.. Ah.." having to stop to think.. "..Jack!.." lost in her charm.

"What was bothering you, Jack?.."

"Well, it's.. it's an awful long story.. I mean I could try t'.."

"Do.. Do tell me.. for I care!.. Truly I do!.. Maybe I could help?.."

"Well.." Jack nervously fidgeting with his now-removed hat. At last, complying for the desperate need to… "Well.. it's.. it's like this.."

In the beginning, it was beautiful! And everything that Jack had seemed so desperately to need! Romantic love and understanding. An ear to hear. He became more at-ease.. and in so, temporarily relieved from all of his inner despair. It moving to the back of his mind for seemingly better thoughts.

His shack.. like his life.. were overall-ed. Put into order! Yes, right from the moment Kare-Angel arrived in his Antarctic Homeland, she began in. Straightening everything. She seeming obsessed with arranging it! But then again, it was a total disaster area! Soon Jack accepted this as her nature. At first, it was hard for him to understand.. he, being one to be more-often-than-not totally unconcerned-'n-lax with such matters. But, yes.. the more he thought on it, the more it did seem the 'Perfect Match'! Besides, he was always much more involved with things like 'The Quest' and 'his plans for it' and so forth. So, her 'hitting the home-front' made total sense!

As for 'being in love', Jack felt very uncertain of himself and his emotions. Or at least, in being able to admit to them. Though fact was, he did love her! But as a result of his (still haunting him) former tragedy (with Angel Jane and all of the agony it had resulted in), he was (to say the least) very cautious now! The separation and loss of his children (in the former), as well, played on his mind. Constantly, too! Making the new relationship all the harder. But he did want to love. He was just sincerely afraid! Too.. knowing all-too-well his own shortcomings and imperfections.. Well, he was (to-the-max) confused in how to put his finger on what he was truly (and internally..) experiencing. So, to try to put it into some kind of focus, he labeled it as being a 'Real Special Feelin' ' .. and left it at that!

Either way, his spirits were obviously lifted now. At least, back to a level of performance. And in this, he knew his earthly quests would be resumed. Though in fact, he wondered now at his intentions, considering all that had transpired in the Musical City of-recent. Despite, he would return to it.. And try to figure it out along the way. It seemed the only logical thing to do!

So, at last, when the off-season ended, he found himself back 'on the road' again.. Leaving Kare-Angel there in the shack. And this, as much as he hated to! For a great part of him would've loved to have just settled-in with her and let the world go rolling around without him and his forever-being-ignored-anyways Carol.

But feeling reasonably secure in his relationship with her, he went. Little knowing that with his Spring return, everything would be changed. And this, to never be the same again!

Homecoming over the Trans-Antarctic Mountains was a hurried one. It edged-on by his jubilant excitement in 'seeing her' again. The long night was on him.. yes.. but he trudged on forcefully, despite. It had seemed an 'eternity away'! But now, almost over!

Finally viewing below him (in the frozen and otherwise-baron ice valley) the inner light of his dwelling, he began his slide downward.. Through the depthly drifts. Gliding-like (and white covered), he reached the door. Quickly and without delay knocking on it.

When, at last, it swung-wide.. there she stood. Kare-Angel. The love still in her eyes. But now, her appearance.. thinner and paler than ever! And her smile.. still there.. but somehow-seeming 'mustered up' now. Forced-like! Looking as though underneath it all, she was very sad and depressed. This, causing Jack to slump into a sort-of guilt over 'having been gone' for so long. Though this, not being the reason for her woe.

"Hi.." he said, trying to be cheerful and ignore the obvious.

"Hello, Jack.." Then (with another forced smile).. "You're going to be a Father!.."

Startled by the news (Though 'her form' having said so, beforehand), he moved in to hold her in his arms. She seeming so fragile now. And lost-like! He didn't know what to say. He couldn't find the proper words. There just weren't any! So instead, he surrendered it to silence and tried 'actual comforting' as an alternative. For she obviously was very upset. And had been without question 'for a time' before his arrival.

No matter how hard Jack tried to revive her (in the days that followed), it was to no avail. It just seemed useless. For she had become totally lost in her depression. And with all that Jack had been through (in his existence).. and having done so much, despite it.. he found it extremely hard to understand the reasons for it. The only logical one he could find (After much thought on it) was.. the 'Pre-Birth Blues'. And in the deduction, he tried desperately to convince her of this. And as well, that after the baby's arrival all would change for the better. But it didn't take! No matter how hard he tried to comfort her!

And at last, with Angel Boy's entry into the world, it still hadn't took! This, of which, totally confounding Jack.. for he'd felt so certain of himself in it. Yes, his theory! But now disproved, he gave up on any further attempts at trying to sell it to her. And as well, to himself! No, it hadn't held water! For nothing.. no, nothing changed! It only seemed to get worse. But the boy.. well, what could Jack say of that? For most every male dreams of, one day, having a son. And now, here he was! And, he.. blonde.. just like his mother. Beautiful? Yes, beautiful beyond belief! The little shack would never, ever be the same! It.. taking on a new (as never before..) 'warmth', if that were possible! Why, Jack even cut-out some windows.. to 'let out' some of the son-shine!

At times (in the season's to come), Kare-Angel did seem to be enlightened. At least, by the child. Though deep down, the otherwise always remained. And after much consideration, Jack thought it to be 'their location'. Antarctica. For it was obvious, by her gradually-deeper withdrawal, that she was very unhappy there. And probably with fair reason. But it was Jack's home! What could he do? His entire world centered around it! He couldn't imagine living elsewhere, short of, maybe.. Heaven? But no, there was more to do here on Earth! No, he wasn't done yet. Although in truth, he wasn't quite sure of what it was? Still, he couldn't leave. 'Least, not yet!

Instead, he would try his best in other ways to please her. And try to make her life there more bearable. Though (when tested), even this seemed useless! Yes, it was as though she were dying. Yes, dying! Slowly, but surely! And it (compounded by his multiple-other problems) ate at Jack constantly! What would he do? He worried so!

Yes, times were rough. For both of them. Though despite all, love was still there. Only now, seeming to become buried in 'the Great Antarctic Chill'! And that, a true test!

Regardless (and in all of it), Jack had committed himself and hung in. Waiting and hoping for her to return to her 'old self'. Though painfully knowing, deep down, that it might possibly take years to get to that point.. If ever? And would they have the time? For she seemed to be fading fast!

Throughout everything, Jack still contemplated his next-of-moves. Yes, the new hymn especially.. and its perplexing-him dilemmas. It.. haunting.. in the back of his mind.. and seeping through his mental-blockade-of-it constantly (more and more) during the 'whenever'-let-ups in his immediate worries. Often times.. and many hours were spent.. sitting out-'n-away somewhere alone, in the ice valley; contemplating this and the (due to it) confusions of his soul. And when, at last, he left for his next-of Quests, he was already 'well-worn emotionally'! Starting out early.. for he felt, if he didn't, he would never make it (inner-wise) to his normal departure time!

Depressed-to-the-max, he now stood, searching out over the rough and turbulent Antarctic Waters; wondering (still) where he might begin his trip. In it, he.. thinking of the events of his more-recent visit to the Musical City. What had it all meant? I mean, he had made a deduction.. But was it right? He really didn't know! His initial feelings.. Were they true? Or distorted somehow, by the pressure he had been under at the time? Or maybe it had been due to the 'ecstasy'-of-the-moment and his surroundings? The music and so on! It had been such a 'profound revelation' to him.. that now, in his more-present endeavors and trials, he had 'pushed it aside' for fear.. as well as for his day-to-day business. But now confronted with it, he agonized on just how important and crucial it could be! And too, what it could mean to the Earth.. and 'all of mankind', in turn! This.. if it (his feelings) were right! If not, how wrong he could be! Yes, he was becoming more and more afraid of 'the vision' and what he 'felt in his heart' with each new analysis he made. Or even 'considered'! If only he had consulted with the other Herald Angels, when they had made their appearances. But of course, how could he have?.. he hadn't even conceived of the idea-of-it, at the time! He needed another opinion! Maybe.. several? This all.. was just too much for one being to fathom.. let alone, execute!

Lifting free his hat from its rest, he tremblingly fore-armed-and-pressed his matted bangs.. leaving large sweat-smeared gaps in them. Then with further mind-search and a momentary nervous pace, he (with inner anger) exorcised his anguish with a banging-of-his-hat-on-his-upper-leg.. and simultaneously exhaled and muttered…

"Gosh, this is crazy!.."

Pouting and fumingly, he started back and away from the iceberg's ledge (As if to be returning to his shack). Stopping after several feet in it, he turned back and exploded-out in an echoing scream…

"WELL?… WHERE TO, NOW?… HUH?… WHERE TO?…"

- WISE MEN -

It was into the middle of a silent night, when Jack (at last) ended his hurried journey. Having passed (in his trip) the town of Capernaum and its historic-(now)-and-land-marking monastery, he recalled the shepherd boy that he had once (centuries before) passed and enthralled (or at least, believed he had!) with his Carol. Yes, the very one that had fled for warmth, at the time! But now at his destination, all thoughts of it were miles-behind. This, for his at-present location and the importance of it to him. And this, being.. Calvary! Or at least, what had once been Calvary! For now, the entire site was surrounded and capped with a Church. And a very huge and massive one, at that!

'Why he had returned here?' was as much a mystery to him, as it probably would've been to anyone else. But here he was! Maybe somehow, he had hoped that it might supply an answer to his turmoil? Or at least, that-of and pertaining-to 'his Carol' and its more ultimate purpose! He really wasn't sure? But regardless (as I'd stated), here he was.. standing at the end of the seeming-thin passage-way of Via Dolorosa.

Mournfully (by the memory of days past there).. and worn tremendously from 'the road', he began in closer to the enormous church's site. The latter of which, he felt sure to be the correct location (?). For with all of the changes-of-time (as well as this great architecture itself!).. Well, he had to admit, it was all very questionable! Deceiving! Not to forget, the blackness of the late-night-hour, making it all the harder to decipher!

People were passing him, on occasions. For now (unlike in the many years past), this was the center of a city.. and the whatever-hours did not deter all. No more than it would have in any metropolis! Yes, it had all changed.. and so much at that! It was hard to believe.. and Jack marveled in its comparison.

Reaching (what seemed like) a main entrance, he paused to peer about himself.. Checking his alone-ness. All was quiet and as he'd hoped!

Touching and trying the door's cold handle, he found it to be locked. Then (before he could even turn back and move away in the discouragement of it..), he heard a sound beyond-it and inside. This, alarmingly coming at him.. and (in a matter of seconds) unlatching the inner lock. And then, astoundingly-enough, this (whomever?).. moving back-in-a-soft-bustle (as much as he could hear), leaving Jack all-the-more confused at the 'who' and 'why' of his benefactor!

Nervous (and frightened for its strange-ness), Jack, at last, regained himself to again attempt entry. And now (as expected) it opened. Yet, in spite, he found it extremely difficult to even peek-in, let alone enter. Finally, peering about (and inside), he noted it immediately to be very heavily dim and solemn. And very architecturally adorned and arrayed. His 'whomever'-benefactor.. was now nowhere in sight.. Having disappeared somewhere into the veiled, inner sanctums.

Eventually his courage built enough to step in, letting the very large (at least, to him!) door click-in, closed behind him. Starting forward (only to come to an immediate stop), he cringingly noted the loud-echoing-'squeak' of his tennies. Almost 'SQWOOSHING' for their volume in the surrounding chamber and its absolute silence! But and despite them (in his wait), no one came forth. So, as light-footedly as possible, he began further.

Soon enough (Though it seemed 'forever' to him!), he was at an altar. But before he could make a fair study of it (Having held his breath inward for fear, among other more-obvious reasons), he turned aside to exhale for relief.. In so, flapping-frantically the pages of a stand-supported, opened-flat Bible (at the right-hand-side of the altar).. Blowing it clear to the final pages of the Book! This.. somehow alarming him.. and in so, tugging him in its direction.

When squeakingly there.. and after pulling to its front a nearby chair for elevation, he hopped up and squintingly (for the dark) gazed upon it. His eyes being drawn to its Fourteenth Heading. Reading to himself, he marveled in it. And wondered if it were not just 'he, himself' and 'his interpretation of it' (in the way that he was presently feeling), that made it so (?). For it seemed to be 'so relevant' to him! And his more-recent conception of his Carol! Yes, hitting in a very personal way! Maybe everyone that read it, found it to be that way? He wondered. Applying it to themselves? He momentarily peered about himself in thought, growing a bit more fearful and confused.

Nibbling now at his fingernails, he returned.. continuing on through its text. It was all so compelling! He couldn't pull himself from it. For it seemed to speak to him.. And answer.. or at least, make sense of. all that he'd been feeling deep inside! 'Was he reading-into-it?', he quizzed himself in the electrifying intensity-of-it.

Flipping back to the beginning of the Book's final and concluding section, he began reading forward (and back to where he had already), for better analysis of the whole. Again and still, it seemed perfectly clear! He gasped in it!

Reaching and finishing two chapters beyond his original starting point (and all-the- more now amazed at its un-coverings), he was stopped. This, due to a sound in the further chamber. Peering up and in-the-direction of where the 'alarming'-sound had originated, he waited. Shakingly!

Hopping down from his elevation, as quietly as possible, to the floor.. he began cautiously in the direction of it. Through the lingering dark, he made. Slowly. Trembling in his tennies, every squeak of the way!

Finally coming to what-appeared-to-be an enclosed tomb-type entrance (about a stone's throw away-and-from his beginning point.. And this, adorned with an arched-like entranceway), he stopped. Cold. Staring in. Though it was totally engulfed in black, for the even-greater-here dark of its area.. Feeling reasonably assured that it (or better yet, 'inside it'..) was and had been the 'source' of the sound he had heard moment's prior.

In the wait, he felt a bolt-of-fear shoot through his inners.. and tremblingly responded in its aftermath. Should he enter? No.. he'd hold fast.. and hoped 'it' would eventually 'show itself'!

After a short (but seeming very long..) pause.. with no further sign of movement (from within), his mind began to drift back to the text.. and he studied introspectively on it. This, 'til (in his startled amazement) 'it' began to blow on him! Yes.. a sort of wind.. coming from the engulfed entranceway! It.. bringing with it a tremendous light.. that shone (as would a gigantic spotlight!.. or even yet, as would the Sun itself!) on his person. Jack falling back from the piercing blur (and power of it) onto the floor. Squinting and barely seeing for its absolute brightness (Not to forget, its 'eye-lashing'-winds), he fought desperately to address it with his sight. But it was nearly unbearable!

At last.. with it.. came a sort-of voice. Though not actually a 'spoken' one! Just.. one.. understood! Its sender, telling Jack something of 'great-and-mind-shattering'-profoundness! But this.. again.. only being 'understood'. And in so, un-record-able! So it must remain unstated here-in.

When at last, 'it' dimmed and settled into the earlier (and again..) dark-silence and cold-of-the-room, Jack (dumbfounded) trembled in great fear. This, despite 'its' only-second's-before warmth and comforting!

Scanning about himself (in the haze of his mental perplexity), he re-affirmed his location and whereabouts. Then jumping up (in the tremor of it), he shot for the exit. This, void of all concern.

After rapid 'SQUOOSHINGS'.. he pulled the door free (in a snap).. and was gone!

Having fled directly (and non-stop) back to his earlier starting point (the coastal shore of Antarctica and his exact-earlier location), he sat now on the iceberg's ledge. Even after all of his travel, still in the blur 'n tremble of it all! Totally lost in what had happened! Despite his seeming-to-be-looking-out-stance (at the cold waters), head-forward.. he was completely absorbed and pre-occupied!

After much time and meditation, he snapped himself to.. and momentarily 'out-of-it'. Wondering if he should return to his shack? And family? No, he had to do something concerning this tremendous dilemma! Besides, it was much too early yet in his Quest for return. Not even Christmas! No.. not home. But.. Where?

He needed, so badly, to discuss 'all that had transpired' with someone. But someone related to it all, that could truly understand. And afford an explanation. Kare-Angel just wouldn't be able to fathom it. But then, how could she? It was hardly her fault.. but well, he needed to maybe confer with another.. say.. yes.. Herald Angel! But, who?.. 'n where? Leah?.. Well, Heaven knows where she'd be now! And Len.. well, him too! Or Johnny? No.. but.. but well.. what about... Yeah!.. That was it! .. Nick!.. Yes, Nick!.. The North Pole!

- MRS. SANTA -

Through the trees (after trees, after trees, after towns, after towns, after cities, after cities..) in his northward hurry, he ran. He must exert extra now.. for (though uncertain of the exact date) he knew it to be coming-on-to 'the big night'! And, Nick.. well, we all know of his duties then! And after all of this effort.. Well, Jack just hated to think of missing him and his take-off. Yes, he must be a true light-foot!

Throughout it all, he couldn't help wonder if Nick would even speak with him, after all of these years. Yes, the other Herald Angels had seemed 'pleasant enough' in his of-recent encounters with them. But, this.. well, this was different! For Nick had been accessible all along.. and, up to now, Jack had never once approached him. For that matter, he'd dodged him! So, it was with little wonder that

Jack had his reservations. But he must! There was no other choice in the matter, but to step on his pride. And only hope that Nick would overlook the past.

After tremendous travel and time, he landed himself on the very ledge that he'd once 'rested in thought' on (After his first departure from Bethlehem on that first-of Christmas's).   But looking down through the night now.. and across the same valley (that he'd once 'iced'!), it had all changed. And very drastically at that! A crystal-like, snow-decorated metropolis lay there now! And sparklingly beautiful it was, too!   It.. initially astounding Jack into a self babble!

When recovered from the shock, he began down and into its narrow street-ways.. Dodging and darting (as usual) his way, through the scattered mounds and glassy-like doorways. The latter of which, adorned in outlandish Christmas arrays!

Undiscovered, he made his way to city center. Then and there, finding out the reason for the deserted-ness of all the streets prior. Yes, ahead in the huge court were all of the entire population! And they (squeezed together in a gigantic-and-massive body), all awaiting Santa's departure.   And this.. sending an immediate 'bolt of nervousness' through Jack, as he watched from the darkened doorway he'd weasled himself into.   He must act!.. and now!   For encircled (by the great numbers), there he stood.. on his sleigh now.. the Angel of Musical Mirth himself.. in full attire (Or at least, the attire the world came to know him by)! Either way.. it was Nick! And he must act! Or miss him! Yes, there he was.. standing there in his forever jovial-ness.. smiling away. And fortunately-enough (for Jack, at least!), awaiting something? Or someone? Jack couldn't tell. But whatever.. he knew he must move forward promptly.. and do something... or he would surely miss him. Yes, before he'd take-off! But somehow, a sort-of paralysis had come over him.. and he fought inwardly-now to take the first step. Yes, after all of his travels, he just couldn't do it! Having serious second-thoughts over whether-or-not he really wanted to see (and talk to) him, after all. Still snuggled in the darkened doorway, he fidgetingly tangled with himself...

"Should I?.." chewing on his cracked-knuckle.. "Nah!... Well.. maybe?.."

Before he could argue another point-on-it with himself, the door behind him sprung open! With its unveiling light (Which, in a flash, burst-out goldly upon him!) came the catching-him sight of.. of...

"Mrs. Santa!.." He, blurting-out in the embarrassment.

Yes, Mrs. Claus herself! And saying (very nonchalantly, as was always her way)... "Oh.. hi, Jack.." period-dotting-it with her warm, smirky-like smile.

How did she know him, he wondered. He gulped heavily in his tracks. For now, with her arrival (and as a result of it, the all-eyes-on-him of the courtyard elves.. not to mention, Santa's himself's!), he realized that this.. yes, she.. was (and had been, all along) 'what' they'd all been waiting on. Yes, it was obvious now. A bad choice of doors! And Jack literally trembled in it all.. Uncertain of what would become of 'his discovery' there.

At last, he regained himself enough to mutter in response and smiling-like flush...

"H.. Hi... M... Mrs. ... Mrs. Santa..."

Coming forward, she took his arm (in ceremonial-type fashion) and began out into and through the crowd. Jack fumblingly escorting her (or kind-of!.. for she really doing more-of-the-leading than he!), despite his shakey-ness. Something of her kindly-ness and general-acceptance-'n-sweetness supported him in it.. Comforting and giving courage, as well. And in so, he began to somehow relax a bit. At least, enough to follow!

The surrounding elves (Though initially he would've thought otherwise..) seemed to accept him. And in so, smiled as the twosome paraded by. They, as well, clearing a way in the couple's forward movement. In this, Mrs. Santa (with her always contented-like chuckle) turned to Jack, saying...

"You're probably wondering how I know you!.. And they, as well.." sort-of nodding-away at them in her fixed-otherwise gaze.. "Well.. we were all there.. at the creation of the Herald Angels!.. Yes, all there!.. Remember?.."

Jack simply nodding numbly in his confounded state. Then, cracking a nervous smile.

Finally, at center court.. and as well, to the waiting, large-'n-brim-filled sleigh, Nick (having watched them in smile, all the way) offered in a jolly, but firm tone...

"Jack.. Jack Frost!.." He, chuckling in a moment. Then.. "How are you?.."

"Fine.." returned the addressed, meekly.. for still-fear of his surroundings. And he, fidgetingly glancing about at the audience (all still staring in smile).. "Ah, fine.. I guess?.."

"You guess!.. Ho.. Ho.. Ho!.. Come.. " Santa putting his arm out at the above -them sleigh seat.. "Come.. and talk with me.. I've still a few moments left!.. And, Mother.." glancing at his wife.. "Come, now.. and give me my goodbye kiss". All the surrounding sprites covering their mouths and giggling in this.

Both boarding up, she fulfilled his request. This, being met with the almost-comical-sounding (for the high-pitched-ness of their voices) "Aw.." of the miniature onlookers. And following (upon completion), their massive pit-a-pattering applause. Then, boarding down, she awaited aground.. still staring-lovingly-back-up at him. He, there-upon, telling Jack to have a seat. And the latter, complying in fumble.

"Now.." Santa seating himself, as well, beside him.. "Tell me, why have you come?.."

"Well.. I.. I…" nervously peering about-and-around the sleigh at the still-staring-up crowd.

Santa assuring…

"Don't worry.." clicking his fingers (As though in so, to make a sort-of invisible wall or sealing between them, magically.. that the others outside-of-it could no longer hear their conversation). Jack was astonished by the all-of-a-sudden 'dead-silence' about them, that followed. And as well, at the still perfectly-visible movement of the crowd, despite it. At last, recovering himself…

"Well, I.. I.. I don't know where t' begin.. I mean, I realize you ain't got much time.. 'n well, there's just so much to tell!.. I.. I…

Well, I guess.. t' make a long story short.. if.. well, if you.. if you had somethin' t' do.. f' God!.. 'n well, it scared y' somehow.. Y' know, doin' it!.. Well, like you were uncertain of.."

"I'd do it!.." Nick smiling.. "Unquestionably!.. Yes, I'd do it!.."

"Whatever it was?.. I mean, I know you're doin' your job here, as is.. But well, y' know.. it ain't nothin' too scary or.. or.. well, I don't mean t'.. Well.. " Jack fumbling for the guilt of making Nick's job seem easy (or less complicated or dangerous, etc.).

"Yes.. I understand!.. Don't worry, I know what you mean!.. But well, we all have different tasks!.. And we can't run away from them.. Especially if they're important!.. And even greater, if they're the Lord's!.."

"Well.. " Jack, still uncertain.. "I'm just not really so sure that.. Well, f' one.. I just really don't see why the Lord's given it t'.. t'.. Well, it just don't seem t' make sense.. 'n.. well.."

"Jack.. the Lord works in mysterious ways!.. Haven't you ever heard that said before?.."

"Well, no.." truly having not!.. "Anyways, Nick.. Maybe you could help me on this?.. I mean, it's really important t' me t' complete it.. 'n, well.. I dunno.. maybe you could.. could…"

"Jack.. Time has run out!.. I must leave!.. For I have MY job to do, too!.. You understand, don't you?.."

"Well.. well.. " Truly not.. though trying to.. "Yeah.. Sure, Nick.. I do!.. But.. but.."

"Just have faith, Jack!.. Why, just look at Jesus.. Why, He was afraid too!.. But He didn't back down.. or run from.."

"But He was the Lord, Nick!.."

"Yes, I know!.. But He was human too!.. and had feelings of Great Fear, as well!…. But He knew what must be done!.. Yes, God, the Father's Will!.. And if you truly feel it that strong in your heart.. y' know, about this 'work' that you feel you must do.. Well.. then.. you must comply!.."

"But, I.. I…"

"Jack.. I really must leave now!.. Do come back though.. say, sometime after the Holidays.. And when I've had time t' get my rest!.. And then, we can talk some more.." Then, snapping his fingers again (Before Jack could prolong it), the crowd's volume came back to the air. And in final statement (in his rising to begin his trip), he turned back, saying (in a smiling, yet serious way)…

"Remember, Jack.. it's like the Lord said.. " referring to his own task.. "..'Feed the Children First'!.. Yes, that's what He said!.." with a wink.

Jack.. unseating himself and climbing down (with these words of the Lord's still ringing in his ears), turned back in-a-flash and said up…

"Nick.. if I don't get t' finish it.. Will y' help me?.." The addressee.. never answering.. only smiling back in the further-hurry of his exit.

When aground, Mrs. Santa re-escorted him back through the crowd. This, to the cheers of Santa's take-off.

At the doorway, they both turned to watch Nick's far-off-now climb into space. Then, unexpectedly, Mrs. Claus invited Jack in. He, awkwardly complying. And in so doing, accompanied with an influx of a number of scampering-in, as well, elves.

- 301 -

Inside, the living room was aglow and beautiful! Adorned with a fair number of Christmas Trees (All trimmed and glistening!). As well, there were hanging decorations and toys everywhere about the room. And of course, a radiant fireplace! Mrs. Claus motioning him to the latter, unthinkingly. This of which, he tried (for courtesy).. but within minutes, asking to be excused to a further-away seat, near the window (at the kitchen table, just beyond the front-door entry). Mrs. S. offering, in her off-handed, accommodating way…

"Oh, yes.. I forgot!… Please.. Please do!.." pointing back in its direction with her freshly-poured cup of hot chocolate. And proceeding there, as well.

With his 'sit-down', the table top frosted with a mist. At this, he giving her a look of embarrassed- apology. She offering in justification.. .

"Oh, don't worry.. we're use to the cold!…

Well, anyway.. Maybe you'd like to talk with me.. of why you came?.. You can, you know.."

"Yes.." Jack having taken an immediate liking-to and trust for her. And who wouldn't have.. For she being a dear and pure sweetheart!.. "Well, it's an awful long story!… But, well.. y' see.. it all sort 'a started in this graveyard.. in North.. ah?.. North Cambridge!.. M.. Massachusetts!… Y' know.. in the New England part 'a the United States?.. Well, anyways.. I mean, at least, this new problem I been havin'!.. I mean, you do know I've been here.. on Earth.. for.. well.. you did know that.. right?" Her silent (but, nodding..) 'yes' clarifying.

"Well, anyways.." He resuming.. "When I was there.. in the graveyard recently.. Well.. well.. God.. He sort 'a.. well.. He told me somethin'.. yeah, somethin' He wanted me t' do!.. Well, it wasn't exactly verbally.. but, well.. I felt it!.. Super strong too!.. And, well.. I just.. just…" getting upset. Then, catching himself with her supportings.. "Anyways.. I dunno if I can do it, all by m'self!.. I mean, it's a big.. big…" pausing briefly to try to find the proper words… "Well, besides.. it really didn't seem t' fit into my plans 'n all!.. 'n well…" Jack stopping again, though this time to momentarily note the elves about them (and under the table), who were playing in child-like unconcern Then, resuming with…

"But, it's.. it's important!.. Real, real important!.. 'n I can feel it with all 'a my heart!.. I just.. just…

Well, more 'n more, things keep happenin' t' make me see that it.. it's…" He breaking down in mid-sentence to tears.

"Jack.. it'll all work out!.. You have to give it time.. " She offering with such kindness and concern, that Jack couldn't keep from lifting his head to listen.

In the course of the following discussion, she told Jack a story of her own. Yes, of her own trials and tribulations. And how patience and belief had carried her through. This, having been such a touching tale, that Jack had become totally lost in it.. finding himself (in its conclusion) with tear-in-eye. Yes, it was so beautiful and heart-rendering! Somehow she had made it sound 'so captivating' that he couldn't have dodged the enthrallment if he'd tried. With a painful lump in his throat, he forced…

"Geez, Mrs. Santa.. I believe.. Yes, I believe I'm gonna try 'n accomplish this thing!.. As scared as it makes me!…

Maybe you're right!.. Maybe I just need t' give it all.. some time!.. Yeah.. more time!.. Maybe I just ain't received all 'a the messages yet.. 'least, t' put it all together properly in my mind!.. Y' know, t' make complete sense 'a it all!.. But, I believe I'm gonna.. 'cause, it's important!.. and that.. I do know, f' sure!…

..'n, well.. Somebody's gotta!.. Right?.. 'n I can't, for the life 'a me, figure 'why me'!.. But, neither here, nor there!…

Anyways, will you explain it all t' Nick?.. 'n if, f' any reason, I don't get t' complete it.. Well, would y' try 'n explain it all t' him?.. the importance of it, too?.. 'n how I'd really appreciate it, if he'd, at least, try 'n help?.. Y' know.. 'n finish it?.."

She, smiling (Though never really responding). Regardless…

"Thanks, Mrs. Santa!.. Really!.. " Jack, sad-like.. "Well, I better get goin'!.. It's getting awful late.. 'n well, it's truly been great talkin' with y'!.. Really!.."

This being met by the elves' (Whom he'd completely forgotten about, for they hadn't seemed to be paying attention before, anyways..) sad-disapproving-"Aw"-'s. And, these.. startling Jack momentarily.

"Well, anyways.. I best get movin'!..."

"Yes, I understand.." and she, so sincere in it.

"Well, thanks for listenin' 'n takin' interest, Mrs. Santa!.. Y' know, I.. "

"That's okay.. We all need that, sometimes!.. Besides, I enjoyed it myself!.. I hope you feel better now?.. You can always come back and visit with us anytime you want.."

Jack nodding gratefully, in his up-'n-departure. Nervously picking at his hand-held hat in it, as he went.

When gone (and throughout all of his running-homeward), the words of Nick (Actually, the Lord's..) echoed constantly in his mind...

'... "Feed the Children First"...'

He thought of Angel Boy.. and how important that all was. He'd always been happy and close-with-him, but maybe there was more he could do? Yes, much more! After all, he'd lost so much 'time' with his daughters. Yes, precious time.. and all of the 'little things' that they could've (and should've..) shared together! Now.. gone forever! He felt so awful about it! But maybe there was still time for the boy? Maybe he should concentrate on him for awhile? Besides, he felt so uncertain of all the things pertaining to his Carol and the Quest! Maybe he should just 'put it all aside' for a bit? Give it all 'a rest'! And make effort in another direction? Yes, with his son! For this was important too! Very, very! He was so confused now, he could hardly apply himself to his work anyhow. Yes, he needed a break.. and badly! Time to think! Sort it all out! He'd been rushing everywhere.. 'n for so long now.. that he'd tied himself up into a 'ball of total confusion'! Though, in another way, he was truly unsure of whether-or-not he could do otherwise? It was all 'such a habit'! Could he? He really didn't know? Still.. he must try! Yes, he had to! For the boy's sake, if for anything! Besides, he could just no longer go on like this.. Wearing himself any thinner and fragile-er than he'd already done! Yes.. 'Feed the children first'.. That he would do! For, oh.. how important they are!

All throughout the Trans-Antarctic Mountains, he had kept seeing shadows moving in the approaching snow mounds. Oddly frightening him. The moon.. possibly being responsible? Or was it due to 'his condition?', he wondered.

In a state of absolute exhaustion, he (at last and literally..) fell down the hill that edged his shack.. breaking down and passing out on the iced (yet, cleared..) entranceway. This.. in a total flop!

Finally.. through his delusion and blurred vision, he beheld the images of Kare-Angel and Angel Boy. They, over him and helping him afoot. How long he had been there?.. He truly didn't know! Puzzling on this, in his awakening.

Very weak-'n-ill-ly, he arose. And ever-so-slowly at that! Numb-foundedly gazing about himself (in the same) at the totally bleak-'n-gray-tinted world surrounding him. This, of which, having a tremendously-whipping-'n-hissing-howling wind in it.. that clung threateningly! Shaking-'n-wobbling (outwardly, as well as inwardly), he hugged his little family. Crying in a cheerless-happiness (as well as sadness) for the sight of them.

In his faint-'n-dizziness, they supported him into the shack. And there, numerous days and nights were spent in slow recovery. Despite all, Jack made extra-effort now to be 'even closer' to them. Yes, greater than ever before! And Kare-Angel, seeming more receptive and patient in this, despite her own condition. Yes, she being 'more drawn' than ever! Yet now (with Jack, as he was), she seemed to become more focused on him (and his recovery) than herself. And in so, it healing her somehow!

Seasons upon seasons passed in this.. and all-the-closer they became. Though it was obvious to Jack that Antarctica was still taking its toll on Kare-Angel. At times (and in so) he felt, as though, 'the whole world were closing in on him' from the pressure of it. Complexing his recovery. This, as well as the still-festering thoughts of his Carol and its greater purpose! Yet he tried desperately to be patient in it (as Mrs. Santa had inspired him to do) and hoped for the best, ultimately. Still though, it haunted him!

With the long lay-off (Though he still did go places to pursue his Carol.. But now, always returning promptly there-after from his immediate business), he felt (at times) as though a sort of 'rigor-mortis-of-defeat' were settling into his bones. And into his total spirit, as well!   He knew he was still trying, all-'n-all.. but somehow, it ached at him. It was a hard thing to explain (or even put his finger on, exactly..), but there'd just been so, so many failings before-hand. Not to mention, his of-recent fall through.. that he could hardly (if any longer?) find the initiative (and energy!) to go on. It all just seemed so fruitless and never-ending! His existence.. a total failure! All of the unfulfilled dreams (in his lay-off.. and with all of this time to think..) preying on him unmercifully!   Its 'paralysis' seemed to becoming a part of his inner and total make-up with the further-ment of time. And it was painful to accept! His momentum had been broken! He tried desperately to ignore it.. and go about his new business of 'raising Angel Boy properly' and 'being as good a partner as possible to Kare-Angel'.   Still, it un-welcomedly lingered in his thoughts. He.. trying with all of his might to maintain his faith throughout. Yes, that all would get better and back into 'gear' in time! Yes, everything would be all right!   He must believe!   Still, it was extremely difficult!

These days were special though, in other ways.   Experiencing things he had never had the time to before.   Like hours spent in ice-skating games and so forth, in the hidden valley with Angel Boy. Snowball fights.. Sleighing.. Building Snow Angels. Yes.. and a new kind of inner feeling was discovered. One that seemed to, somehow, make him feel more akin to God.. and how He must feel of His children. Yes, an 'all-around' better understanding of Him!   Maybe it was just 'the times'?.. but whatever, Jack realized he was changing. And he could truly 'feel it' now, unlike when 'the Angel of the Musical Spirit' had noted it to him (in the Garden of Prayer). Yes, there were just so many pro's-and-con's to all that had been happening to him! It was confusing! But this he knew, if anything.. 'If he could change.. well, then.. anyone could'!

Still though, it all sort of scared him. Yes, knowing that he would never be the same again. As before! He wondered if these changes would affect his performance level.. or even his 'whole attitude' concerning his for-so-long (prior) goals and dreams? It had to! He felt sure! Would he ever be able to view-it-all in the same way as he had? Could he? Did it really matter? Yes, somehow it did! Still! Yes, despite everything, the whole Quest was still 'right there' on the tip of his heart-'n-mind.. Awaiting his next move! None.. yes, none of the desire, nor fire of it had passed. Or been lost. And he could forever feel it pumping.. Below his skin! As 'heated' and 'ready' as a bull trapped in a pen, awaiting the gate! But, as I'd said.. now things had changed. And drastically! And just the same (and in the same breath), he hoped they wouldn't change back (If that makes any kind of sense?). I mean, he'd never felt so good inwardly as now! At least, concerning his home life. Yet still, another part of him 'ached' for 'the old'! And it beckoned.. making him feel to be slipping behind. Becoming lazy towards it! Finding it extremely difficult to muster-up the enthusiasm (he knew it took) to go on with it. Yes, everything was all so confusing now! Like always, I guess.. just in a different way! What exactly did he really want anymore? Well, whatever?.. it must all wait for the time being. Yes, that.. and that, alone.. was all he really did know, for sure!

And so it was. Days passed.. after days, after days. His trips now (as stated).. minimal. Very to the point! Almost seeming done out of a 'pure inner duty'. Not very exciting. For more and more, they only seemed to be 'back-trackings'.. 'Re-enactments'. Yes, somehow (for either fear or confusion) he couldn't seem to make a forward move. Towards the 'New Work'. He was just so uncertain of it all!

Throughout everything, Kare-Angel continually weakened. And (in the later days) it was becoming all-too-obvious to Jack, that it was a result of their location. It had to be the reason! Yes, it was just too cold and isolated in Antarctica for her. Slowly but surely, it was killing her! And Jack was realizing more and more, that if you love someone, how wrong it was to cage them for your own convenience. And this, only to watch them die! Yes, he knew this.. and all too well! Things were coming to 'a head'.. and he realized (beyond a doubt) that something must be done. Compoundingly, this too was preying on his mind. And constantly, along with all else! Yes, he must somehow regain his strength and initiative-to-pursue again.. and in so, conclude his quest. Get it done! And over with! Time was running out! The inevitable was lurking! He must act! This, if he truly wanted to keep and maintain 'what he had' with Kare-Angel and the boy. A move from Antarctica was becoming inescapable. So, as worn and weary as he was, he knew he must re-build himself and attack it one more time. Yes, once and for all!

- ANGEL BOY –

On the floor now, he lay.. drawing pictures with Angel Boy. Kare-Angel couched and sleeping beside (and in so, above..) them. All the while, Jack inwardly considering his plans. Re-vamping his more of-recent events. The Lorraine Village. And the happenings of-and-at the old Fiddler's cabin with Leah. The latter, bringing to mind (again) the sign that he had seen (and fretted over, then and since!) in the snow (outside the cabin on that last-of-nights). The 'confounding sign'! He still couldn't help but puzzle over 'exactly' what it had meant? Maybe

Angel Boy's child-innocence might afford a truer, more in-tune-with-the-Infinite interpretation of it? He wondered. And with that, he devised a little game of...

"Here, son.. If I was to draw this" (meaning 'whatever'..) "simple bunch 'a lines.. How would you.." (Angel Boy) "complete them into some sort of a picture?"

This working finely enough.. For Angel Boy (who had a natural knack for Art.. and as well, a great sense of creativity) became immediately engrossed in it.. and in so, turned out some interesting interpretations of his Daddy's 'rough lines' and offerings.

Once into the game, Jack attempted his 'initial reason' for starting it all.. and laid-out in front of the lad 'the symbol'. Yes, the very sign! The child eyeing-it-up unconcernedly.. and with that, promptly-enough flipping it sideways. Then undertaking 'how he would make it into a picture'. This of which (along with the child's explanation), amazing Jack. For what he had composed.. was the image of a man who was blind-folded! And his hands.. tied to something! And this man ironically-enough, looking reasonably-'n-pretty-much like Jack! Yes, it was almost as-if the child's drawing was, in fact 'n somehow-or-another, 'more profound a statement' than the 'sign itself' had originally been a mystery! At least, it seemed so to Jack!

As the little game continued, Jack contemplated on this. And what it had meant to him personally. Angel Boy, at last, became bored with it all (as children often will) and (like his Mother) soon nodded-out to sleep on the floor.

After toting him off to his bed, Jack returned to the scraps of paper, retrieving 'the one'.. And taking it to his seat (at the new window), he studied it again. Staring out then (at the large valley), he scanned the deep-set night. Thinking. It was, as always, a cold night. Often he'd do this in his mind-searching. But now, his pensive and pre-occupied mind was hardly there. Nor his eyes. They, truly seeing nothing of the vast engulfment. No, instead.. millions of thought-visions away!

For one of many, many things.. Jack had finally learnt the true meaning of love. This, in regards to his new relationship with Kare-Angel. For unlike the Romeo-'n-Juliet-ness of his first relationship with Angel Jane (Which had had a beautiful, story-book send-off.. only to slam-crash its pages down on him in short time).. this, on the contrary, had started out immediately with its troubles and turmoil. Yes, it had been true work!.. From the git-go! But now, ultimately it had paid off. And a tremendous lesson had been learned. Yes, this was real love! 'Cause, Real love is Sacrifice! 'Giving things up'.. 'Giving of Yourself'. Sometimes even 'Giving up yourself' for someone else! Yes, like Jesus had! Now (in his slightly better knowledge of the Lord) he could see this.. And perfectly too! Yes, for Jesus had offered the 'greatest show of love' ever! The perfect example! Yes, love was someone who never backed-out on you. Devotion! Even to the end! Yes, now Jack could truly understand. And as well, it wasn't so much 'who you loved' that mattered.. But greater, 'who loved you'.. and was truly willing to follow you and suffer whatever losses came with that end. And this is what Kare-Angel had done.. left Heaven and all of its comforts to stand by Jack.. in what he was and did! Accepting all of the failures and trials that came with him. All the way to the end too (And it was sure seeming close to that, at present)!

In realizing all of this, he wondered at 'how he could have said what he had to Angel Jane then and not meant it'? It seemed hypocritical now. Well, fact was, he had meant it! It wasn't a lie. He just simply (at the time) truly didn't understand what love meant to begin with. He just really didn't know. But now that he did, he could easily see that his love for Kare-Angel was real and true! Yes.. and true in the more-educated sense! And this said, in no ill-reference to Angel Jane. No, never. Simply fact!

And it was for all of this (Not to mention, his deep and devout love for little Angel Boy) that a great anguish came over him, when he began (and fully realized that there was no way around..) making actual plans for his next-to-be 'lengthy' Quest. Yes, grieving inwardly with all of his might. But something.. yes, something had to be done! For things were becoming too desperate! Kare-Angel (despite all her love) was not long for the Antarctic. All arrows pointed elsewhere. Yes, one way or another, it was going to end. Unavoidable! Somehow he sensed that (once into his Crusade) she would be leaving. And upon his return, he would find her gone. Out of pure survival! And with that, taking Angel Boy, as well! Yes, he could just 'feel it'! And for that.. on his night-of-departure, he made more 'excuses' than ever to detain his leaving.. Finding almost anything to do to dodge its eventuality.

At last (When Kare-Angel and the boy could no longer remain awake to give him his send-off.. having tired-out exhaustedly from watching him in all of his antics), Jack (alone now) sat still-stalling at the kitchen's table.. Staring out the fogged window at the cold-iced and dark lowland. Kare-Angel's earlier words rang in his head now…

"Window Panes"

'... "If that's what you've made up your mind to do.. then you've got to go with it, for whatever good or bad comes from it!"...'

This, in relationship to his forever Quest and his despite-all-odds 'still belief' in it. And this, of which, he had already known, quite honestly. But now, it served as a good reminder (after all of the self-doubt that he'd been experiencing of-late). It rang again. And he listened to it in his ear. It was true! Though sometimes, hard to practice! Especially when you've been beaten-down and fruitlessly-trying for as long as he. Who, in their right mind, would've gone on? Though, he knew he must! It was all too important!

Looking back now over the time he'd spent with Kare-Angel and the child, he re-evaluated how hard it had been. Super trying! Still and yet, he (as well) knew he'd have never done otherwise! Nor in the same, been elsewhere! Yes, time (like everything else) had moved onward now.. But the past there (with them) had been precious! In a different way than he'd ever known! Yet still, precious time! And his 'Love', it was only stronger than ever! Yes, the hardships had made them closer. He knew that. Difficulties will! Yes, it had all (Despite his inner perplexities) been worth whatever-time he might've lost (if that were the case?) in the Quests. No, he'd have never changed it for anything!   No regrets!

In the tremendously-windy turmoil, yet absolute-inner quiet of the middle-night, he (at last) lifted himself to fetch a paper and pen. Writing a very-melancholy note of love, he re-read it (soft, but aloud) to himself...

"... Dearest Kare-Angel (Thief of my Heart)...

... Impatience.. is a 'hurts- you'...

... In patience... 'n True Love...

... Forever... beyond all time...

...'n when we're together again...

... (at last!!) you'll truly understand...

Jack Frost

... P.S. And... I'll Wait for You !!!!... "

Dearest Kare-Angel (thief of my heart)

Impatience .... is a 'hurts-you' ...

In patience .... in True Love. ....

Forever ...... beyond all time... ...

'n when we're together, again ...
(at last!!) you'll Truly Understand .... .

P.S. And .... I'LL wait for You !!!! !

He slid the note away to center-table. Finally in agreement with himself (that
he must make the move or never), he eased himself free of the seat and crept off to
kiss his slumbering two. And then, at last, he was off! Into the bitter night. The
long.. cold.. whirling-darkness beyond.

Many locations were hit. In the old fashion. Yet somehow, the nebulous-like feelings surrounding his Carol (and its 'newer' light) remained throughout, havocing and distracting him terribly. Why did he trouble over it so? Why did he fear it, as well?.. and so greatly as he did? Why couldn't he just make a move on it? With all of the Will-'n-Power he'd been blessed with, why was he so-lacking now in Faith? Yes, to go forward with it? And stop the back-tracking! Well, for one, he felt so unworthy! Yet on the other hand, who on the face of the Earth (Short of the Lord Himself) ever really was? Or would be?, for that matter! Still somehow, even that justification didn't hold water (or 'ice', however you'd have it!) to Jack. Yes, it was just all, so.. and, too.. confusing!

In light of all of the mentioned, it was with 'no wonder' that on late Christmas Eve, he found himself again (as on the first of these such nights) at Bethlehem. And again (as on the same), in the very spot and location of his years-'n-centuries-before visit. But as with everything and everywhere else, there had been changes. Yes, many and great! Regardless and despite them, standing on the very ledge, he inwardly studied it all, as he had once done. The night seemed identical with its Peace-on-Earth stillness! And a huge and bright Star was in the sky now, as was then! He sighed heavily in the memory of days-past, seeing (in a fleeting vision) the former view.

With his at-last descent into the lowland beyond him, rather than rocks and palms trees, etc. to dodge (Though some were still there obviously!), there were now homes and so forth. Yet still, in the very fashion as before (and as always), in-'n-out of them, he went. Scatting, dodging and darting his way through 'the new'!

Now on the very site of the Lord's birthplace (the manger) was instead a shrine. Reaching it, he began promptly towards its entrance. But as would've been expected of the extremely late (or 'early' Christmas morning..) hour, it was locked. Oh, dang! After all the travel!

Turning back behind him (to verify his solitude, considering the noise he had made in his attempt), again (as had been the similar and earlier case in Jerusalem) came soft footsteps inside, towards him and the separating-them doorway! Startled, Jack (in absolute awe) watched and listened as the lock was undone. This time though, as well, the knob was turned.. and the door pushed forward towards him slightly, several inches. Then, all went silent again inside. Jack's heart.. pounding viciously throughout!

Considering and remembering what had transpired at the Holy Sepulcher, he wondered if he really wanted entry now-'n-after-all? But.. well.. he'd come so far for this already.. and deep down.. somehow.. he knew he really did want in.. so…

His entire frame 'rattling' from nerves, he began. Peeking in first, of course! But the sparse and dim-glow (from the early morning behind him) didn't shed very much light on the absolute-blackness there-in. Creeping as softly as he could manage.. and leaving the door 'wide' for a momentary search of light, he (at last) located a means to this end. In so, the hanging chandelier affording thinly-illumination to the tight-'n-tunneled- like chamber. As he'd have expected, no one was there!

Scurrying back to the door, he closed it.. But not entirely, in case a 'quick escape' became necessary. Then immediately in the direction of the above-and-golden-glowing light, he proceeded. Just beyond it, lay an altar-like, adorned cavity. A railing protected it. And to this, he went.. eye-searching its beyond enclosure and interior. Yes, this had been where it had all taken place, ages before! He remembered! And was certain! Despite all the additions and years!

Kneeling down and leaning on-'n-over the rail to fold-and-cup his hands, he closed his eyes in the same breath. Re-picturing. And seeing it, as clear as-if through a mental telescope. Oh, how intense-a-night it all had been! Greatly 'moved' by his surroundings (as well as by the recall), his focus became gradually-to-very-heavily-doused with sentimentality. And melancholy, as well. Tears, at last, rimming his eye lids. Yes, how 'eventful' it had all been! And beautiful, despite all that he had been going through, at the time! And well, after all, he had had his way in it.. Whistling his hymn first. Yes, he realized that despite it all (the before-'n-since pains), he'd, at least, accomplished that!

Oh, so many, many times since, had he whistled his Carol. Yet never, never in all of his practice-makes-perfect-like replays, had he ever felt he had even 'near-matched' the sensitivity-'n-beauty of its delivery on that very special-of occasions! For though it had been 'new to him' at the time.. Well, still.. it.. it was.. just.. just.. so.. Well, y' know!

He thought on, of his 'new, envisioned hymn'.. And how, if he was 'right' to his feelings (with its execution), what a 'glorious and monumental event' that could herald! And bring to the world! Yes, what ecstasy he could feel in mentally picturing and hearing it. But why now, unlike then, was he so uncertain of himself? And afraid? What had happened to had changed him so? Was it 'knowledge'? For then, in his naïve-ness and innocence, he just acted on impulse! Was it 'the world' and his running away that brought him guilt and all of this complexity? Whatever? The Hymn had been just so beautiful then.. and could be even more-of-a-rapture in its refrain. This, he did know! Yes.. and in its simplest form now, he (to himself) began it. Yes, whistling softly in his still-kneeling stance.

But no sooner did he get 'into it', when came the flap (again) of the to-his-right stand-held Bible! This, startling him into a dead stop. Had he done that? No, he felt sure! How could he have? Why, he knew 'for certain' he'd been facing forward throughout it all. As mentally-spaced-and-far-away as he'd been.. still, he did know that! No, there'd been no way he'd been responsible for it! Short of.. maybe.. a.. a.. ricochet? Nah, even with that, he'd hardly been exhaling 'that strongly' to have caused such a flapping!

Up and very shakingly, he wobbled his way towards the Book.. supporting himself (on brief occasions) with the on-his-left-now altar rail. And this, for the fear-filled sensation of 'faint' mounting in him.

Finally at it.. and finding a stool placed near-at-hand, he rumbled it over-to and underneath the stand. Very unwillingly (but feeling 'called to'), he began up. Extremely light-headed now (for the intensity of it all), he hoped (all the way up) that he wouldn't find the pages opened to the same spot as he'd found them in Jerusalem.. For he couldn't take it now! Please.. Not that! At least, not now! Please!

Beneath the yellow-ish, dim glow of the chandelier's light, he read softly-in-whisper- to-himself the page opened.. and to where his eyes automatically led him…

"Pslams.. 22..."

In this, remembering how the Lord had said these same (and beginning lines and..) words, when he'd seen Him on the Cross. Then studying to its end, he marveled at the text and its precise depiction (and in so, disclosure) of the events of that day. Yes, now (all of a sudden), he understood! It was so obvious! Feeling warmly comforted and encouraged by it all (and remembering something he had read in the Fifteenth Chapter of Revelations, of recent, back in that huge church on the once-site of Calvary), he flipped the pages to its end location. There.. and feeling 'the Spirit', he intuitively ran his eyes down to the Third Verse.. Reading up to the Fifth. But before he could go on.. in an instant and flash.. and without any 'breath' or effort on his part.. the pages again flipped! In a rightward-going, fanning flutter. Jack snapping back in the shock of it! Watching them!

When, at last, they re-settled to their stop.. Jack (eyes, fearfully stuck in upward stare) gulped in conclusion.. Afraid to lower them to the text, for what he might find! But with nothing else happening there-after, he (in surrender) finally did; reading in-so (and in the same hush-tone as before)...

"Exodus.." at the top of the page. Running his eyes down to the First Heading, he read... "Fifteen..". Not but a slight way into this chapter, it took off again! Jack watching it, this time, as it instead reversed its direction.. All happening so-flappingly-fast, he didn't have time to raise his eyes away! He gulped again, reading now...

"Matthew..." at the page top. His eyes again leading him to a large, bold typed...

"Twenty-Five.."

Starting there and reading down, at last he came to Verse Fourteen. From that point on, somehow it became very interesting.. Or at least, more-related and directed towards all that he'd been feeling and 'worrying-about' for so long. Yes, concerning his Carol and the more-ultimate possibilities and importance of it! Or better yet, that of his executing it.. and to the best of his limited abilities! All of this, relaxing him now. And it (inwardly).. as well as in the reality (outwardly) of the moment and his at-present whereabouts. Yes, no matter how things were to turn-out (in the outcome), he knew now that he must try! And just trust in the Lord!.. Even if anyone were to misunderstand him and his intentions.. As long as he himself knew them to be true and sincere (in regards to God, Jesus and the Holy Spirit and so forth..), he must not hold back any longer! Yes, and in the same, he must not be afraid! He must be brave instead! And in all his moves, leave it in the hands of God. And His Providence! Yes, he must move forward to the new! It was his 'duty' and 'responsibility', as well! Yes, no matter who or what he was! That was totally insignificant to the cause. Yes, the importance was.. for the overall.. and mankind! And whether or not, it helped him personally (in his existence and final outcome).. Well, that too must be left to fate.. and God's Will. But whatever.. and no matter what.. he must try now. He knew that! And for sure!

Through the remaining chapter, he read on. It (as well) touching him profoundly. When done, he paused in deep thought over it all. Stepping down from his platform, he began out.. glancing back over-his-shoulders, once more, upon 'the exact spot' (of Christ's birth).. Then out he went, in his pensive-ness. In so, forgetting to 'close shop'.

- JESUS IS THE REASON -

The coastline of Israel found him still-in-thought. Through the blur of it all, he glanced down (in his walking), noticing the Swiss-cheese-like and too-numerous-now holes in the horizontal, red-'n-green stripes of his socks. They.. heavily spotted with the cold-pale flesh-tones of beneath. Like he himself now.. worn! To the absolute end! And grossly-faded, as well! The frustration of 'not succeeding' still ached in his arteries. At least, 'succeeding' by his own terms. Yes, despite all-and-any attempts to thwart it mentally, it still preyed. And remained firm, no matter how he tried to justify it! His whole being still agonized with the thoughts of it. Even after all this time! And somehow, even making him feel worse than before-or-ever. And to think, now there was even greater need to succeed! Yet, how tired he was! And beat! Could he do it?

Somehow.. despite all now.. the 'new order' (Which had, up to this point, seemed to be 'disorder', in regards to his more recent pages) was making 'better sense' than anything previous. Yes, somehow all of that had come together. In Bethlehem! All that he had (for so long) dreaded and dodged, had come to a 'true calm'. How it had happened exactly.. well, he really wasn't sure? But it had.. and he marveled in it still. Relieved.. at least, in that way! But now, knowing (as well and in the same) that 'this work'.. yes, this 'new work'.. was hardly near its end. Yes, hardly! Now he was no longer afraid or opposed (in any way) to undertaking it. Though this, if only he could find the energy! The storm.. yes, it had cleared. The seeming forever one! All was plain! Yes, all he needed now was a little time (If he had it?) to do the groundwork. If not, he would (at least) try his best to lay-it-out for the others. Yes, the other Herald Angels!

No sooner had the latter thought occurred in his mind, when (like it had been some sort of telepathy or premonition) did he view, up ahead.. sitting on a sea-side boulder.. Will. Yes, Will! The Angel of Notes himself! Jack couldn't believe his eyes!.. Rubbing them.. in that, it all might be a mirage! Brought on by his former contemplation!

But even after the brief, knuckling massage, in the re-focus.. yes, there he was. Will! Up ahead, in his robe-full-'a-musical-insignias-'n-all! Yawning.. 'n well, just every-bit-'a-him-sleepin'-self!

Running across the cold, hard-matted sand, he called out (in the nearing)…

"Will!… WILL!…" The recipient, in hearing, turning to him to wave a welcome.

When (at last) upon him, Will (still turned in his direction) saying, real casual-like and with another slight yawn…

"Hey, Jack.. How y' been, kiddo?…"

The addressed, too out-of-breath to answer. At last, choking out…

"Fine.. I guess!.. Yeah, fine!.. 'n how 'a you been?"

"Swell.." Will, smiling a bit in it.

"Well, I'm glad!.."

They looking at each other, uncertain (for a moment) of 'what to say', after all of this time. Or, at least, Jack!

"Well, Will.. Wh.. Wh.. What y' doin', anyways?.." motioning a quick look out at the pounding-to-shore waves. Then, back… "I mean.. y' know, Whatcha up t'?.." Nervous, for the joy of seeing him again.

"Lookin' f' seagulls!.." very matter-of-factly.. "I like seagulls!.."

"Yeah.. well.. " Jack accepting that… "Me, too.. I guess.. Always sort 'a re-minded me of.. big doves!.. Can I join y'?.."

"Sure.. help y' self.." palming towards the place on the rock beside him.

"Thanks!.." Jack, doing so.

After a fair silence, Jack offering…

"I like the Sun, too!.. I mean, y' know.. y' probably wouldn't think I would, but.. somehow now, I do!.. It's beautiful, huh?.."

"Yeah.." Will momentarily glancing up at it.

"Here Comes the Sun.." Jack to himself… "saw that somewhere once"

"Hmmm.." Will responding non-complacently.

"Y' know, Jack.." Will, at last and out-of-nowhere-like (tiring of the 'small talk') and taking serious… "I know you didn't see me.. But I remember you in your darkest hour!.. Yeah, I was right there!.." Jack (in this) looking at him to listen with full focus. Though Will, still staring-out.. and continuing on with… "Yeah..'n your vision then, as well!.. Yeah.. 'n f' that matter, I know why it ends where it does!.." at that, turning to Jack.. who, in so, smirked a quick-like smile back. Then, re-swinging forward to the tide, he resumed… "Yeah.. 'n just what you were trying t' lead folks to!.. 'n the greater reality of it, as well!.. Yeah, I know exactly where it picks up again!.. Yup, your tale.. Well, it was only a finger pointing at it.. right?" Jack nodding at his again brief glance. "Yeah, Jack.. it's all in there.. and in the memory of those times!.. 'Guess you could say, 'I was taking notes of it'.. Huh?… get it?.." chuckling slightly to his side. Concluding…"Yes, sir.. it all makes perfect sense in my mind!… I read y' loud 'n clear, partner!.."

Jack.. into the remaining silence…

"Well, I guess y' know then, that it was all.. and only.. f' Him!.. Yeah, He.. was the reason!.. and really is and will always be!.. I mean, even I used t' think it was f' myself.. but.. well.. well…

Anyways, that was His original idea, wasn't it?.. For all 'a us, in the begin-nin'!.. 'n ultimately!"

"Yeah.. you got that right, partner!.. " Will agreeing in a sigh.

"I mean, Will.. Ain't none 'a it for 'my glory'.. or.. 'our glory'.. but, His!.. 'n well, if it ain't then.. y' know.. ain't much gonna ever really come 'a it anyhow!.. Right?.. " Will nodding. "Even if the whole world was t' think it so.. Hey, what's that?.. Really?.. 'cause, y' know.. if it weren't f' Him .. Well, none 'a us would 'a been t' begin with!.. Right?.."

"Yep.." Will again, in soft reverent-like agreement.

".. 'cause, You, Will.. Well, you know what I am!.. 'n have always been!.. So I mean.. well.. y' know how people are.. They always get t' worshippin' everything-'n-anything.. except f' what's the right thing!.. Well, y' know.. like Money!.. Fame!.. 'n People!.. 'n well, y' know.. Earthly Glory!.. 'n well, I'd just hate t' think.. that they.. they.. Well, y' know what I mean.. 'cause, in the end.. what's all 'a that anyways!...

Shoot, Will.. He's forever!.. 'n ever 'n ever!.. 'n, well.. that was what our job was, t' begin with!.. Y' know.. to herald His comin'.. 'n all!.. Right?.. Yeah, 'n that's our job!.."

There was a long pause. Of meditative thought. Jack intended to go further into his words on it (Uncertain of his point being made), but before he could mouth-form another, Will offered…

"Christmas time is here again.. huh!.." This, distracting Jack into a smile to greet Will's. So he offered (with a head-shaking nod) instead…

"Yeah.. it is!.. Ain't it!.. I can feel it strong!.. 'n it's beautiful, huh?.."

Will re-turned and said.. "Yeah.." Then re-swung back out to the water. Jack (in the sentimentality of it all) getting emotional…

"Will.. if.. Well, I'm just gettin' so really tired-'n-weary of this place any-more!.. 'n well, I mean.. just everything seems t' be all so in-vain here anymore!.. 'n y' know, I'm gettin' t' think that nothin's ever gonna be right here!.. Ever!.. 'least, not f' me!.. I'm just so unhappy here.. 'cause I just can't seem t' get it to-gether!.. 'n, no matter how hard I try.. Everything just seems t' make me feel fur-ther-'n-further away from.. from.." pausing to catch himself in a breath.. "Well, anyways, Will.. if, f' any reason, I don't get t' finish my Carol.. Well, maybe you could.. could help?.. Well, y' know.. d' y' think you could tell the others?.. 'n, y' know, get 'em t'.. t'…

'cause, well.. it's.. it's just awful important!.. 'n I wouldn't ask, if it wasn't!.. Y' know, nobody else 'd be able t' understand!.. or care!.. 'n, well.. it's just gotta be.."

Will cutting in… "Why?.. I mean.. Do you think I don't have anything better t' do?.." He turning firmly to Jack in this. Jack was totally taken back. Where was Will coming from, to be so abrupt and cold to this open-show of sincerity of his? It just.. just didn't make sense! Jack felt a start of anger-'n-hurt come up in him. But before it could near-erupt, a thought 'snowed' down on him. Yes, entering his mind, as does the slight flurry's-begin on a winter's day. Yet, in spite of its subtle invasion.. in the outcome, it hitting him as poundingly, as were the waves that were presently hitting the before-him shoreline! Yes, with a manifestation as strong. Yes, he could see now (in the dawning), how.. in a way, ole Gabe had been right! Or at least, sort 'a right. Will was 'just like Jack' in a way. Or even better yet, in this very moment. Maybe it was due to.. well.. that they had an even-more 'human-ness' about them, than the other Herald Angels? He really didn't know! But whatever.. he could see now, just how cold.. bitter.. and ultimately, as a result, unforgiving he (himself) had been! Yes, then.. and all along!.. Towards God and everyone back in Heaven! And just how 'off-base' and wrong (in the same) he was. Yes, it all seemed so obvious to him now! And now 'seen', he couldn't help but feel grateful to Will for helping him in the discovery! Maybe this had all been an act?.. Yes, just to 'show him'! He wondered. Then Will interrupted his thoughts with… "Well?.." This, with the same hard edge.. Making Jack all-the-more uncertain. Wanting greater to find the 'better' in Will, he fumbled out in a gulp…

"Well, ah.. no.. but…"

"Then, tell me.." Will continuing.. " Why?…"

Jack recoiling and softly responding (Though more 'to and for' himself)…

"Well, I guess.. 'cause, it's for.. for the Lord.. Y' know?.."

Will turning back out to the water in silence. Then, after a minute, pivoting again…

"I already got something I gotta do for the Lord" in this, glancing down to his cupped hand. This, making Jack note (though he hadn't prior) that Will had been holding something all along. In the latter's serious-look, the hand was opened..

and Jack eyeing its contents. And with his after-review of Will's face, offering only a gulping nod.

Following a chilling aftermath…

"Well, Will.. I bet 'a go.." Jack starting up.. "There's something I gotta do too!.. yeah, I think I gotta go.."

After ten feet or so, Will speaking out to him…

"Well, see y' around…"

Jack looking back to again give him a nod.

The Angel of Notes returning it.. and in so, re-swinging back out to the gulls.

Jack still facing him, calling out in his backwards walk…

"Good luck with it all.. See y' in Heaven.. 'k!.."

Will saying something, but this going unheard by Jack for his greater retreat.. And its consuming distance. But the waving of his hand answering 'satisfactorily enough' for Jack.

Yes, and into the far and its haze, he went.. never again looking back.

THE THIRTEENTH AND FINAL CHAPTER
~ (CONCLUSION OF AUTHOR'S INTRODUCTION) ~

~ VOICES IN THE WIND (OUT OF BACKWARDS) ~

.... Locking and checking the parlor door behind me, I fumbled my way down the few porch stairs (for the beginning of snow and its extreme slippery-ness).. And in the same, as well.. slid myself awkwardly down to the chain-linked fence's small gateway.

Outside of it (in my leftward hurry), I crossed the immediate-driveway's mouth.. Turning back to see (in my moment's-later angular-crossing of Rindge Avenue), my family 'car-loaded' and entering into it. In this, I turned and gave them a wave. They (as well as I could see) returning it through the wiped-glass-fog, in their continuing leftward swing and entrance into the drive.

Trembling somewhat (in my return-to-myself and introspect), I edged on, despite it.. working my snow-slushy way across-and-towards the Our Lady of Pity Church's circular driveway. In a brief flash of this, turning my head through the huge-falling flakes to see Phil's Barber Shop. This interrupted by (what I ini-tially thought to be..) the sudden sound of screeching automobile brakes coming from behind-me. At least, that had been my first thought and impression.. But, in fact, I quickly came to realize (in sharper focus) that it had, in all actuality, been the violent-like shrill of Jack's whistle!.. This, fearfully stopping me cold in my tracks, for a snapping-and-swinging-forward moment to re-listen! But, nothing followed.. Short-of, more-mounting of my already-high anxiety! It had seemed-to-me to be coming from.. Yes, around the huge, affront building in the little chapel's direction! Forcing forward-and-out my right foot, I began again.. Only slow now. For as anxious as I was, something seemed to demand it. Something very internal! At last, pass the entranceways of the Main Church, I crept.

With the dark, hazed-like sight of the chapel coming into view (in my con-tinuing-swing around the cornering bushes), I nervously raised my hand to find 'anything to do' to thwart my becoming-too-intense fear.   In so, reading my wristwatch…

"Seven, Forty- Seven.."   This reminding me that I had forgotten to re-place the child's time-piece back onto the shelf (in my parent's living room). Quickly feeling through my pockets to confirm, I found I had been right.. it was there!.. Dang! I thought to return it.   But 'Why?', on second thought! Surely no one

was going to miss it before my return. Well, maybe.. still.. I should (Looking for any excuse to dodge the inevitable)?

Then suddenly (to distract my inner debate), it returned.. Jack's whistle!.. Ahead, from the chapel! Pleading-like! Almost demandingly howling at me! Forward again, I moved.. Unwillingly, but onward.. feeling and hearing the loud crunches of the mounting-now snow beneath my feet. The violent 'increasing-drastically' bitterness of the night was hardening all-about!.. and all-within, as well!

The closer I came to the chapel-front, the more I felt 'the pounding of his

wind' on me. It.. thrashing my face and clothing in climaxing fury. I fought to keep breath and myself afoot in it, for it was absolutely crashing me!.. Lashing my ears, eyes and nose, in painfully-cold-like whips and gusts! This, ending with-and-in a powerful, electric-type shock, as I 'footingly'- touched the top stair of the chapel's few. It.. zapping me so violently-and-traumatically, that I fell forward (in my absolute daze), grasping the doorway's brass latch-handle for not-to-fall. But collapse I did, despite the attempt. Yes, to my knees, yet still holding a grip to it!

Somehow (out of this momentarily 'unconscious-ing and electrocuting' experience), there came a feeling of peace? Yes, a very ecstatic-like sensation of inner tranquility!.. That slowly (but very surely) surfaced in my spirit! It.. like 'a birth' of-sorts! Or, whatever?.. Hard to explain.. but regardless, it came! In the outcome, filling my total being with silence and rest.

In the 'totaling' of it, I lifted myself up with the door-handle's assistance. Looking back out at the night, I saw it.. as if, it.. it were.. Spring? Yes, some-how.. miraculously.. it had all transformed into a very pleasant Springtime night! In so, I could smell the sweet fragrance of flowers all about me in the stillness.. The balm-ing rustle of the trees and leaves swaying! And songbirds, as well! They.. 'very-weirdly-enough' seeming to be 'chirping' Jack's melody! I shook my head in it. It was absolutely mind-blowing!

Re-shaking my wits (in a downward-and-away fashion), I again tried to clear my mind. But on re-looking, it was all still there. Very peaceful!.. and beauti-ful!.. but hard to accept and appreciate! It (in longer surveillance) reminding me of a very special and fond memory of my youth. Yes, of a time far-forgotten, when all of the world was at perfect ease.. And harmony. Lazy-like. Yes, a very long, long ago-'n-mystical time!

As hard as it was to drag myself away.. inside, at last, I went.. through the chapel's vestibule, cracking (in so) the further-set, secondary doors. Peeking in. It was all dim and darkened.. and solemn, in my following eye-search of the chamber. And vacant.

Upon the altar were great bunches of beautifully-assembled flower arrangements, arrayed in every color. These, affront of a white-clothed-and-draped background. All.. glowing.. as though my eyes were viewing them through a (somehow?..) smearing, wide-angled-type camera lens. Radiant-'n-dazzling beyond belief!

Shocked for it (Though no longer scared or fearful in any way, despite the strange-ness of it all!), I began myself forward. Down the center aisle. Slowly and right-handedly touching each pew-end for support, as I went.

When reaching just-before halfway point, I stopped. And looking ahead and to my left (at the seating that I had always-before-and-by-habit taken), I instead pew-ed on the right-hand side.. On occasion there-after, glancing (directly-) over at it, in my continuing study of the 'pin-drop' quiet inners.

In my sitting, I came to think again of the child's wristwatch, now being replaced in my pocket. And so I dug for it. But it was gone? Then to my immediate amazement and side, I saw it.. lying there beside me on the pew-seat! I hadn't put it there! I was sure! Picking it up, I noted it as reading… "Eight-o-Seven!.." This, confounding me terribly (and even worse)! For there was no way that I had put it there!.. Nor that 'the time itself' had flown by, so fast! No, there's just no way that 'that amount of time' could have passed, just coming from the house to here! Why, in re-considering it now.. even the last time I'd look at it (in the churchyard) seemed totally illogical and in-accurate, as well!.. making it all 'that much more confusing'! I turned back at the door in my extreme perplexity, as if to try to re-count it .. As well, as all of my actions throughout. Swinging back, I said to myself (again, aloud)…

"There's no way!.. 'n it couldn't be that late!.." checking my own wristwatch for sync. But it too said… " Eight-o-Seven!.."

After a few more second's dismay…

"What is this?… What's going on?.." whimperingly followed by.. "Geez!.." with a deep sigh.

Feeling upset-enough to cry, I placed the watch on the pew-seat again and bent forward to lower the kneeling pad. And in that, slid forward to do so and say a prayer. This (with the very touch of my knee), being met with…

"I see you've returned.. " from the altar. This, spoken solemn.. But loving-like and warm.

I quickly raised my head to greet it.. Answering slowly, softly and carefully back…

" Yes.. ah.. Yes, Sir!.. "

"For help?.."

"Ah.. well.. Yes!.. I mean.. I guess?.. I.. I…"

"Jack no longer needs that!.. Nor, You!.." His tone, the same as prior (and this, throughout).

"Well, Sir.. he still is on the Earth, right?.. 'n.. I mean.. well, he's still try-ing to…"

"Not for much longer!.. That work is nearly completed now!.. he's coming back to me.."

"But.. but.. Why?.. I mean.." trying to think of some great reason for not.. "What'll happen to.. to.. Antarctica?.. Will it.. it melt?.. And Winter?.."

"I determine that!.. You've truly no need to be concerned over it anymore!.."

"Well.. What.. What of his hymn?.. 'n.."

"I have plans for that, as well, my child!.. I always did.. from the very start!.."

"Can I ask, Sir.. What they are?.. I.. " truly curious.

"No.. but you can be assured that they are good!.. And you've no need, any longer, to be worrying over Jack!.. Nor, his hymn!…

Now.. What of you?.. What can you say for yourself?..

And what have you learned as a result of it all?.. Let's speak of your life!.."

This.. sending me into a sudden panic and nervous-ness.. and in my perplexity, I fumblingly scanned down to see.. still sitting there, pew-seated.. the child's wristwatch. It somehow bringing me to say…

"Well, f' one thing, Lord.. I realize now that.. Well, I truly wasted so much time!.. in regards to my daughter, especially!.. Precious time!.. Gone now forever!.. All for my obsessive desire to succeed in my career.. And for my fear-of-failure in it!.. And.. well.. though my intentions might've been sincere.. 'n not-necessarily selfish, in so.. Still.. all the things we could've shared together.. yes, now.. they're gone!.. Lost forever in her growing up!.. I mean, I truly never-ever meant to ignore her or anything.. as I did try to always do the best I could, under the circumstances.. But, just.. well.. being apart, most 'a the time.. I.. and both of us, ultimately.. lost a lot of the little things we could've shared!.. I'm truly sorry for that.. to her.. and to you, as well, Father!.. Yes, I'm really sorry!.."

Nothing was returned in the momentary silence. So I resumed…

"… 'n well.. for another thing.. I guess I learned that.. well, no matter how much you want something in your life.. if it's not of your will, Father.. Well, then.. it just never will be!.."

Uncertained of whether or not I was even 'near-answering' His question, but continuing on regardless in it (for what would've-otherwise-been 'deathly silence'!)…

"… 'n well, if I ever.. 'n well, I know I have many times.. But, y' know, gone against your will.. then I'm sorry!.. Truly, truly, truly sorry!.. 'cause I never ever meant to.. purposely…

Well, I guess I admit that I have!.. And maybe often at that too!.. But I'm really, really sorry!.. 'Cause I didn't mean t'.. 'n well.." a pause to regain myself.

"Like.. y' know.. the times I thought that You were being unfair to me?.. Well, when I really thought about just how lucky I was.. 'n all.. Well, considering the other truly less fortunate folks in the world!.. the Cripples.. 'n Homeless.. 'n so on.. Well, y' know, I realized the opposite!"

Boy, was I babbling on! I knew it! But…

"… 'n those times, when I went against Your Will.. " back-tracking, but for confusion… "Well.. it was out 'a weakness.. 'n not defiance!.. I hope you'll believe that?.. 'n understand, as well?.. I swear!.. Pure weakness!.. 'cause I do love you!.. more than anything or anyone!.. It's just that.. well, y' know, the world.. y' can't help getting wrapped-up in it sometimes.. 'n forgetting!.. Y' know.. like.. What's really important!.. And maybe by knowing better, it makes y' all-the-more guilty and responsible ultimately?.. But, well.. I just hope you'll forgive me, when my.. my..."

A pause came.. for an overcoming, momentary 'blank-ness' hit me.. due to the distracting-and-disturbing thought. Catching my breath and fighting it, I proceeded...

"... I... I... I realize now.. too.. that.. well.. I could've had it all.. Y' know, everything I'd wanted.. if only I had done what you had wanted me to do!.. Yes, your way!.. But I just.. just couldn't see it then!...

.. 'n.. as well, in that.. 'n everything else.. that it was I.. yes, I.. that was to fault for every single bad thing that ever came my way!.. Yes, they were all a result of my own mis-doings!.. I.. myself.. created them!"

Hanging my head, I paused in the sad revelation of it all.

At last, distraught-and-forlorn, I resumed.. in a sort of conclusion...

"Well.. to tell the truth, God.. Sir.. I really don't know what more to say for myself?.. or my life?...

I guess I'm.. well.. just sorry for all the people I ever hurt in it!.. Whether consciously or not!.. 'cause I sincerely never enjoyed hurting anyone, f' sure!.. Oh, I dunno!.. " Truly confounded at what more I could say in defense. But the following silence seemed to demand it...

"Well, anyways.. most 'a all, I guess the only thing I can add.. 'n I know I already have, but.. well.. again.. I'm sorry!.. To You, above all!.. 'n my children and their mothers!.. My parents.. 'n family.. 'n, y' know, just everybody I ever let down in any way!.. I never meant to fail them.. That I do know!"

I went blank.. Totally lost for any further words.

A cold silence followed. And after all I had voiced, I awaited now a reply.

But nothing came!

In its dragging-out aftermath, I considered that I might've 'over-talked' myself.. and 'bored Him to tears'.. and ultimately, 'into leaving', if that were pos-sible? I mean, I couldn't figure it? There was only pure.. absolute.. pin-drop silence! Maybe something 'more important' had come-up somewhere-else-in-the-Universe.. and He had had to leave?.. and attend to it? I just couldn't make any sense of it!

So at last, removing myself from the pew (and feeling extremely guilty and uncertain, in so doing!), I began my exit.. Hearing in it (as I made my way back up the aisle) Jack's outside-whistle! It immediately crossed my mind, how.. at last-'n-finally.. Jack's toils were over. I felt so happy for him! Relieved.. and greatly, at that! Only, I just somehow wanted to see him one more time, before he would be gone. Yes, just once more!

So, hurrying a bit (But trying not to appear as-so), I reached the first set of (in-ner) doors. When practically through them, it struck me that.. for all I had lived and experienced-in-it (as well as 'learned'!), there seemed to be 'one more thing' that I could say to God for it. If, in fact, He was still there? But either way, it had to be said. So peeking my head back in (in my anxious-ness) and hoping He would (Regardless of where He was?) still hear, I yelled out...

"THANKS GOD.. SO MUCH!.. FOR EVERYTHING!.. I LOVE YOU, SO MUCH!.. THANKS GOD.. 'N JESUS.. 'N HOLY SPIRIT, TOO!.. YES.. JUST.. WELL.. THANKS SO MUCH!.."

Through the vestibule, I flew.. stopping at the cold touch of the inner (and out-side's, in the same) door latch. In this, feeling the door itself, for the startling note of its 'change-back'! Opening it (in a flash), I marvelingly saw...

"Winter!.." Yes, it was back! It.. blowing in on me in a violent gush of enter-ing wind.

There.. beyond the further-set bushes and towards the front of the Main Church (in the now-descending darker night), I saw...

"Jack!.." Or at least, his silhouetted image! Yes, standing there in solid jet-black stance, for the further-distant streetlight's backing.. With his scarf.. 'a blowin'-'n- flappin' to his side. His hat, on head.. 'n well, just lookin' as much-the-same as I'd ever seen him before! Waitin' for me, I was sure!

So without delay, making my way towards him, I began. In awful hurry! Or at least, as much as the slippery ground would allow me!

Maybe twenty-or-so feet from him, I remembered that I'd (again!) left the child's wristwatch on the pew-seat. Stopping momentarily in confusion, I considered a 'quick return' for it. But Jack, in this.. making a bolting dart away.. As if, reading my mind!

I couldn't wait (Nor, return!).. I must pursue, before he would be gone forever!

So chasing him, I went.. around the bushes and passed the main church's entranceways.

With Phil's Barber Shop ahead, I saw (in forceful squint) him.. making his sharp, left turn down the avenue.

Just as I reached the street myself (in all of my mental confusion), I heard it.. The loud.. ear-piercing squeal of brakes!

Then.. the crash.. that sent him flying limb-lessly up and towards the opposing sidewalk! This.. to conclude.. with his head (on his right side) hitting the stone-ledge stair of Phil's Barber Shop! Yes, the very tip and hard-pointing edge of it! This.. all happening so fast and crazy-like that I knew not what to do! All I could feel.. was the 'impact'.. and the 'tremendous agony of its smashing'! And.. the pain! The awful, excruciating pain of it!

Through streaming-wet, smeared eyes.. and the coming of a 'great cold' in the night.. I blurred ahead, in my paralysis.. at my reaching-out and forwardly-stretched (Though, bent-) arm.. focusing-in and seeing (upon it) my watch.

Then.. into this long, numbed-like and continuing spacey-ness.. I heard and felt the around-me howling wind.. with its spinning cyclonically-upward whirl. I called Jack's name!.. and, then.. again! At last, surrendering it for my second's-earlier focus.

Only now.. beyond the reality of my arm's-stretched wrist.. I saw into what-appeared-to-be a lifting haze, all about me! This.. like a strange vision!.. Or memory!

Echoing in the far-corners of my mind, I heard distant whistling. It.. seeming to increase rapidly!.. Like a beckoning bugle, calling me!

There.. on what-would-have-been the surface of this ascending fog.. I (in forceful squint) saw.. my hat.. lying, up-turned. On impulse, I felt to reach for it.. But immediately became distracted by the sounds of nearing-me voices. They.. calling his name. I felt to answer .. but (in my fearful and confused paralysis), could only recoil.. and, in this, I re-focused to my arm's end.. Seeing.. again.. the face of my watch. It.. reading (through the fluctuation and furthering disjunction)…

'Eight..'

'Infinity'

THE ABSOLUTE FINAL STATEMENT

All that is written and told by Man is Fiction…

God's Word is the only Forever Truth!…

So revert now to His continuing and actual 'Revelation' (Chapter 14)…

And then, work your way forward and back to 'The Beginning!'…

Where 'He' will show you the true way to…

The End!

Many, many thanks to you, my little friends.…

Mark Brine

P.S. And, yes.. if there ever truly has been a 'Frost' (Webster's meaning: #3.. A failing enterprise).. then it has unquestionably and most-surely been I! But then.. 'Ours' is not to question or want.. But, instead to locate the 'Jack' in our lives.. and have 'Him' lift us up.. to make the total best of what (and all) we have been given.. Yes, our gift to give!.. Whatever it might be (in the eyes of the World!.. or even more importantly, ourselves!)!.. So, in that.. May 'Yours' be.. even more fruitful! And, now…

It is Done!

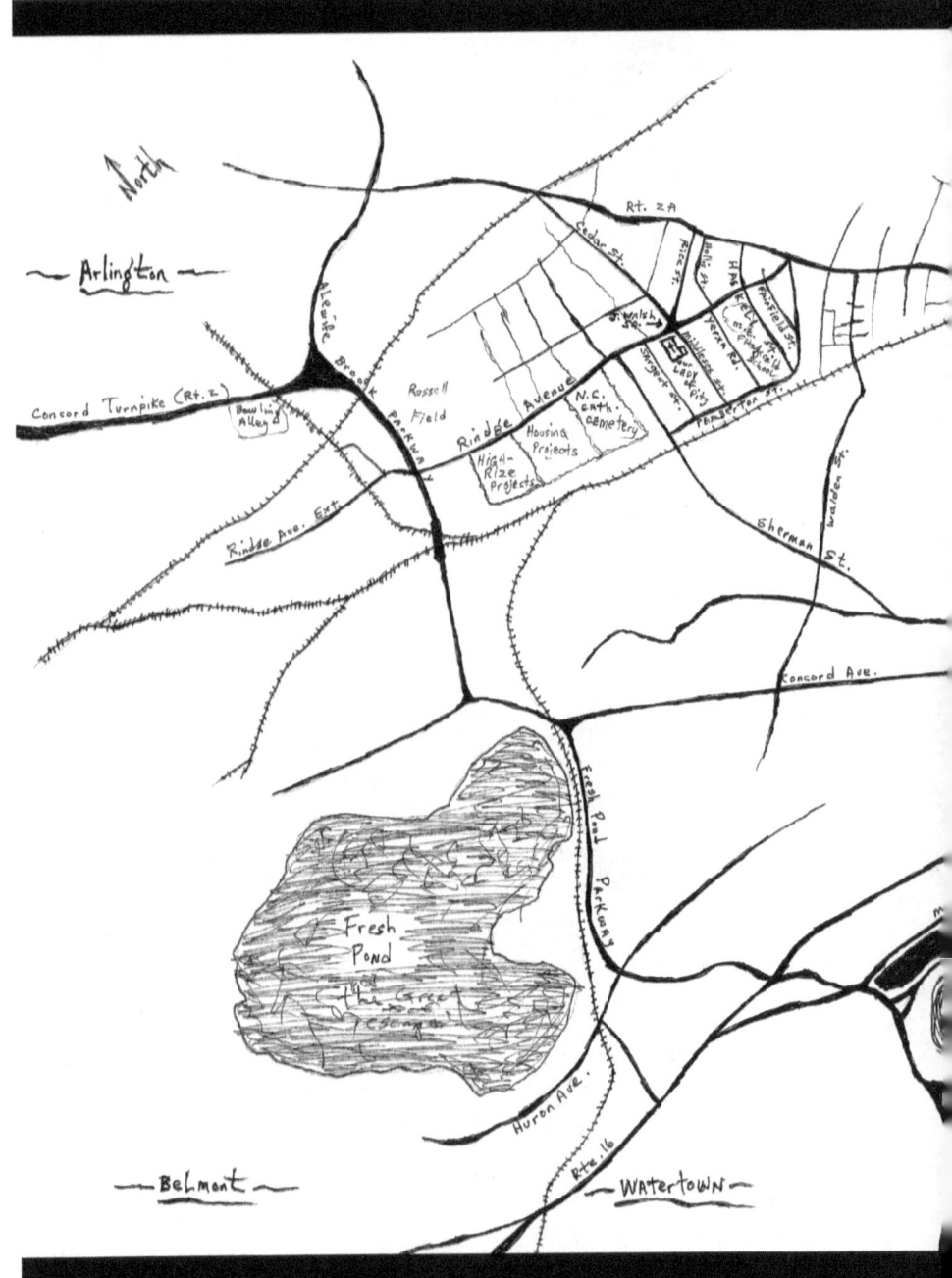

North

Arlington

Rt. 2A

Cedar St.

Walsh

Rice St.

Hall St.

Hackett's Field (Bloody Bucket)

Fairfield St.

Whittemore Ave.

N.C. Cath. cemetery

Vernon St.

Pemberton

Sargent St.

Middlesex Liquors Lady Grey

Consord Turnpike (Rt. 2)

Bowlin Alley

Alewife Brook Parkway

Russell Field

Rindge Avenue

Housing Projects

High-Rize Projects

Rindge Ave. Ext.

Sherman St.

Walden St.

Concord Ave.

Fresh Pond Parkway

Fresh Pond

The Great Dedman?

Huron Ave.

Belmont

Rte. 16

Watertown

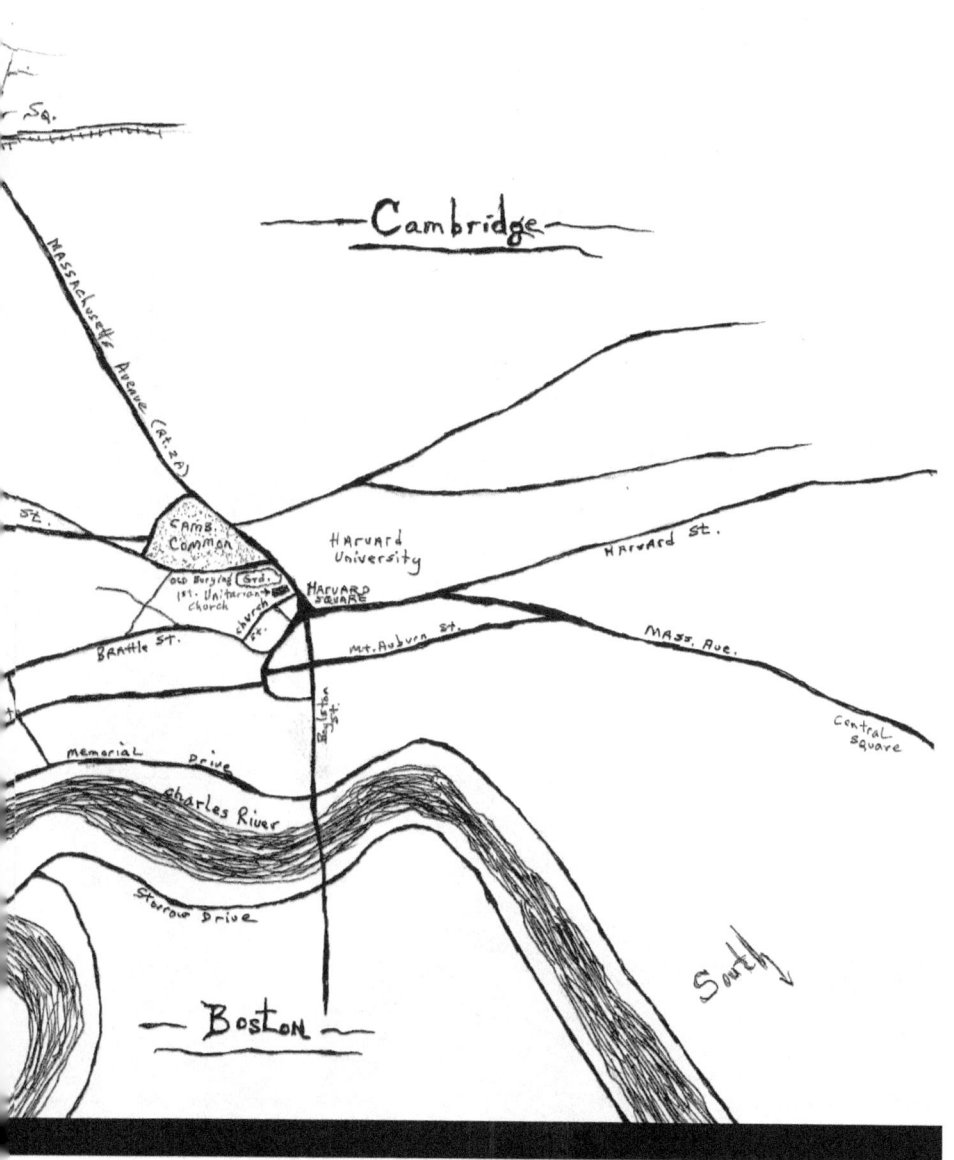